BD

P9-BZI-755

Praise for the Bubba Mabry series
by Steve Brewer

"Brewer's insights about the delusions of the people who make their living in newsrooms and about the homely city that lives in the shadow of its beautiful sister, Santa Fe, show grit and intelligence."
—*Albuquerque Journal*

"Bubba is like [Sue] Grafton's Kinsey Millhone, bogged down with life's vicissitudes and bothered by all-too-human frailties.... Let's hope Bubba keeps on stumbling around in the Land of Enchantment."
—*Arkansas Democrat-Gazette*

Praise for the Faith Cassidy series
by Catherine Dain

"Really a delicious book, one to savor."
—Gayle Lynds on *Death of the Party*

"Faith is a strong and gutsy heroine whose flaws make her even more likeable."
—*Booklist*

"...a wonderful mystery that entertains from start to finish."
—Harriet Klausner on *Follow the Murder*

The LAST NOEL

STEVE BREWER

CATHERINE DAIN

MAT COWARD

LINDA BERRY

WORLDWIDE®

TORONTO • NEW YORK • LONDON
AMSTERDAM • PARIS • SYDNEY • HAMBURG
STOCKHOLM • ATHENS • TOKYO • MILAN
MADRID • WARSAW • BUDAPEST • AUCKLAND

THE LAST NOEL

A Worldwide Mystery/November 2004

ISBN 0-373-26509-3

Printed in U.S.A.

CONTENTS

SANITY CLAUSE ·   9
Steve Brewer

FINDING CHARITY   93
Catherine Dain

DEEP AND CRISP   185
Mat Coward

THE THREE WISE WOMEN   277
Linda Berry

SANITY CLAUSE

by Steve Brewer

I MUST'VE BEEN CRAZY to take a job at a shopping mall in December. All the things I hate about Christmas—crowds and Muzak and shopping and greedy children and forced merriment—collide at shopping malls during the seasonal gift-buying madness. Normally I'll do anything to avoid such a mob scene, up to and including purchasing my gifts on Christmas Eve at the nearest 7-Eleven. People always need batteries.

But this year, I was trapped at the mall. And not just any mall, either, but the Rio Grande Mall, the newest one in New Mexico. Ninety stores clustered around corridors as long as airport concourses, every shop gushing Christmas cheer.

Albuquerque loves the "new" the way a monkey loves a shiny penny, so the new mall—only a couple of years old now—drew throngs of Christmas shoppers with feverish eyes and overflowing carts and the steaming pressure of approaching deadlines.

A shopping mall in December isn't the place to see humanity at its best. Kids scream and harried parents curse and smug clerks jangle cash registers and little old ladies hip-check each other out of the way to reach the "bargain" tables.

In this merry melee, there's one island of relative calm and true holiday spirit—Santa's Workshop. Filling thirty yards of wide, tiled corridor at one end of the mall, it's a world of gaping children, twenty-foot Christmas trees, fake snow, plastic workbenches and spritely elves. And Santa Claus himself, all red fluff and polyester beard, seated on a golden throne, taking one squirming child after another up onto his lap.

What follows is the best little drama in the whole mall. Will the child cry? Happily babble about baubles and toys? Draw a blank? Pull off Santa's beard? Wet Santa's lap?

It's a regular soap opera, played out on Santa's knee, and the dramatic tension is just right. The kid comes through, more often than not, so you get a happy ending and proud parents and a beaming tot. One damned Kodak Moment after another. It's a scene you'd think you could watch forever. Again and again, little kids and Santa, ho-ho-ho.

Try it for eight or ten hours straight sometime. With the crowds jostling and the kids wailing and the Muzak *pah-rum-pah-pum-pumming* and the encircling kiddie train whirring dangerously around pedestrians, tooting its little horn in a hair-raising shriek every time you've got a cup of hot coffee in your hands. Try that on for size. See how much you like Santa's Workshop then.

Spending all day, every day, amidst this joyful noise was the task assigned to me, intrepid investigator Bubba Mabry. I was supposed to blend into the crowd as much as possible and conduct surveillance on the entire Santa's Workshop decorative complex. Change hats and coats regularly to keep undercover. Watch for shoplifters and pickpockets and lost children. And, most of all, keep a close eye on the various impostors playing Santa Claus and his skinny little elves. Make sure every man keeps his hands to himself. Make sure nobody shows up intoxicated.

I was just eyes. I didn't have to *do* anything if I saw something go wrong, unless it was a real emergency. I had a small walkie-talkie clipped to my belt. If I saw somebody up to no good, I'd radio Milt Jablonski, head of security, who'd send one of his uniformed goons swooping in to remedy the problem. That way, I remained undercover and could keep watching Santa and his crew.

Not that the three Santas, who worked four-hour shifts, or the elves, who were around even more, didn't notice me. I mean, they must have. I'm standing around the mall all day, eating funnel cakes and sipping coffee and changing hats, and they don't notice? Eventually? Probably thought I was some kind of pervert, eyeballing the little kiddies. I suffered through every shift with the fear that someone would start screaming for the cops, pointing at me, getting *me* arrested. As a pervert. At Christmas. Not the best thing for business when you already have a shaky reputation as Albuquerque's hard-luck private eye.

I hadn't thought of all these drawbacks when Milt Jablonski offered me the job. Milt called me up the first of December, asked me to come down to his nondescript office at the Rio Grande Mall and offered me the gig out of the blue.

I needed a job. Badly. My wife, Felicia Quattlebaum, had been dropping hints that all she wanted for Christmas was a new laptop computer. For weeks, she'd left sales brochures and circled ads lying around the house. Felicia drops hints like somebody else drops anvils. Anyway, with that big purchase on the horizon, along with the standard calendars and flannel shirts for my folks back in Mississippi, I needed some quick cash. Milt's gig had seemed a Christmas blessing, just in the St. Nick of time.

Milt admitted it was an unusual assignment. Lots of things could go wrong among the hordes at the mall, but you'd think Santa's Workshop would be the one safe haven. Not so. The year before, a Santa had shown up for work with a snootful of Irish whiskey and proceeded to blearily sing, curse, scare the children and dump one brat off his lap onto the floor. This just as a news crew was setting up the camera for a local weatherman to do his remote report amid the fake snow in Santa's Workshop. Drunken Santa was the top story on the evening news. And a front-page headline the next morning. Mall management, still smarting from the bad publicity, made Milt swear that nothing of the kind would happen this year. He told me his job was riding on it. That's why he hired me, the funnel-cake-eating secret agent. One more set of eyes to help Milt keep his job through Christmas.

"I'm an old man, Bubba," Milt said, smiling. "This is my retirement job. Twenty-five years on the force, finishing as a by-God decorated sergeant, my whole career in uniform. And what've I got now? A blue blazer and a wall full of video monitors, a bunch of cop wanna-bes on the payroll and my job riding on whether Santa Claus tries to grope the little girls. This is my retirement and it's the shits. But it's all I've got. This shitty job and three ex-wives. Merry frigging Christmas."

Milt said all of this flatly, his expression never changing. You've got to understand about Milt: He's the happiest-looking guy you've ever seen. He has this face, all arcs and half-moons, that simply looks happy. His wide mouth curves upward naturally and his plump cheeks crease with smile lines and his dark eyes twinkle. Milt's still got most of his curly hair, though it's gray now, and thick black eyebrows that arch expectantly, like he can't wait to see what happens next. He just looks happy as hell.

But Milt, in fact, is not that happy. I've known him for years, and he's always crabbing about how his back hurts or his arches have fallen or his ex-wives are hosing him. But he looks so happy while he's complaining, you can't take him seriously. You're too busy catching that contagious smile. Milt's bitching about something and you're grinning like an idiot, marveling at what a happy guy you've had the pleasure to encounter. It's weird.

Anyway, Milt's smiling and complaining, and I'm smiling and nodding along, and he offers me the job: Go under-cover, monitor Santa's Workshop, keep the Rio Grande Mall out of the freaking headlines. Three weeks at a thousand dollars a week. Enough to buy Felicia's laptop, pay all the Christmas bills and have some left over. How could I turn it down? How tough could it be to keep an eye on Santa Claus?

Clearly tougher than I'd expected. I hadn't counted on the noise, for one thing. Or the tedium. Or how it's tough to simply hold your ground in a moving crowd without being conspicuous. Or how even funnel cakes lose their appeal after a while, but you can't escape that aroma. With the Christmas cash waving in front of my nose, I hadn't even paused to consider all the potential hazards. I just said, "yes," and took the paycheck.

In my haste, I'd even overlooked the biggest problem of all: Santa Claus gives me the creeps.

There, I've said it. I'm sorry. I know you can't be a Real American and fear Santa, but I can't help it. I had a bad experience with Santa Claus when I was five years old, and I never really recovered. We don't need to go into detail, but let's say vomiting was involved. In front of about fifty people.

Ever since, a costumed Santa gives me the willies, the same way some adults are inexplicably terrified of clowns. I see Santa Claus and I get a shiver down my spine and a quiver in my belly and a sudden burst of fight-or-flight adrenaline that gives me a headache later. I've tried to rationalize this fear away, telling myself Santa isn't some kind of a stalker because he "knows when you are sleeping and knows when you're awake," that he isn't a loud, jolly home-invader who'll make me puke. No, Santa is about giving and joy and happiness.

It doesn't work. Nothing hangs on tighter than a clutching phobia.

Essentially I'd doomed myself to three weeks of this sensation. I thought it might be a good way to overcome my fear, witnessing Santa shift changes and being constantly reminded of the man behind the beard. But every ho-ho-ho sent a chill through me, and the constant cacophony of carols and crowd noise made me all the jumpier. I was so wound up most of the time, it was all I could do to keep from throwing myself onto the tracks in front of the shrieking kiddie train.

I was standing by a jewelry store on the last Monday before Christmas, dabbing at the spilled coffee on my shirt, when I saw the next Santa arrive for his shift. Daniel Gooch lanked into the mall in jeans and sneakers, a garment bag slung over his shoulder. The overhead lights glinted on his bald head and his gold-rimmed glasses. He was already smiling and he wasn't even on duty yet.

I knew Gooch from the files Milt had shown me. All the Santas had undergone rigorous background checks and he was the best performer on what Milt insisted on calling "our Santa team." The guy was simply great at playing Santa Claus. He was so slim, he must've worn thirty pounds of padding under his red suit, but he never seemed to break a sweat. One awed kid after another climbed up on his knee, and Gooch always said just the right thing or made the right little joke to keep the kid happy. Beneath the fake white hair and beard, Gooch had real mirth in his eyes the whole time. He came closer to embracing the role of St. Nick than anyone I'd ever seen. The other three Santas on the team—including the swarthy guy, Arguello, who was finishing up his four-hour stint—did a good job, but Gooch was the real deal. I always felt a little sorry for the kids who came at the wrong time of day to catch his act.

Gooch went through an anonymous gray door off a short, dead-end hallway that branched off the main mall near Santa's Workshop. Milt had shown me around back there when I started this job, and I'd seen a room with a couple of

benches and gray lockers and a shower and bathroom. A
place for the Santas to change into their gear and clean up
afterward. There was only one other way out of that room,
a door on the far wall that opened into a scuffed service corridor that ran behind a bunch of the stores, and Milt had said
that door was kept locked.

Arguello sneaked a peek at his wristwatch. His shift was
over, but a dozen kids and parents still waited in line where
the green-uniformed elves kept them herded behind red
plush-rope cordons. I knew the drill: Gooch should stick his
bald head out the door and give a signal. Then Arguello
could leave his throne, go into the locker room, and his re-
placement would come out. You can't let the kids see two
Santas at the same time. It blows the whole illusion.

But Gooch didn't come out. Arguello wearily put a few
more cranky kids through their paces, but he kept glancing over
to the hallway, waiting for the signal. Finally he leaned over
to the elf who was in charge of setting kids up on his knee and
whispered in his ear. The elf—perfectly cast for the role with
a pointy little beard on his pointy little chin and a wide forehead capped perfectly by his pointy green hat—leaped down
from the throne platform, the bells on his pointy toes jingling,
and ducked under the ropes to go over to the locker room.

I kept an eye on that hallway, still waiting for Santa, but
nobody emerged for several seconds. Then the skinny elf
burst out the door, his eyes round and his face bright red. He
was screaming.

Everyone in the crowded mall whipped around at the noise.
The elf wasn't screaming anything coherent. Just mindless,
high-pitched, random screaming. His mouth grappled for
words until he locked on to a phrase, which he repeated over
and over, louder and louder, as the gasping crowd took up the
chant.

"Santa's been *murdered!*"

TWO

Maybe I've been married to a newspaper reporter too long, but the first thing that flashed through my mind was that "Santa's been murdered!" would make a damned good headline. My heart seized up at the thought. The one thing Milt Jablonski had made clear was that the mall couldn't get *any* negative publicity during the Christmas shopping season. A murdered Santa's about as negative as publicity gets.

Before a second thing could come to mind, my feet were moving. I weaved between stunned shoppers and weeping children and screaming mommies, bumping people, knocking them aside. My eyes never left that dead-end hallway, where the elf still screeched. Nobody went in or out of that locker room, not until I pushed the elf out of the way and burst through the door.

I saw nothing out of the ordinary until I took a step around a bank of gray lockers that jutted from the wall. There was Daniel Gooch on the concrete floor, already in his padded red suit and shiny black boots, but not yet wearing his beard. Instead, wrapped tightly over his head was a clear plastic shopping bag gaily decorated with red reindeer and green Christmas trees. Inside the bag, Gooch's blue eyes bulged behind twisted glasses and his tongue drooped thickly from the side of his mouth. He was sprawled on his back, one foot up on a wooden bench, his arms splayed wide. Deader than a Christmas goose.

Asphyxiated. The word came into my head unbidden. A horrible way to go. People do it all the time, though. Why go to exotic means to kill yourself when you've got plastic bags lying all around the house? If you're serious about it, you can be dead in minutes. As long as you don't mind those agonizing final moments of no air whatsoever.

A quick look around told me the locker room was otherwise empty. Gooch's street clothes hung neatly in an open locker near his head. No sign of anyone else.

I backed out of the locker room and bumped into the elf, who was jingling around, hands clutched together, feet doing the Anxiety Shuffle. I turned toward him, scowling, only to find scores of people gathered at the mouth of the hallway beyond him. Customers and clerks and wide-eyed children, all staring at me. Waiting for news of Santa.

I tried to play it deadpan, tried to keep the look of shock and tragedy off my face. But you try it sometime, with an entire mall's worth of Christmas shoppers staring you down. A great wail went up from the assembled, and they all started babbling about murder and mayhem. A goodly number scurried for the exits, which is the last thing the mall management would ever want to see.

Before I could radio for help, Milt Jablonski and two uniformed guards pushed through the milling throng. Milt's face was bright red and he was puffing hard from the sprint from his office.

"What the hell is going on here?" Milt sounded angry, but he looked like he was smiling, of course. Some people in the crowd started to return the smile, despite their tears and alarm. Milt was here, with that happy face, so somehow everything would turn out fine.

I leaned close to him, hoping to keep the others from hearing.

"Gooch is dead," I muttered. "Bag over his head."

"Holy shit!" Milt growled. People nearby smiled and nodded along, agreeing with this assessment from merry Milt.

"Set up a perimeter," he said to the guards. "I don't want anyone else in that room until the cops get here."

A couple of other gray-uniformed guards came huffing up about then, and Milt set them on the crowd, getting people to move back, urging them to return to their shopping.

"And keep any media out of here!" Milt barked happily.

Over at Santa's Workshop, parents and children still stood behind the red ropes, craning their necks to see what all the ruckus was about, but not giving up their hard-earned places in line. Arguello still sat on Santa's throne, but he, too, stared. The kid in his lap chattered away, not noticing Santa's distraction.

A couple of cops arrived, bulling their way to the locker room in their black uniforms, their gunbelts and attitudes bristling. One of them opened the locker room door just enough to step inside and get a glimpse of Gooch, then he got on the radio and called the homicide unit.

Milt moaned. Homicide meant headlines. You might sandbag the media with a Santa suicide; nobody wants to report a story like *that* during the holiday season. But a suspected homicide would have reporters baying at every mall exit.

While Milt dealt with the cops, I drifted away. I felt woozy, to tell the truth, and thought I'd better sit down. People bumped into me and murmured and stared, but I was tuned out. I found a spot on a wooden bench and sat down and rested my head in my hands.

O, holy night, what a mess. Daniel Gooch, the mall's best Santa, dead, possibly slain. Now there'll be a storm in the news media and Milt will get fired and I'll never get paid and Felicia won't get her computer and I'll never hear the end—

"Hey, there."

I looked up. I don't know how long I'd been sitting there,

my head in my hands, but it must've been a while. The crowd around the hallway had thinned, the cops were stringing yellow crime scene tape like tinsel and business was getting back to normal. Felicia stood over me, a notebook in her hand.

"Hey," I said. "What are you doing here?"

"I heard what happened. Thought I'd better get over here right away."

"Thanks," I said. "It was pretty traumatic and I'm—"

"I'm not here for *you*. I'm here for Gooch."

I blinked at her. Couldn't process what she was saying. I'd had too much mental and emotional input.

"Daniel Gooch? He's dead, right? I was driving across town with a photographer when we heard it on the police scanner. We were here in minutes."

"But—"

"Do you know what happened?"

"But—"

"Come on, Bubba, snap out of it. I've got a lot of people to interview here. This guy's big news."

"Gooch?"

"Don't you know who he is?"

I shook my head.

"Do you ever *read* that newspaper that comes to our house every day? Gooch! He's been written up everywhere. Big-shot inventor, takes the plunge out of the corporate world, starts giving fistfuls of money to charity. A real nut for Christmas, but a good guy, you know?"

I think my mouth was hanging open. "Gooch?"

"The scanner said he's the guy who's dead here."

I nodded. "He was about to play Santa. Already in his red suit. I found his body."

"You did?" Felicia went on alert, her pen poised above her pad. "What did it look like? How was he killed?"

"Wait a minute! Are you interviewing me?"

"No, I'm washing your car. Of *course* it's an interview. You're a witness."

Sitting on the bench, I was at a disadvantage, though Felicia's much shorter than me. I would've liked to look down at her while I said what had to come next. Or, at least, be able to move out of striking range. But I was a sitting duck, and I winced in anticipation of the storm to come as I said, "No comment."

"What?"

"I can't say anything, honey-bunch. Not until I've talked to Milt anyway. See if it's okay."

"See if it's okay to talk to your own *wife?*" Felicia's face flushed and her eyes flashed.

"Look, sweetie, I've got a conflict of interest. You can see that. And I'm upset already. Milt's all mad. The guy's dead and all and he was a really great Santa—"

"Bubba. You're babbling."

"I'm sorry, honey. I just—"

"Bubba?"

The voice came from behind me. Rarely have I so welcomed the authoritative baritone of homicide's Lt. Steve Romero. I turned on the bench, away from my steaming sweetheart, and said, "Yes, Lieutenant?"

"You and I need to talk."

"Okay." I stood up from the bench. Felicia didn't step back to make way, and it was a tight fit.

"Now *wait* a minute," she said. "I had him first."

"Nope," Romero said. His square face split open and a grin spilled out. "I get him first, Felicia. He was first witness on the scene. He's all mine."

"The elf really was first," I said.

Both of them said, *"What?"*

I sighed and slinked around the end of the bench, putting

the heavy, anchored, wooden slab between Felicia and me. Just in case.

"The elf found the body," I said. "I ran in there after he started squealing about dead Santas and panicking the whole mall."

Felicia scribbled furiously on her pad, taking down every word in her cryptic personal shorthand. Romero gave me a look and we edged away. We'd covered a good twelve feet before she looked up.

"Gotta go," I said.

"Bubba!" she shouted.

It froze me in place, but Romero, beside me, said out of the side of his mouth, "Keep moving."

"Should we run?" I asked.

"Just back away slowly. I've got guys here with guns. They'll keep her off us."

"Yes, but for how long?"

"Long enough for you to tell me all about Daniel Gooch."

"I knew you were going to say that."

We kept backing up. Felicia crossed her arms and glowered at us. She gave me a look that said I'd hear about this later. Gave Romero one even worse. We reached the crime scene tape and ducked under it, and I felt temporarily safer. Felicia kept glaring at us. Other people bustled around and a photographer I hadn't even noticed before fumbled with a lens beside her and kids wailed and Arguello was back in the Santa business. But all I could see was the smolder in my sweetie's angry eyes.

Beside me, Romero said, "Let me guess. You're gonna request protective custody."

THREE

ROMERO USHERED ME to a corner, out of the way of some arriving evidence technicians, and stood too close, facing me. Wide-bodied as he is, it felt as if I'd been walled into the corner.

"Tell me what you saw." The grin he'd given Felicia was gone. Romero was all business. His dark eyes watched my face unblinkingly, waiting for the little physical clues of a lie. I knew this, knew how keen were the lieutenant's powers of observation. Which, naturally, made me itchy all over and gave me facial tics, so it would look like I was lying, even when I told the truth. Romero has that effect on people.

"Gooch goes into the locker room and never comes out," I said. "*Nobody* comes out. Finally the elf goes in to look for him, and comes out screaming."

"Which elf?"

"The hysterical one. Over there."

"Right. You saw no one else go in or out that door?"

"Nobody but the elf. And I was watching, too. This hallway was empty."

The short hall was pretty full now, with uniforms and evidence techs and photographers and bawling witnesses all huddled together behind the crime scene tape. It was making me claustrophobic.

"There's another door," I said. "Out the back of that locker room."

"I know. Goes to the service corridor. But I talked to Milt and he said he's been steady eyeballing the security monitors for that hall for the past hour. Nobody went into that locker room."

"Says Milt."

"That's right. Milt says nobody went through the back door—which is still locked—and you say nobody came out the front door. No other way out of that locker room, right?"

Romero cocked an eyebrow at me, waiting.

"Hey, I saw what I saw. Maybe Milt blinked or something. But I was watching the front door the whole time."

I don't know why I was so adamant. What did I care who went through which door? The murder was Romero's problem now, not mine. I've danced backstage at enough murder investigations, I know I don't want any part of them. I should've told Romero whatever he wanted to hear, agreed with whatever line of bull Milt was spreading, gone with the flow. But I've got this contrary streak and when I'm right, dammit, I'm right. I cling fiercely to every such moment of professional pride. They're so few and far between.

"I'm telling you," I insisted, "nobody went in after Gooch and nobody came out."

Romero said, "Then I guess he killed himself."

"What? No. Not Gooch. He was the happiest guy I've ever seen."

"I thought Milt was the happiest—"

"Not like that. Milt just looks happy. This guy Gooch was really, truly happy. Down deep. When he went in that locker room, he was already smiling."

"Maybe he was smiling because he'd decided on suicide."

"Come on. You don't believe that."

"It's Christmas," Romero said. "Busy season for suicides."

"Not this guy. He was having the time of his life, playing Santa Claus. Felicia says he's loaded, so he was doing this gig just for fun! He *chose* to spend every day in a freaking mall, playing Santa. That's no kinda suicide I've ever heard—"

A baby-faced detective in a blue suit tapped Romero on the shoulder.

"Lieutenant?" he said as Romero turned toward him. "Medical examiner removed the bag and looked over the body. Victim's got a dent in the back of his head."

A muscle twitched in Romero's jaw. "From the fall?"

"M.E. said it looks like somebody hit him with a pipe or a blackjack or something. He said the victim was probably unconscious when he suffocated. He said to tell you they'll know more after they roll him downtown. He said call him in a couple of hours."

"He say anything else?"

The kid pondered a moment, then shook his head.

"*You* got anything to say?"

The junior detective blushed, shook his head again.

"Then run along. I'm talking here."

As Romero turned back to me, he shoved his fists deep into the pockets of his black bomber jacket and frowned. Another homicide to solve. Santa Claus, no less. Romero was officially having a Bad Day. Could there be a less opportune time to say, I told you so?

"I told you so," I said. "I knew Gooch didn't kill himself."

Romero didn't look directly at me, but that jaw muscle pulsed a warning. I shut up.

"We'll need you to come down to the office and make a statement," he said tightly. "I'll meet you downtown in a couple of hours. I'm going to be here a while."

I said, "Okey-dokey," sidled past him and slithered away.

From behind me, he said, "Milt was looking for you."

I winced, then got hold of myself and ducked under the crime scene tape and put some space between me and Romero.

A couple of fat-assed security guards stood outside the tape, watching eagerly as the real cops did their work. I asked one where Milt had gone.

"Back to his office." The guard smacked his gum, grinning. "I think he was having a heart attack."

He elbowed the guard next to him, and they both chortled merrily. Apparently it hadn't sunk in that somebody had been killed right here. They acted like they were watching a cop show on television. Idiots.

I let it go, and trudged off down the mall toward the waiting Milt Jablonski. No sign of Felicia lurking in the crowd, which was just as well. Let her go interview somebody else, make somebody else miserable for a change.

I heard yelling as I opened the door to Milt's office. He sat behind his desk, smiling while he berated two of his uniformed guards. They stood across from him, their shoulders slumped, staring at their toes.

"Get out of here," Milt shouted. The pair slunk out of the office, leaving me in Milt's line of fire.

"Bubba. Sit your ass down."

I pulled a straight-backed chair out from the wall and set it across the desk from Milt. Sat down. Took a deep breath. Started talking.

"Look, Milt. I talked to Romero and I don't know what you think you saw, but I was watching that locker room door the whole time and nobody went in or out. Nobody but Gooch. You sure nobody went out the—"

"Hey, Bubba?" Milt beamed at me. "Shut up, okay? Before I climb over this desk and jump up and down on your head."

"But Milt—"

"I'm not kidding, Bubba. I am not happy. Do I look happy to you?"

"Well, jeez. Yeah, you do, Milt. I mean, you always look happy—"

"I am not happy. Trust me on this."

"Okay, you're not happy. You look happy, but you're not happy. On the inside."

"That's right. And you are a big part of my unhappiness."

"Me? What did I do?"

"I gave you one simple job to do. Keep an eye on the Santas. Make sure they come and go on time and behave themselves. One thing. That's all. And what happens? Somebody gift wraps a dead Santa Claus. While you're watching!"

"I didn't see anybody—"

"I'm screwed, Bubba. That's all there is to it. You just blew my retirement right out of the water. I'm gonna be homeless by New Year's."

"Take it easy, Milt."

"Hell with 'taking it easy.' I'm supposed to be enjoying my golden years. This is what I get?"

"Kinda louses up Christmas, huh?" That's me, always saying the right thing.

Milt growled and snarled and snapped, looking like the happiest rabid dog you've ever seen, and sputtered out, "You're *fired!*"

He pointed a thick finger at the door behind me. It seemed like an excellent suggestion.

FOUR

THREE HOURS LATER, I got home, depressed and unemployed and weary of police interrogation. Near as I could tell from their questions, Romero and his boys didn't have a clue who killed Daniel Gooch or why or how the killer might've escaped. I was too tired to care.

I unlocked the front door of our redbrick bungalow near the University of New Mexico and let myself in, craving only quiet and solitude and rest. Felicia skipped in from the kitchen, talking excitedly, gesturing at me with a flapping bologna sandwich.

"Just stopped by for a bite," she said through a mouthful. "I'm on my way to the newsroom."

I tensed, expecting her to unload on me for giving her the slip at the mall, but she went on talking. "This is a great story. Probably gonna be working late tonight, filling in the gaps."

I thought of the headlines to come, and felt a sharp pain in my belly. Felicia apparently noticed my discomfort.

"What's the matter, Bubba? They give you a hard time down at the cop shop?"

"You said it."

"And Milt? What did he say?"

"Something about me being fired."

She frowned. "Too bad."

Then she brightened right up again and said, "Don't sweat it, Bubba. It's a big story. You'll get your name in the paper."

"As the guy who let Santa Claus get murdered, right under my nose."

"No such thing as bad publicity, right?"

I didn't think that was right at all, but I was too whipped to argue. I slumped past her, headed for the kitchen and a nice cold beer.

Felicia followed right behind, chattering away.

"Listen to this. Gooch was this big inventor, right? He holds like a hundred patents. All kinds of stuff, but mostly for various gizmos involving lasers. Farmers use them to measure land and make sure their fields are level and stuff like that."

I couldn't possibly tell her how little I cared, or how little I wanted to hear another word about Daniel Gooch. I plopped onto a kitchen chair and slugged beer.

"A couple of years ago," she said as she sat across from me, "something terrible happened. Gooch's wife was killed in a car wreck."

I let that sink in. What came to mind was a kindly grandma type, with fluffy white hair and eyeglasses and round cheeks. Mrs. Claus. Dead in a car wreck. I shook my head, trying to get the image from my mind. Gooch wasn't really Santa Claus, dammit, he was a rich inventor. His wife probably looked like a Vegas showgirl.

While I tried to untangle my thoughts, Felicia said, "Gooch took her death hard. He stopped working. Stopped inventing stuff. Nobody sees him. Then, after a few months, he's done grieving and he's a new man. Not interested in work anymore. Wants to save the world instead. He starts giving huge amounts of money to charity, especially those connected to Christmas. Made cute headlines. 'Real-Life Santa,' blah, blah, blah. But Gooch was about to take the whole thing a step further."

I sighed, tired and confused. Felicia didn't pick up the cue.

"He wanted to *sign over* the patents. Give them all to one particular charity, this group that buys Christmas meals and gifts for needy families every year. All the money earned by the patents in the future would go to this one group, called Joyous Noises."

"Joyce's Noses?"

She ignored that. "All this has been going on behind the scenes, right? But there's a problem with this wonderful gift. Gooch signs over the patents and it essentially puts Gooch Enterprises out of business. The patents will get picked up by other companies, which will pay the charity, so that's all fine. But his employees get the shaft."

I couldn't take it anymore. I erupted. "How do you *know* all this stuff? The man's been dead, what, four hours? And you already know everything about him and his company and the latest gossip."

She waggled her eyebrows at me.

"Information's what I do, Bubba. I'm damned good at it."

"Sure, honey, but—"

"We've had a few stories about this stuff in the *Gazette*, so some of it was in the newspaper's library. I looked it up on the computer."

I blinked at her. "Oh."

"Then I made a couple of calls. People who knew Gooch. The head of Joyous Noises. They told me more."

"Like what?"

"Like Gooch had a business partner, a lawyer who's been with him since the beginning and handled all the patent stuff over the years. Guy named George Marley. You know him?"

I shook my head.

"I've seen him around. Gray-looking guy. Gray hair, gray face, real skinny. Looks like he's dead already."

"That makes two of them," I said.

Felicia rolled her eyes. "Marley's been putting together

a legal action behind the scenes for months now. Word is he was planning to have Gooch declared incompetent."

"Because he gives to charity?"

"They say he was out of his head. His wife's death gave him a nervous breakdown. He started thinking he *was* Santa Claus, giving everything away."

"Could they prove it?"

"Who knows? Now they don't have to. He's gone. The patents haven't been turned over. Marley keeps control of the company."

"What about Gooch's estate? Does the charity get that?"

Felicia shook her head. Her glasses slid down her nose, and she pushed them up with the back of her wrist. Somehow, amidst all the talking, she'd polished off the sandwich. I don't know how she does that without choking to death.

"Will hadn't been changed, or so I hear," she said. "We'll check probate tomorrow. But if everything still goes to his next of kin, it'll be his younger sister, Carol Tannenbaum. She'll get millions."

"And the charities get screwed."

"Merry Christmas, huh? It's a great story. Slow time of year. I'm gonna be on the front page with this thing for weeks."

I moaned.

"Cheer up, Bubba. It gets better."

"Couldn't get any worse."

"I was talking to Donna Hanratty, the executive director of Joyous Noises, this afternoon. You'd like her. She's tough as nails."

That's what I need. More tough women in my life.

"She's not going to roll over on this deal," Felicia said. "She wants to hire an investigator to make sure her charity gets what's coming to it."

I met my wife's eyes. "She wants to hire me?"

Felicia tossed a business card onto the table in front of me as she got to her feet.

"She said you already knew about the case. Long as you don't bring the cops down on her, she's willing to give you a try."

"A vote of confidence."

"Take what you can get. After all, you're the man who stood by while Santa Claus was gruesomely murdered—"

I growled and made as if to get up from the table. She laughed and danced away.

"I've got to go," she said. "We're updating the story for the second edition. All the gory details."

I groaned and settled back at the table. Heard Felicia slam the door on her way out and her car crank up outside the kitchen window a minute later. Heard her tires squeal on the asphalt as she whizzed away at her usual breakneck speed.

I registered all this, but I wasn't paying attention. I had only one thing on my mind: Front-page headlines. The possibilities were endless, and Felicia's smartass co-workers would have a field day. Kris Kringle Killed. Santa Claus Slain. Ho-Ho-Hold It! I'm Dead! Another Santa Claus Gets Bagged at Rio Grande Mall.

The talk of the town tomorrow. People will read every word. And there they'll find my name. Bubba Mabry, the man who failed Santa.

I fingered Hanratty's card, thinking, I'd better call her first thing in the morning. Before she sees the *Gazette*.

FIVE

I WAS WAITING at Donna Hanratty's office on Lomas Boulevard when she arrived for work Tuesday morning. Low gray clouds threatened a storm, and Mrs. Hanratty wore a tan trench coat over a blue pantsuit as she climbed out of her four-door Ford. She bent over to get her briefcase as I hurried across the little parking lot carved into what once had been the yard of a brick bungalow similar to the one Felicia and I call home.

A lot of the old houses along Lomas have been converted to offices, but this time of year, they're decorated and glowing, putting up the Christmas pretense that this remained a regular neighborhood.

We've got this funny tradition in New Mexico of decorating at Christmas with *luminarias,* which are lighted paper bags. You put some sand in the bottom to hold the bag in place, set a votive candle inside and torch the wick. Assuming the bag doesn't burst into flames in the process, a *luminaria* makes a nice, mellow light. Set them all around the perimeter of your yard, and the place looks like a postcard. Of course, those little candles are only good for one night, so you only see the real ones on Christmas Eve. A few years ago, some jackass invented plastic "paper bags" with electric lights inside. Now, you can see *luminarias* throughout the Christmas season, but somehow it isn't the same.

Anyhow, the office of Joyous Noises was decorated with strings of the electrified bags and, under the darkening sky, they looked merry as hell.

Donna Hanratty appeared to be in her fifties, and she wore her short hair brushed back into frosted flames and lacquered into place. Realtor hair. She wheeled and her face flushed when I spooked her, coming up behind her in the parking lot, but she quickly pulled herself together. Her firm handshake confirmed the feeling I'd gotten over the phone. She was a competent, forceful manager of people and resources. A leader. The kind of person who always brings out the worst in me.

I stammered my name and reminded her who I was—though we'd talked by cell phone only minutes before—and generally acted like a goof, and Mrs. Hanratty smiled and ushered me into the building. A couple of young secretaries greeted us as we passed through the living-room-turned-lobby, then we went into Mrs. Hanratty's office, which was decked out for the holidays, right down to a three-foot Christmas tree in the corner. She shucked her trench coat and hung it on a rack, then gestured me into the guest chair while she sat behind her neat desk. I pulled out a pen and my little notebook. Crossed my legs. Tried to look alert.

"So," she said, "from what you told me on the phone, your wife's given you a pretty good summation of where our situation stands."

"Yes, ma'am."

"Don't get the idea that we don't trust the police," she said, her voice low and businesslike. "That's not it at all. They'll catch whoever killed poor Daniel Gooch."

I nodded vigorously.

"But we need someone looking after our interests," she said. "If the paperwork had gone through as planned, Joyous Noises would've become the most prosperous charity in town. There's no end to the good works we could do with the regular income from those patents."

She paused, seemed to be waiting for something. I stopped nodding long enough to say, "It's what Gooch wanted."

"That's right. That's why the timing of his death is suspicious. A couple more days, and all the legalities of the transfer would've been complete."

"I heard his partner wanted him declared crazy. Wanted to invoke some kind of sanity clause."

"There is no sanity clause," Mrs. Hanratty said with a perfectly straight face. "George Marley was blowing smoke with that whole gambit. Their partnership was set up so that Daniel maintained the final rights to all the patents, with no provisions for his mental health. They were Daniel's to handle as he wished. He was the one who thought up all the inventions. Marley just leeched off the profits."

"You're not crazy about him," I suggested.

"I don't like him, no, but I'm trying not to let that prejudice me. Because of the timing, though, we have to consider that Marley might've had something to do with the murder."

"Absolutely," I said. "I'd thought of that already."

"Frankly, it would be best for us if Marley were involved. We prove he had Daniel killed to stop the transfer of ownership, and we can still end up with those patents."

I caught myself nodding again. Probably looked like one of those bobblehead dolls.

"The police are required to look at every suspect," she said, "but they're more likely to overlook something if local big shots like Marley or Carol Tannenbaum are involved. We want you to make sure that doesn't happen."

"The sister's name is really Carol Tannenbaum?"

Mrs. Hanratty smiled. "Funny, isn't it, this time of year? Bill Tannenbaum was one of Carol's ex-husbands. Second or third, I'm not sure. 'Carol Tannenbaum' stuck in everybody's mind, so she's used that name ever since."

"Carol Tannenbaum. Jeez."

"Beats her maiden name. Gooch."

"True. Which husband is she on now?"

"I think she's between commitments at the moment," she said, "but we're talking five or six so far. And counting."

Mrs. Hanratty fondled the wedding ring on her own hand. It was a sizable rock. I read her as the lucky type who'd found her soul mate on the first try.

"I don't really think Carol would kill her brother," she said, "but she's another person you'll need to check. If she's involved, it would negate Daniel's will. Still good for us, though we're probably talking a long court battle with Marley to get control of those patents."

"Right." I wrote in my notebook "Marley" and "Tannenbaum." That was all I had so far, and the page looked a little naked.

"Anybody else?" I asked.

"I did think of one person. Jeremy Hopwood. Heads up the Holiday Food Bank. He's been extremely upset the past few weeks over the patents. Daniel had given generously to Jeremy's program and other charities over the past couple of years. They all worried the tap would shut off once we got Daniel's fortune, but Jeremy's been really vocal about it. Really angry."

"You think the *food bank* guy killed Santa?"

She laughed and said, "Lord, let's hope not. Think of the headlines then!"

I winced. Guess she'd seen the *Gazette* after all. And the front-page banner: Mall Santa Murdered. Pretty restrained for the *Gazette*. But anyone who read the whole story—and who wouldn't?—found my name in there. The undercover man who showed up too late. The fact that Mrs. Hanratty was hiring me, despite the way I'd been depicted in the newspaper, made me like her all the more.

"There might be others," she said. "You'll figure out who as you go poking around. But always look to the suspects who'll do Joyous Noises some good. The worst thing possible would be if Daniel's murder was a senseless, random act. If they're both in the clear, then Carol gets everything and Marley keeps running Gooch Enterprises and we'll end up with a big fat nothing."

I felt as if my life—at least the next few weeks of it—had been mapped out for me. Mrs. Hanratty was accustomed to setting a course and having others follow. She had the force of personality that comes with command. I was ready to run right out and do her bidding.

It helped that she also handed over a retainer check.

Outside, it was spitting sleet, and I hurried over to my red Dodge Ram, got inside and turned on the heater. I had several appointments to make, and what better office than a nice warm truck with a cell phone?

My first call was to Milt Jablonski. Not that I wanted to talk to Milt. It was, in fact, about the last thing I wanted. Without the cushion of his happy countenance, Milt's sharp words might be too piercing to take. But I had to call him as a matter of professional courtesy. I was about to go splashing about in his muddy scandal, and he had the right to know. Besides, he might know more about what angles the cops were pursuing.

I listened to some Muzak about sleigh bells glistening or some such crap while I waited for Milt to come on the phone. The music abruptly stopped and Milt snarled, "The hell do you want?"

"Just checking in," I said. "Wanted to tell you that I'm investigating the Gooch murder."

"Say what?"

"Gooch. I've been retained to investigate."

"My ass. By whom?"

"Donna Hanratty. She's the director of Joyce's—"

"I know who she is. She hired you? Doesn't she read the damned newspaper?"

I cleared my throat. "She wants to make sure her interests are represented."

Listen to me. I was channeling Donna Hanratty.

"Yeah? And what are her interests?"

"Those patents. She wants to pin the murder on Marley or Tannenbaum so her charity still walks away with the patents."

I was giving up something for nothing here. But I figured Milt already knew about the behind-the-scenes struggle over the patents. If I let him in on what I was doing, maybe he'd say something in exchange that would help.

"Listen, loser," Milt said. "I've already heard from Marley *and* Tannenbaum *and* their attorneys. They're ready to sue the mall over the security breach that got Gooch killed. In case you don't remember, that breach centered on *you*. If you know what's good for you, you'll go sit quietly somewhere until this thing blows over. You don't want to get caught in a feeding frenzy."

He was right about that. Lawyers scare me worse than Santa Claus. But I'd already taken the retainer from Joyous Noises. I had to move forward. The lawyers were probably a smokescreen anyway. Marley and Tannenbaum were fat cats, just as Mrs. Hanratty had said. Naturally they'd insulate themselves in layers of lawyers. That type always does.

"Sorry, Milt, but I'm on the case. I'll try not to make a mess for the mall, but I'm looking into who killed Gooch. Soon as I get off the phone with you, I'm calling Marley."

"Don't do it, stupid. I'm warning you: Stay out of it."

"No can do, Milt."

He cursed and fumed, then there was a repeated loud slamming over the phone line that I took to be him banging the receiver against his desk. The line went dead.

Milt, clearly, was still not happy.

SIX

I CHASED AROUND TOWN all morning and even worked through lunch—a bowl of immediately-regretted spicy beef chili at a diner—gabbing on my cell phone the whole time, getting nowhere.

People seemed to be dodging me right and left. It was as if everyone I needed to see was in the same darting school of fish. Just ahead of me swims a shark, clearing a path. I come along in its wake, wondering where everybody went. I had a feeling the shark was named George Marley.

Sometimes, boldness is the only path. Around three o'clock, with hours of frustration churning the chili inside me, I went to Marley's uptown office.

I barged right in, a fullback hitting a line of tacklers. I made it through the first two waves of intercepting receptionists, and dodged a weakass arm-tackle thrown by a jowly secretary who couldn't have been a day under seventy. I'd just reached the goal line—the door to Marley's inner sanctum—when I was pulled up short by an attractive blonde who emerged from a hall to my right and reached for Marley's doorknob at the same time.

She was nearly as tall as me, lean and well-tended, wearing a festive red dress and bouncy hair that reached to her shoulders. She had enormous blue eyes, curling black lashes and a pert nose. The only thing marring her good looks was a long upper lip that threw everything out of proportion, even when she smiled. Something about her face was familiar, but I couldn't place it right away.

She said, "Excuse me," and stepped back to let me go first. Politely, pretending she didn't notice me staring or the herd of howling receptionists behind me.

I couldn't stop gawking, my mad dash to Marley half-forgotten. Had I met her somewhere before? Her smile went a little stiff as she waited, and a hard glitter arose in her eyes. And that's when I recognized the resemblance. The big eyes and that long lip and that smile that curled up on the ends. She looked like the Grinch, the green critter who stole Christmas in the Dr. Seuss classic.

Okay, maybe I had Christmas on the brain. But that smirk of hers made me nervous. She looked like the type who'd try to ruin everybody else's holiday, particularly if there were money to be made from it. The type who'd steal gifts from little children. The sort of person who'd put antlers on a dog.

I was trapped there with her and the secretaries closing in, so I took the only appropriate course of action. I stuck out my hand and introduced myself.

She shook hands. What else could she do? We were keeping it polite.

"Carol Tannenbaum."

Oh, ho. I just hit a two-bagger. Marley and Tannenbaum in the same place. Half my legwork done at once, as long as I didn't let the office staff drag me outside.

"So glad to meet you," I said. "Mr. Marley inside? I need to talk to both of you. I've been leaving messages all over."

She looked me up and down, and her wry grin cocked up on one side. Like I *amused* her.

She glanced past my shoulder and fired off a dismissive look that quieted the baying receptionists. Then she opened Marley's door and we walked right in.

George Marley was alone in his office, a long way off across a savannah of beige carpet dotted with crouching furniture. He sat behind an ornate antique desk, looking as gray and hollow-cheeked and cadaverous as Felicia had described. His thick eyebrows arched when he saw us enter, and he unfolded from the chair and up onto his feet like the hinged bundle of bones he was.

"Who the hell is this?"

"Bubba Somebody," Carol Tannenbaum said. "I found him outside, trying to bust in here."

Marley's gray eyebrows jumped around some more, ended up low over his eyes as he glared at me.

"You're that private detective," he said. "The one in the newspaper."

I tried smiling, but I don't think it worked. "That's right."

"You think you can just barge in here without an appointment?"

"I called first. It wasn't getting me anywhere. I thought the direct approach—"

"I could have you arrested for trespassing," Marley said coldly.

"Aw, you don't want to do that. I just need a few minutes of your time. And Mrs. Tannenbaum's, too. Then I'll get out of your hair and we can all get on with our Christmas shopping."

Marley wore a black suit, and he tugged at the cuffs, pulling himself together. He looked like an undertaker.

Carol Tannenbaum still appeared amused. Their eyes met, and she lifted a shoulder, as if to say, "What could it hurt?" Which was, of course, exactly what I was hoping.

"Very well," Marley said, but he didn't sound happy about it. He folded back into his chair and gestured for Carol and me to sit across from him. The big desk sat between us, but we were still within shouting distance of each other.

"First," I shouted, "let me say I'm sorry for your loss. From everything I've heard about Daniel Gooch, he was a good man."

"He was a saint," Tannenbaum said dryly.

Her expression gave nothing away. Marley still glowered at me. They weren't having me arrested, but they weren't exactly overcome with holiday welcome, either.

Milt's warning sparked through my mind. Marley and Tannenbaum and their lawyers, already circling the mall and Gooch's fortune. I needed to tread easily here, try not to upset them any more than necessary. Last thing I wanted was to be dragged into court.

I carefully skated out onto the subject of Gooch's patents, braced for the worst, getting no more than the occasional nod from Marley and zero from Tannenbaum. Everything I said was from the public record, and they both knew that. Finally Marley interrupted me.

"I take it, from the questions you're asking, that you've been retained by Donna Hanratty and her miserable little charity."

That set me back a little, but I nodded and tried to take up the questioning again.

"She wants you to find some way to pin Daniel's unfortunate murder on me," he said. "So she can get her hands on his fortune, now and forever. Isn't that right?"

I gaped at him.

"If you can't find a way to implicate me, then you're supposed to target Carol here. That would be second best, for sure, but I imagine Donna Hanratty will take what she can get."

If he hadn't scored such an absolute bingo, maybe it wouldn't have rattled me so much. I stammered and backtracked and squirmed as the pair of them watched me, frosty smiles on their faces.

Marley leaned forward in his chair, which was a form of rescue, and I shut up and let him take the lead again.

"Here's what you can write in your little notebook," he

said archly. "For the record. Carol and I are mourning Daniel right now, and you came here uninvited and made our sorrow worse."

They didn't seem to be mourning to me. Looked instead like I'd interrupted a little conspiracy klatch, Marley and Tannenbaum picking over Gooch's bones, figuring ways to maximize profits and sock away the loot.

"Also for the record," Marley continued, "both of us can account for our whereabouts at the time that Daniel met his demise."

I poised pen over paper to show him I was listening.

"I was at a business meeting, looking after Daniel's interests, right here at the office," he said. "There were twenty people present and we spent the entire afternoon here."

I wrote some gibberish on the page. Might as well have said, "Bubba's screwed."

"Carol spent the entire day at a health spa, getting massaged and painted and exfoliated for the holidays. Surrounded by attendants all day. Right, Carol?"

She nodded, which made her hair bounce. Still smiling, though clearly she didn't mean it. This is the woman who's been married four or five times? Sure, she was attractive, in a polished, expensive sort of way. But hadn't those men seen her inner Grinchiness? I could see nothing else now, and it gave me the willies.

"We've already told all this to the police," Marley was saying. "We've got nothing to hide."

I nodded glumly.

"But we've also got no reason to cooperate with you. Particularly since you're working for a charity that we may end up facing in court somewhere down the road."

More nodding. What could I say? He was right.

"Now take your little notebook," he said firmly, "and get up out of my chair and walk out of my office. Right now. If you so much as look back, I'll consider it an assault and will call the police. Clear?"

Flushing furiously, I did as I was told, skulking out the door and past the glaring secretaries. I didn't exactly have my tail tucked between my legs, but only because I don't have a tail.

A few minutes of deep-breathing exercises in the cab of my truck, and I started to feel normal again. Marley had been so smooth, telling me off and showing me the door, it had taken my breath away.

Ah, well, it wasn't a total loss. I'd registered their alibis, which I found to be suspiciously airtight. I'd confirmed the status of Gooch's patents and his fortune. I'd gotten a sense of what sort of money-grubbing, string-pulling, lawsuit-filing vermin I was dealing with here. If I'd had to eat a little humiliation to get that far, then, hey, that's why I was getting paid. All in a day's work.

Best way to recover from such a skillful putdown was to go right out and interview somebody else. Get back on that horse and ride.

Ten minutes later, I was outside the Holiday Food Bank, which was in an old warehouse off Second Street north of downtown. The building was painted with a mural of a towering Santa Claus, driving a sleigh shaped like a giant cornucopia, with all kinds of food spilling out. Creepy.

Slow, random snowflakes began to fall as I parked at the curb. I zipped up my light jacket and hiked around the windowless building until I found the entrance, dodging a couple of street people who wore so many layers of clothes, they looked like the Michelin Man. It wasn't much warmer inside, but the bustling office workers didn't seem to notice. Through an open double door, I could see a large warehouse stacked with pallets of canned goods. Workers in aprons and gloves and flannel shirts rearranged the stacks and sorted through cans, filling boxes with what I supposed were holiday meals for the indigent. The people working in the warehouse looked content, if extremely busy, and I couldn't help comparing their virtuous jobs to the grubby things I do for a living. By the time I reached Jeremy Hopwood's private office, my bad mood had gotten worse.

Hopwood bounded up from his desk as I came through the door and hurried over to pump my hand. He was younger than I'd expected—maybe thirty—ruddy and energetic and dressed like a lumberjack. He had the reddest nose I've ever seen. A deep, peeling sunburn that looked several layers deep. His forehead and the lower half of his face were sunburned, too, but they couldn't come close to his nose. It was red as a stoplight. You could even say it glowed.

He caught me staring after we introduced ourselves, and said, "Sorry about the nose. Went skiing last weekend in Taos, and forgot my sunscreen. Bad burn, but it's getting better."

"Ouch," I said.

"Forgive the clothes, too. Usually I greet people in a suit and tie. But we're shorthanded in the warehouse this time of year. I was working in there when you called."

Once he finished apologizing for his appearance and I was done assuring him it mattered not a whit, we sat and got down to business.

I didn't dance around it this time. Told him right off that I was working for Donna Hanratty. I figured, hell, they're in the same business. They're probably all friends. Maybe dropping her name would get him to speak freely.

Instead Hopwood's face reddened until it was approaching the hue of his beak.

"That witch sent you over here to *interrogate* me?"

Oops. I started over. "Mrs. Hanratty believes—"

"I don't give a rat's ass what she believes. Or what she

says. She'd do anything to get Gooch's patents and that's the bottom line."

Now that he mentioned it, that had pretty much been the upshot of Mrs. Hanratty's instructions to me: Do anything to make sure the right people get implicated in the Santa murder. Put flatly like that, away from the context of her personal charisma, it all seemed a little *calculated*.

"Donna Hanratty's on thin ice," Hopwood said. "If she doesn't secure those patents, Joyous Noises will go out of business. She thought she was all set, seducing Daniel Gooch into handing them over, but everything's different now."

I needed to back up a step. "Did you say *seducing?*"

Hopwood's ruddy face had lightened some, but now the red glow dawned again in his cheeks.

"Let me clarify. I don't mean physically seducing. I wouldn't know whether anything like that was going on. But their relationship was extremely cozy. And she used that relationship as leverage to get him to hand over the patents to Joyous Noises and cut the rest of us out. To me, that's worse than some tawdry affair."

I let that soak in, then said, "You've been very angry about this, haven't you?"

"I've been upset. And I felt I needed to speak out. Nobody else would do it. They're all afraid of making a scene. Busy playing their little games."

"What do you mean?"

"Charity organizations are a funny business, Mr. Mabry. Very courteous, very circumspect. Never do anything that might upset the donors because they'll take their dollars elsewhere. There's a limited pool of giving out there, and an ever-growing number of charities trying to survive. Out front, everything's sweetness and light, but behind the scenes, it's a cutthroat business."

I asked him a few other questions, including his whereabouts at the time of the murder—working in the warehouse with a dozen others—then folded up my notebook, ready to leave. Hopwood had given me a lot to think about, in particular the motives of my own client. He gave me a parting shot as I turned toward the door.

"If you want to find the person who killed Daniel Gooch, you'd better take a hard look at Donna Hanratty herself. I heard a rumor last week that Gooch might've had a change of heart. That some of my carping to the media had gotten through to him, and he might be leaning toward keeping all of us charities fed. Nothing definite, but there was something going on."

I put my hand on the doorknob. "That's what you've got? Rumors? That maybe Gooch was splitting up the Christmas pie? You think that's reason enough for Donna Hanratty to kill him?"

Hopwood rubbed his sunburned nose, then winced with pain. He blinked a few times, then focused on me again. His blue eyes were steady.

"I said she'd do anything, didn't I?"

SEVEN

OUTSIDE, FAT SNOWFLAKES the size of half-dollars spilled thickly from the sky, as if nature had hit the jackpot. It was sticking, too, which meant it was colder than I'd realized. My sneakers slipped in the slush as I hotfooted it back to my truck through the gathering dusk.

We don't get much snow in Albuquerque. Lots on the looming Sandia Mountains, but not much down here in the river valley. Which is exactly the way I like my snow—at a distance. Pretty to look at, but I want it *over there* somewhere, not here in the city, slicking up the streets and generally making life inconvenient and damp.

Driving in Albuquerque during a snowstorm is a thrill ride exciting enough to thaw Walt Disney. Because it snows so rarely in town, we don't get much practice driving in icy conditions.

Motorists fall into three types: One, those aggressive drivers who grew up somewhere else, like the Midwest, and who know their snow. That's Felicia. Two, timid Sun-Belt types who've never felt comfortable behind the wheel in a whiteout. That would be me. Three, reckless lunatics who rumble around New Mexico in their four-wheel-drive trucks with giant tires. These guys go eighty miles an hour wherever they go, and they don't see any reason to change that, just because there's a little ice around.

The three driving styles make for a lively mix at intersections and on the freeways. Which is why, when I'm forced to travel in snow, I look for routes with as few stops and lunatics as possible. In this case, that would be to go up Broadway past the warehouse district and hit Odelia over by Albuquerque High School. Odelia turns into the long uninterrupted stretch of Indian School Road, which I could use to get across town and approach my house from the north.

All I wanted was to get home, where it was safe and where, I hoped, people wouldn't bark at me anymore. It had been a long day.

I inched up the long, four-lane hill on Odelia, clinging to the right-hand lane while assorted maniacs roared past me on the left. The hill was steep, but I had no trouble getting traction in my pickup truck. The snow wasn't deep. Yet.

Besides, I was more worried about stopping than I was about going. That first layer of snow mixes with spilled motor oil and antifreeze and various other leakages that bake onto the roadways during the dry months. Get it all wet and stir it up, and it can be slick as a Popsicle, making every braking an adventure.

One vehicle got right on my ass as we climbed past the high school. It was a big Chevy Tahoe four-wheel-drive rig with whip antennas and oversize tires. The Lunatic Special.

I slowed even more, giving the Tahoe room to come around, but it stayed right on my tail, its headlight beams bouncing off my mirrors and blinding me.

As we neared the I-25 overpass at the top of the hill, the Tahoe swung around me to my left, passing me finally, and I sighed in relief. Then the SUV swerved right and nearly clipped my fender. Idiot! I hit the brakes too hard and my Ram fishtailed on the slick pavement. I spun the wheel and eased off the brake and got the pickup under control, just as the Tahoe swept at me again.

Its rear bumper crashed into my front fender from the side, and the jolt nearly knocked the wheel out of my hands.

The Ram slid sideways. Its tires hit the curb and we jolted back in the other direction, thundered again into the roaring Tahoe.

The SUV shuddered and slid, but the driver goosed it forward, and the big tires threw slush, water and mud all over my windshield. My wipers were going, but not fast enough to handle the deluge, and I could see nothing for a moment.

I had my foot off the gas, but the Ram still rolled forward. I didn't want to hit the brakes again. I'd had enough thrills already.

My heart pounding, I thought: What's with this guy? I couldn't see the driver through the Tahoe's tinted windows, but he must be drunk or crazy. Whamming into me on these messy streets. Had I done something stupid in traffic to anger him? We see a lot of road rage around Albuquerque, particularly when the city's in the grip of the snow crazies. I couldn't think of any error I'd made. If anything, I was too cautious. Had that set him off?

The windshield cleared just in time for me to see the Tahoe braking and swerving to its left, into the oncoming lanes. There were headlights far away up ahead, but no other cars right around us and I slowed some more—to maybe ten miles per hour—trying to give the maniac the whole road.

The slowing Tahoe suddenly veered toward me. I saw in a flash what was happening. The overpass had concrete walls on either side and tall wire fences, curved inward on the top, to keep pedestrians from jumping. But just before the safety walls began, there was an opening, with only a flimsy metal rail offering protection from the forty-foot plunge to the busy freeway below.

Just as I registered the situation, the Tahoe crunched into the side of my slow-moving truck. It hit me just right, the passenger door of the Tahoe even with the front end of my truck, all the momentum on his side. The Tahoe pressed up against my cab obscenely, pushing the Ram sideways on the slick street, steering me directly toward the edge of the precipice.

While visions of plummeting danced in my head, I fought back the only way I could, yanking at the steering wheel, slamming my truck into the SUV, trying to get it *off* me. It dawned on me to hit the gas, and the Ram lurched forward, its wheels spinning. There was a long, painful shriek of metal-on-metal as I squirted between the Tahoe and the sturdy concrete guardrail. Onto the overpass, where it was slightly safer.

The Tahoe smashed the Ram against the guardrail as we scraped and slid across the overpass. Sparks flew up from my right fender, mixing with the falling snowflakes into a blinding hallucination. Horrendous crashing and grinding overflowed my ears, so that I could barely hear myself screaming.

One level of shrieking dropped away as we reached the end of the concrete wall. My truck shimmied sideways, then thudded into a steel guardrail that angled away from the abutment. The Tahoe kept coming, a terrible weight to my left, and I felt the Ram lift off the ground, its tires roaring as they tried to grasp air. Then my truck went crashing through the snow.

The Ram slowly rolled two or three times. Mud and slush and weeds flashed past the windshield as the truck tumbled into an empty lot in front of St. Paul Lutheran Church. The church's roof swoops above the hilltop like a three-cornered hat, and the roofline glowed with *luminarias* that dipped and spun crazily through the cracked windshield before the truck stopped flip-flopping on the ground.

I was safely buckled into my seat belt, so the wreck didn't knock me out or send me flying out the window. I'd hit my head, though, and I was dizzy and in pain. I felt out of breath and achy all over, as if the seat belts themselves had given me a good beating. Plus, I was covered with smaller, sharper pains from all the missiles that had rocketed around the cab while the truck mocked gravity: My cell phone, a flashlight, some cassettes, a few ballpoints, loose change and old sandwich wrappers. The truck ended up lying on the driver's side, so all that junk settled around me where I lay strapped in my seat.

The engine conked out. I must've hit the radio buttons with my knee when I was flailing around, because the cab filled with Bing Crosby crooning "White Christmas."

I fumbled for the button, cursing, and cut off the music. I popped myself loose from the seat belt and swiveled around in the detritus until I was sitting on my own window against the ground. I stretched and got hold of the passenger-side door handle and forced the crunched door open.

I stood, pushing the door all the way open with a squawk. I had to hold the door because it wanted to slam shut at that angle. *Sure, now I've got gravity working against me. Where was it when I needed it? Not keeping the Ram's wheels on the ground, that's for certain.* I was so busy with the door, I almost didn't notice the roar of an engine up on the road. I looked up in time to see the Tahoe drive away.

So not only had the jackass run me off the road, he'd stuck around to see if I survived. Clearly no accident, whatever the road conditions. That Tahoe was out to get me.

I knew two things as I climbed out of the mangled cab: No matter how much I hurt at the moment or how cold and wet it was out here, I was lucky to be alive. And somebody really wanted me off the case.

EIGHT

OVER THE NEXT TWO HOURS, the empty lot was illuminated by so many flashing lights from cop cars, a wrecker and an ambulance, it looked like a disco.

Overworked officers, bundled against the cold, stomped around in the mud and bitched about the snow. They dutifully recorded my story about being forced off the road, but seemed to lean toward the notion that the wreck was just another accident on a snowy night in Albuquerque. They promised, however, that the case would be passed along to detectives once the storm was over. Since I hadn't gotten a license plate number or a look at the driver, they told me, the prospects of an arrest were dim.

Two emergency medical technicians examined me and declared me more or less intact. They suggested I go to a hospital to be checked over thoroughly, but I declined, so they shrugged and declared me an idiot and turned me loose.

My red pickup hadn't fared as well as me. After the heavy-duty tow truck pulled the Ram onto its feet, it was clear my old steed was a goner. The body was mangled, the frame was bent and the tires hung off the rims like muddy rubber bands. If I'd had a pistol on me, I would've given the truck a farewell shot to put it out of its misery, like in that old Bill Mauldin cartoon from World War II.

Just as well that I wasn't armed. Too many cops steaming in the snow, looking for clues, to be shooting motor vehicles. They might get the wrong idea.

Instead I retrieved my cell phone from the cab, gave the keys to the tow truck guy and sent my red Ram off to the auto graveyard without ceremony.

A cop gave me a lift home. This wasn't any great courtesy, seeing as how he made me ride in the back on the hard-plastic, hose-off seat, and there was evidence that a holiday reveler had hoisted the old egg nog back there recently. Still, it was better than hiking home in the snow.

The cop handled the slick streets with daring and skill, and in no time I was skating up the sidewalk to my front porch and he was racing off to some other holiday emergency.

I hurt all over, bruised and nicked and limping. My clothes were soaked and muddy. I still suffered the disorienting aftereffects of the crash—a jittery daze, partial deafness and an adrenaline headache. I creaked up the icy steps onto the front porch, and let myself into my warm house, wanting only quiet and rest.

A powerful evergreen fragrance hit me in the face and almost sent me reeling. I turned to the right and nearly poked my eye out on the branch of a huge Christmas tree, which had been planted squarely before the front window. Furniture had been moved out of the way to make room for this needled monster, and its top reached the nine-foot ceiling. It filled half the room, and seemed to be growing, soon to take over the whole house.

The tree was strangely decorated. From about six feet down, it was thick with tinsel and balls, candy canes and little red bows and strings of lights that weren't plugged in at the moment, which explained how the thing had managed to sneak up on me. A note was speared onto the end of one branch. I cautiously snatched it off and read its scrawl:

Bubba,
I decorated as high as I could reach. You do the rest. Put the angel on the top. I've gone back to the news-

room. Couldn't really spare the time to get the tree, but I knew *you'd* never get around to it. You Scrooge.

Ho, Ho, Ho

F.

The note left several questions unanswered: Why did Felicia have to overdo the Christmas tree, the way she overdoes everything? How did she get this mammoth sequoia home through the snow? How did Felicia, a relatively tiny, if dynamic, woman, get the tree through the front door and erect on its stand, and the furniture rearranged to accommodate it? And if she was mighty enough to accomplish all that on her own, how come she couldn't get a ladder and finish the decorating? Could I possibly lift my battered arms high enough to put the angel on the tree?

I could not. I shambled to the kitchen, trying to shake off the feeling the tree was following me, and took the one sure remedy for all pains and distresses: I drank a beer. Standing at the kitchen sink, too tired to change out of my wet clothes, staring out the window at the snow blanketing the backyard, I finished the whole beer—then opened another. Then I squished into the spare bedroom that passes for my office and sat at my desk in my damp clothes. It was dark in there, but I didn't feel like reaching for the desk lamp. I just rocked in my swivel chair, sipping my beer, comforted by the warmth and the silence of my home.

The phone jangled—naturally. I fumbled for the receiver in the half light. Pain stabbed my shoulder when I brought the phone up to my ear, so instead of hello, I answered, "Ow!"

Nobody on the other end. I gritted my teeth and said "hello" a couple of times, wondering how much it would hurt to reach over and hang up. Then a voice floated over the line.

"Mr. Mabry?"

"Yeah?"

"This is George Marley. Are you all right?"

Granted, I'd sounded funny when I answered, but something in Marley's tone told me he was surprised I was up and around at all.

"I'm fine."

"From the way you answered the phone, you sounded like—"

"Ow? It's Chinese. Traditional greeting. I've been trying it out."

"Yes, well, that's fine. Listen, I wanted to follow up on our meeting this afternoon—"

"Was that you in that Tahoe?" I blurted. "Or somebody you sent?"

"Excuse me?"

"I was nearly killed in a car wreck a couple of hours ago, as if you didn't know. Somebody forced me off the road over by Albuquerque High. Rolled my truck."

"So sorry to hear that," Marley said. He didn't sound sorry at all. Sounded a little smug, in fact.

"You behind it?" I asked. "Trying to throw a scare into me?"

"Not me," Marley intoned. "Not my style, I assure you. If I had a problem with you, I'd take you to court. That's the way civilized men settle their grievances."

He had a point. I flexed my neck, trying to get a hitch out of it, taking a moment. Then I said, "Would've been awfully easy for somebody to follow me away from your office this afternoon. Wait for the right moment, in the snow, then run me off the road."

"When did you say this happened?"

"Around dusk."

"So it wasn't immediately after you left my office."

"No, but—"

"You must've gone elsewhere during the interim."

"Well, yeah. I was at the food bank—"

"Isn't it more likely that someone followed you from the— What did you call it? A *food* bank?—rather than wait for an hour or two and then give you the bump at dusk?"

I said nothing, too occupied with processing it all.

"See, Mr. Mabry, this is the way the legal mind works. Find the inconsistencies, the gaps in the timeline, the everyday errors of human life. Use them to your advantage. Resolve your grievances before the court. See who comes out on top."

I didn't think much of this lecture, but I was too busy slugging beer to respond.

"This is the type of mind you're going up against," Marley said. "One, I don't hesitate to say, that's far superior to yours. You don't want to end up in court against me."

I suppressed a burp and said, "Is that a threat?"

"Not at all," Marley said. "I believe you've already been warned to call off your little investigation. This car wreck, if it wasn't a simple accident, might be a more serious warning. I'd be careful, if I were you."

"Thanks for your concern," I said flatly. "Why were you calling again?"

Marley cleared his throat. "It came to my attention after you left here this afternoon that your wife is Felicia Quattlebaum, the reporter for the *Gazette*."

"So?"

"I was calling to give you notice that I'll be watching her stories very carefully to see if there's any indication you're feeding her information about me or Gooch Enterprises or Carol Tannenbaum. The slightest falsehood or allegation will be considered grounds for a libel suit."

"I can't control what she writes—"

"I'm not sure the court would see it that way."

"Buddy, you don't *know* how little I control around here. I couldn't keep Felicia from writing whatever the hell she wants in *any* story. No more than I could keep a nine-foot redwood out of my living room."

"What?"

I took a deep breath.

"Look, Marley, you can stop worrying about me. I've got nothing on you. Not yet anyway. And what I do get, I won't hand over to Felicia. That's between me and my client."

"Better keep it that way," he said. "I'll be watching."

That got my hackles up.

"I'll be watching you, too, pal. And if I find out you were behind that wreck tonight, you and I are going to—"

The phone clicked in my ear. I was talking to myself. I gingerly stretched across the desk, moaning over the pain in my shoulder, and hung up. I relaxed into my chair, finished off my beer, let the silent night settle over me again.

Footsteps clomped onto the front porch.

NINE

FELICIA LET HERSELF IN the door by the time I limped into the living room to open it for her. The looming tree seemed to reach its clutching branches toward her as she sidled through the doorway, carrying an evergreen wreath that was almost as big as her.

"Here, take this," she said, and handed the wreath over before I could object. I tried to grab it, but every bruised muscle resisted, and the bow-dotted wreath fell to the floor.

Felicia pushed her hair out of her eyes and looked at me. Her face was flushed from the cold and maybe a little holiday cheer, if you know what I mean. I remembered something about an office party.

"What's the matter with you?" she demanded. "You bent the wreath."

"I don't feel so good."

"You're sopping wet!"

She looked around the room through the steam forming on her glasses.

"And you haven't finished the tree! I left you that note hours ago. I swear, Bubba, ask you to do one thing around here—"

"I wrecked the truck."

"I don't care. I asked you to— What did you say?"

"The truck. Totaled. Some fool ran me off the road over by Albuquerque High."

"Get *out*."

"It's true. They towed the truck off to the junkyard."

"Oh, shit. That's what we need. To buy a new car. Right at Christmas."

"Sorry. I'm fine, by the way."

She caught herself and pushed the wreath out of the way with her foot and came closer to look me over.

"You're not hurt? You look hurt."

"A little bit. Nothing that won't heal on its own."

She poked my chest a couple of times with an exploratory finger, making me jump and say, "Ouch." I backed away, out of reach of Dr. Feelbad, and headed for the kitchen, yearning for that time—only a few minutes ago—when all was calm around the house.

Felicia bustled along behind me, pressing for details and clucking over my wet clothes and muddy shoes. I let her steer me toward the bedroom and some dry jeans. While I changed, every movement sending panic attacks of pain through my body, I told her about the wreck and my day full of interviews. I finished up with the phone call from Marley.

"That's all he threatened you with?" she asked when I paused for air. "Court?"

"Yeah, but he suggested tonight's wreck might've been a warning for me to mind my own business."

"He denied doing it himself?"

"Who can believe a guy like that?"

We trooped back to the kitchen, where I took the last beer from the fridge.

"I still think Marley's our murderer," Felicia said brightly. "He had the most to lose if Daniel Gooch kept walking around. And he seems like the type who'd kill to get what he wants."

"Marley's an easy guy to dislike," I said.

"You said it. So creepy and gray. Almost like a ghost."

"I get the feeling he's haunting both our lives for the near future."

Felicia popped the top on a Coke and we sat at the table,

batting around theories, oohing over my aches and moping over our departed red sled of a truck.

"You know," I said finally, "Marley said something on the phone that kinda struck me funny."

Felicia had finished her soda and was deliberately crumpling the can into an ever-smaller ball. I couldn't watch for fear she'd slice open a finger. She didn't look up from her project as she said, "What's that?"

"He said something like, 'I believe you'd been warned to call off your little investigation.'"

"He meant with the car wreck."

"No, *before* the wreck. He said I'd already been warned, and tonight might be the second warning."

Felicia pushed her ball of aluminum away. "So?"

"So what did he mean, I'd been warned? He didn't warn me off the case at his office. He just said he knew what I was up to, working for Mrs. Hanratty, and then sort of danced circles around me and sent me spinning out the door. Who's he talking to, says I was warned off the case?"

"Turn it around," she said. "Anybody give you such a warning?"

"No." I thought back. "Hell, I don't know. People are always warning me and threatening me and telling me to mind my own business. Eventually it all blurs together."

"Think about who you've seen since the murder," she said. "Who said anything like that?"

I ran the past twenty-four hours through my mind, ticking off the people I'd encountered—everyone from Marley to Romero. Only one person came to mind who had issued a warning. Milt Jablonski.

I told this to Felicia, who thought it over before pronouncing that it didn't make any sense. How would Marley know that Milt had warned me about anything? Why would Marley and Milt be talking to each other, now that lawsuits had been threatened and the mall people were scurrying to cover their assets?

"Do you think Milt maybe told Marley about the warning as a way to distract him?" she asked. "Put his attention on you instead of having him sue the mall?"

"Maybe. But the timing's all screwy. Milt said he'd heard from Marley and the rest. *Then* he warned me to stay out of it. Which means he must've talked to Marley after I was fired. Why tell him anything about me then? I was out of the picture."

We chewed on it for a few minutes. Felicia said, "We need to talk to Milt. Find out what he said."

I looked at the clock on the kitchen wall. It was after eight. The mall would close soon. Even if we could get there through the snow before the mall was shuttered, odds were good that Milt had long ago gone home.

Felicia was looking at the clock, too, doing the same calculations.

"Get your shoes on," she said. "I'll drive you over."

TEN

FELICIA'S TOYOTA is just the right size for her, but it's a little cramped for a long-legged guy like me. It hurt all over to squeeze into the car. I whined and yelped so much, it sounded like an opera.

Things didn't get any better after we got underway. Felicia was as casually reckless and distracted behind the wheel as she always is, zipping fearlessly along the snowy streets. I spent the drive to the mall in a state of apprehension, bracing against every little slip and slide, aching all over.

"You're gonna stomp a hole through the floor," she said. "You don't have a brake pedal over there. Give it up."

"I don't know what you mean." I busied myself looking out the window at the winter wonderland of snow and streetlights, trying to ignore the lack of traction or the fact that Felicia was driving too damned fast.

"Hey," she said, "you think Marley bought Milt off?"

"Like how?"

"Getting him to say he saw no one on those security video monitors. The whole mystery here has been how somebody killed Gooch when no one was seen going in or out of that locker room. But if Milt was *lying* about that, then Milt knows who killed Gooch."

"You think Milt saw somebody leave that room. That Marley paid him off to lie about it?"

"Maybe Milt saw Marley himself," she said. "Marley could've come in the back way, killed Gooch, then gone out again before the elf found the body. But only if Milt was paid to look the other way, and to say he saw no one."

"I don't know, hon," I said. "Doesn't sound like Milt. And besides, Marley has an alibi for the time when Gooch was killed. He was in his office with a bunch of other people."

She chewed on it for a minute while we slid around potholes full of water and icebergs.

"He could've paid them off, too," she said. "Or, he could've sent somebody else to kill Gooch while he had a convenient alibi."

"I don't know—"

"How else to explain it? You're sure nobody went in the front, right?"

"I was looking at that door the whole time."

"So Milt's lying. Either he saw somebody and is lying about it, or he wasn't watching the monitors for some reason and somebody got past him and he's lying about *that*. Until we know which is true, we don't know if we can nail Marley or anybody else. If Milt saw the killer, the cops should be able to squeeze it out of him. But if he was squatting in the crapper the whole time and too embarrassed to admit it, we've still got no killer."

My sweetie. Always the perfect lady.

Felicia wheeled us into the parking lot at the Rio Grande Mall, throwing up a rooster-tail of slush. Snow still fell steadily, and the parking lot was mostly empty, a white blanket crisscrossed by the tic-tac-toe of tire tracks.

In Albuquerque, everybody races home at the first sign of snow, trying to avoid all the other speeding lunatics. Some pause long enough to make a run on supermarket shelves, stocking up for the big blizzard that never lasts more than a day or two. But the mall shoppers were gone, and the arc lights in the parking lot showed only a few snow-covered cars that probably belonged to store employees.

The only vehicles moving around in the snow were a couple of big black SUVs, tricked out with antennas and big tires. They were unmarked, but clearly were mall security vehicles, still patrolling.

Okay, every third vehicle in Albuquerque these days is a freaking SUV, all right? And they all look alike to me. But these looked identical to the Chevy Tahoe that tried to send me to my death earlier in the evening.

I pointed this out to Felicia. She clenched her jaw heroically, gripped the steering wheel and zoomed on a beeline toward one of the SUVs to get a better look. She had to tell me when we were close because I had my eyes closed, muttering prayers.

I pried my eyes open and checked out the circling patrol car. Ho, ho, ho, a Tahoe.

I told Felicia it was identical, and she whipped the steering wheel around. The little Toyota did a slow, sliding pirouette on the slick pavement, all the way around, coming to a graceful halt inches away from the curb outside the glowing mall entrance.

Once I could get my breath, I said, "Did you mean to do that?"

"Do what?"

A row of lights along the mall's exterior wall winked out.

"They're closing," she said.

"I'll run inside. Check Milt's office."

"I'll go with you."

"No, wait here. I'll just run inside. Run right out again."

"I'm going with you."

"Just wait right here. I'll be back in a flash."

I flung open my door, determined to go it alone, but I was too creaky and achy to leap out of the little car. By the time I was on the curb, Felicia had shut off the engine, got out, come around and was standing on the sidewalk, watching me.

"Need any help?"

"I'm fine," I muttered.

More lights shut off as we walked toward the entrance.

"We need to hurry," she said.

"That's what I'm doing."

"This is hurrying?"

"Best I can do."

I grunted and gritted and hobbled faster.

"Good thing you've got me along," she said.

"If it weren't for you, I'd be snuggled in bed right now."

"This will only take a minute," she said. "Then you can run right home and jump under the covers."

ELEVEN

HERE'S THE TRUTH: The only reason I consented to slip-sliding across town with Felicia was that I figured Milt Jablonski wouldn't be at the mall. A man of his age and position hanging around until closing time? Not a chance. Not even with all the bad publicity keeping them busy with spin control at the Rio Grande Mall. Milt would be home, drinking beer on the sofa, his sore feet propped up on pillows, watching a football game. Which is exactly what I would've like to have been doing myself.

But no, I was marching through the mall, limping along to the rhythm of the pulsing Christmas Muzak, as weary shopkeepers pulled steel gates shut across the fronts of their stores. No one tried to stop us as we went through a door marked Employees Only and walked down a corridor toward Milt's office.

I'd seen the determined light in Felicia's eyes when she'd announced that she'd drive me to see Milt. She gets that look, I might as well go along. I can agree to whatever wild whim has grabbed her, or I can agree after I lose the argument. Felicia's too smart to outwit and too dogged to outlast. She says we'll go see Milt, sooner or later we'll go see Milt.

I went along because I expected he wouldn't be there. I thought we could scoot over to the mall, find Milt's office locked, maybe talk to a security guard, then go home. Felicia would feel that she'd made the good effort. I could, eventually, go to bed where I belonged. Everybody wins.

So I was more than a little surprised when Felicia knocked

on the office door and it was flung open by Milt himself. His curly hair was mussed and his necktie was pulled loose, as if he'd had a long day, but he otherwise looked as happy as usual.

"We have some questions for you," Felicia said, and steamrolled right past him into his office.

Milt's eyes went wide, then he glared at *me,* who'd done nothing but stand in the hallway like a geek.

"The hell you want, Mabry?"

"I brought you a Christmas present."

Milt tried to scowl at me, but it was, of course, the happiest scowl you've ever seen, and I couldn't take him seriously.

"What present?"

"The pleasure of my wife's company."

"Thanks a lot."

He stepped back and let me in, then closed the office door. Felicia already sat in a straight-backed chair in front of Milt's desk. I pulled up another chair and Milt went around to his own chair and fell into it with a weary sigh.

"You're here late," I said.

"There's a lot of shoveling after a shitstorm."

"You look pretty happy about it," Felicia said.

"He always looks like that," I said. "He's not really happy."

"Not happy at all," Milt agreed.

"Whatever," Felicia said impatiently. "We wanted to ask you about those security monitors."

She pointed at the eight flickering screens on a rack beside Milt's desk. They showed various angles of the emptying mall and the blank-walled service corridors of the shopping center's backstage world.

"What about them?" Milt said.

"You told the cops you were watching them the whole time."

"That's right. I knew the shift change was coming up, so

I was watching for any hitches. Saw your husband on one screen, spilling coffee on his shirt—"

"What about the service corridor behind Santa's locker room?" I interrupted.

"One screen's kept on that corridor all the time. When you get employee theft, that's the kind of back entrance they use to haul stuff out. I was looking right at it the whole time, and nobody came or went."

"Not possible," Felicia said. "Bubba was watching the front and saw no one there. Somebody had to leave that locker room after Gooch was killed. One of you would've seen him."

Milt ran his plump hands along the edge of his metal desk. "Excuse me for saying so, but who are you gonna believe? A retired cop, or your husband, who, frankly, couldn't find his way out of a revolving door without help."

"Hey—"

"Better yet, who do you think the police will believe?" Milt looked happily smug. "Me or him?"

Felicia, I noticed, didn't answer.

"What about George Marley?" she said. "You've been talking to him. What's that about? Was Marley the one you saw in that corridor?"

"I haven't talked to Marley."

"Yes, you did. Marley said Bubba had been warned to stay out of the case. The only person who'd issued such a warning is you."

"Probably everybody's been telling him to stay out of it. Certainly the police must've warned him away. He's a loose cannon. You don't need that in a murder investigation."

I was beginning to resent Milt's remarks.

"There's another investigation," I said. "The one into who tried to kill me tonight by shoving my truck off the road."

Milt's expression, naturally, didn't change.

"We just got a look at your security vehicles outside," I said. "They're identical to the one that forced me off the road. I'm guessing the cops will check them out, find one hidden away. One that's got body damage all around from the crash."

"You think it was one of our vehicles?"

"That's right. I think it was you behind the wheel, too. Or one of your guards. Somebody you sent after me."

"That's crazy talk."

"We'll see what the cops think," I said. "They'll be coming around to check the trucks."

Milt fingered the edge of his desk some more. His eyes darted from me to Felicia.

She leaned toward him, moving in for the kill.

"Who are you covering up for, Milt?" she demanded. "Who did you see in that corridor?"

"I saw nobody."

"Somebody pay you to keep quiet? To let them slip in and do their dirty business with Gooch and sneak away again? Was it Marley? He's got the bucks to arrange something like that."

Milt said nothing.

"Was it Carol Tannenbaum?" I asked. "Did she get to you? Make wild promises so you'd cover up for her?"

Milt's hands stopped moving. He leaned back in his swivel chair, putting a little distance between us, but he still kept quiet. Weathering our onslaught.

"Or was it *you,* Milt?" Felicia said.

That pulled me up short.

"Did you go down that corridor yourself?" she said. "You could've killed Gooch, then run back to your office, so you could pretend to have been watching the whole time. Maybe it's your own ass you're covering."

Milt's eyebrows arched even higher than usual. Felicia, it seemed, had hit a nerve.

"Who paid you to kill him?" she persisted. "Was it Marley? He wanted Gooch out of the way. The transfer of the patents made it urgent. Maybe Marley found just the guy to help him out of his problems. A retired cop who knows the mall inside and out. One who has all the *keys*. One who can create his own alibi and testify about empty corridors should the need arise."

Milt was very still. She was cornering him. It was a beautiful thing to watch, but I was nervous as hell. If Milt *had* killed Gooch, wouldn't he kill again to cover his tracks?

I suddenly wished I'd brought a gun with me. I wished we had stayed home. I wished I'd taken that ambulance ride to the hospital. I wished I was anywhere but here.

"You know what will happen," she said. "Marley will make a deal. He'll talk and he'll walk. He'll get an early retirement. You'll get Death Row."

Milt seemed to deflate. He closed his eyes and lowered his head and sagged in his chair.

My heart thumped. Felicia crouched on the very front edge of her chair, looking as if she were preparing to pounce across the desk.

Milt took a deep breath and looked up at us. The defiance had gone out of his eyes.

"All right," he said. "But it's not the way you think."

"Tell us about it," she said.

"First, let me show you something. It'll help make it all clear."

He pulled open the middle drawer of his desk, and his plump hand wriggled inside and came up with a snubnose revolver.

I stiffened all over, which hurt. Felicia froze.

"See there," Milt said happily. "That makes everything clear, doesn't it? Now you two sit still, or I'll shoot you. Clear?"

TWELVE

MILT STOOD US UP against a wall, patted us down and found our cell phones. He took them away and put them in a drawer of his desk. Milt was very professional the whole time, very thorough, looking happy as all get-out.

After checking his video monitors to make sure the coast was clear, he marched us out of his office and down the long service corridor. He stopped outside an unlabeled blue door and kept the gun on us while he fished keys out of his pocket and unlocked it.

"Inside," he said, smiling.

We did as we were told, and Felicia just managed to find a light switch before Milt slammed the heavy door shut.

The overhead lights revealed a storeroom, windowless and jam-packed with naked mannequins and old store displays and decorative kitsch. A couple of tattered tables. Stacks of crates and boxes. Holiday decorations from around the calendar—cardboard Thanksgiving turkeys, plastic jack-o'-lanterns, furled American flags and even a few Christmas items too worn or broken to grace Santa's Workshop this year.

Felicia immediately began poking around the room, rummaging through stuff. I checked the door. Of course it was locked, but you never know.

"I can't believe it," I said. "Milt really did it. You pegged him exactly."

"I was fishing," Felicia said. "Thought he'd get so busy

denying the murder that he'd say something about who paid him off to keep quiet."

"You didn't know he did it?"

"Not for sure. But he looked guilty to me. Nobody's that damned happy."

"But why would he kill Gooch? What's he gain?"

"A big payoff from Marley. I'm guessing Milt discovered he didn't like spending his retirement as a shopping mall cop."

She might be on to something there. I remembered our conversation when Milt hired me, him complaining about being stuck at the mall in his golden years.

"But how would Milt even know about Gooch and the patents and all that?"

"Couldn't have been too hard for him to put it together. He interviewed all the Santas this year and did background checks, right? He would've known who Daniel Gooch was, after he showed up here, wanting to play Santa as a lark."

"I don't think it was a lark for Gooch. He was serious about being a good Santa."

"Whatever." She still rifled through the holiday displays. "The question I'd like answered is whether Milt went to Marley or Marley came to him. I still think the two of them are mixed up in this together. Why else would Milt bump Santa?"

She tossed aside a large cardboard rocking horse that had a hole gouged in one side.

"But why hire me?" I protested. "If Milt knew he was setting up Gooch, why hire an extra set of eyes to watch the Santas?"

She gave me a pitying look, and it hit me: I'd been a diversion, a smokescreen, a shill. Milt had hired me because it would make him look better once Gooch was killed. Prove that Milt was doing all he could to protect the Santas. Give him a fall guy, if necessary. I felt bad that I'd been duped this way. Felt even worse because it's happened before.

Felicia grabbed a large plastic reindeer out of the pile of Christmas rubble and stood it up.

"What are you doing?" I asked.

"Looking for something to help get us out of here."

"We can't get out of here. There's only one door, and it's locked. We can bang on it, see if somebody hears us."

"Nobody will hear us," she said. "He would've thought of that. We have to get out on our own."

"But that's impossible."

She pushed up her smudged glasses. "It's like this, Bubba. We get out of here before Milt comes back or we're dead. He's just waiting for everybody to clear out of the mall. He could be back anytime."

That made a chilling amount of sense. "Okay," I said. "Let's get out of here. How?"

"The ceiling?"

I looked up. The ceiling was twelve feet high, constructed of those perforated white tiles you see everyplace, suspended on white aluminum frames. Something above it, but no way to know what until somebody climbed up there.

"That reindeer looks sturdy," I said.

"It's only got three legs."

"We can prop it up with something. Put it on one of those tables, climb up on its back."

"And dash away home?"

I made a face. "We can at least see what's up there. I don't see any other option."

It sounded easier than it was, but pretty soon, with me steadying Blitzen and a wooden crate replacing his missing leg, Felicia was able to lift away a ceiling tile and pull herself up. She turned around up there and peered down at me through the square hole.

"Nothing up here," she said. "Just some pipes and wires and things. It's pretty dark, but we can crawl around, find a way out."

She sort of bounced on her arms a little bit. I started, thinking she might be falling on me, but she was just testing her weight.

"Ceiling's pretty flimsy," she said. "I'm not sure it'll support both of us. You want to try it, or should I go get help?"

"I'll go with you. Better than standing around here, waiting for Milt to come in and shoot me."

I climbed up on the reindeer, teetering and twitching, and managed to get hold of the ceiling trusses.

"Watch out for the antlers," Felicia said.

Every muscle hurt like hell as I pulled myself up through the hole, and the ceiling gave precariously as I clambered up onto it, but pretty soon I was crouched next to Felicia. Up by the rooftop. Ho, ho, ho.

We began crawling, the ceiling flexing and bowing under our weight. I tried to land my hands and knees on the places where the supporting frames came together, figuring it was stronger there. Pretty soon, I was splayed out like Spider-Man.

"Think we oughta lift a tile?" I whispered. "See where we are?"

"Let's go a little farther. I want to put some distance between us and Milt."

The ceiling stepped up a couple of times. We'd pull ourselves up a wall four or five feet, then it was back onto the "dropped" ceiling, which I feared would live up to its name. We were climbing ever higher, and I had a strong sensation of the unseen floor beneath us getting farther and farther away.

The mall Muzak was even louder up here among the acoustic tiles. "Joy to the World" and "Silent Night" and "The First Noel" and I don't know what all. Annoying as hell.

Felicia moved through the crawlspace the way she does everything—full-tilt and reckless. I was barely keeping up when we heard a loud crack.

We froze. Waited.

The ceiling seemed to sag beneath us more than before, but it didn't make any other noises. Felicia took a deep breath and gently lifted her knee and moved it forward, shifting her weight. The ceiling held. All was well.

She glanced over her shoulder at me and grinned. Started crawling.

I began to follow. A truss cracked loudly under my knee. Everything gave way.

There was something almost fluid about the way we spilled from the ceiling. The aluminum supports peeled away and the tiles tipped and slid and Felicia and I went screaming downward. Sudden and swift, like riding down a waterfall.

I was immediately swallowed up in pointy plastic pine needles, which stabbed me all over. I'd landed on one of the giant, ornately decorated Christmas trees that flanked Santa's Workshop.

Fake branches ripped and shiny baubles flashed past and strands of lights and tinsel grabbed at me, trying to break my fall. Foliage slapped me in the face all the way down, but I snagged to a halt, a string of lights caught under my right arm, before I hit the floor. I dangled there, my sneakers two feet off the floor, while I listened to Felicia finish crashing down the other side of the giant tree.

"Sweetie?" I called hoarsely. "You all right?"

Someone shouted off to my left. I whipped my head around and saw Milt Jablonski gaping at me, fifty feet away down the mall, beyond the tracks of the miniature train that encircled Santa's Workshop. Two gray-uniformed guards were with him.

"Burglars!" Milt shouted. "Get 'em!"

The chunky rent-a-cops pulled nightsticks from their belts and sprinted toward us.

THIRTEEN

THE TWO GUARDS were almost upon us by the time I untangled myself from the Christmas tree. I looked around for a weapon but was overwhelmed by the possibilities. This was Santa's Workshop. Junk was *everywhere*. Gift-wrapped packages and fake workbenches and velvet-rope stanchions and life-size rocking horses and giant candy canes and chunks of foam snow and broken tree branches and every type of toy and bauble and ornament a person might like to throw. The embarrassment of riches stunned me for a second.

The first fat guard was close enough that he'd cocked his nightstick over his shoulder, ready to brain me, and I still stood there, helpless and stupid. A giant Christmas gift came hurtling through the air, its green bow flapping, and smacked into his red face.

Granted, it was just an empty box. But it was the distraction I needed. I dodged away before he could recover.

Out of the corner of my eye, I saw Felicia coming round the Christmas tree. Her glasses were cockeyed and she had tinsel in her hair, but she didn't look injured from the fall. She looked, in fact, a little dangerous, a murderous gleam in her eyes. That gave me hope.

I turned as I reached the rows of velvet ropes used to corral anxious kids waiting to see Santa. The guard Felicia had bopped with the big gift was right behind me. The other one had peeled off, headed toward Felicia, who darted away, knocking over displays and casting gifts in her wake. The guard was gaining on her. I felt sorry for him.

My immediate problem was the rent-a-cop swinging his billyclub at my head. I ducked and heard the nightstick whistle past. Threw a looping right low into his soft belly. He oofed and stumbled backward a couple of steps.

I grabbed one of the brass stanchions used to support the red velvet ropes. I lifted the heavy stanchion and lunged forward, swinging it toward the surprised guard's head like a baseball bat.

The problem with your velvet-rope stanchion as a weapon is that it's still attached to the velvet ropes. Which in turn are attached to a bunch more stanchions. Which means you can't get very far. I swung the stanchion to within inches of the guard's head before the ropes and the weight of the long line of poles snatched me backward. The guard stood gaping, only slightly less surprised than I was.

The ropes acted like bungee cords, yanking me back, using my own momentum against me. Some ropes snapped loose and came hurtling at my head. Brass stanchions crashed up and down the line. I lost my footing and went down in a snarl of red velvet snakes.

While I squirmed and flailed, trying to get free, the guard snapped out of it and saw his opportunity. He closed in, his nightstick raised, half bent-over so he could reach down and clobber me.

My arms were still ensnarled, but my feet were free. I kicked like a Rockette, hitting him in the knees and the shins, making him dance away. He tripped over a fallen stanchion and fell flat on his fat ass.

I got free of the ropes and leaped to my feet. I looked around for Felicia and saw her over in the workbench area. She had one of the long plastic workbenches between her and the other guard. The two of them, winded, ran around and around the bench, back and forth, trying to outfox each other.

My guard was on all fours, trying to clamber to his feet. I took two long strides and swung a foot up into his gut like a field-goal kicker. He curled up on the floor, both hands grasping his stomach. His nightstick lay on the floor beside him. I picked it up and gave him a tap on the head. To relax him.

With the guard out cold and a nightstick in my hand, I suddenly felt better about things. I turned toward where I'd last seen Felicia, just in time to see her swing a four-foot plywood candy cane at the rent-a-cop's head. He went down like he was shot.

Felicia spun the rest of the way around, carried by the weight of the candy cane, before she could stop. Gasping, she dropped the plywood. Our eyes met across Santa's Workshop. Felicia smiled triumphantly.

Her guard was laid out flat. I looked down at mine, saw that he was smiling contentedly, unconscious. Hah.

Then it dawned on me. Milt Jablonski was still around somewhere. He had a gun. And Felicia and I had just knocked out the only two potential witnesses.

I whirled, looking for Milt. The nightstick in my hand suddenly wasn't such a comfort. Unless I could figure out a way to bat down bullets with it.

Someone must've stumbled over the switch that started the miniature train. It was only seven or eight feet away from me, puffing on the tracks, ready to go. For no reason at all, the train chose this moment to emit that shrieking whistle it automatically blasts at certain intervals. I nearly jumped out of my skin.

I looked at Felicia, who was maybe twenty feet away, but she didn't seem to have noticed my nervous start. She stood by the red-and-green levers that controlled the train. Her mouth was open and her eyes were wide. She was pointing at me. No, not at me. Past me. Behind me. Aw, shit.

Wincing, I turned around. Milt Jablonski, looking jolly

as hell, was near the front of the puffing train, standing atop one of the two-foot-high railroad cars, taking the high ground. Which meant his pistol was pointed directly at my face.

I opened my mouth, but no words came. I could see Milt's finger tighten on the trigger. Jiminy Christmas, I was about to die.

Something clanked behind me, and the train jolted forward. Milt went tumbling.

Each car was a little bench for the kiddies, and Milt fell across a couple of them, howling and kicking. His gun flew into a nearby Christmas tree. The little train puffed away.

I glanced at Felicia and saw she had hold of one of the levers that controlled the train. She was grinning.

Milt was thirty feet away on the train, heading into the far turn, struggling to get to his feet. I took off after him. It hurt to run, but I slogged ahead, the nightstick in my hand, trying to catch the train.

The curve helped. I cut across Santa's Workshop at an angle, running around reindeer and cutting around candy canes, and caught up with Milt just as he got his feet under him. I swung at him with the nightstick, but he dodged the blow and the little train carried him out of reach.

I couldn't run anymore. A glance told me Felicia was yanking on the controls again, but the choo-choo showed no sign of stopping. I didn't have a choice. I jumped onto the moving train.

I nearly lost my balance, but I caught myself and stood flatfooted on top of the rattling train, facing Milt. The train consisted of a dozen cars. Milt was up near the engine. I was back by the caboose.

Milt looked happy to be facing off on top of a moving train, like two outlaws in a Western. He stepped onto the next two-foot-high car, coming toward me.

I jumped to the next car in line, caught my balance and moved to the next. Milt was still coming. He wants to meet in the middle and duke it out like John Wayne, it suits me. I'm the one with the nightstick.

The train took a curve, and Milt and I leaned over to keep from falling off.

We still had one empty bench between us, but Milt recovered from the curve before I did and leaped nimbly forward. Suddenly he was too close to be in handy baton range. He caught me in the belly with his fist.

I tried to whack him with the nightstick, but it glanced off his shoulder, and he hit me in the ribs. I was already one big bruise all over from the truck wreck. I didn't need this guy pounding on me.

I cocked the nightstick back by my hip and thrust it forward, driving its blunt end deep into Milt's plump belly. His eyes and mouth went round, and he looked for a moment like a jolly snowman. Grabbing one end of the baton in each hand, I swung it up sharply, catching him under the chin. Milt's head snapped backward and he dropped onto the bench seats. His eyes rolled back in his head.

I stood above him, gasping and wheezing, aboard the rocking train. I passed Felicia and gave her a weary thumbs-up. She still yanked at levers. The train jerked and brakes squealed and I pitched forward.

Fortunately, Milt broke my fall. I landed on his soft belly and bony knees, and bounced off onto the floor. Probably hurt Milt worse than it did me, but he was too unconscious to know it.

I sat up and found Felicia standing over me.

"Found the brake," she said.

"Good timing."

"Sorry. Nice work there. On the train."

"Thanks."

"You in any condition to tie these boys up?"

I stared at her.

"I'll do it," she said. "Go find a pay phone. Call the cops."

I struggled to my feet and handed her the nightstick and slumped off down the mall.

The Muzak was still going. "God rest ye, merry gentlemen . . ."

Sounded good to me.

FOURTEEN

BY THE TIME I GOT BACK to Santa's Workshop, Felicia had Milt and the two groaning guards tied up beautifully in strands of Christmas lights, fuzzy tinsel and six-inch-wide ribbon she'd ripped off the oversized gifts lying all around. She was just finishing with Milt, who still lay on his back on the railroad cars, his hands tied together at his belly and his feet sturdily bound. She slapped a big red bow on his chest.

"Nice touch," I said.

"'Tis the season."

She gave me a quick hug, which hurt my bruises. I staggered to the little train and sat next to Milt, checking first to make sure Felicia was nowhere near the controls.

"You know," she said, "I was thinking."

I moaned.

"We still don't have the connection to Marley. Unless the cops can turn Milt, we might not be able to prove anything."

"Don't worry about it. Romero's on the way. He'll sort everything out."

Felicia started to say something more, but someone shouted down the way. We turned and saw another gray-uniformed guard approaching.

I was too tired to get up and fight another rent-a-cop.

Felicia said, "I'll handle this."

She bent over and plucked the nightstick off the floor, then walked with purpose toward the guard.

"Sweetie," I said. "You might want—"

"Hey!" she yelled at the guard. "Stay where you are. Things are under control here. The police are on the way."

The cop, uncertain, took a couple more steps. Felicia brandished her baton and growled at him. He raised his empty hands and kept his distance.

A flashing squad car pulled up outside a minute later, and a couple of wet-booted cops came slip-sliding through the mall's glass doors. Romero was right behind them. He wore his bomber jacket over a maroon sweatsuit and sneakers. Not his usual look, but then it was late at night. He'd probably been relaxing at home.

Romero stalked straight to me, his dark eyes taking in Felicia, the gift wrapped guards, the fallen ceiling, the denuded Christmas trees and the wrecked displays. Not to mention snoozing Milt Jablonski, all trussed up with nowhere to go.

"Been having fun, Bubba?" Romero said.

"Not so much."

"You injured?"

"Lots."

"Good. I won't have to put the cuffs on you. Want to tell me what the hell's going on here?"

Felicia appeared at my side. "We came to talk to Jablonski about the Gooch murder," she said. "He kidnapped us at gunpoint. He's the one who killed Gooch!"

"I know," Romero said.

We both gawked at him, then Felicia said, "We think George Marley paid him to knock off Gooch so he could keep control of the patents that were going to charity."

Romero said, "That's right."

Felicia looked stunned. She hadn't dealt with Romero as much as I had. The man's always like this. Uncanny. Frankly, he gives me the heebies.

"You knew all this?" Felicia asked.

Romero's mouth twitched. "We were putting it together."

"Then why weren't *you* here, pouncing on Milt?"

"We do things at a certain pace, follow certain guidelines. It's called *procedure.* Once I had the case against Milt iron-clad, we would've arrested him. That's the way it works."

"How long might that have taken?" Felicia demanded.

He shrugged. "Tomorrow. The next day."

"But what about Marley? How were you—"

Romero shook his head. "That's where you jumped the gun. I suspected Milt from the beginning because of that business with the security monitors. Then we found that he'd left a single fingerprint on the plastic bag that suffocated Gooch, so I had him nailed. But I wanted to arrest everybody at once, before they could lawyer up and do more talking behind the scenes. I even worried that Marley might bump off Milt if he knew we were onto them. But you two couldn't wait."

I tried to look abashed. Felicia still had that glitter in her eyes, which meant she wouldn't let it go.

"You said 'arrest everybody.' Who do you mean, besides Milt and Marley?"

"What about these guards here?" Romero said, grinning.

"Nah," I said. "They weren't part of it. They thought we were burglars."

"Why would they think that? Because you crashed down out of the ceiling like Santa Claus?"

"I think Santa uses the chimney."

"Who else?" Felicia insisted.

Romero turned his steely gaze on her. "How about Carol Tannenbaum?"

"The sister?"

"She put Milt and Marley in touch. I've got witnesses who say she met Milt when he was doing background checks on the Santas the mall was hiring."

· "Bet she gave her brother a glowing recommendation," Felicia said.

"Sure," the lieutenant said, "especially once she saw what kind of man Milt was. Unhappy with his retirement, looking for an opportunity."

"She was in on the whole thing?"

Romero plunged his hands into his jacket pockets and glanced around the mall. Some other cops streamed in the doors, along with a couple of emergency medical technicians, who hustled toward us.

"Looks that way," he said. "I would've had it all put together in another day or two. Might be tougher now. But I imagine Milt will sing, if we cut him a deal. They'll all go down."

Felicia and I looked at each other. Despite the aches and bruises, the trauma and the torn clothes, the ruined mall and the tinsel in our hair, despite even the fact that our whole ordeal was an unnecessary risk when Romero was about to arrest everybody anyway, we were both smiling.

Felicia glanced at her wristwatch, then back at me. "I've got to call the newsroom. We might be able to get something in the late edition."

Romero rolled his eyes, but he didn't try to stop her as she hurried away in search of a phone.

I still sat on the train next to Milt. Two EMTs rushed up to us. One started looking over Milt and the other crouched in front of me. She was a young woman with buzz-cut hair and dangling earrings shaped like Christmas trees. The look didn't instill much confidence, but she proved capable, gently checking me over.

Romero wandered off, ordering people around, directing traffic. Next to me, Milt came awake to smelling salts, moaning and struggling against the ribbons that bound him. His head turned from side to side as his eyes focused and he took in the wreckage and the strangers all around.

I waited until his gaze settled on me before I said, "Hiya, Milt. Merry Christmas."

FIFTEEN

'TWAS THE NIGHT BEFORE Christmas, and I was feeling pretty good about myself.

I was in our kitchen, sitting at the table in my pajamas, wrapping Felicia's laptop computer in gilt paper. I was making my usual sticky-tape, ragged-edge mess of the gift wrapping, but it didn't matter. Felicia would go through the paper like a leaf-shredder in the morning. And she'd be thrilled I'd gotten her exactly what she wanted.

The past few days had been a flurry of arrests and interrogations and headlines. Milt and Marley and Carol Tannenbaum were behind bars. Romero came off like a hero on the news, and Felicia and I didn't make out too badly ourselves. The embarrassed mall managers showed no interest in suing us for crashing through their ceiling and wrecking Santa's Workshop.

Donna Hanratty was my happiest client ever. She was certain, with Marley and Tannenbaum out of the way, that Joyous Noises would end up with those patents and the riches they'd bring. She had enough preliminary documents to prove Daniel Gooch's good intentions, and the actions of Marley and Tannenbaum reinforced her claim.

Mrs. Hanratty was so happy, in fact, she gave me a bonus. That hardly ever happens. Usually it's all I can do to force timely payment. I'd only gotten a bonus once before—a wealthy client, who died a short time after I helped her, remembered me in her will. Her legacy to me? My red pickup truck.

It seemed fitting that the bonus from Mrs. Hanratty, along with my regular fee, was enough to cover Felicia's computer *and* help with the down payment on a new car to replace my Ram. As soon as the insurance settlement for my departed truck arrived, I could do a little after-Christmas shopping of my own at the used-car lots. Maybe get something a little more anonymous this time. Let's face it: A big red truck isn't the most covert vehicle for surveillance. I should buy something ordinary and bland, something so common that it won't draw a second glance on the streets of Albuquerque. Maybe an SUV.

I whistled a tune as I tied ribbon around Felicia's gift. I realized it was a Christmas carol, which made me cringe, but I kept whistling, feeling a little holiday spirit.

I'd come out on the side of the angels this time, no question. Despite my earlier qualms about Mrs. Hanratty's apparent avarice and the cutthroat charity business, Gooch's money was going to end up in the right place, helping families at Christmas. Just as he would've wanted.

Daniel Gooch had embodied jolly old St. Nick so well because he really believed in the spirit of giving and the wonder of the season. Nice to know there are people in the world who believe in giving it all away.

I'd served his memory well. So had Felicia. If we ended up getting a little something out of it ourselves, a bonus for our labors, then Merry Christmas to us.

One thing I knew for sure: Gooch had opened my eyes to Santa Claus and the giving spirit behind that symbol. All the imagery of Christmas would have a new meaning for me now. I'd no longer fear Santa, his red suit, his loud bluster and his beady-eyed reindeer. No longer worry about the intrusion of a fat burglar coming down the chimney. No longer get queasy at the sight of a white beard.

That childish phobia was gone, replaced by a renewed Christmas spirit.

I heard a noise outside. A jingling. Sounded like sleigh bells. Carolers? Holiday revelers? An ice cream truck?

Something *thump-thumped* on the roof. Hey, now. Another *thump,* and my stomach turned to jelly.

Moved by the old Christmas spirit, I leaped up from the table and hurried to the bedroom. Felicia was sound asleep, a curve under the covers. No help there.

More clatter on the roof. Oh, shit.

I jumped into bed and pulled the blankets up over my head.

Damned squirrels.

FINDING CHARITY
by Catherine Dain

ONE

"YOU HELP OTHER PEOPLE! I know you help other people! Tori told me when she said I should come talk to you. So you gotta help me, too! You don't think I'm good enough or something? Is that it? I'm as good as Tori! I'm as good as anybody you helped! What do I got to do to get help? Kill somebody?"

Charity Jackson stood in the center of my office, yelling like the disturbed teenager she probably was at heart, no matter that she was technically an adult, and at that moment I didn't care how good Charity thought she was. I didn't even care if she killed somebody. I didn't want to help her. I wanted to slap her.

Instead I sat there, looking up at the shouting woman, elbow on the arm of my chair, chin propped on my knuckles, waiting for Charity to stop ranting.

Charity did need help, of course. I knew that. I simply had a different idea of what kind of help Charity needed, and what kind of help I could offer. And that depended on whether Charity stopped yelling and whether I could muster the compassion to help her at all.

"Those guys I saw are the ones who killed somebody, and I'll bet people are helping them." Charity's voice became even louder, and I hadn't thought that was possible. "They put a body in a big silver car and float away, and you think they gonna have problems? No, I'm the one with problems! And who's gonna listen to me?"

When Charity finally paused for breath, I said, my voice oozing patience, "I am listening to you. I am doing my best to help you. Now please sit down so that we can discuss this calmly."

Charity wavered, body swaying, long arms quivering down to her red acrylic fingertips, one of which pointed accusingly at me. I waited.

And wished I had never agreed to see the young woman at all.

Charity Jackson had come to the clinic where I volunteered not because she thought she needed therapy, but because she thought she might have witnessed a murder, or at least the aftermath of a murder. I, of course, suggested that she go to the police. And that was when Charity started yelling.

I tried to explain that the one time I had intervened in the case of someone who had information about a murder and was afraid to go to the police, that same Tori Sanchez who had sent Charity to the clinic, I had special knowledge of the crime. This time I didn't.

Charity, however, was more interested in the fact that Tori, the witness in that case, the woman I had helped, was a hooker, as was Charity. Or at least she implied she was. She had been vague about that, along with other details. And hookers don't walk willingly into police stations.

Not that Charity looked like a hooker, at least no more so than thousands of other L.A. twentysomethings with angular bodies squeezed into midriff-baring T-shirts and midcalf leggings. What made Charity stand out was the combination of beaded cornrows and burnished bronze skin, the high cheekbones and hawklike nose and the large, round, dark eyes. Plus the tattoo of the Madonna—the original one, not her more recent namesake—on her right shoulder. The Virgin Mary seemed to me a curious choice for a hooker's tattoo, unless Charity was playing into the irony of the Madonna/whore dichotomy, the idea that women are either angels or devils, which led some men to buy sex from "bad" women because they have trouble associating lust with "good" ones.

Unfortunately I didn't have the opportunity to ask her about the symbolism of the tattoo. The conversation had deteriorated too quickly.

Even though her face was now flushed with rage, Charity was stunning. I could understand why she was afraid that someone might have seen her and remembered her, could understand why she didn't want to go to the police.

Nevertheless, all I was willing to do for her was what any therapist would do. Listen. Maybe give some practical advice.

I was not willing to go with her to the police.

I was even less willing to go to the police in her stead, which was what Charity wanted me to do.

Not only that, but I was tired, I didn't want to be yelled at, and I found myself unaccountably on the verge of yelling back.

Charity stopped wavering. The accusing finger with its blood-red tip came closer to my face.

"We got nothing more to talk about, you fucking bigoted bitch. I hope you die. Slowly." She spat the words, and then she smiled. She knew she had managed a gut shot.

I lost it on the word "die."

I jumped up and pushed the finger out of my face. "You hope I die? You come in here asking for my help, and when I suggest we talk about it, you call me names and say you hope I die? And you don't think you need therapy? You think that behavior works for you? You think arrogance and hostility are going to get you help?" I didn't realize I was screaming until the door opened.

"Okay. That's enough. Both of you." Wendy Kormier, the director of the family clinic that housed my office, made it an order.

"I'm just leaving." Charity drew herself up so that she looked like an Aztec queen, glanced at Wendy and turned back to me. "Have a merry Christmas."

She shoved Wendy aside and stalked out.

Wendy started to follow, but when she was certain that Charity wasn't coming back, she turned to me, straightened her glasses and said, "Want to tell me about it?"

"I'm sorry," I said, feeling uncomfortably like a disturbed teenager myself. "I don't know how that happened."

"Then tell me what led up to it." Wendy sat down on the ratty sofa where clients usually sit and gestured toward my chair. I sat, awkwardly assuming what was normally a place of authority.

"Charity's a hooker," I said. "Or I think she might be. She described a hypothetical situation in which she was doing a john in a car on a side street off Sunset, oral sex, and when she was through, she looked out the window and found herself face-to-face with one of two men carrying a body, presumably a dead one. They tossed it into the trunk of a silver Mercedes. She got out of the john's car and ran, hid in a backyard, so frightened she didn't even wait to get paid. She heard somebody looking for her, but he triggered some motion sensor lights that scared him away. I'm not sure how much of that is true, how much a story. I think there really was a murder, though. And she doesn't want to go to the police. She wants me to go for her. Which I can't do."

"Of course you can't. Could she identify the man?"

"She thinks so. More important, she thinks he could identify her. And she's scared. I believe that."

"I don't blame her." Wendy's tone indicated that I shouldn't blame her, either. "How did she find you?"

"She knows Tori Sanchez, one of my clients. Tori sent her to me."

"That's nice." Wendy smoothed her skirt and nodded. "I like it when clients refer people."

"Me, too," I said, feeling a little less awkward and embarrassed. "Anyway, I told Charity that I couldn't go to the police because I had nothing to tell them, but that I would be happy to offer whatever therapeutic support I could after she talked to them. And then she started to yell at me."

"Clients have yelled at you before, Faith. This is the first time you've yelled back."

"I know, and I can't tell you how awful I feel about it." I paused, hoping Wendy would leap in and say my behavior wasn't that bad. She didn't. So I continued. "I was okay until she said she hoped I'd die. Slowly. That seemed such a personal attack."

"And you felt…" Wendy prompted.

"Scared. Because I know what it feels like to think I might die slowly. Even though I denied what was going on at the time, later I knew how scared I had been. And when Charity said she wanted me to die, I got scared all over again. But I couldn't let her see I was scared. So I got angry."

Wendy nodded. "You went through a very tough experience when you helped Tori and the murderers went after you, Faith, and it hasn't been that long since it happened, maybe not long enough for you to have worked through it. I thought then that you ought to take some time off."

"It was months ago, and I did take some time off," I argued.

"You canceled appointments on days when you absolutely

had to, days when you were talking to the police or had court appearances. And it still goes on, reminding you every time you have to talk about it. It was months ago, yes, but the trial is starting soon. Isn't it?" She looked questioningly at me.

"Soon. Right after the first of the year."

Wendy nodded. "I thought you should take a vacation then. I still do. When was the last time you took a vacation?"

"I went to Maui for a few days a couple of years ago."

"Faith, take a vacation. I'd tell you to go somewhere for Christmas, but that's still three weeks away. I think you ought to take a vacation now." Wendy was only a few years older than I, and since I was a volunteer, not an employee, Wendy had no real right to give me orders. But Wendy had the presence of someone whose orders were going to be obeyed. There was something about her short, curly graying hair, untouched by dye or peroxide, and her round, serene face, untouched by makeup, barely showing signs of crinkles around the eyes and mouth, that reminded me of a nun.

Not that I know much about nuns, and I thought Wendy's heritage was Jewish, although we had never discussed it. But Wendy had that unshakable sense of the rightness of her mission that I always associated with nuns. And the clinic was Wendy's mission. So Wendy gave orders and expected them to be obeyed.

I, however, have never liked orders, no matter who was giving them. I took a breath before reacting.

"My clients need me, Wendy. Especially this close to the holidays. All my clients get tense around the holidays. And I really can't afford to cancel my private clients for a week. Plus I have no place to go and no one to go there with."

"Your clients need a therapist who isn't so stressed out that she's yelling at them. And it's better to cancel a week now than to cancel a month later, because the stress isn't going to go away by itself. As for a place to go and someone to see, why don't you go see your parents? An early Christmas surprise. How long has it been since you've seen them?" Wendy asked in innocence, the kind of innocence that someone who has good family relationships always has when speaking with someone who doesn't.

I knew that, and I still had to beat down an angry answer. In fact, I was working so hard to stay in control just talking with Wendy, who was a colleague and almost a friend, that I knew she was right. It was time for a vacation.

"My father and stepmother live in Arizona," I said, surprised at how calm my voice sounded. "You'll have to believe me when I tell you that seeing them wouldn't be a vacation. And my mother is dead."

"I'm sorry. Then what about your friend—"

"Thank you." I cut her off because I couldn't bear another suggestion. It was all I could do to bear her sympathy. "You're right. I need some time off. I'll see my two clients this afternoon, and then I'll tell Mary to cancel my clients here for the next week. I'll figure out something for my private clients. But I can't go anywhere. I haven't mentioned it, but I'm doing a play. We've been in rehearsal since early November, and we open in a week."

"A play?" Wendy sounded as if she had never heard the word.

"Yes. I'm going to be playing Mrs. Cratchit in *A Christmas Carol* at a small theater in North Hollywood. I'm looking forward to it. But I haven't been on stage in more than ten years, and I'm a little nervous about it."

I stopped myself before I could go into a long confession, letting her know that one reason I was looking forward to it was that we would be playing over Christmas, which gave me a family for the holidays, the Cratchit family. When we were rehearsing, the Cratchit family felt more real to me than my own.

"That's wonderful, Faith." Wendy still sounded puzzled. "I'd forgotten you used to be an actress. But that's another source of stress, even though it's good stress. One more reason to take a vacation."

"I know. I had thought about taking a few days off around the weekend the play opens. I decided not to because I just didn't want to let theater interfere with my professional life. And I'm sorry I've never told you much about my past. I guess it didn't seem relevant."

Wendy nodded. To her, my past wasn't relevant. I wasn't her client. "Stay home and take care of yourself, Faith. Go to your rehearsals rested. Take a week off, more if you need to. Don't think about it as theater interfering in your professional life. Just think of it as taking care of yourself." Wendy held out her hand, and I reached over to take it. "Read. Sleep. Hug your cats. And I'll tell Mary to cancel your clients."

"No. That makes it sound as if you're punishing me. I need to tell her myself." That was better. I was back in control.

Our hands swung lightly, as if we were two little girls on a playground. Wendy squeezed my hand, dropped it and the moment was lost.

"Okay. You tell her. Are you sure you're all right to see your afternoon clients?"

"I'm sure. I have time for a quiet lunch, and I'll be fine this afternoon," I said.

Wendy got up and started toward the door. But I wasn't quite ready to let her go.

"Wendy?"

Wendy paused in the doorway, clearly ready to get back to work.

"I'm sorry," I said. "It won't happen again."

"Good. I'll see you in a week." Wendy gave me a little wave and smile, then disappeared into the hall.

I shut my eyes for a moment, wishing I could go back and replay the last hour, rewrite the scene so that I hadn't yelled back at Charity Jackson. I opened them again and decided that I needed lunch if I planned to face my afternoon clients with equanimity.

I picked up my heavy black leather bag, swung it over my shoulder, and prepared for the next step—facing Mary, the clinic's receptionist. Mary knew everything that went on in the clinic, and she had surely heard the argument. Just as surely she knew that Wendy had gone in to talk with me about it.

Mary was on the phone when I reached the outer office, so I stood next to the desk and waited. I was grateful for the small blessing that the argument had occurred close to lunchtime, and no one was sitting in the plastic chairs waiting to see a doctor or a therapist.

"Everything okay, Faith?" Mary asked, once she had taken care of the client on the phone.

She was looking at me seriously. I had never seen Mary looking serious before. In fact, I thought Mary had taken a vow against being serious around the time that she had pierced her nose and eyebrows and dyed her hair burgundy.

"Sort of," I replied. "I lost it with a client, and there was no excuse for that. Wendy and I agreed that I should take a week off. I'll tell the two clients who are coming this afternoon. Would you mind getting in touch with the others?"

"No problem," Mary said, still looking concerned.

"Thanks. I'm all right, Mary, I promise. Just a little stressed. And I'll be better after lunch."

Mary buzzed me through the security door. I walked out of the clinic, head consciously held high, and stood there, not sure what to do next. Lunch, of course, but where?

The clinic was in a minimall on Sunset Boulevard right around where Silver Lake becomes Echo Park. The residential areas to the north and south were an uneasy mix of single artists and Latino families, with the balance shifting almost block by block, even though there were more artists north of the boulevard and more Latinos to the south.

The commercial establishments to the east and west were heavily Latino, including a Cuban bakery and a Guatemalan grocery in the same minimall as the clinic. The Laundromat and the shoe repair store, the two other occupants of the minimall, had signs in both Spanish and English. This time of year that meant both Merry Christmas and *Feliz Navidad*.

Someone had sprayed a snowy mural, adorned with holly and berries, on the windows of the Laundromat. Since it never snows in L.A., the mounds of white paint looked absurd. More like cake frosting than snow. But fake winter Christmas displays always look absurd to me. There ought to be a way to claim Christmas for Southern California, a nonwhite Christmas, in all senses of the word, but I don't know what it is.

If I wanted lunch within walking distance, my choices were pretty much limited to the bakery, a taqueria across the street, or an old French restaurant a couple of long blocks away that had somehow managed to remain neutral territory, attracting everyone who had a few dollars for a good bowl of soup and some terrific bread.

The sky was a little dreary for early December, gray and gloomy, with a threat of rain, and the air just a little too cool for an Angeleno weather wimp to be comfortable walking very far, even in low-heeled boots. But the thought of the bottomless bowl of soup, maybe a thick, creamy potato-watercress soup, refilled ladle by ladle until my need for comfort was sated, lured me toward the restaurant.

I had only taken a few steps when I heard a shout for help that sounded very much like the voice that had just been yelling at me.

At the end of the block, too far away for me to intervene, Charity Jackson was being forced into a silver Mercedes.

I dashed back into the clinic.

"Call the police!"

"What?"

Mary looked so startled that I decided calling them myself would be easier. I quickly punched 911 on the clinic's phone and explained to the operator that one of my clients had just been abducted by force, almost in front of the clinic. The operator responded calmly, professionally and quickly.

Explaining the situation to the police officer who showed up fifteen minutes later was a little more difficult.

"You saw a hooker get into a Mercedes on Sunset Boulevard," he said, "and you think she was abducted by force?"

"I understand your skepticism," I began, then trailed off. The thing was, I did understand his skepticism. And I knew there was no point in arguing with him. Even if he had believed she witnessed a murder, a notion he shrugged off.

So I thanked him for coming and apologized for taking up so much of his time.

He left, shaking his head in exasperation.

"Are you really worried about her?" Mary asked.

Since I had talked to the officer right in front of Mary's desk, she had heard the whole thing. Mary was worried, but whether about Charity or about me I couldn't tell.

"I don't know anymore," I told her. "I'll have to think about it, and I'm too hungry to think clearly."

"I hope you can think clearly in ten minutes," Mary said. "That's when your next client will be here."

"I can get a *chile relleño* and be back in five," I answered. "This day has got to get better."

It didn't.

TWO

"At least you made it through the afternoon without yelling at anyone else," Michael said, topping off my glass of Chardonnay from the bottle that sat between us. The small table tilted precariously as he set the bottle back down. He stuck the toe of one sandal under the offending table leg.

I envied Michael his sandals, jeans and loose, striped T-shirt. Well, not the sandals. My low-heeled boots were more appropriate for the day, given the threat of rain. But I felt overdressed for life in a cotton skirt and ruffled blouse. My quilted jacket barely protected me from the cold, but Michael looked as if he had never been cold in his life. He was too free to be chilly. Too free to care about clothes at all. No one would mind if I wore jeans to the clinic, and I couldn't figure out why I had clung to some sort of semiprofessional dress code. I was at least going to be free of skirts for a week. I could think about clothes after that.

"I barely made it. Both of my afternoon appointments had serious dependency issues. How could they have been so upset just because I'm taking a week off?" I asked, not really wanting an answer.

Michael offered it anyway.

"They depend on you because so little in either of their lives is stable. That's why they come to the clinic. And then you freak out and take off for a week, just before the holidays. How did you expect them to react?"

"With smiles. Wishing me well. Understanding that I have a life of my own. I don't know. I know Wendy was right, though. I really need a week off." The words came out a little louder than I intended. I glanced around, but nobody noticed. That's L.A. Everyone is too involved in their own lives to notice yours.

"People in therapy never understand you have a life of your own," Michael said, as if confirming my unspoken observation. "They pay you not to have a life of your own, you know that. When they do see you as someone with a life, they're ready to leave."

"Is that why you burned out?"

Michael didn't answer. He closed his eyes and turned his face to the tiny bit of late-afternoon sun that peeked between clouds.

I took a sip of the Chardonnay. Not bad for an inexpensive wine at an actor's hangout.

I had called Michael between the two afternoon appointments, about the time the *chile relleño* from my fast lunch had started sending danger signals up my esophagus. He had agreed to meet me at a bistro on Santa Monica Boulevard, one that a lot of actors frequent, the unknown, the sort-of known, and the once-famous. It was reputedly the place where Quentin Tarantino had the lunch with Robert Forster that gave Forster his second act in life. Sitting on the patio, watching the parade of seminaked buffed bodies, young and not-so-young, all impervious to cold, I began to relax a little.

I was watching bodies because the only other choice was cars. Like too many restaurant patios in L.A., this one was too few feet from a busy street. The carbon monoxide fumes had to be every bit as bad for the body as second-hand cigarette smoke. But car addiction is the habit Angelenos refuse to admit is a problem.

Never mind. No complaints. I had a week away from the clinic. I was in rehearsal for a play. And with a bit of effort, I could start to look fit again. That's something else I could think about once I wasn't stressed. Looking fit. Even becoming fit.

"Are you going to cancel your private clients, as well? You should, you know," Michael said.

"I know I should. But then I won't have any money coming in, and I have to think about whether that raises my stress level more than a week free of clients lowers it."

Michael nodded wisely. Or he looked wise to me, anyway. The trouble with having a trained therapist for a best friend is never being certain whether the wise face is real or not. We learn to do that, look wise, whether we feel wise or not.

I took another sip of Chardonnay.

"Maybe I'll see how tonight's rehearsal goes," I said.

"Are you rehearsing every night now?"

"Tomorrow is my last night off until the show opens. As you know, my part is small enough that I haven't had to be there for every rehearsal, but Saturday and Sunday are tech rehearsals, and then we have four dress rehearsals, and then it opens. But that's another reason I'm hesitant about canceling private clients. My two Saturday afternoon clients were already unhappy about the way I've juggled them around rehearsal. I have to move them to morning the two weekends before Christmas because we have matinees on both Saturday and Sunday. If I cancel them for a week, I might lose them altogether." I took another sip of wine. Friendship and wine are the two most comforting things in the world, maybe after cats but certainly ahead of food and sex, or at least it felt that way at the moment. "And the awful thing is, right now, I'm having trouble caring."

"Then you have to give yourself the week. In fact, you should have given yourself two." Michael shrugged his shoulders, the wise look gone. "When you stop caring about clients, it's time to take a break. That's what I did, and it worked."

"Well, it worked, in that you never went back to being a therapist, except for two clients, and I can't live on two clients. I'd talk to Amy and Mac about getting work, but they just don't have Elizabeth's style."

"Not every cat can be a television star," Michael said. "In any case, you surely have enough money saved to get through the next week. Please tell me you aren't down to your last dollar."

"I could even handle a couple of months without clients if I had to. But it would make me nervous," I said. "One week of no clients will get me through the opening of the show. Then I can go back to seeing clients with renewed energy."

"Good. I hope it works that way." He hesitated, then continued. "I almost wasn't going to say this, in case it puts ideas into your head. I have to say, though, there's one good thing about your stressed-out state. I was afraid you were going to tell me you were thinking about looking for Charity. Your would-be client, I mean, not help. I would have expected you to be so guilt-ridden over her possible abduction that you'd be tacking up flyers on telephone poles right now instead of drinking wine with me."

I had to think about that.

"I'm tired, I'm stressed and I'm still angry at her," I told him. "And it just isn't my job to save her."

Michael's eyebrows went up in surprise.

"Since when? Last week you would have thought it was."

I shook my head. "Not this week. Besides, what would the flyers say? I don't have a photo, and a description wouldn't do her justice. I thought fleetingly about cruising the hills above Sunset, looking for a silver Mercedes, but I don't know what I'd do if I found one. I was too far away to see the license plate, and probably too stressed to notice it anyway. I told the police officer that Charity thought she witnessed a murder, and he didn't care. So I have no way of following up on that. The only action I'm going to take is to let Tori know what happened when I call to let her know I can't see her next week."

I didn't tell him that Mary would be calling Tori along with the rest of my clients from the clinic. I somehow felt I had to call Tori personally. After all, Tori was involved in the stress that was causing me to take a week off in two ways—she had been there when both our lives were threatened, and she had sent Charity to me.

"I can hear it now," Michael said. "'Hi, Tori, thanks for the referral. I yelled at her, she walked out, she was abducted and I'm taking a week off. And how are you?'"

"I'll do better than that." I hated the way he made it sound. "I don't have to call her until tomorrow. And I'll think of something to say to her that'll make it all right."

Michael gave me a wise nod that I knew was fake.

"I see," he said.

"How are you doing? Anything I can get for you?" Our cheerful waiter, a young man in jeans and a white shirt with a bright, brocade vest, appeared beside the table.

"We're fine, Chad," Michael said.

I managed a wan smile, and Chad flashed a much brighter

one. He bounced away, doing a waiter's version of broken-field running as he slipped between the small tables scrunched together on the narrow patio. I still had to respond to Michael.

"I'll tell Tori I'm sorry about what happened. And that's the best I can do."

"Very good! I'm proud of you!"

Michael may have been proud, but I felt guilty.

"And I'll tell her if she needs to see me, she can come to the apartment," I said.

"Faith, Faith, what am I gonna do with you?" Michael asked, doing a lousy Brando imitation.

"I don't know. In fact, you don't have to do anything with me. But what I'm going to do with me is play as much as I can, at least for a week. Play in the play. I earned this play, and I deserve it, and I'm going to have a good time, and my clients—most of them anyway—will just have to take care of themselves for a while." My voice was so firm I began to believe myself.

"I hope you mean it," Michael said. "I hope you take care of yourself and do a great job in the play. You're too talented to walk away from acting for the rest of your life. I remember how wonderful you were the first time I saw you on stage, in *Two for the Seesaw*. And you were still in college then."

"Thank you. But I don't want to think about past triumphs, if I can even call them that." I wished he hadn't mentioned that play. My former co-star and college sweetheart had been murdered, I felt partly responsible, I probably hadn't grieved properly, and I wanted to cry. "I was so young and enthusiastic then. I thought all things were possible."

"They still are." He regarded me thoughtfully. And he surely noticed that my eyes were filling. "Do you want to talk about Kirby?"

"No. He's been dead almost a year now. Let's leave him that way."

Michael nodded. "And you're alive, and far too beautiful to play Mrs. Cratchit, who really should be a plain little Brit housewife. Not to mention that you are far too talented for such a small part."

"There are no small parts…" I said.

"Only small actors," Michael finished.

"Playing a small part was a way I could handle getting back on stage after all these years. If I can do a small one, then I can think about doing a bigger one. And there are no plain little Brit housewives in L.A., nor actresses to play them," I said, and the tears began to dry as I shifted to theater-talk. "Actresses are not plain. And thank you for the compliment, but I'm not beautiful. Maybe ten years and twenty pounds ago, on a good day, but not now."

"You're not getting older, you're getting better, or however that goes. You were ten pounds too thin when you were on television, and your face had that lean and hungry look. Cocaine does that, whether you admitted it at the time or not. You wore too much makeup and you were too blond. The muted color suits you better."

He paused to take a sip of his wine, and I jumped in. I didn't want to be reminded of dead boyfriends, and I didn't want to be reminded of the cocaine use that had shortened my television career. Much more of this and I could be sorry I called him. "Thank you so much for the kind words. The not-so-kind ones, too. And for the record, I like that touch of gray in your hair. Ten years ago, you looked a bit like Tony Curtis in his prime, but you're aging much better than he did."

"Thanks, I guess," Michael said. "But I'm not aging. I'm only thirty-nine."

"Michael, dear, you've been thirty-nine for at least two years now. This is the twenty-first century. It's okay to turn forty, even in L.A., as long as you aren't an actor or a writer. It just isn't okay to turn fifty yet." The topic of age was always sure to distract me, whatever was going on. "I even plan to celebrate my fortieth this year, believe it or not."

"I'll believe it when you invite me to the party. And that's enough about age, which I don't believe in anyway. Back to *A Christmas Carol*, which you really haven't told me much about."

"You've been busy and so have I," I said, with a twinge of guilt. Theater had not only interfered with my professional life, it had interfered with a very important friendship, one I needed. "I haven't intentionally left you out of anything."

Michael patted my hand. "I know, dear. So tell me now. Don't you feel somehow antifeminist doing that part?" He added just a touch of needle to the words.

"Not at all. Mrs. Cratchit holds the family together, even as Bob works hard and Tim's health fails. She's a brave woman, if traditional. It is a romance. There isn't anything wrong with romance." I bristled at the idea that there might be.

"Are there possibilities for that in the cast? Has that been distracting you?"

"Unfortunately, no. The actors playing Bob Cratchit and the Scrooge/Dickens part are both wearing wedding rings, although Scrooge is a flirt and maybe more than that, and the others are either too old or too young. You'd think Scrooge would be too old, but since the play is written with Dickens narrating and playing Scrooge, and since this is Hollywood, or North Hollywood anyway, the actor is in his prime. I'm not into married men or father figures, and I'm not in the mood for cradle-robbing. Even the director is about fifteen years younger than I am—and gay. He told me his mother used to watch me on television. For this group, I'm a star." I laughed as I said it, but I wasn't sure it was funny.

Michael granted me a polite smile. "Might I have heard of any of them?"

"Scrooge—Ryan Slade—was on a soap for a few years and shows up doing day work on television now and again, but I don't think he has done anything memorable. Bob Cratchit—Ted Reed—was on a glass cleaner commercial that played forever, the guy who got a better shine than his wife. That's his only claim to fame. The others are wannabes, like the guy playing Marley, who just started taking acting lessons when he retired from a long career as a commercial airline pilot."

"What does the director wannabe?"

"Johnny is right out of the UCLA Theater Arts department—I suspect that his MFA is framed and hanging on his bedroom wall. First stop, North Hollywood. Next, Broadway musicals. Except that North Hollywood may be a long stop. He owns the building where the theater is, and he doesn't seem too interested in making a living."

"You're right. No good possibilities for romance in the bunch."

"Anyway, there is something so much like family about this cast, something that gives me a sense of what really being home for the holidays is like, that romance would somehow mess it up. I don't know how to explain that." I took another sip of wine. The glass was less full than I remembered.

"You don't need to explain a deep longing for family. We all get that at Christmas. You do, however, need to eat something before you go to rehearsal." Michael pointed at the wineglass to make certain I understood. "Think about what you want, and I'll catch Chad's eye."

"You've already caught Chad's interest," I said. "And I'm having trouble thinking about food after the way lunch backfired."

"An omelet," he urged. "You can always eat an omelet."

"Will you split it with me?"

"No. I have a dinner engagement."

I waited for more, but he didn't volunteer.

"With whom?" I finally, and formally, asked.

"A friend. I'll introduce you if he becomes important."

The new friend. That was why Michael had been too busy to hear about the play until now. "If you have a new friend, why are you flirting with Chad?" The words came out with more irritation than I intended.

"I'm not flirting with Chad." Michael said it so calmly that I knew he meant it. I felt annoyed with myself for being wrong, and added that to my annoyance with the rest of the world. All the world that wasn't the stage. Michael raised a hand, and when Chad looked our way, waved him over.

"I changed my mind," I said. "I'll have a mushroom omelet."

"Right away," Chad said. He made a note on his pad and trotted purposefully toward the kitchen.

I closed my eyes and had to resist an urge to put my head down on the table.

"How did Nancy Drew do it?" I asked. "Didn't the death and destruction have to get to her sometime?"

"Yes, if she had been real. Nancy Drew was a fairy tale. And did anybody ever die?"

"I don't remember. It's been too long since I read the books."

"I don't think anybody ever died. And Nancy Drew didn't have to process her emotions. You do."

"I don't know how. I don't know how I got through grad school and got my therapist's license without learning how, but I did."

"A lot of people learn from their families, when they are growing up, but we won't go there, will we?" Michael was wearing his therapist expression again.

"Oh, God, I want to cry."

"More than you want to go to rehearsal?"

I snapped myself out of it.

"No. Where's my omelet?"

"Coming. You know, it's good that you want to cry."

"No, it isn't. It would be good if I were doing a tragedy—I could use it. But *A Christmas Carol* is an upbeat morality tale. I have to get over it."

"Enjoy!" Chad dropped a warm plate of food in front of me and dropped a basket of warm bread folded in a napkin with a little tub of butter perched on top in front of Michael. He was gone before I could thank him.

I had only taken one bite when I happened to catch sight of the time. I don't wear a wristwatch because I don't like them and there are always plenty of clocks around. In this case, a watch was on the wrist of a well-muscled young man at the next table whose sleeves were rolled up just under his elbows.

"Oh, God, I have to hurry," I said with my mouth full of omelet.

"Fine," Michael said. "You eat, I'll talk."

He told me a long and rather pointless story about the negotiations for Elizabeth's next Pretty Kitty cat food commercial. But that was fine. All I had to do was nod occasionally as I scarfed the omelet. He was right. I needed the food.

I started to pull money out for the check, but Michael stopped me.

"I'm going to sit and finish the wine," he said. "I'll settle the check when I'm ready to leave."

"Bless you," I said.

I grabbed the big black leather bag that holds most of what I need in life and dashed off.

My apartment wasn't exactly on the way to the theater, but I wanted to stop and feed the cats before rehearsal. Traffic inched along so slowly as I maneuvered from Santa Monica Boulevard to La Cienega and finally to Laurel Canyon that I was afraid they might have to subsist on whatever dry food was left in their bowls until the end of the evening.

Once past Mulholland Drive, though, it was a little easier. I made it down to the Valley floor, turned left on Ventura Boulevard and inched along again until I reached Coldwater Canyon. From there it was a hop, skip and jump to my apartment building.

I pulled into the carport, slammed the car door in my hurry, dashed around the building and up the stairs.

Where I stopped short.

Tori Sanchez was sitting on the front step, right in front of my apartment door.

"What are you going to do to help Charity?" she asked.

THREE

I STARED AT TORI, struggling to come up with an answer to her question, hoping she was only following up on the referral, wondering whether Mary had told her about Charity's abduction, feeling guilty and incompetent. I'm not certain how long I stood there with my mouth open, without a voice. When I finally found words, they were lame ones.

"Tori, I can't help her," I said.

"You have to. Please." Tori's large black eyes began to fill.

"Oh, God, Tori. This isn't a good time. I have only a few minutes. I have to be somewhere." Tears ran quietly down Tori's cheeks. I couldn't stand it. "Come in and we'll talk while I feed the cats."

I opened the door and found Amy glaring at me, with Mac right behind her, looking soulful. Mac was Amy's boy, bigger than she was, but not as bright. The two long-haired, sable-coated cats were clearly from the same gene pool, although Amy had kept the smart ones for herself.

"I'm not that late," I said to Amy.

Tori followed me inside, then stood uncomfortably, surely remembering the last time she had been there. Actually, thinking about the man with the gun made me a little uncomfortable, too. I had done all the things they tell you to do to reclaim your space, from burning sage and ringing bells to hosting dinner with friends, but I didn't feel the same way about my living room as I had before.

I didn't want to move again—I had been living in the apartment less than a year—but I could feel it coming. Dealing with the holidays was worsening my discomfort with the apartment. I hadn't even been able to think about decorating.

"Sit down, or come with me to the kitchen. Lock the door if it'll make you feel better," I said. "No one's after you this time."

Tori still stood there, looking uncomfortable.

"Please tell me that no one is after you this time," I added.

The small kitchen area was only a few steps away, not much more than an alcove in the large space I used as living room, dining room and office. I pulled out a can of something that was supposed to be shredded chicken and salmon and proceeded to open it. Mac rubbed against my leg. Amy waited by her dish.

Tori couldn't seem to make up her mind what to do. She compromised by leaning against the back of the pink-and-blue Santa Fe sofa, bought when the style was in and I had money, that divided the living area from the dining space. In jeans and a faded yellow T-shirt, with her curly black hair loosely knotted on top of her head, she looked like a college student. Every time I saw her like that, I hoped again that she would become one.

"I don't know," she finally said. "I don't think so. But someone is after Charity, I'm sure of it. That's why I told her to call you. And then when I got home this afternoon, there was a message from the clinic saying that you were taking a week off. What's going to happen to Charity?"

I added a handful of tartar control treats, put the dishes of cat food down and watched both cats go to work on them. I tried to figure out how to tell Tori what had happened in twenty-five words or less. I couldn't.

"Tori, I'm in a play, and I have to go to a rehearsal, right now." The words didn't register, as if she was one more person who had never heard of a play. But then, therapists aren't supposed to have their own lives. "I could talk to you later tonight. Is there something you could do for a few hours? I'll meet you at ten-thirty, and we can talk then."

"Where?"

"How about Argento's? It's a coffee shop on Ventura Boulevard, just a few blocks from here." I wouldn't want coffee that late, but the place would be clean and bright and safe. And it would get her out of my apartment.

Tori wavered.

"Please," I begged. "You can go to a movie, go to the mall, something. But I have to leave now."

"Okay. I'll see you at ten-thirty at Argento's."

"Great." I grabbed my bag, and I practically pushed her out the front door. "See you then," I called, as I ran down the stairs ahead of her.

With luck, I could still make the rehearsal on time.

The traffic gods were with me. I zipped up Coldwater Canyon to Magnolia, zoomed along to Lankershim, and dropped down to within a block of the theater, all without hitting a red light.

And then the parking gods smiled on me. A space opened up right in front of the building.

It wasn't really a theater, or not originally one, at any rate. In fact, the building had started out as a rather modest little church, complete with bell tower. Wide concrete steps led up to heavy wooden doors that opened into a small lobby decorated with theatrical posters. More wooden doors opened into a larger space that held the original pews, fortunately padded, now with metal tags marking off the seats. The altar was gone, though, and a stage had been installed in its place. The choir loft was now a balcony. Johnny Galliano, who was directing the play, had inherited enough money from somewhere to buy the building and fix it up so that he could live in back and direct plays in front. Not a bad setup for a kid.

I liked the idea of a church becoming a theater. Theater had stayed alive after the fall of the Roman Empire, after the barbarians stormed the gates, only because of the church. An Easter pageant, the *Quem Queritas* trope, was the earliest example of what passed for theater in the Dark Ages, if I recalled my history of the theater class correctly. There was still, for me, something holy about setting foot on stage. Easter, Christmas, and every other day, as well.

"Yo! Wait up!"

I stopped at the foot of the steps when I heard the voice. I had been trying to remember what *Quem Queritas* meant, confusing it with *Quo Vadis,* which meant Where are you going, but the Latin wasn't coming back.

Ryan Slade was coming toward me at a slow jog.

"I guess I'm not the last one here," I said.

"Not a chance." Ryan graced me with his perfect smile. It was so perfect that I almost stumbled over the bottom step. I had to remind myself that we were working together and he was married.

But I still smiled back.

From the first read-through of the play, the chemistry between us was so strong that one part of me wished we were doing a different kind of show, the kind where we had love scenes. But the hard part would have been keeping the chemistry on stage. If I had met him ten years earlier, I wouldn't have tried. Sometimes I regret being an adult.

Ryan wasn't exactly the actor I would have expected to be playing Scrooge, the old miser, a part played by actors like an aging Albert Finney or an aging George C. Scott in the movies. I had never watched the soap Ryan had been on, but I knew the kind of stock character he played—the charming heel who finally has to be killed off because he can't get any worse and the writers don't know how to redeem him.

In person, he had black hair, blue eyes, a dimple in his chin, and he knew he was gorgeous.

I wondered how his wife had learned to live with all the women who must throw themselves at him. I was sure he could live with them just fine.

"Come on," he said. "Let's go in."

I followed him up the steps, thinking I really had to get in shape. Ryan was probably in his early forties, but the biceps that drew the short sleeves of his polo shirt taut indicated that he still took his workouts seriously.

He waited for me at the front door, but by the time we crossed the lobby, he was three steps ahead.

"The stars are here, we can start now," Johnny called out, as Ryan paused again at the door to the theater so that I could go in first.

"Are we really late?" I whispered.

"No," Ryan said. "Maybe ten minutes. I don't wear a watch."

Whatever time it was, everyone else was in fact waiting.

The stage wasn't a large one, but it was divided into two acting areas. One was a bedroom for Scrooge, the other a space where most of the other scenes could take place. A platform to the side of the stage, almost in the audience, served as a street. The actors playing the other Cratchits were sitting together on the platform. The Ghost of Christmas Present was sitting in a back pew. The other Ghosts and Scrooge's nephew were scattered around the theater.

Ted Reed, my husband for the show, was eating a sandwich, just as if the stage really was a kitchen. Even sitting on the stage, he looked more like the house husband from the commercial than an actor. There was something real about his smooth brown hair and square-jawed face. Not that actors aren't real. It's just that sometimes the ones in L.A. look too charismatic to be true.

"Let's take it from the top," Johnny said, with more volume than was necessary in the small space. He was short, wiry and young, but he did have a commanding voice.

I took a seat in the front pew, and Bobby Spitzer, the boy playing Tim, came over and sat next to me, grabbing my hand. I squeezed it and smiled. I am not particularly maternal, and I knew where W. C. Fields was coming from when he said he didn't like acting with children, but I was willing to embrace this one for our time together. In fact, it surprised me how much I wanted to embrace him.

Ryan climbed the steps to the stage, then moved to the podium he used as Dickens the narrator.

"And, lights!" Johnny called.

I sat there breathing quietly as Ryan started the play. I felt myself releasing the tension of the encounter with Tori, and I worked all the way back to the blow-up with Charity. By the time they got to my entrance, I was at peace with the world.

Early in the rehearsal period it had become clear who the professionals and who the amateurs were, not in the sense of who was paid and who wasn't, because none of us got paid, but in the sense of who was trustworthy on stage, who was dedicated and serious, and who was liable to screw up. One Ghost and two children were on my watch-out-for list. Ryan and Ted were both professionals, and I still remembered what being a professional was like. My time on stage with them was pure joy.

The rehearsal was three hours long, but it was the shortest three hours of a long day. Almost before I knew it, Bobby Spitzer had cried, "God bless us, every one," echoed by Ryan, and I was walking out that same heavy wooden door and down the steps, with more energy than I had when I walked up, thanks to the adrenaline surge from being on stage. I even had a little glow of Christmas spirit.

Ryan was next to me by the time I hit the second step.

"I'd suggest we go for a beer and get to know each other better, but I promised my wife I'd come straight home." He flashed that perfect smile, and I got all the messages.

"I couldn't go anyway," I replied. "I'm meeting a friend for coffee. What I really need, though, is a little hot cocoa, to calm me down. I'd forgotten what a night owl I used to be, and why."

"We're all night owls in the theater." He dropped his hand on my shoulder and squeezed gently. "See you Saturday."

I got into my car feeling the little glow that comes from flirting, even when you know you're not going to act on it.

When I turned on the ignition, the digital clock lit up, and I was startled to discover that it was already ten-thirty. I was late to meet Tori.

A light rain had begun to fall, barely more than a mist on the windshield, but I turned on the wipers.

I retraced my path, from Lankershim to Magnolia to Coldwater Canyon to Ventura Boulevard, hoping she would wait, rain or no rain, because I wouldn't be able to stand the guilt if she didn't.

The flashing red lights were my first cue that something was wrong. I was a couple of blocks away when I noticed them, but at first I didn't realize that the police cars and the ambulance were parked in front of Argento's. I turned onto a side street to find a parking place, hurried back to Ventura Boulevard, and trotted as quickly as I could toward the crowd that had gathered just beyond the yellow tape marking a crime scene.

"What's going on?" I asked, gasping for breath.

"A drive-by shooting, in Sherman Oaks. Can you believe that?" A short, middle-aged woman wearing a light jacket and a rain hat looked at me and shook her head.

"Who was it, do you know?" My stomach began to knot, even as I asked the question.

"Some young woman," she said, shaking her head again.

I pushed past her, looking for a police officer.

One stopped me before I got much closer.

"I was supposed to meet someone here," I told him. "A young woman, curly black hair, probably wearing a sweatshirt and jeans. I don't see her."

His mouth got tight. I felt my hands clench, and I prayed it was somebody else, not Tori. The rain was beginning to firm up, now more than a mist. Drops splashed my face and hair.

"Come with me," he said. "They were just about to take her away."

He led me over to the ambulance.

"Are you ready to look?" His eyes were steely, too steely for someone so young, and I had to nod.

I climbed into the ambulance, and the attendant pulled back the blanket covering the body.

As soon as I saw the hair, I knew it was Tori.

I dropped to my knees and began to cry.

FOUR

THE YOUNG OFFICER HELPED me out of the ambulance. We walked into Argento's together, his hand under my elbow, holding me up. He pulled a chair away from a table near the door, and I sat.

The heavy quilted jacket that had seemed perfect for the December evening when I put it on was now damp, and I had trouble deciding whether I would be more comfortable with it on or off. I finally pulled my arms out of the sleeves and left it around my shoulders.

A waiter—in fact, the sole occupant of the restaurant—started in our direction, but the officer shook his head.

"Will you wait here while I find Detective Pierce?" he asked.

I nodded.

"Are you sure I can't get you something?" The waiter, a pleasant young man with a friendly face, was at the table as soon as the officer moved away.

"Could I have a cup of hot chocolate?" I asked.

"Would you like it made with steamed milk?" he asked.

"Yes, please."

He zipped away to fill the order.

Argento's was one of those throwbacks to a gentler age that are amazingly common on Ventura Boulevard—a small, family-owned business, in this case a restaurant, with friendly service. I suspected that the young man who waited tables, steamed the milk for my hot chocolate and otherwise took care of things was the owner's son. I had only been in a few times, and he was always there. I had never seen it this quiet.

I watched the crime scene investigation through the heavy glass storefront as if it were a television set with the sound muted. The rain acted like a soft-focus lens, blurring features, distorting lights. The officer, undistracted, found the detective, who nodded and glanced in my direction.

My cocoa arrived before the detective did.

I was feeling a little better by the time he finished his conversation with someone else, walked into the restaurant, and sat down in the seat across from me.

"I'm Pierce," he said. "What can you tell me about the girl?"

"Her name is Tori Sanchez, and she was my client," I said. "My name is Faith Cassidy. I'm a therapist."

"Do you always meet your clients this late at night?"

"No, of course not," I snapped. I took a second look at Pierce.

He was middle-aged, probably close to retirement, and on the hefty side, a bit out of shape for the LAPD, which prides itself on its paramilitary muscles. His sweater vest didn't quite conceal the bulge of his stomach over the top of his pants. The bulge of his shoulders under the lightweight raincoat was enough to make the point that he wasn't slowing down.

And his eyes had the gaze of somebody who had seen too much.

"I was meeting her this late because she came to my apartment at a time when I couldn't talk," I said. "Somebody had threatened her a few months ago—threatened both of us—and she seemed concerned that she might be in danger again. But I thought it was about Charity, I really did."

He frowned, then nodded. "Tell me what you know."

I told him how I met Tori, that she had witnessed the murder of a man named Craig Thorson, that both of us were threatened by the murderers, that the people who had threatened us then were out on bail, and that the trial would be starting soon. I also told him about Charity, who claimed to be a witness to a different murder, or at least to the aftermath.

"So this Tori Sanchez has just been eliminated as a material witness in a murder case," he said.

"Yes, but I don't think it's about that. There was another witness, and one of the conspirators is cutting a deal. Eliminating Tori really shouldn't make a difference to that case. I think it's about this thing with Charity."

"Forgive me, Miss Cassidy." Pierce sighed, a deep been-there-done-that sigh. "But I think the officer you talked to this afternoon was right. A hooker got into a Mercedes on Sunset Boulevard. She'll turn up. In the meantime, I'll see what's going on in the murder case. The first one. The one about to come to trial."

"Did anybody see who shot Tori?" I didn't really expect an answer, but I had to ask.

He surprised me by answering.

"Somebody in a light Mercedes, nobody saw a face," he said. "But before you add two and two and get five, let me ask you something. Was somebody in a Mercedes involved in this murder case, the one Tori Sanchez was a witness in?"

"Yes." I had to tell him.

"That's the thing, Miss Cassidy." He was nodding at me again. "This is L.A. You know the old joke? Why is a Mercedes like a hemorrhoid?"

I nodded, but he finished it anyway.

"Sooner or later, every asshole gets one," he said. "No offense."

"None taken. I don't drive a Mercedes."

Pierce stood up, pulled his wallet out of his back pocket, fumbled for a business card, and handed it to me.

"I want you to call me if you think of anything that might help. And I'm going to ask an officer to accompany you home, just in case there's a message on your answering machine, from Tori Sanchez or anyone else, that we should know about. Is that all right?" he asked.

"That's fine." I looked around for the waiter, so that I could pay for my cocoa. I held up my purse and waved.

"No charge," he called, from across the room.

I thanked him, then followed Detective Pierce out of the restaurant.

The sound came up immediately, but only to the level of whispers. The ambulance had gone, but the crime scene investigators were still checking the place in the street where Tori's body had lain. And the crowd still watched.

Pierce found the young officer I had first talked with, and he agreed to follow me home.

It was a fruitless trip.

There was nothing suspicious in the vicinity of my apartment, and only a couple of messages from clients on my answering machine.

I said good-night to the officer, grabbed the cats and went to bed.

In the morning, as I sat down to make the phone calls to cancel my private clients for a week, it occurred to me that at least now I had a legitimate reason for doing so. Nobody could expect me to keep to my regular schedule after one of my clients had been murdered.

But that was hardly a message I could leave on another client's answering machine.

I went to the kitchen and fixed myself a second latte—the first had been consumed as I glanced at the *Times,* headlines passing through my brain unheeded—and struggled with the wording of a "personal emergency" message.

It took me only ten minutes to make the calls. This was the first time I considered myself lucky when none of my clients answered their phones. The machines were easier to deal with.

With the calls out of the way, the rest of the day was mine. Friday, my last day without a rehearsal until we opened. Obsessing about Tori's dead body wasn't going to do anyone any good. Nevertheless, I had to tell Michael what happened.

I was grateful to all the gods that he was home.

"I'm glad to hear that," Michael said, when I ended the story by assuring him that I wasn't obsessing over the murder. "Still, even though you didn't know Tori well, the two of you were in the same foxhole—metaphorically at least— some months ago when the enemy snipers were shooting at you. That tends to encourage bonding, even among people who don't have much in common. And she was your client. Are you certain you can let this drop?"

"No, of course I'm not certain. I just don't know what else to do."

"Talk to me about Tori," Michael said. "Get it all out now. Or would you rather do lunch?"

"No. No lunch. I don't even think I'm going to get dressed today." I paused, thinking about Tori. "She wanted to be an actress, and she really did have some talent. That's how she dealt with the men who paid her for sex—as if she were an actress, and they were paying for her talent as a performer. Part of her was untouched, and that was what made her so likable, but also vulnerable."

"You think she was murdered because she was vulnerable?" Michael asked.

"Oh, God. I have no idea why she was murdered. I'm afraid it's because of something Charity told her, though."

"Faith, if somebody kidnapped Charity, and that's a big if, why wouldn't they just kidnap Tori, too?"

"Because Charity could be bought and Tori couldn't?" I countered. "I just don't know."

"That's it. You don't know Charity, and you don't know Tori all that well. If I were you, I'd be more concerned that Tori was killed because she was a witness to the Thorson murder. In fact, your insistence that this has something to do with Charity sounds suspiciously like denial. Are you taking steps to protect yourself?"

"Denial?" My heart started thumping, and I struggled to stay calm. "Oh, God, I hope not. What if it is? Do you think I need a bodyguard?"

"Not really. After all, you weren't an eyewitness. You only heard the confession. But maybe you ought to stay inside for a day or two, and check the street."

"Oh, Michael, no. Don't say that. I have a rehearsal tomorrow afternoon, and I'm going to be there." I could hear the fear in his voice, and I remembered how close he had been to the murderers. I wasn't the only one who had been in danger then, and I wasn't the only one who was stressed out now. "We both need to take deep breaths and hope that Tori's murder has nothing to do with us."

"Are you sure you don't want to do lunch? We could hold hands, like Hansel and Gretel in the forest."

"I'm sure. I'm going to check the dead bolt on the door, take a shower and relax. Which is what I intended to do today." I liked the sound of conviction in my voice.

"All right. Let me know if you hear from that detective, Pierce."

"Michael, are you all right? I mean, you really aren't in danger, whatever is going on. They'd come after me long before they would think about you, if it is connected to the Thorson murder trial." I was so used to Michael as the stable person. I needed him to be all right.

"Of course I'm all right. If you can keep going, so can I."

I hung up the phone, but it took me a moment to get up from the chair. Talking to Michael hadn't helped as much as I had hoped. He was there for me so often, but this mess had gotten to him.

Taking a shower and washing my hair cleared some of the fear. I picked up a book, a fat thriller, sat down in my big living room chair, curled my feet up under my bathrobe and settled down to read.

I gave up fifteen minutes later, unable to get involved in someone's fictional perilous situation. I shut my eyes and thought about Tori, remembering the therapy sessions, trying to pull up anything that might help me figure out what was going on, why she had been murdered. I refused to believe it had anything to do with the Thorson murder case.

When the idea came to me, I didn't understand why it had taken so long. Tori lived with her older sister, Letty, and Letty's five-year-old daughter Rina. Letty and Tori were estranged from their mother and had never known their father. If Tori had confided in anyone, her sister would be that person.

I had met Letty only once, when I had been chauffeuring Tori to and from our meetings with law enforcement. Most of the time Tori would wait for me on the street, away from Letty. The one time I met her I had the sense that she was nursing a deep-seated rage toward life, a rage she took out on who-ever was handy.

Tori's death wasn't going to help Letty with her emotional problems.

I thought about calling, but I knew Letty would just hang up on me. I would have to drive over there if I wanted to talk to her. Letty had a straight job, working as a data entry clerk for an insurance company, and I would have to hope that she had taken the day off. Surely she would have stayed home and let Rina take the day off from school.

But I didn't have to find out that instant.

I needed breakfast first. I scrambled a couple of eggs, toasted some Italian sesame bread and poured a glass of organic grapefruit juice. The food calmed me down and fortified me for the drive to Hollywood.

The next step was putting on some makeup, then getting dressed.

Finally I looked better, I felt better, and I couldn't postpone the trip any longer. I grabbed a water-resistant jacket and a hat with a sloping brim and went out into the rain. Last night's gentle mist was today's downpour.

I almost changed my mind. All those jokes about L.A. drivers slowing down in the rain from eighty-five miles per hour to eighty-three miles per hour are true, except for the hours when traffic is gridlocked, and I hate getting on the freeway when the sun isn't shining. L.A. drivers get crazy in the rain. Driving on the same road with one is a risk of life, limb, and automobile. But I got in the car anyway.

The Hollywood I drove to bore no resemblance to the Hollywood of film fantasy. This was the Hollywood that bordered Koreatown, an area that was less a land of broken dreams than of shattered ones. No dream that landed there could ever be put back together again.

The single-family homes were mostly bungalows badly in need of paint, as were the cars parked in front of them. One house was strung with Christmas lights, but they weren't turned on, as if the attempt at cheer had failed. The apartment buildings had cracked stucco facades and bars on the windows. Waking up in this neighborhood would depress the rosiest of spirits, even on a sunny day. The rain made it feel as dark as one of the circles of Hell.

The apartment building where Tori had shared quarters with her sister Letty looked like a converted motel—two stories, cracked stucco that might have been painted white shortly after World War II, on a lot split down the middle into half building and half parking area. No landscaping. It was no better and no worse than the other buildings on the block.

I parked the car in front of it, wishing for a moment that my car had an alarm. But when I stepped out of the car, I inhaled a pervasive sense of despair. Nobody on that block would have the energy for car theft.

The sidewalk was slippery, and I picked my way carefully. I climbed the cracked concrete stairs and rang the bell to the second apartment. When there was no answer, I rang again. I thought I could hear movement inside, and I didn't want to leave if Letty was there.

Finally a muffled voice said, "Go away."

"Letty, it's Faith Cassidy," I replied. "I thought you might want to talk to a therapist."

That was true, and I was perfectly willing to act as a grief counselor in exchange for some information.

The door opened a few inches, with the chain still in place.

I saw one red, tear-filled eye and a portion of a red, bloated face.

"I know who you are," Letty said. "You didn't do Tori any good. She's as dead as she would have been if she'd never listened to you. Why would I want to talk to you?"

"Because you need to talk to somebody," I answered.

The door began to close. I held my hand against it, and Letty waited.

"Letty, I am so sorry about what happened to Tori, and I know you must be grieving for her. Don't try to handle it all by yourself. Let me in. Let me hold your hand for a while." I looked into the bloodshot eye with all the compassion I could muster.

"Why would you want to help me?" she asked.

"Because you were Tori's sister, and I cared about her, too."

That did the trick. Letty unlatched the chain and opened the door.

Tori had told me about the apartment. The layout was a bit like mine, in that the room I walked into was a combination living room, dining room and efficiency kitchen. An open door led into a bedroom. My apartment was easily twice as large, though, and several times as bright. The only light in this one came from a single barred window next to the front door. The resemblance to a motel was heightened because neither Tori nor Letty had made any attempt to decorate the place, turn it into a home. They slept and ate here, that was all.

Even that little bit of sharing had been done uneasily. Letty and Rina had the bedroom, and Tori slept on a sofa bed in the living room. Tori baby-sat Rina while Letty was at work during the day, then left when Letty came home. I could see Rina through the open door, thin little body sitting crosslegged on the bed, pinched face making no move to see who the visitor might be.

I had asked Tori why they hadn't tried to turn the apartment into a home. She told me they believed it was temporary. They had believed it was temporary for the six years they lived there, ever since shortly before Rina's birth. Rather than buy anything for that apartment, each woman had saved what she could, which wasn't much, hoping to get a place of her own.

"Want to sit down?" Letty asked.

"Yes, thank you," I replied.

When I looked at Letty, I could see the family resemblance in the hair and the skin and the eyes. But Letty probably outweighed her sister by forty pounds.

"Can I get you a glass of water or something?" she asked.

"No, I'm fine."

Letty nodded. She gestured toward a small table with three chairs, one of those round tables with leaves that drop so that you can set it against a wall. This one was right next to the kitchen.

I picked the chair farthest from the kitchen. Letty sat in the only padded armchair, a torn leather recliner next to the ratty sofa bed, halfway across the room. She wasn't about to get cozy with me. I took off my damp jacket, draped it on the table and turned so that I could face her.

"I know this must be a shock to you," I began.

"No, you don't know," she said, interrupting. "I had to look at her body, tell them it was her. You don't know what a shock that is."

"You're right. I'm sorry." I faced her, unblinking, and waited.

She gave in. "The policeman said she was supposed to meet you. Tell me what happened."

"I don't know. She was waiting on my apartment stairs when I got home, a little before seven. I had to be someplace, I didn't have time to talk, so I told her I'd meet her for coffee at ten. When I got to the restaurant, she had already been shot." The words sounded so lame. I wished all over again that I had talked to Tori before the rehearsal.

"You were late, right?" Letty asked.

I struggled with the answer. "Yes. I was late."

"See, you say you cared about her, but she came to you for help, and you sent her away till later, and then you didn't even come back on time. If she hadn't been on the sidewalk, waiting for you, she might be alive." Tears were rolling down Letty's face from unblinking dark eyes.

I bit back all the retorts. I didn't get Tori into trouble, and I didn't ask her to come to me, and I didn't ask her to wait on the sidewalk. But saying that wouldn't help. It wouldn't even ease my guilt.

"You didn't even help her get off the streets," Letty continued. "She's been seeing you for months, saying you're going to help her get her life together, and then she's still out there fucking creeps to pay her share of the rent. How can you say you cared?"

I bit back more retorts, like all the times I had picked Tori up to take her to the police and the attorneys, the time I had driven her to the community college to pick up information, the encouragement I had given her to look for a straight job, or even take an acting class. The truth was, Letty was hitting a nerve because I already feared I was failing with Tori. And I felt that even knowing, as Letty surely did, too, that change takes time.

"I did care. I was doing my best. Tori would have stopped—stopped exchanging sex for money when she was ready." I hoped that was true. "Did she tell you what kind of trouble she was in?"

"You were going to say, 'this time,' weren't you?" Letty asked. "What trouble was she in this time?"

"Yes. I was."

"Tori didn't tell me much. We lived together, but she stopped telling me her problems when I got pregnant with Rina. I didn't do anything but cry and eat for months." The thought of that period when she had cried so much started Letty's tears again. We both waited until she had them under control. "Tori stopped spending time in the apartment unless she had to be here with Rina. I found out after a while what she was doing. She said it was the only way she could make enough to keep our bills paid. I hoped when I got a job, when Rina was old enough that I didn't have to be here all the time, maybe Tori would get one, too. But she didn't. And she wouldn't talk to me about it."

"Tori had to lead her own life, Letty. You did what you could." I reminded myself that I had done what I could, too.

Letty shrugged.

"If I hadn't got pregnant, it would all have been different," she said. "I'm glad I have Rina now, otherwise I'd be all alone. But I'd have had a different life if I hadn't got pregnant."

I hoped she wouldn't say that too often in front of the little girl. No sounds came from the bedroom. I hoped Rina had fallen asleep.

"If you need help with education or job training—" The disdainful look on Letty's face stopped me.

"Or a surgeon to bind my stomach? You got it all?"

"No, Letty, I don't. But I do want to help."

"Yeah, I know. You're one of those people, always want to

help, feel bad when you can't. You have an alcoholic mother or something? Tried to help her and couldn't? Get screwed up when you were a kid?"

I didn't feel the need to respond to that. Letty's anger was directed at me simply because I was the only person in the room.

"Well, you can't help here," she continued. "You can't help me find a way to get out of this rathole. You couldn't get Tori off the streets, and now you can't bring her back. And you can't even help find out who killed her. The cops will give up after a while, one more Mexican whore gone and who cares, and that'll be that."

That I had to respond to.

"I'm going to do my best to see that every effort is made to find Tori's killer. And you can help me there. I think there's a possibility that the police are looking in the wrong direction. Did Tori ever mention a young woman named Charity Jackson?" I leaned forward, mentally crossing my fingers for luck.

Letty laughed. "Mention her? She practically lived here for almost a week, until yesterday. With Tori dead, I guess she knew better than to come back." The laugh disappeared. "You think she knows something? How did she know Tori was dead?"

"I don't know what Charity knows—I don't know where she is. I think Charity is in trouble, and I think Tori's murder may have something to do with that."

"The cops think Tori was shot because somebody doesn't want her to testify about that guy who was killed a few months ago," Letty said, clearly unwilling to take my word over that of a police officer's, no matter how much she might distrust the police.

"The police may be wrong," I replied.

Letty had to think about that.

"When I asked Tori how long Charity was going to sleep in the chair, she said she didn't know. She didn't tell me what was going on." Letty rose heavily from the chair and moved to the kitchen. She pulled the lid off a plastic trash can and began rummaging, bracing herself with one hand against the counter. When she straightened up, her face was red from the exertion, and she had a crumpled, greasy piece of paper in her hand.

She brought it to the table and laid it out for me to see. A name, Ollie, and a phone number. That was all.

"One of them left this beside the phone yesterday, either Tori or Charity," she said. "I don't know which one. That's the only thing I have to offer. Do you think I should tell the police?"

"Why don't you give me the number? I'll give it to the police," I said.

"Okay. It's yours."

"Thank you. Are you sure there's nothing I can do for you?"

Letty shrugged again, a shrug that started at her shoulders and worked all the way down her body.

"I'll let you know. Don't call me, I'll call you. Isn't that what they say?"

"That's what they say."

I had all I was going to get from Letty. I thought about going into the bedroom to check on the little girl, but I didn't really believe that my checking on her would make any difference in her life.

Letty watched as I put my damp jacket back on and let myself out, piece of paper with phone number in hand.

I would turn it over to the police. But first I wanted to know who Ollie was.

Once I reached my car, I pulled out my cell phone and dialed the number.

When a deep, male voice answered, I said, "I'm looking for Charity Jackson."

"So am I, baby," he said. "So am I."

My cell phone picked that moment to die.

FIVE

THERE WAS NOTHING TO DO but drive home. I suppose I could have looked for a pay phone, but the thought of it made me tired. Ollie, whoever he was, didn't know where Charity was anyway.

The middle of the day, Friday. Driving back up the Hollywood Freeway to the Ventura Freeway in the rain was easier than driving in. The mass exodus from the city hadn't started yet, and traffic was light enough to move smoothly.

For the first time since I had moved there, I had a warm feeling for Sherman Oaks, glad that my apartment was there, cozy, and not in Hollywood.

Once inside, I dropped my jacket on the kitchen floor to let it dry, grabbed Mac, and sat down in the chair I used when clients were there. Near me on the wall was a Maxfield Parrish poster of a young, joyful woman looking as if she were about to soar into the sky. The chair and the poster were part of my professional costume. I sat there wanting to feel strong and professional and capable of joy. Loved, too, that's what Mac was for.

But Amy wanted to investigate my jacket, and Mac struggled until I let him hop off my lap to join her. Strong and professional were also out of reach. As for joy, it might as well have been a word in a foreign language.

I thought about calling Ollie again. But that was pointless, since he didn't know where Charity was. Thus, there probably wasn't any point in alerting Detective Pierce to Ollie's existence. Still, I had promised Letty I would turn his number over to the police. Besides, I had to do something to end my focus on Charity's abduction and Tori's death. So I decided to call Pierce and then release the whole mess for the rest of the day.

Pierce, of course, wasn't there. I left a message, with both my phone number and Ollie's phone number, hoping that my explanation was sufficient.

I hung up the phone and picked up the thriller.

Much to my surprise, I was able to focus on it after all. When I was ready to put the book down, the afternoon light was beginning to fade.

I had been ignoring phone calls, letting the answering machine do its job, but now I checked messages. They were all from clients, expressing concern, mostly for themselves, but two had the grace to be worried about me. Pierce hadn't called me back.

That didn't mean he hadn't checked out Ollie, of course. I couldn't expect a detective to keep me up-to-date on the investigation. Still, I had a gut feeling that Pierce wouldn't check out anything but the Thorson case. I hoped I was wrong.

I stared at the phone. Ollie or Pierce.

I picked up the phone and dialed Ollie.

This time a machine answered, a machine with that gravelly male voice, offering no information I didn't already have. I couldn't decide what sort of message to leave, so I hung up without leaving one.

As I sat there with the phone still in my hand, eyes shut, wondering what to do next, I suddenly remembered that I wasn't supposed to be doing anything. I was supposed to be taking a week off, doing nothing but dealing with stress. Of course, that was a couple of stresses ago.

If I were advising a client in my situation, I'd tell her to take a hot bath, have a light dinner and a glass of wine, watch a videotape and go to bed early.

For once, I took my own advice.

Not only did I go to bed early, but I woke up early, with the sun streaming through the Venetian blinds. The storm had passed sometime during the night. The sky was bright blue, and the foliage was that rich green shade you see in Southern California after the first rains of winter, a vibrant green that lasts into the early spring, before everything turns brown for the summer.

I fed the cats, made a latte and went out onto the deck. I hadn't thought to bring the cushions in, so the chairs were too damp to sit on. I stood there, appreciating the quiet and the beauty. The surrounding trees wrapped me in leafy protection. A stressfree life was possible, I could sense it. A week with nothing to do and nowhere to go except rehearsals. I would be a new woman by the end of it. Maybe I would even decorate the apartment for Christmas.

When it was time to leave for rehearsal, I was still feeling good.

I was feeling so good that I almost didn't notice the man standing across the street, watching me walk down the stairs and head toward the carport.

But I did notice him. He was African American, wearing a black trench coat, and built like a football player. He would have stood out in a crowd, had there been one. In this case, he was the only person on the block, and he just leaned against a tree and stared at me.

The thought of going back to my apartment flitted through

my mind. But if I went back, what then? Call the police? Tell them what?

He wasn't making a move toward me. So I hurried to my car, got in and drove away. If he was still there when I got back, that was the time to call the police.

Maybe he wasn't staring at me anyway. Maybe he was waiting for someone, and I just happened to enter his line of vision. Maybe.·

I drove to the theater—the church—with one eye on my rearview mirror. Not that I really believed anyone would follow me. All I could see was the normal flow of traffic.

My own parking space was waiting for me in front of the door, as if it had been reserved. I rushed up the stairs to the heavy wooden doors, glad to be there.

Somehow I had managed to be early.

The lobby was deserted, except for the collection of framed posters on the walls. The one in the place of honor, straight ahead as I entered, was from *Phantom of the Opera,* signed by Michael Crawford. The others were an eclectic collection of musicals and dramas, many autographed. Jason Robards in *Hughie.* Hal Holbrook in *Mark Twain Tonight.* Clearly Johnny had been a fan long before he had become a director. He had designed his own poster for *A Christmas Carol,* a sketch of Ryan holding an old book in his hand, surrounded by sprigs of holly, with one limp piece of mistletoe hanging over his head. It was a strange mix of traditional England and postmodern L.A.

The theater was deserted, too. I walked down the aisle to the stage.

"Johnny?" I called.

He appeared from behind the set, coffee cup in hand.

"I don't believe it. Miss LATV is the first one here."

"I'm eager to rehearse. And I'm not that early, am I? It's almost one."

"Right. But it's too bad you didn't check your rehearsal schedule. We're starting at two." He smiled triumphantly, as if he had just scored a bull's-eye in darts.

I was caught off balance, and my stress started to return. I straightened up. I could use the edginess, Mrs. Cratchit's annoyance at Scrooge.

"Darn," I said, smiling as innocently as I could. "I guess I'll have to be more careful next week."

Johnny nodded, pleased with my response. "Pour yourself some coffee. There's a fresh pot in the kitchen. The real kitchen, that is."

The real kitchen—Johnny's kitchen, as opposed to what passed for one on the set—was behind the stage, next to what had been the church's administrative office, and was now the greenroom, where the actors hung out. The kitchen was bright and airy, and I could imagine the women of the church fixing buffet lunches for the congregation to eat after the services. Or maybe for wedding receptions. Christmas parties. All kinds of celebrations.

I wondered if Johnny ever celebrated. And what the rest of his life was like. I knew he had more space on the second floor, but he had never invited me up. Probably never would.

Johnny didn't keep me company, and I drank a second cup of coffee before the other actors arrived, all except Ryan. He showed up before the grumbling became severe, and Johnny put us to work.

Somewhere in the art of the actor is the art of healing the soul. I know it, and if I could truly figure it out, in a way that I could share with troubled souls everywhere, I would be the best therapist in the world.

Even though my entire part in the play was only two short scenes as the center of a loving family, I began to think that maybe love wasn't so far out of reach. If grace was possible for Scrooge, maybe it was possible for me.

For a moment I could dream of a happy family celebrating Christmas.

The afternoon would have been tough—tech rehearsals are never easy—but everyone had such goodwill, and the young actors were so excited about being in the play that no one complained.

I found myself holding Bobby Spitzer's hand whenever we had a break.

"I think I'm getting a puppy for Christmas," he whispered to me at one point.

"Awright," I whispered back. "Puppies are great."

He nodded.

I wondered briefly what Rina would get for Christmas. I got rid of the thought as quickly as I could.

When Johnny said, "That's it for today, good work everybody," I discovered that I was holding hands not with Bobby, but with Ted, my stage husband, and had been ever since our scene ended. I would have to leave the dream for a while.

I dropped Ted's hand and glanced over at Ryan, who winked. And I remembered that it really wasn't Ted or Ryan I was dreaming about anyway.

"See you all tomorrow," Johnny said. "Two o'clock, Faith, we start at two."

"I'll be here, Johnny," I said.

I grabbed my bag and headed for the lobby, hoping I looked as if I had some purpose in life other than to wait for it to be time to come back to the theater.

I stopped short just outside the heavy double doors.

The man in the black trench coat was standing across the street.

"Watch it," Ryan said, clapping a hand on my shoulder. "I almost ran into you."

"That man is following me." The words were choked and strange, and the voice saying them didn't sound like mine.

"I'll talk to him," Ryan said.

I tried to tell him to wait, but he was down the steps and halfway across the street before I could bring the thought to form.

Ryan had the same kind of presence walking across the street that he had walking across the stage, and added to that was the confidence that came from having been in front of the camera five days a week for years. No one was going to intimidate Ryan, not even a scowling guy in a black trench coat who outweighed him by a hundred pounds. I used to have that confidence. I wondered what had happened to it.

The man didn't move as Ryan approached. I watched them talk, a picture without sound, one more time. I sensed the other actors leaving the theater, heard someone say goodbye. Nobody else seemed interested in what was happening across the street. The man pulled out his wallet and showed something to Ryan, who nodded. They both started back toward me.

I met them at the bottom of the stairs.

"He's a P.I.," Ryan said. "He wants to talk to you."

"About what?" My heart was pounding, and my stomach was churning. I was reacting out of all proportion to the words.

"About Charity Jackson," the man said. As he stood next to me, I had a sense of what standing next to Refrigerator Perry must be like. "My name is Ollie Burke. I think you wanted to talk to me, too."

I struggled to sort out what he was saying, why I might want to talk with him. Then the gravelly voice registered, and the name Ollie.

"Ollie?" I asked.

He nodded. I took a closer look at his features, his round, unlined face, the color of chocolate pudding, his small, calm, black eyes. The top of his head was smooth and shiny, but there was a light stubble on his cheeks. He wasn't scowling. I had just thought he must be, when I saw him across the street.

"You're really a P.I.?" I asked.

Ollie nodded again.

"Why are you looking for Charity Jackson?" I asked.

"Why are you?"

"Who's Charity Jackson?" Ryan asked.

"It's a long story," I said. "And I know you need to go. Thank you for helping me. I'll be all right now."

I reached out and touched his arm, instinctively, then took my hand back.

Ryan hesitated, the kind of hesitation that meant he really did need to go.

"I promise I'll be all right," I added.

"Okay. See you tomorrow. And you have to tell me the story then."

I watched him walk to his car, resisting the urge to call him back.

Ollie waited for me to turn to him, waited for my attention. When he got it, he said, "I'm Charity Jackson's brother."

I thought back to the slender woman with burnished copper skin.

"I don't believe you," I said.

"We both take after our fathers," was the calm reply.

"None of this makes sense." I shook my head. "If Charity had a P.I. brother, why was she asking me for help?"

"Can we sit down some place and talk?"

"Yes. Right here." I sat down on the stairs and grabbed my knees, huddling to keep as much of myself as possible away from the chill of the concrete. Ollie seemed to be a reasonable person, but I wasn't confident enough of that to risk going somewhere with him.

I wondered what Johnny would do if I called for help. I couldn't imagine him rushing to my defense, but he might have the presence of mind to call 911.

"Okay. If this is what you want." Ollie eased his bulk down to the concrete, on the other side of the metal rail that ran up the center of the steps.

"Start with how you found me," I said.

"You called me," he answered. "And I got a little machine that displays numbers, even when people don't leave a message. It didn't take much of an Internet search to discover that the number belonged to one Faith Cassidy, a therapist. Your address is listed, too, and that might not be such a good idea."

"I know. I almost delisted it when I moved." Next time, I would.

"But the number just made it easier. I would have found you by Monday. The last message I got from Charity said she was going to a clinic to talk to somebody named Faith. She knew she was in trouble, she didn't know how bad. I would have called every clinic in L.A. until somebody answered to Faith." He said it so calmly, I knew he meant it.

"Charity called you from Tori Sanchez's place, and now Tori is dead. Did you know that?"

"I know that." He nodded slowly, weighed down by the

gravity of the thought. "And I know the police don't think it had anything to do with Charity."

"But you do."

"Well, I don't know. And so I don't know it's any of my business. But I need to find my sister, and I want to find her alive. So why don't you tell me what you know?"

I told him about my encounter with Charity, what little I knew. And why I had followed up with Tori Sanchez's sister. He sat there, scowling—and this time the scowl was real—as I talked.

When I finished, he said, "Charity wasn't entirely honest with you. As far as I know, she did a little sex-for-money a while back, but I don't think that's what she was doing the other night. She knew that man, the one she says she saw carrying the body. But she wouldn't give me a name, either the dead man or the possible killer. I haven't been able to turn up any leads. I was hoping she had given you some information that would help me find out who the guy is, where he is. And finding him would get me to her."

"If she had you, why did she involve me at all?" I asked, fighting down anger at Charity, anger doubled now that I knew just how much she had lied to me, anger that wouldn't do me any good with her brother Ollie.

"Because my help came with strings attached," he replied. "I've bailed her out too many times, each time worse than the last. I told her the only way I was helping this time was if she left L.A. We got a cousin lives in Atlanta. I told Charity I'd pay for a one-way ticket."

"Moving to Atlanta wouldn't have changed her if she didn't want to change," I said.

Ollie lifted his eyebrows, softening the skepticism with a half smile. "You think I never been to a twelve-step meeting?

I know that. It was just all I could think to do. Get her away from the life she was leading."

"What kind of life was that?"

"Maybe she wasn't a hooker, but she was sure involved with the wrong people. Drugs for a while, now murder."

"I'm sorry she wouldn't listen."

Ollie shrugged. "Me, too."

I closed my eyes and let my forehead sink into my hands, elbows on my knees. The cold of the concrete steps was starting to seep through my jeans. In another minute, it would be traveling up my spine. Was there anything I needed from him? Did I care who the man was, the one Charity saw with the body? I didn't.

"Okay. If I have this straight, you're a P.I., and you're looking for Charity, and the police are looking for Tori's murderer. If you find out anything that will help them, you'll let them know. Right?" I lifted my forehead and turned to him, feeling hope for the first time in days.

"Right," Ollie said, nodding.

"Then there's nothing more for me to do."

"Right again."

I wanted to watch him nod for a while, but I was getting seriously cold. I stood up, stretching the chill out of my legs.

And then the words came out before I could stop them.

"Let me know when you find her, will you?"

"Sure thing," he said.

Ollie Burke was still sitting there, nodding, when I got into my car and drove away.

SIX

I WOKE UP SUNDAY MORNING after a good night's sleep to a vision of a clear blue sky just beyond the sheer white curtains that covered my bedroom window, two sable-furred cats sleeping in a lump at the bottom of my bed, and a light heart.

I fed the cats and fixed a latte. And picked up the phone and called Michael. I had to let him know that my stress level was at an astonishing low, now that I had turned Tori's murder over to the police and Charity's problems over to her brother.

Michael was gratifyingly amazed.

"You really were due for some good luck in all this," he said. "But discovering that Charity's brother is a private investigator—and that he was looking for her anyway—is beyond what you could have hoped for."

"Especially since I still have five days of vacation ahead. That's five days with nothing to do but sleep and go to rehearsals. And then we open."

"Yes. And you'll be playing through Christmas, which is another piece of luck for you. No hard decisions on how to spend the day, or at least the evening," he said.

"Michael, it's really luck for you. You don't need to worry about me when you're in Northern California seeing your mother. I'll be celebrating with the other Cratchits. Bobby Spitzer's real mother has been grumbling at the thought of driving him to the theater right after Christmas dinner, but I suspect she'll end up staying for the show. If every cast member but me has a couple of people coming, we'll be sold out." Other people may have visions of sugar plums for Christmas. I had visions of a full house. All of them applauding.

"I'll come to the opening, Faith, this Friday."

"With your new friend?"

"With my new friend. We'll have a drink after."

I hung up with an even lighter heart. Christmas is normally as difficult for me as it is for most of my clients. Not close to my family, only one close friend, always the question of what to do, even whether to decorate or not. Walking through decorated malls with piped carols blaring, so that I can buy token presents for my father and stepmother and something special for Michael, can induce a full-blown anxiety attack. Some years I have thought about hiding my head under the covers for two weeks, the whole holiday period, until after twelfth night. Those years I kept going because the cats needed to be fed and in the last few the clients needed to be tended to. This year *A Christmas Carol* was doing as much for me as it ever had for Scrooge.

Somehow the image of the happy Cratchit children blended with my sorry image of myself as a lonely child, and alongside it popped up a third image of a child, one worse off than I had ever been—Tori's niece, Rina.

So there was another thing I had to do. Or two, really. I had to tell Letty about Ollie Burke. After all, she had given me his telephone number. And then I needed to buy gifts for Letty and Rina, two people who needed everything they could get to have a better Christmas.

But I could put off Letty and Rina. Rehearsal this afternoon, and tomorrow afternoon I would go see Letty. Calling her would be too impersonal. I needed to make the effort to see her.

The thought fell like a cloud across the sun.

I fixed myself a second latte and picked up the Sunday *Times*. Nothing was going to spoil my day.

My light heart was fully restored by the time I was ready to leave for rehearsal.

Considering that it was a second tech rehearsal for a play with children, the rehearsal went easily. For all his snippiness with adults, Johnny was good with children. The four young Cratchits were as comfortable with Johnny, Ted and me as they were with the parents who dropped them off and picked them up. I spent the afternoon hugging Bobby and holding hands with Ted and ignoring Ryan, who didn't seem to notice. He didn't even follow up on his request for the story of Ollie Burke.

When I found myself standing on the steps outside the church, having said goodbye to everyone, I felt lost and alone, the old Christmas funk returning. I heard Johnny lock the door behind me. And I had to do something useful.

I decided not to put off seeing Letty and Rina after all.

With the short December days, the sun was low in the sky when I got on the freeway to go over the hill. The edges of the clouds were muted coral, not the spectacular red of the old L.A. sunsets. I used to love those blazing red sunsets, until I discovered the colors came from smog. Cleaner air has meant more sedate sunsets. I tried to make a metaphor of that, wondering if the city was growing up. But I don't think it is.

The street where Letty and Rina lived looked even drabber in the twilight than it had during the day. The one house with Christmas lights had turned them on, making the others more depressing by contrast. I began to have second thoughts. I was probably going to catch them at dinner, an interruption about as welcome as a telemarketer.

Nevertheless, I parked the car, climbed the stairs and knocked.

As before, I had to knock again and announce myself before the door opened a crack and Letty peered out.

"What do you want this time?"

"I wanted to thank you for giving me that telephone number," I said. "Ollie is Charity's brother, and I gave him the information I had. He'll be looking for her, so she'll be taken care of. And I wanted to make certain you're all right."

Letty shook her head. "All right. How am I going to be all right? No, Miss Glib, I am not all right."

"Did something else happen?"

She pulled the door open enough so that she could fully confront me.

"Not exactly. Just a phone call to prove you wrong. That detective called after you left on Friday, to let me know that the killers Tori was going to testify against had alibis. He asked if I thought the killer could have been an angry pimp. I told him no. He said to let me know if I thought of anything, because they don't have any more leads. It's like I said. One dead Mexican whore, and nobody cares."

That was not what I wanted to hear.

"Letty, I'm sorry. Can I come in?"

She had to think about it.

"Okay." She pulled the door open and stepped aside.

One look and I knew how hard the last two days had been on Letty. There were dirty dishes in the sink, and a few articles of clothing scattered around, as if picking up after herself had suddenly become too much trouble. No sign of cooking, no dinner in process.

I caught a glimpse of Rina, still curled up on the bed.

Letty gestured toward a chair, and I sat.

"What can I do to help you?" I asked.

"I don't know." She plopped into the big chair across from me. "Can you make the police investigate?"

"No. But if you can think of anything that would help, maybe I can encourage them to pay attention."

"She was your client," Letty said. "She talked to you. Why can't you think of anything that would help?"

The question stunned me. Why couldn't I? I couldn't because I had been thinking about looking for Charity, who was not my client. Because I hoped the police would follow up on Tori's murder.

"Do you know where Tori met Charity?" I asked, hedging. Since the Thorson killers had alibis, I felt that my original sense of Tori's murder was validated. Her death had something to do with Charity's disappearance. So maybe there was a lead in the connection between the two.

Letty frowned. "How would I know that?"

"I thought since Charity stayed here, they might have talked about it."

"They joked about a party, some party this turned out to be, that kind of thing. Maybe that's how they met."

"Was it recent? Or were they old friends?"

Letty shook her head. "I don't think Tori had any old friends. And there was something desperate about Charity coming here. Charity was desperate. I wish I had paid more attention. I just thought it was more of the same old shit."

She put one hand up to cover her eyes, but I had already seen the tears forming. I reached out to take her other hand.

"Don't blame yourself," I said. "You didn't know what was going to happen."

"Is that how you get out of it?"

I retrieved my hand.

"If I were out of it, I wouldn't be here."

Letty made an effort to compose herself.

"You want a look through her things?" she asked.

"Yes. Thank you. That's a good idea."

Letty pointed at the daybed.

"Everything Tori had except for her clothes is in those boxes underneath."

"Didn't the police already go through them?" I asked.

"No. I told you, they aren't trying."

I got down on my hands and knees and looked under the daybed. There were two cardboard boxes, both falling apart. I pulled them out.

"What about her cell phone and her fanny pack?" I asked.

Letty shrugged. "I guess the police have them."

Tori traveled light, no purse, nothing that might be easily taken from her. I don't think she carried much in her fanny pack except a driver's license and a little cash.

In the first box, right on top, was a manila envelope. It wasn't sealed. Inside, there was a lot more cash.

"Give me that!" Letty cried.

"Wait a minute." The envelope had been mailed to Charity Jackson, at this address, just three days before she had disappeared. There was a Hollywood postmark and no return address. "It's not Tori's money. It's Charity's."

"I don't care. And you don't know that."

She was right. I didn't know that. I only knew the envelope had been Charity's.

"Let me see how much there is." I counted out loud, all the

way to five thousand dollars, mostly in twenties and fifties, some hundreds. "Do you know where the money came from?" I asked when I had finished.

"Saved it up. Tori must have saved it up."

Letty shifted restlessly, and I thought she might dive out of her chair to grab the money.

"Letty, there's no way Tori could have saved this much money, especially without you knowing. We have to tell the police."

"No, we don't." She started to sob again.

I thought uncomfortably about the difference five thousand dollars would make for Letty and Rina. Five thousand dollars wasn't much in the grand scheme of things, but it would be one huge Christmas present for the mother and child.

"Okay. Listen. Let's order pizza, for the three of us, my treat, and we can think about this."

Letty perked up slightly, enough to dry her eyes and reach for the telephone.

"No meat," I added, when it was clear she knew the number of the nearest pizza place and wasn't going to ask what I wanted.

She glared. "No meat on half."

I figured that was as close to thanks as I was going to get.

While we waited for the pizza delivery, I sat on the floor and looked through the rest of the boxes. The manila envelope stayed tucked under my crossed ankles.

The depressing thing was that there was nothing to find. Tori didn't have much of a life, or at least hadn't chosen to save many memories. She had kept some old clothes, including a pair of worn pink baby booties. With the booties in the second box was an old Christmas card, a manger scene, with the inscription "Love, Mom," inside. One good memory, from before things got bad.

There were a few old photographs with wrinkled corners showing Tori at various stages of development, some with a young girl that was a thin version of Letty. There was even a manila envelope with a few eight by ten glossies, Tori looking overposed and over made-up in a sad attempt at a publicity shot.

I looked at the manila envelope again.

This time I found a piece of paper that had been stuck in the crease at the bottom.

Charity—
This is all I can come up with right now.
Zach

The note was printed, as was the address on the envelope.

"I'm sorry, Letty, but I have to call Charity's brother," I said, handing her the note. I knew we were messing up the possibility of finding fingerprints on the paper, but if Ollie turned it over to the police, which he might, they would just have to live with that.

Letty glared, but this time she didn't argue.

I left a message on Ollie's voice mail, letting him know where I was and what I had found.

"Don't you think it's time Rina joined us?" I asked. "The pizza should be here any minute."

Letty didn't move.

"Rina!" she called. "Wash your hands and get out here! We're gonna have pizza!"

There was silence in the bedroom. I was thinking about going in to check on the little girl myself, but there was a knock at the door, and I busied myself paying for the pizza.

Rina was sitting quietly at the table when I turned around

with the box in my hand. She stared at me, still silent, with eyes so large and sad that I was reminded of an old painting.

Letty still wasn't moving, so I took charge, getting clean plates out of the cupboard, finding a spatula, tearing off some paper towels in lieu of napkins.

"Thanks," she said, when I handed her a plate with a large slice of pizza, from the half with sausage.

Rina didn't even say that. She looked from me to the pizza, picked up her slice, and took a tentative nibble. Tori had told me Rina was shy, but this was beyond shyness.

I was annoyed at Letty all over again for not being more loving to the child.

Letty was obviously hungry, Rina wasn't talking and I was getting tired of the whole situation. Nobody spoke until we were finished eating and I had put the last two slices of pizza in the refrigerator for someone's breakfast.

"All right," I began. I'm not sure what I was going to say after that. I was saved from having to figure it out by another knock at the door.

Letty frowned. "I'm not expecting anybody," she said.

I found myself unaccountably nervous.

And relieved when the visitor turned out to be Ollie Burke.

"I figured it was easier to come on by," he said, looming in the doorway.

I invited him in and introduced him to Letty. Rina had retreated to the bedroom again.

Letty gestured toward the daybed, and Ollie sat, taking up most of it.

I handed him the envelope with the money and the note.

"Zach," he said. "Damn."

"Damn what?"

"Well, that's gotta be Charity's ex-boyfriend, Zach Miller.

I thought she hadn't seen him in more than a year. I would have gotten around to checking on him, but he wouldn't have been anywhere near the top of my list." Ollie shook his head slowly.

"So what about the money?" The question burst from Letty, spilling forth like water over a dam.

Ollie regarded her thoughtfully before he answered.

"For now I got to hold on to it," he said. "Until I find Charity, see what's going on. But seeing as how you took her in, let her stay here for a while, I think part of it should go to you. Something for your trouble."

Letty struggled to make sense of that.

"Can I trust you?" she asked.

"Probably more than you can trust most people." Ollie smiled at her, and Letty visibly softened.

"Does Zach live in the hills above Sunset and drive a Mercedes?" I asked.

Ollie lost his smile and Letty was back to her glare.

"No," Ollie said. "But he might know somebody who does. Zach's a gaffer, made good money a couple of years, worked on a couple of movies with names you would recognize. But a little too much of the money went up his nose, and the business isn't what it used to be, not enough jobs for reliable people even."

I didn't react to Ollie's comment about Zach's cocaine use. But I felt a twinge of sympathy for Zach and his messed-up career.

"Nobody had drugs in here," Letty said. "House rule, and Tori only did a little socially anyway. Or so she said."

"That's true. Tori didn't have a habit." That I would have known. There are things one can hide from a therapist, things one can't. Especially when the therapist had herself been a user.

"And ain't none of us able to cast the first stone, right?" Ollie was smiling again.

"Right."

"Charity got into cocaine for a while to stay thin," Ollie said, and I had to work harder to keep from wincing. "But she was working too hard to stay healthy to do too much dope. That girl was vain, and in her case it saved her. I thought she got away from Zach. So I have to wonder what she was doing back with him."

"You're sure it's the same Zach?" I asked.

"Just how many Zachs do you know?"

I didn't bother to answer.

"I thank you ladies for your company," Ollie added, "and the information. I gotta go look for Zach."

Ollie rose, blocking all the light in the room, and I wanted to tell him not to go. But I didn't.

"Remember I'm trusting you," Letty said, softening again.

Ollie nodded and said goodbye.

"That didn't help find Tori's killer, did it?" Letty asked, when Ollie was gone. She looked as tired as I felt.

"Maybe it did. I'll check with Ollie tomorrow and see what he finds out." I was starting to feel stressed and guilty again, and I didn't like that.

"Well, do something, can't you?" She made the mistake of raising her voice.

"Go to hell."

For the second time in less than a week, I snapped in front of somebody who needed help.

Without apologizing, I walked out.

SEVEN

ONCE IN THE CAR, I tried everything I knew to get my anger and my heartbeat under control. I closed my eyes and concentrated on my breathing, taking slow, deep breaths, in through the nose, out through the mouth. I visualized my pounding heart and then visualized it relaxing. But I could hear my own pulse, thumping above my ears. I decided I wasn't too angry to drive, but the cheery sounds of Christmas music on the slow jazz station I keep the car radio tuned to almost made me stop.

When people talk about seeing red, that's literal. The blood pounding in your head affects the colors of the world.

What had happened to my vacation?

The guilt I felt over thinking about myself when Tori was dead, Charity was missing and Letty was dealing with problems far worse than mine overcame my anger. My heart calmed down, slowly.

A honking horn reminded me the light had turned green.

When I got home, two hungry cats were waiting for me.

After I fed them, I didn't know what to do. I was wired, still, from the anger and stress, even if my blood pressure was borderline normal. I tried a hot bath and television, but I wanted to do something, anything that would help.

I was awake much of the night, so restless that Amy moved to a chair, unwilling to put up with a bouncing human, and

Mac joined her. I was so envious of that double mound of fur that at one point I picked Amy up and brought her back to the bed, but she shook herself, glared at me and went back to the chair. Mac blinked and went back to sleep.

Nothing had changed in the morning. As soon as I thought it was a reasonable hour, shortly after nine, I called Ollie Burke.

"I need to help," I told him. "I'm sorry, but I can't just sit around and wait."

There was silence on the other end of the phone, then a sigh.

"I tried talking to Zach Miller last night," he said. "Nothing. He said he owed Charity money from a long time ago, and he just got around to paying part of it now. She just happened to call and give him an address when he had a little cash. He don't know nothin' about no murder, and he ain't heard from Charity. Didn't know she was missing. So he says."

"You don't believe him."

"Well, I believe he's scared and he doesn't trust me. So maybe he knows something, maybe he doesn't, but I'm not likely to find out what it is."

"And you think I could?"

"Maybe. I'm willing to let you try, if you want to do that. But this is a measure of how desperate I am to find that girl, that I'm willing to let you try."

The adrenaline surged again, but this time it felt good.

"Of course I want to try. How do I find him?"

"I can't promise he'll be there today, but Zach used to have lunch a lot when he wasn't working at a little place on Third Street, an old Hollywood hangout called the Shanghai Café. You know it?"

"I know it and a lot of others like it. Eight by ten glossies all over the walls, overpriced food. He probably has a late lunch, I should get there about one. How will I know him?"

"There's a supermarket half a block away, on the other side of the street. I'll meet you just inside at quarter to one, with a picture."

I got off the phone feeling high, a good high, the kind of high I used to get from just a little blow, or a couple of glasses of wine. I had discovered a while back I could also get it from walking into a strange situation, one with the possibility of just a little danger, not too much, and I wanted more of it. I couldn't rest until it was time to get ready to drive to West Hollywood to meet Ollie.

My new addiction. High risk behavior of a special kind. I was going to have to examine it at some point, but not today.

Clothes and makeup took a little time. I had to have the right loose, actressy appearance.

Black jeans, olive sweater, heavy makeup. If I were younger, I'd go with no makeup, but actresses who are just a little too old to be ingenues almost always wear too much. I'd fit right in.

When I left the apartment, I discovered a bright December day, the kind that reminds me, after all these years, why I love Southern California.

I drove to West Hollywood humming along with the Christmas carols on the radio.

The freeway wasn't bad. The supermarket parking lot was, partly because a hunk of it was taken up by a roped-off area devoted to a stand of would-be Christmas trees, scruffy pines dying in the balmy December air. I had to navigate carefully, looking for a space. The parking god must have taken the day off, because when I found one, it was in a far corner, and I was wedged between two SUVs. I sent a short prayer asking that there be no dents when I got back, and went to look for Ollie.

I was momentarily distracted by the smell of the pine trees. There is something about that fresh, crackling scent, something that wakes longings for a happier holiday, even among those of us who don't have many memories of happier holidays. I snapped back to the task at hand.

Ollie was standing just outside the front door, watching for me, not far from a Santa with a jingling bell and a Salvation Army pot. He was wearing that same black trench coat, far too heavy for the day. I motioned him inside. He was simply too big to be unobtrusive, and I didn't want to be seen talking with him so close to the café.

Of course, he didn't want to be seen talking with me, either, and I had to follow him to the produce section before he started to talk.

"I figure our guy isn't the healthy type," he said, grinning. "Even if he is in the store, he's not likely to be picking out apples."

"So where's the picture?" I asked.

Ollie took out his wallet and flipped it open.

"Just showing you my grandkids."

In fact, the picture was one of Charity hugging a guy who looked like any average gaffer. Curly rust-colored hair, pale skin, blue eyes, narrow nose. Battered leather jacket over a nondescript T-shirt.

I was struck all over again by Charity's beauty. What could she have seen in him? She was smiling in the picture, though, obviously happy, a long way from the woman who had come to my office. I looked more closely at her sparkling eyes. Maybe she was just stoned.

"Can you give me the name of something he worked on while he was seeing Charity? At a time when she might have visited the set?"

Ollie nodded. "*Trial by Fury II*. Shot it a year and a half ago, streets of L.A. You think you might have visited that set, too?"

"I was thinking in that direction. Any old character actors in that one? I didn't see it."

"Derek Stern. Played an old, alcoholic cop who died in the second scene."

I nodded. "Actually, I have met Derek, and the old, alcoholic part fits."

Ollie nodded in return. He flipped his wallet shut and stuck it back in his pocket.

"But what happens when Zach doesn't remember meeting you?"

"I was on television for five years, Ollie. Everybody thinks I look familiar, even though they have no idea who I was."

He granted me a courtesy laugh.

"You might want to know that Charity was starting to look around then, getting ready to drop Zach," he said. "She left him for James Rowe, the guy who directed it. I had hopes for that one until I started hearing stories about more drug use."

"Everybody's heard stories about James Rowe. So what happened?"

He shrugged. "Life, I guess. I don't know for sure. Anything else you need?"

I shook my head. "Where will I find you?"

"I'll keep an eye on the door to the café. I'll find you."

He seemed amused by my enthusiasm, so I had to ask another question.

"You don't really think he's going to talk to me, do you?"

"No. But I think you may spook him into doing something that might lead me to Charity. Wherever he goes after he talks to you, I follow."

I left him there, examining the avocados.

There didn't seem to be any point in moving my car, so I navigated my way out of the store, walked to the corner and waited for the light. A slight breeze had come up, and I wished I had worn a heavier sweater. By evening, Ollie's trench coat would make sense.

I crossed the street and headed for the restaurant, heartbeat elevated just enough to feel good.

The Shanghai Café looked like a miniature pagoda, bright red with green trim. The year-round Christmas colors now, during the appropriate season, somehow seemed out of place. I had remembered it as shabby, but it looked beyond that, as if its better days had been around the time of Johnny Weiss-muller. In fact, his was one of the eight-by-ten signed gloss-ies on the walls, along with a lot of other stars from the early to middle part of the twentieth century. The newer pictures were of nobody anybody had ever heard of. Or at least I hadn't heard of them.

Inside, the restaurant was narrow, black leather booths on each side and tables for two down the middle, with hardly room for a waitress with a tray to navigate between. Some of the booths were occupied, but even though it was prime L.A. lunchtime, the tables were empty. Of the few people in booths, none appeared to have star quality.

I didn't see Zach Miller, so I sat down in a corner booth. I was still looking at a menu when he came in, wearing the same battered leather jacket that I had just seen in his picture. He stopped just inside the door, and looked around.

All of a sudden this whole thing felt more complicated. I had to decide quickly how I was going to start a conversation with a man I didn't know.

He was about to walk down the aisle past me. I dropped the menu and slid out of the booth, almost bumping into him.

Zach Miller stopped short, and we were face-to-face. There was a dusting of freckles on his pale skin. His eyes were smaller and colder than they had looked in the photo. I almost changed my mind.

"I'm sorry," I said. As he nodded and started to ease by me, I added, "Wait. I know you."

He stopped again, frowning, trying to place me.

"I don't forget names and faces, not after interviewing as many people as I did, but sometimes it takes me a moment to access the right file on the inner hard drive." I kept talking, and he quit trying to slide past. "I think it was on a movie set, downtown L.A. Indie action flick, a year or so ago. I had just stopped by to say hello to an old friend, Derek Stern. I do that when I'm out of work, like a lot of other actresses, hang around sets looking for possibilities, and I ended up chatting with your gorgeous girlfriend for a while."

Zach Miller was suddenly alert.

"Zach, isn't it? And your friend's name was Charity?" I smiled, as if pleased that I had remembered.

"Who the hell are you?"

"Faith Cassidy. So how is Charity?"

His mouth opened, but nothing came out. Something that was happening behind me distracted him, and his already white skin turned bloodless as snow. Before I could turn to see what it was, a man's body was pressing up against my back, hands on my shoulders.

"Who is she and why is she asking about Charity?" The voice was low, barely more than a whisper.

"Don't get excited," Zach said. "It's nothing."

I struggled to see who was holding on to me, but I couldn't turn.

"That's two people in two days," the voice said.

"A coincidence." Zach was clearly scared of this man, and my confidence was starting to falter. "She says she met Charity on the set of an indie film, had to be *Fury II*. Said she was looking for work."

"Coincidence, hell." His hands tightened on my shoulders. "You want to see Charity? I'll take you to her."

Before I could answer, the man was propelling me not toward the front door, the way I had come in, but toward the kitchen.

I thought about getting the attention of the waitress, or one of the patrons. But I knew Ollie was outside, waiting for Zach to come out, and I figured that trying to get his attention would be a better plan. Somehow we would have to get around to the front of the building, to the street. So I allowed the man to take me through the tiny kitchen, past three people so focused on preparing food that our passage didn't seem to register, and out the employees' door to the parking lot.

It occurred to me that I might have made a bad decision when I realized that I was being shoved into the back seat of a silver Mercedes.

Only after I caught my breath did I manage to get a good look at the other man. He had unwashed black hair hanging limply around his neck and ears, brushing the collar of a black sport jacket. His face had the pallor of a druggie who doesn't eat too well, and he hadn't shaved it in a day or so.

But this one I recognized from having glanced at the occasional article on Hollywood up-and-comers. He was James Rowe, the man who had directed the indie movie whose set I had just claimed to have visited.

Zach pushed his way in next to me, and James Rowe slid into the driver's seat. He turned around to look at me.

"She looks familiar from something," he said, "but not from any film of mine. If she had been looking for work, I would have remembered her."

"I didn't talk to you," I said, working to keep the edge of desperation out of my voice. "Derek said I was too old, that there wasn't a part for me. I believed him."

"Derek only had a couple of days work, and he was drunk the whole time. He wouldn't have had the vaguest notion what the film was about. I don't believe you." James Rowe turned his attention away from me and started the car. "So let's go talk to Charity."

As we pulled out of the parking lot and onto Third Street, I looked for Ollie, feeling frantic, while trying to appear simply nervous. I didn't see him. So I wasn't simply nervous, I was over the top, out of my mind nervous. Frantic. And there was no way out of the car.

James Rowe turned left on La Brea, heading for the Hollywood Hills, the area above Sunset where Charity had seen the murder. I tried to remember what I had read about him. I had a sinking feeling that I had read somewhere that he was nuts. Creative, but nuts. Not nuts in a good way, but nuts in an even-his-friends-worry way.

Next to me, Zach Miller was sweating. I could see the film of perspiration on his pale skin.

As if he might think James Rowe was crazy.

We took La Brea to Franklin, took a left, then turned right

on Nichols Canyon. The Mercedes wound its way up the narrow road, past what appeared to be modest homes mostly hidden by foliage of one kind or another. There was, of course, no such thing as a modest home in the Hollywood Hills. We were passing million-dollar fixer-uppers.

We turned onto an even narrower road, and stopped in front of a small, stucco house, painted a light brown that caused it to fade into the hillside, further obscured by heavy plantings of juniper.

James Rowe hit a remote, and a garage door opened. The silver Mercedes glided inside, and the garage door closed.

I hadn't seen any signs that anyone might have been following us.

The two men got out of the car. James Rowe stood there, jingling his car keys, until I was standing next to him.

"Charity had better know you," he said softly.

He took my arm and guided me through the door from the garage to a kitchen so sparkling clean that I didn't believe anyone had ever cooked in it.

The kitchen had only a counter separating it from a surprisingly large living room, furnished in brown leather and antique oak. One wall was glass, looking out on a patio even larger than the living room, and the hillside beyond. Another wall was taken up by an entertainment system, including the kind of big-screen television that I thought only existed in commercials.

James Rowe pushed me toward one of two sofas that faced each other, smack in the middle of the floor space, square table in between. I sat.

"Charity! Get your ass in here," he called.

"I'm right here."

At the end of the wall with the giant TV, a few stairs led up to an open hallway. Charity stood there, regarding me. She was wearing a long, red silk robe, as if she might have been taking a nap before we arrived.

She looked well cared for, still stunning. Nothing about her suggested that she might have been taken by force or held against her will.

"What's she doing here?" Charity asked, looking at me with no sign that she cared one way or the other.

"She was looking for you," James Rowe answered. "I thought I'd let her find you."

"You stupid bitch." Charity shook her head, then turned from me to James. "You want to kill somebody, kill her."

Weirdly enough, at that moment the meaning of *Quem Queritas,* the Medieval church trope, popped into my head. *Whom are you seeking?* What had I found?

EIGHT

"YOU WANT TO KILL somebody, kill her!"

The words hung there for a minute before they fell like acid rain on my ears.

"Wait a minute," Zach said. "We don't need to kill her. We didn't even need to bring her here."

Neither James nor Charity seemed to hear him. He backed into a chair and sat down, resigned to defeat.

"I want to know why you were asking about Charity," James said softly. He was jingling his keys again, a vaguely threatening action.

I considered telling him that I had seen Charity forced into his car, considered building up my concern for her, but I didn't think it would help. So I told the truth.

"Tori Sanchez," I answered. "When Tori was killed, I had to find Charity. She was the only person I could think of who might know something." Turning to Charity, I added, "I know you don't care about me. But you must have cared about Tori."

Charity blinked. "I didn't want anything to happen to Tori. James got scared."

"I'm not scared!" James shouted, then realized he didn't want to do that. "I'm not scared," he said, his voice soft again. "I just made a mistake one night, and I don't like the idea of anybody talking to the police."

"A mistake. Oh, honey, it was more than a mistake," Charity said. "And even if you want to call killing Evan a mistake, you can't say that about killing Tori."

"Evan?" I asked, not sure I really wanted to know.

"Evan Corbin." Charity paused, then decided to go ahead. "He was a friend of Zach's, a low-level dealer, and he sold James some bad dope. James went out of his head and beat him to death. James and Zach got rid of the body. I ran out of here, ran to Tori, and that got her killed. James was afraid I said too much."

"Not afraid," James whispered. "Just making sure."

"Don't do this, Charity." Zach was starting to sweat. "Don't talk about it, not even here. He'll end up killing all of us."

James looked at him as if he might be considering it. But then he looked at Charity. Her eyes challenged him.

"Not Charity. Not you, babe, I won't kill you," James said. "I love you, you know that."

I should have stayed out of it, but I was confused on top of being nervous, so I opened my mouth.

"Wait. You were here when James killed a man? This is the murder, the one you were afraid to go to the police about? What about that story you told me, about doing the john in a car?" I asked.

"What?" James was shouting again.

"A lie," Charity said quickly. "I turned a few tricks a long time ago, when I was doing heavy speed, but I had stopped long before I met James. It just sounded like a good cover, for why I didn't want to go to the police. And I didn't want to tell you how much I had seen because then you'd want too many details. I didn't want to tell everything. And I was scared. You know that. I was scared."

"Don't lie about turning tricks! I gotta know the truth about that!" James yelled.

"You had a right to be scared," I said to Charity, but I was including James, as well. Anybody doing that much dope has a right to be scared, deep down terrified by the chemical changes in his body, by the waste of his life. And he had killed somebody. He had to be terrified now, and that made him dangerous.

"You know where I was when you killed Evan, honey. I was right here." She walked over and put her arms around him. He calmed down when she touched him. "And you know I don't turn tricks, any more than I do drugs. I'm taking good care of me now. Me and the baby."

"I wouldn't have hurt you," he said. "I want to take care of you, too. And the baby."

"I couldn't be sure. You were too crazy for me to take the chance."

"Baby?"

"I'm pregnant," Charity said. "That's why I'm not doing drugs anymore. And why I tried to get away."

"You aren't going anywhere with our baby," James said, hugging her.

I was having trouble imagining James and Charity as loving parents. I decided to move on.

"How did he find you?" I asked. "And how did he find Tori?"

"Money," Charity said, dropping her arms away from him. He reluctantly let her go. "He spread money up and down Sunset, money and a phone number and a promise of more, and somebody saw me go into the clinic and called him. So he got me. I made the mistake of telling him where I had been. So he followed Tori that night, out to the Valley."

"She was meeting somebody," James said, "and she knew too much. I can keep an eye on Charity, keep her here, but I couldn't let that dumb friend of hers run around talking."

I didn't think it would help to tell him that Tori had been meeting me. The expression on Charity's face meant she had already guessed who Tori was meeting.

"Your brother is looking for you, too," I said. "And he knows I was hoping to find Zach at the restaurant. People saw us leave, and Ollie will talk to them. It won't take him long to find this house. If James kills me, or Zach, or anybody else, this is only going to get worse."

Inside I was close to gibbering. The words sounded to me as if they were coming from someone else. I prayed I was right about Ollie, that he was on his way to this house.

"Ollie?" Charity frowned. "I don't want Ollie hurt. Maybe we should let her go, honey, so she can tell Ollie I'm all right, tell him to leave us alone."

"And then she goes to the police!" James lost control of his voice again.

"How many people do you want to kill?" My voice was as low and soft and calm as I could make it.

James looked around wildly, as if an answer had to be written on some hidden cue card. He abruptly sat down on the other sofa.

"Nobody. I didn't want to kill Evan, I didn't want to kill that bitch friend of Charity's. But I can't go to jail, I'd go crazy in jail." His eyes were twitching, unfocused.

I wanted to state the obvious. He was already crazy. I tried to come up with better words for it.

"You'll go crazy killing people, too," I said. "Look, I'm a therapist. In my professional opinion, you're too distraught to be able to think rationally, so you couldn't aid your own defense. So they couldn't make you stand trial. You could get help."

I was hedging. He knew right from wrong, and after a few weeks in rehab, his sanity wouldn't be an issue. I just hoped he was too whacked out to think of that.

He was.

"You're telling me a good shrink could get me off?" he asked.

Charity started to say something, then changed her mind.

Zach sat frozen to the chair, mouth gaping like a fish, but he didn't say anything, either. It hit me that he had problems of his own. James probably didn't know he had given Charity money to help her get away.

"Find the right shrink," I said, hedging again. "You have a chance. And that has to be better than killing me, killing Zach, killing Charity's brother when he comes around."

"I don't know." He got up and started pacing the room. "I don't know."

I took my first deep breath since I had entered the house. And I looked around for something, anything, that could be used as a weapon. James had a gun somewhere, he had used it on Tori, but I hadn't seen it yet. The others were scared of him—I was scared of him—but it would be three against one. Maybe there was a way we could subdue him.

He was standing over me before I knew it.

"I don't trust you," he said.

"Then what's your solution?" I asked.

James started pacing again. His twitchiness made it clear he didn't have one.

I was struggling for a follow-up question when the doorbell rang.

James froze.

"See who it is," he whispered to Zach.

Zach rose from the chair and took a moment to steady himself before he crossed to the door and looked through the peephole.

"Shit," he said. "It's Ollie. She told the truth."

"Let him in," James told him.

There was a gun in his hand now. Somehow, while I was watching Zach at the front door, James had drawn a gun.

"Don't do this," Zach whispered.

"Let him in," James said again.

Both of them were pale and perspiring. I thought Zach might take him on, but he backed down again, turning to open the door.

As the door opened and Ollie's bulk appeared, James raised his gun.

With one swift motion, Charity picked up a brass lamp with a Tiffany shade from the table beside the sofa and crashed it down on his head, shattering the glass. James staggered and dropped the gun. She hit him again with the base of the lamp, and this time he fell.

"Enough is enough," she said. "You aren't killing my brother."

NINE

I MADE IT TO REHEARSAL on time. It was touch and go, because the police took a while to find the house after Ollie called 911, and then the officers took much, much longer interviewing all of us. Eventually they took Charity, James and Zach to the station and told Ollie and me that we could go. Ollie went to the station anyway, to be with Charity.

So I made it to rehearsal on time.

I felt a strange kind of emotional disconnect, setting aside everything I had just been through so that I wouldn't upset the others. Especially so that I wouldn't upset Bobby Spitzer. I suspect that's as close as I'll ever get to understanding what it's like to be a mother.

Another kind of disconnect came out in my interaction with Ryan. I couldn't flirt with him. When he asked what was wrong, I told him I was tired, which was true. The bigger truth was, I wasn't interested. Or at least I wasn't interested in the illusion of a romantic relationship, which was all I would ever have with him. I wanted to put all my illusions into my stage family.

I still had several days of my so-called vacation left, and I spent them doing nothing but sleeping and rehearsing—and, of course, going to the arraignment. James and Zach were both held without bail, despite the efforts of the celebrity defense attorney that James retained. I knew that a celebrity shrink would be on the team, and I wondered if he really could plead insanity and get away with it. Ollie bailed Charity out, and he told me he was hopeful that she could arrange a plea bargain, probation, no jail time, for testifying against James. He figured Zach would cut a deal, as well.

I invited them all—Ollie, Charity, Letty, and Rina—to come to the opening night of the play, not really expecting them to accept. But they did.

One of the dividing lines between professional theater and all those other kinds is the accessibility of the actors. When the actors aren't paid money, they tend to head right out to mingle with the audience members after the show, to collect a little love and approval.

So I walked out to the lobby after the curtain call to meet Michael and his new friend. And I found myself with four more friendly people to greet.

Ollie wrapped me in a big bear hug.

"You were great," he said. "Thanks for the tickets. And thanks again for helping me get my sister back."

Charity thanked me. Letty thanked me, even as she grabbed Ollie's arm to pull him back in her direction.

Rina said the first words I had heard out of her mouth. She pointed at Bobby Spitzer, who was across the lobby, surrounded by his real family, and shouted, "God bless us, every one."

Bobby looked at her and nodded.

"Merry Christmas," he said.

Looking at the cheerful people surrounding me, I thought we had a shot at it after all.

DEEP AND CRISP
by Mat Coward

ONE

"BLOODY HELL!" said Detective Constable Frank Mitchell. "Has the Anti-Terrorist Squad been alerted?"

The uniformed P.C. chuckled; he'd achieved precisely the response he'd been hoping for. "No, don't worry, Frank—they're not urban guerrillas. It's some sort of social club. The guy did explain, but he was in a bit of a state and I wasn't really listening."

"So where are they, then, these heroes of the 25th December Resistance Movement?"

"Four of them are over there," the P.C. said, nodding toward the road, where four patrol cars were parked close together. "They're all in a state, shaking and gibbering and that. And the fifth is still lying where we found him—over there, in the middle of that big stand of holly. He awaits your ministrations."

Frank checked his notebook. "Paul Alsop, right?"

"That's it. White male, midtwenties."

"And what were they all doing in a public park on Christmas afternoon, do we know? Playing with their new toys?"

"Apparently," said the P.C. whose face revealed that this was quite the most enjoyable murder he'd attended in some time, "they were playing hide-and-seek."

Oh well, thought Frank, at least Don will enjoy this setup.

He went to have his first look at the body in situ. "Afternoon, Doctor," Frank said.

Sam Walker, kneeling on the ground next to the corpse, looked up at the D.C. "Merry Christmas, Frank."

"And you," said Frank, who'd never quite got used to the everyday manner in which people in his line of work exchanged festive greetings, no matter how inappropriate the circumstances. In his first year on the job he'd been helping to collect body parts after a rather nasty accident, when an ambulanceman's watch had bleeped. *Midnight,* the guy said, *Happy New Year, each,* and he'd insisted on shaking hands all round.

It had been a rather dull day, though dry, and as Frank glanced around Jubilee Park, he saw that it was deserted—if you didn't count members of the emergency services. It was getting dark, and the scene had been secured pending a full area search at daybreak.

"Cause of death," Mr. Walker told him, "is being whacked on the head, hard—probably with that bit of tree branch, there. Hit from the front side, not from behind."

Meaning Paul Alsop saw his attacker coming, Frank thought; and didn't, presumably, know he was an attacker. "No chance he just walked into a tree, or something?"

The doctor shook his head. "No, he was hit with some force—twice."

Frank studied the ground around them, using his torchlight. "Not much bleeding?"

"Not externally, no. He'll have been unconscious immediately, and dead pretty quickly."

Walker groaned as he rose to his feet, though Frank noticed his movements were fluent enough. Perhaps groaning was like wishing Merry Christmas—the done thing.

"You on your own today, Frank?"

"No, the D.I.'s on his way."

"Of course. Which D.I.?"

An answer proved unnecessary. From nearby, came the sound of a young constable cheerily wishing someone "Happy Christmas, sir," and the someone replying with a muttered *"Bollocks."*

"Ah," said Walker. "It's Mr. Packham, is it?" He winked at Frank.

As Don Packham entered their pool of light, the doctor took him warmly by the hand. "Detective Inspector Packham, may I be the first to wish you all the compliments of the season; not merely a Merry Christmas, but in addition a happy and prosperous—"

"Show some respect, Doc," said Don. "There's a dead bloke lying here, in case you didn't spot him."

The doctor gave Frank another look of complicity, though without a jolly wink this time. "Oh," he said, quietly, "it's one of those days, is it?"

"Afternoon, sir," said Frank. "There are four witnesses; they've been separated in the patrol cars by the north entrance."

"Which one found the body?"

Frank checked his notes. "Greg Mulford."

Don nodded. "Right, then he's chief suspect. We'll have a quick word with him in the car, he'll probably cop to it straight away, then we can all go home. Except him, obviously."

GREG MULFORD WAS FAT, aged about fifty and spoke with a strong Bristol accent. He was visibly in a state of nonclinical shock, which was only to be expected, and which, as Frank well knew, meant nothing in regard to his innocence or otherwise.

"We're treating this as a suspicious death," Don told Mulford, "and officers will take a formal statement from you later, but for now I just wanted to ask if there's anything you can tell us?"

"Like what?"

"For instance, did you notice anyone in the park, earlier?"

"No," said Mulford. "The place was deserted, we had it to

ourselves. Oh, Jesus," he added, as he realized what he was saying.

"Well, it never does to jump to conclusions," said Don. "Have you got another cough, D.C. Mitchell?"

"No, sir."

"Let's hope not. Lot of viruses around, this time of year. Now, Greg—what were you and your friends doing here this afternoon? My colleague mentioned something about a resistance movement?"

Mulford frowned for a moment, as if he was trying to remember how he came to be in this car, talking to these strangers—which, Frank thought, was probably precisely what he was doing.

"Yeah, that's right, it's a club we all belong to. We always have lunch together on the 25th of December."

"So the same group always spends Christmas Day together?"

"Well no, that's the point, see?" Mulford seemed to focus on the conversation properly for the first time. "It's December 25, not—"

"Yes, thanks," Don interrupted, "we can talk about that later. What were you actually doing here, in this park—not having a picnic, presumably?"

Frank had been looking forward to this bit. He deliberately hadn't told the D.I. what the friends claimed to have been up to, so as not to spoil the surprise.

"No," said Mulford, "we were playing hide-and-seek."

"Right," said Don.

And then he looked at Frank. It wasn't much of a look— just a quick flick of the eyes to the left, nothing showing on the face, the whole thing no doubt invisible to a casual onlooker.

How does he know? thought Frank, as he felt a familiar and unwelcome warmth spread across his neck and cheeks. It was all he could do not to blurt out that he was sorry, that he'd forgotten to mention the hide-and-seek.

"Now, the deceased—Paul Alsop, is that right?"

"Yeah. Paul, yeah."

"He's a member of your club?"

"Yes, that's right." Mulford nodded his head, and then repeated, "Yes, that's right.

"Do you know if he's married, lives with anyone?" Don asked.

"No, I think he lives on his own. Pretty sure."

He'd better do, thought Frank, if he spends Christmas Day with a bunch of blokes in a park.

"Age?" Don asked.

"Twenty-five, twenty-six, round there."

"Does he have a job?"

"Not sure," said Mulford. "Casual work, I think. Maybe temping or something, that's what a lot of the youngsters do these days, isn't it? No such thing as a career anymore."

"How did you come to find his body?" Don asked.

"Well—" Mulford tugged his jacket tighter across his belly "—we'd finished our game of hide-and-seek—"

"Who was hiding?"

"What? I think I was. Anyway, the game was over. Everyone was back at the starting point—that's the drinking fountain—except Paul. We shouted out for him, but he didn't answer. So we sort of wandered around looking for him, and…"

"And you found him."

"I found him." Mulford sat up straight, stared at the roof of the car for a moment, and then out of the window. "Look, I'm sorry—I think I want to be sick. I mean, I think I'm *going* to be sick."

Don and Frank jerked away from the big man, as far as they could within the confines of a cop car. Don scrambled out of the passenger door, and called over a uniform to "See to Mr. Mulford, please."

The sounds of a man taken unwell, of a policeman exercising his swearing muscles and of an unwell man apologizing—and almost choking to death in the process—faded as Don and Frank walked back across the grass toward the center of activity: the tent covering the hollow circle of holly bushes.

Don summoned a uniformed sergeant. "Have you found me any witnesses yet?"

"Sorry, absolutely none. We've done a complete sweep of the place, and the surrounding streets, and there's not a soul around."

"What, *no one?*"

The sergeant shrugged. "Just one old dear walking her dogs, right over the other side of the park."

Don smiled at Frank. "She's been cheated out of her Christmas fun."

"Sir?"

"It's usually dog walkers who find the body, isn't it? Tradition, that is. But someone's beaten her to it—she'll be livid when she reads about it in the local paper."

You're cheering up, Frank thought. Must be the fresh air.

"Anyway," the sergeant concluded, "she reckons she hasn't seen anyone since she came out."

"Typical," said Don. "No danger of any useful security footage, I suppose?"

"Nothing in the park at all, sir. The nearest cameras are up at the junction by the cinema, so we can check for cars fleeing the scene. But apart from that, zilch."

"Ah, well," said Don, as the sergeant returned to his fruitless search, "looks like we'll have to detect this one the old-fashioned way."

He didn't seem too distressed by the thought, Frank noticed. "So, you reckon it was one of the friends? One of the 25th December lot?"

"I don't know, Frank. Could be someone lurking in the bushes, I suppose—a mugger, a madman, a flasher, whatever. We'll have to see if any of the other Decembrists remember seeing anyone; get uniform on to that, in the all too likely event that they haven't thought of it themselves."

"Will do."

"But if not, then it certainly looks rather like an inside job. The fact that he was hit at very close range is suggestive, too. And no real struggle, isn't that what the doc said? So presumably he didn't think he was about to be conked on the nut with a Yule log."

"So," said Frank, looking across the park at the quartet of patrol cars. "Are we inviting them all to accompany us to the station?"

Don lit a small cigar as he thought about that. One of his regular smokes, Frank noted; nothing special for Christmas. "No. No, I don't think we will at the moment. I really can't face spending half the night at the bloody nick."

"Right you are," said Frank, wondering what Don had been doing when his mobile or pager had interrupted him with a summons to Jubilee Park. Frank himself was on the rota today, but Don was merely on call. The D.I. was wearing jeans and a sweater under a leather jacket, so no clue there.

"Besides," Don continued, "police stations are no place for informal interviews. No: we'll let the Scenes people have a look at them, see if they need them for any reason, ask permission to take any articles of clothing and so on—and nick them if they refuse—then let them go."

"I'll do that now," said Frank, glad to be on the move as the early evening chill settled on the park.

"Oh, and Frank?"

"Yes?"

"Warn them not to get too involved with the big film premiere on TV—because we'll be along to see them later."

GET FREE BOOKS and a FREE GIFT
WHEN YOU PLAY THE...

SLOT MACHINE GAME!

Just scratch off the silver box with a coin. Then check below to see the gifts you get!

YES!
I have scratched off the silver box. Please send me the 2 free Mystery Library™ books and gift for which I qualify. I understand I am under no obligation to purchase any books, as explained on the back of this card.

415 WDL D346

FIRST NAME	LAST NAME

ADDRESS

APT.#	CITY

STATE	ZIP

7	7	7	**Worth TWO FREE BOOKS plus a BONUS Mystery Gift!**
🍒	🍒	🍒	**Worth TWO FREE BOOKS!**
♣	♣	♣	**Worth ONE FREE BOOK!**
🔔	🔔	🍒	**TRY AGAIN!**

(ML-04-R)

DETACH AND MAIL CARD TODAY!

The Mystery Library Reader Service™—Here's how it works:

Accepting your 2 free books and gift places you under no obligation to buy anything. You may keep the books and gift and return the shipping statement marked "cancel." If you do not cancel, about a month later we'll send you 3 additional books and bill you just $4.99 each, plus 25¢ shipping & handling per book and applicable taxes if any.* That's the complete price and — compared to the cover price of $5.99 each — it's quite a bargain! You may cancel at any time, but if you choose to continue, every month we'll send you 3 more books, which you may either purchase at the discount price or return to us and cancel your subscription.

*Terms and prices subject to change without notice. Sales tax applicable in N.Y. Credit or debit balances in a customer's account(s) may be offset by any other outstanding balance owed by or to the customer.

If offer card is missing write to: Mystery Library Reader Service, 3010 Walden Ave., P.O. Box 1867, Buffalo, NY 14240-1867

NO POSTAGE
NECESSARY
IF MAILED
IN THE
UNITED STATES

BUSINESS REPLY MAIL
FIRST-CLASS MAIL   PERMIT NO. 717-003   BUFFALO, NY

POSTAGE WILL BE PAID BY ADDRESSEE

MYSTERY LIBRARY READER SERVICE
3010 WALDEN AVE
PO BOX 1867
BUFFALO NY 14240-9952

TWO

Not a bad way to spend the evening, Don reckoned, when all's said and done. Poking around in other people's business; if you didn't find that prospect enticing, then you were surely wasting your time working in CID. Better than watching appalling festive television, at any rate. Not that he actually had a telly at the moment, but that was beside the point.

He located the properties officer, and asked whether the deceased had been carrying his house keys.

"That's about all he did have on him, sir," said the officer, an Asian lad Don hadn't met before. "No driving license, just a wallet with a few quid in it. The only thing with his address on was a video rental membership card, in the lining of the wallet."

"That'll do," said Don. "Shine your torch on it, will you, while D.C. Mitchell jots down the details."

Frank drove. Before they left the park, Don warned one of the P.C.s on perimeter duty not to let anyone nick his car: "There's a very valuable item in the boot. And be warned, I know its serial number."

The abode matching the deceased's address turned out to be a single room in Stoke Newington, carved out of a dark, dusty house, which smelled of—what? Don inhaled and rolled the unpleasant aroma around his mouth, before spitting it back out. Dark and dust, he decided; the dark, dusty hall smelled of dark and dust. When he was a kid, the communal areas of such buildings had always smelled of stale food; but, he supposed, no one cooked anymore.

The timer on the forty-watt hall light popped out while Frank was still finding the key to Paul Alsop's door.

"Shit," said Don. "Should have stuck a broken matchstick in the switch."

"It's all right," Frank assured him, "I've got it now."

"It's not you I'm thinking of. It's a matter of principle— you should always waste a landlord's electricity whenever the opportunity arises."

"Here we are," said Frank, as the door opened and he stepped through.

It really was a single room, Don saw; shared loo and bathroom down the hallway, no kitchen at all. Well, that explained the lack of cooking smells; he should be grateful not to smell anything worse than dark and dust. The stale odor was even stronger in here than in the hall; Paul Alsop was not a fresh air fan, apparently.

"It's about the size of a couple of ping-pong tables," Don said.

"Not much more," Frank agreed. "Let as furnished, I suppose."

Sure enough, the tiny room contained a bed, a wardrobe and a hard chair. No table, no lamps, no bookcase, no kettle. Not much of anything, in fact—even the wardrobe was empty but for one old suit, a frayed shirt, and a single set of underwear.

"Where's his toothbrush?" said Frank. "Shaving gear, deodorant?"

Good spot, thought Don; good eyes. He was about to tell the lad as much, but then he remembered it was Christmas, so he kept his compliments to himself. "Taken them with him, perhaps? Maybe he was to crash the night with one of the other Decembrists."

"That'll be it," said Frank. "You can certainly see why he wouldn't want to spend Christmas here, poor sod. I reckon 'casual worker' is a euphemism, don't you? He must be chronically unemployed."

"Why, though? A presumably healthy young man—there's not that much unemployment about these days, is there? We'll have to ask the doc whether he had any debilitating conditions."

Frank took a couple of pictures of the scene—such as it was—with his mobile phone.

"You want to be careful with that," Don cautioned him.

"Oh, yeah?"

"Definitely. Didn't you hear about that DS, in Essex somewhere I think it was? Used his phone to take pics of a corpse found in a car boot in a long-stay car park—pressed the wrong buttons, and sent them out to all his friends and family, attached to an invitation to his engagement party."

"Not to worry," said Frank. "Debbie and I aren't planning any parties at the moment."

I'll bet, thought Don. Unless it's a Tupperware party. "He's either just moved in or is just about to move out, I reckon. Don't you?"

"Could be, aye."

"Must be. This simply cannot be somewhere that someone's lived in for long, or is planning to stay in. There's nothing of him in here—it's like a motel room in one of those American films, where the guy's on the run in a battered old car with a hundred thousand dollars in a holdall in the boot."

Frank looked at him. "Well, it's certainly a bit basic."

Don could feel frustration crawling all over his scalp like lice. Usually a tour of the victim's home was crucial to his understanding of those crimes in which the victim was left unable to speak for himself—such as unlawful killings and, more commonly, serious assaults. But this place told him nothing. Nothing!

"I suppose it tells us something," said Frank.

What was this? Telepathic piss-taking? "Go on…"

"Well, obviously he lived alone, didn't have any money, either unemployed or working for a pittance, doesn't—"

"Yes, but Frank," Don interrupted, trying to keep the annoyance out of his voice, "these are all things we can learn by *asking* people. Yeah? By checking records. By fiddling with computers. What this room doesn't tell us is why someone might hate Paul Alsop enough to smack him to death with a tree."

"Right," said Frank.

There was silence for a while, eventually broken by Don's loud sigh. "We're wasting our time here. Let's see if any of the hide-and-seekers have found their way home yet."

Frank got out his phone again, along with his notebook. "Which one shall I try first?"

"How on earth should I know, Frank!" This horrible little room, a young man killed—probably by someone he thought was a friend—and this damp, dark time of year; what was he doing in a job that had him standing in a shithole like this on Christmas Day, phoning up strangers and asking them if they were murderers? "Just ring one of them at random, for heaven's sake."

"All right," said Frank. "I'll do it alphabetical."

Don glared at him in astonishment, but Frank wouldn't catch his eye—and it took the D.I. a few seconds to realize he'd been had. *Alphabetical…not bad.* And as he heard Frank ask if he was speaking to Mr. Simon Young, Don very nearly laughed out loud.

CHRISTMAS AFTERNOON, Don thought, as Frank drove them toward Wembley, must be the only time of the whole year, these days, that there's hardly any traffic on the roads. Just for a few hours, you could hear something other than the sound of motors.

Even now—he checked his watch—just gone seven, it was pretty quiet, despite the people heading home from having their Christmas dinner at someone else's place.

"Bet they drive a sight quicker going home than they did going out," he said.

"Who do?"

He gestured toward the short queue of cars ahead of them, waiting for a light to turn green. "That lot. Been at the in-laws for the afternoon. They'll be feeling ten years younger now than they did setting off this morning. Full of relief that their real Christmas can begin at last."

He glanced at Frank, but got no response beyond a non-committal grunt, so he carried on. "Get home, get their shoes off, turn the telly on…no more having to be jolly with relatives you can't stand. Having to play games, and engage in conversation, and eat meals from a bloody *table,* instead of off your lap like nature intended. Not being able to watch the TV for several hours on the trot! Don't you reckon, Frank—that moment when you get home and switch the kettle on for a cup of tea made by someone who actually knows how you like it, namely yourself, that's the best moment of the whole season?"

"Aha," said Frank, and Don wondered whether he said it deliberately to annoy. If so, it was working.

"So what do you normally do at Christmas? Make the long trek to Newcastle, do you?"

"Yeah, we go to my family's one year, then Debbie's the next, with vice versa for Boxing Day."

"Very orderly, Frank."

"Seems to work out."

"And do you enjoy it?"

"Yes, thanks."

Don tried counting to ten; got as far as five. "Not secretly relieved to get home? Just a little bit?"

"Always nice to be home," said Frank.

"You drew the short straw this year, then, having to work."

Frank shrugged. "Well goes with the job, doesn't it?"

Don gave up. Honestly, sometimes the lad was so phlegmatic, Don feared for his sinuses.

"What do we know about this bloke?" he asked, as they pulled up outside Simon Young's flat.

"Thirty-nine years old," Frank read out, "divorced, gives his profession as actor."

"Actor, eh? Wonder if he's got himself a pantomime this year? That's when jobbing actors make all their money, you know—Christmastime. Do you take Joe to the panto?"

"We're planning to take Joseph next week, as it happens, for his first time."

"Quite right, too," said Don, with a big smile. "Scar the little lad for life!"

IT WAS A SMALLISH FLAT, Frank noted, but nice; good furnishings and fittings, bit of an arty look to it, but nothing too embarrassing. No Christmas decorations at all—not even a row of greeting cards.

Young himself was slight, with thinning fair hair. Frank couldn't tell whether his face was usually so pale, or whether the deathly coloring, like the tremor in his lips, had its origins in Jubilee Park.

He greeted them with a half-full tumbler of whisky in his hand. "Here, sit down—just shove all that crap on the floor, that's fine. Can I get you some coffee?"

Don made an apologetic face and said, "Any chance of tea?"

"Of course, sure. Won't be a minute."

Yes, you will, thought Frank; tea takes longer to make than coffee, leaving us more time to snoop.

Don, by established custom, was snooper-in-chief; he was in charge of tiptoeing around the room, peering behind things and under things (without actually touching anything; that would be against the rules), while communicating his findings to his colleague by means of nods and raised eyebrows.

Frank's role was, mainly, to receive and interpret these signals—and, incidentally, to keep lookout.

There didn't seem to be much to excite Don's attention in this room; a display of family photos, which included two children but pointedly excluded anyone who might be their mother, only earned a single raised eyebrow, raised only halfway.

Young returned with two cups of tea and a plate of pink biscuits.

"No mince pies?" Don asked.

"I'm sorry, I—"

"Thank God!" Don helped himself to three of the biscuits. "Tell us about this 25th December business, Simon."

"Right." Young looked around for his whisky, realized he'd left it in the kitchen, and for a moment Frank wondered whether he was going to get up and fetch it. But the actor found his cigarettes were nearer at hand, and lit one of those instead. "The 25th December Resistance Movement. It's a sort of anti-Christmas league."

"Oh dear—I'm afraid you've shocked my colleague," Don said, and he reached over and patted Frank comfortingly on the shoulder.

Frank tried to look slightly annoyed, which wasn't all that difficult, because he knew that when his boss put on a show like that, he often had his reasons. Often bloody didn't, mind, but this time he'd give him the benefit of the doubt.

Young recognized the banter for what it was, and relaxed a little. "Ah, well," he said, speaking to Don but smiling at Frank, "your colleague, I daresay, is a married man, looking forward to getting home to his wife and kids."

"Only one kid so far," said Don. "Frank, show the man a picture of young Joe."

"I'm afraid I don't have a picture of Joseph on me, unfortunately, sir." It was only very rarely that D.C. Mitchell lied whilst going about his constabulary duties; he did so on this occasion, however, without hesitation or regret. He was getting a bit tired, after three and a half years, of Don boasting about Frank's son.

"Not to fret," Don told Young, "he can always zap you one later, from his mobile. So, how many people are in this anti-Christmas league?"

"Not many now; there were originally more, a dozen or so."

"When was that?"

"Nineteen eighty-three, I think it was—that was when it started. It began in a pub, you won't be surprised to hear. There was a bunch of guys—young lads, bachelors, divorcés and so on—who all thought Christmas was a pile of crap, to be avoided at all costs. None of them had particular family ties or obligations they couldn't get out of, so they made a point of taking no part in the run-up to the festering season at all."

"How did they manage that?" Don asked, sounding genuinely interested.

"They simply refused to acknowledge its existence. Kept their faces straight. As far as they were concerned, Christmas just wasn't happening." He laughed. "The best thing was when the Sally Army used to come round the pub. You know, on the beg, singing carols, making everyone feel guilty? The lads used to ask them if they did requests, and when they said yes—did they know any Motown!"

"And this has kept going all these years?"

"Well, the central rite of the Movement, if you like, is that we all meet on the twenty-fifth for a drink in a pub, followed by a curry or whatever, then back to someone's place for an afternoon of not watching seasonal telly. We play games, listen to records, go for a walk, whatever. And that has survived. I suppose it's become a habit, more than anything."

"Is it the same people every year?" Frank asked.

Young shook his head. "Over the years, most of the lads have dropped out—got married or whatever. Some come and go, as marriages come and go…" He trailed off, and gazed into his own cigarette smoke for a while. "I suppose you'd say it's a little bit serious, mostly fun. Depends who you talk to."

"And are you a founder member of the Movement?" Frank asked.

"Not a founder member, no. As I remember, I joined a couple of years later; in fact, I was still living with my parents when the Movement started, and I was a bit jealous of the other guys."

"I'll bet," Don said with feeling. Or *apparent* feeling; Frank had learned long ago that talking to people was a skill, and that nobody in the Metropolitan Police Service was better at that skill than D.I. Packham. When he was in the mood.

"You can imagine," said Young. "They were quite a cool crowd in those days—lots of girlfriends, between them, you know. But there was no way I could get out of Christmas with Mum and Dad! Eventually I left home, not on the best of terms, to be frank, so of course I joined the Movement as soon as I could."

"And you've been going ever since," said Don.

"No, as a matter of fact, I had nine years away from it— one year courting, eight years married."

"I see. But you're back with the boys now."

Young lit another cigarette. "Yeah, that's it. Thing is, I'm not allowed to see my kids on Christmas Day, which bloody hurts, and I'm not pretending otherwise. I'll have them for a few hours on Boxing Day, which is very gracious of her. The custody thing is proving a bit problematical. I find the familiar rituals of the Movement help take my mind off things." He started to drift away again, but caught himself just in time. He grinned unconvincingly, slapped his knee, and said, "Besides, the fact is—

and you give any man a truth serum, and I guarantee he'll say the same thing—the lads' Christmases of your youth are always the best, no matter what you might tell the wife in later years."

"I'm sure you're right," said Don.

"Even during my marriage, every Christmas I'd get a twinge of nostalgia for my Resistance Movement days. Especially on Christmas afternoon, having to endure my parents-in-law picking each other to death in front of something awful on the telly, with the smell of overcooked vegetables clinging to the wallpaper." He shuddered. "I'll bet you lot get plenty of overtime at Christmas, don't you? Everyone busy murdering each other, just to break the tension."

Frank was wondering what Simon Young would do with his children on Boxing Day—have Christmas Day all over again, perhaps? But Don was off down a different alley.

"How about actors—are you busy at this time of year?"

"Personally, no. Which doesn't help, of course. I do mostly voiceovers, for ads and corporates, and that."

"A good living?"

"Sure, can't complain." Young looked around him. "Not about that, anyway."

"And have you always been in that game?"

"No. Not at all. Worked in a bank when I left school, then in my twenties I chucked it in and went to drama school as a mature student."

"A man who likes to take risks," said Don, and having said so, nodded at Frank and sat back with his arms crossed. Time for the routine questions.

"Did you see anyone else, other than your lot, in the park this afternoon?" Frank asked.

"No, no one at all. The place was deserted."

From Young's expression—Frank reckoned the actor was going for firm but regretful—it was clear that he understood the implications of his answer.

"And tell us something about the victim, Paul Alsop. Had he been with the Movement long?"

"Well, this is my first year back, like I said, but I gather that this was his second year of attendance."

"Not one of the original gang, obviously."

"No. A friend of a friend, I think."

"So, today was the first time you'd met him?"

"I can't really tell you anything about him, I'm afraid." Young spread his hands. "I think Greg and Neil still see each other a bit during the year, but for the most part we keep it for the twenty-fifth. After all this time, we haven't really got that much in common except…well—all this time."

Both detectives noticed that this wasn't quite an answer to the question.

THREE

As THEY WALKED BACK to the car, Don squinted at the sky and looked distinctly unimpressed with what he saw there. "Too bloody mild for Christmas. It wasn't like this years ago."

For a moment, Frank had no idea what to say. He'd never thought of Don as suffering particularly from nostalgia; nor had he suspected that inside the D.I. there lurked a Bing Crosby sentimentalist.

"Were you hoping for a white Christmas, then?"

Don looked at him sharply. "Who said anything about snow? All I'm saying is, you should be able to tell Christmas from Easter, otherwise you might as well go and live in California. Or is it Florida where they don't have any seasons?"

While Frank phoned the next witness on their list, he speculated to himself about Don's current emotional state. *Changeable* seemed to be the only apt description. Quite early in their relationship, he had given up trying to figure out from unreliable clues, whether Don was up or down at any given moment. However, he had never given up wishing, now and then, that his boss would keep still for a while.

DON WATCHED THE SKY out of the car window, but there wasn't anything there worth looking at. Surely Christmases hadn't always been gray and damp? Seasonal shift, they called it, according to something he'd heard the other day; the seasons creeping across the calendar, making all human traditions look foolish. December was autumn, these days.

Derek Fleet was sixty, and looked older. Like everyone else they had spoken to so far, he looked, in fact, exactly as someone should look in such a situation—shaken, slightly afraid, as if they might be next, slightly disoriented, because the world has suddenly changed forever, and—whisper it—slightly excited. Because we're all human—and that means we're all animals. Don wondered if Frank was aware of that uncomfortable truth, and if so how he dealt with it.

Fleet lived in a spacious terraced house in Watford, which had a Christmas wreath hanging on its stained-glass door. They were scarcely into the hallway, before he managed to get on Don's nerves.

"You'll be wanting a cup of tea, no doubt, if I know anything about coppers?"

"We certainly would," Don replied, with a broad smile, "if it's not too much trouble."

The tea-making offered no opportunity for snooping, because throughout the process Derek Fleet kept an eye on his guests from the doorway connecting the kitchen to the living room. More out of general principle, Don reckoned, than because he necessarily had something to hide. The man was still a little drunk from lunchtime, Don thought, unless he'd continued drinking when he got home. Both, perhaps.

When the tea arrived, Don thanked Fleet for it extravagantly and then set it to one side, and studiously ignored it, using eye-signals to ensure that Frank did the same. If there was one thing Don couldn't abide, it was sarcasm. Well, two things: sarcasm and marzipan.

Frank took the lead. "Did you see anyone else at the park today, Mr. Fleet?"

"It's a park," said Fleet. "Of course there were other people around."

"So you did see someone?"

Fleet took his time putting sugar in his own tea. "Not specifically."

"What does that mean?" Don demanded. "Not specifically?"

"Just that."

"Did you or did you not see anyone else at the park?" Don asked. "And please be as specific as you can."

Fleet shrugged. "I wasn't looking."

"So you *didn't* see anyone?"

"I didn't, as it happens, but my point is that I wasn't *looking,* you understand? I was with my mates. I didn't notice anyone else, but that doesn't mean there wasn't anyone there." He took another drink of tea. "In fact, there obviously was someone else there, because it sure as hell wasn't one of our lot that did the killing."

"No?"

"No chance." He shook his head. "They're all great lads. They're all for one and one for all, and all that."

"What exactly were you doing," Frank asked, "when Paul was killed?"

"We were playing hide-and-seek." Fleet was obviously pleased with this answer; he nodded at Frank and grinned at Don.

"I see," said Frank.

"Well," said Fleet, addressing Don, "perhaps when you retire you'll have time to play hide-and-seek on Christmas Day, too." He managed to make it clear by his tone that he found it hard to imagine the inspector ever doing anything so sophisticated.

"Do you usually play hide-and-seek on Christmas Day?" Frank asked.

"Always," said Fleet, looking happier by the second. "We have to, it's our duty."

Frank opened his mouth to ask what that meant, but Don was too quick for him.

"What do you do for a living?" he asked.

"Retired," said Fleet, still smiling. "Retired at sixty. Not bad, but not as good as you lot, of course."

"Retired from what?"

"Management training." He crossed his arms and met Don's gaze, challenging him to make something of that. Don declined the challenge—for the moment. He could always come back to it, if he felt the need. He signaled Frank to carry on.

"How long have you been in the 25th December Resistance Movement, Mr. Fleet?"

Reluctantly Fleet returned his attention to the junior officer. "Nine years now. Never missed a meeting."

"I take it you're not married?"

"Divorced years back. I make sure I'm between girlfriends at Christmas time, wouldn't want to let the boys down. To be honest, I think they rely on me to get the party mood going. You know, from my professional life," he added, with a victor's glance at Don, "I know how to motivate groups. Anyway, I look forward to Christmas all year round."

"But I thought," said Frank, "that this was an *anti*-Christmas movement?"

Don felt a rush of pride at how well the lad was coming on, but Fleet seemed unconcerned at being exposed as a heretic. With a wave of the hand, he replied, "Oh, you'd have to ask Greg about all that…he could talk for England on that Christmas stuff—not boring, mind, fascinating stuff." He nodded, evidently keen to emphasize this point. "Yes, indeed, there's a lot of sense in what Greg says."

"Such as?" Don asked.

"Oh, you'd have to ask him, get it from the horse's mouth."

Just as I thought, Don told himself; the buffoon knows sod all about it.

"How well did you know Paul Alsop?" said Frank.

"Not well at all," said Fleet, settling his face into an expression at once somber and pompous. "But I shall mourn him. He was one of us. He'd not been coming long, though."

"You don't meet up together apart from on the 25th?"

"Of course we do! We're all good friends."

Keep going, thought Don; you'll convince yourself eventually.

"But you didn't know Paul particularly well?" Frank continued.

"No more or less than the others."

"Nice chap, as far as you can say?"

"Splendid chap. Lovely fellow. It can only be a maniac that killed him."

"You can't think," said Frank, "of any reason why someone might kill him? He wasn't into any heavy drugs, or crime, or messing about with married women, or…"

Derek Fleet stood up—actually *stood,* and Don fought not to laugh out loud. Bloated twazzock!

"If you knew anything about the 25th December Resistance Movement," Fleet proclaimed, looking down at his interrogators, "you would *never* ask such a question."

OUTSIDE, DON CHECKED his watch. "What time is it? Time for one more, I suppose."

He didn't sound especially enthusiastic, Frank thought, which was a refreshing sign of normalcy. Who would be enthusiastic about interviewing witnesses on Christmas evening? "Right you are," Frank said, opening his mobile phone.

"On the other hand," said Don, looking at his watch again, more closely this time, as if to extract more—or better—information from it, "really, you should be getting home to Debbie and Joe."

"I'm on duty," Frank assured him. "Debbie understands

that." He'd hardly spoken before it occurred to him that perhaps Don had been looking to him for an excuse to call it a day. "But how about you?"

"I'm on duty, too, Frank. Did you think I was here because I won a day out with a bobby, in the Coach and Horses' Xmas Raffle?"

"No, I meant…" It was no good. Frank could not think of a polite way of asking the D.I. whether he had anything worth hurrying home for. In the end, he settled on: "Well, perhaps we'll just do the one more, eh?"

Don looked at his watch again, then shrugged. "Oh, well, Frank, if that's all you feel up to, then just one more it shall be."

FOUR

THE CURTAINS WERE OPEN when they arrived at Neil O'Brien's ground-floor council flat, on a small estate in Barnet, so Frank and Don could see in from outside: one large living room, with a decent kitchen off, open-plan style. It looked very comfortable, too, with all the lights on. Bit untidy, perhaps, for Frank's taste; definitely a single bloke's place, but then that presumably went without saying, given that it was occupied by someone who spent Christmas Day in a curry house.

Neil O'Brien was forty-five years old, small, sharp-featured and friendly; perhaps seeming a little less shaken than the others had been. He was also smoking a cigar which Frank felt was very nearly large enough to overbalance him.

"That smells fantastic," said Don.

"It's Cuban," said O'Brien, turning it round and looking at its tip, as all men must when discussing cigars.

"Now that is a proper Christmas smell—that and pine needles. When did Christmas trees stop ponging, does anybody know that? And why?" O'Brien smiled and shook his head.

Don turned to Frank, "Make a note of that, Frank—we need to know when and why Christmas trees lost their perfume. I shall expect a report on my desk by Twelfth Night."

"Yes, sir," said Frank, writing in his notebook.

"I would offer you boys a smoke," said O'Brien, "but I only buy one every year. I won't tell you what it costs. Suffice to say I don't smoke at all the rest of the year! Well, you can't be bothered with anything else after you've tasted one of these bastards."

"I'll bet," said Don.

"I usually smoke it tomorrow, Boxing Day, but I felt the need today, as you'll understand."

"Absolutely," said Don, "and we're very sorry to have interrupted it. You can't exactly stub one of those out and stick it behind your ear for later, can you?"

He sounded entirely sincere in his apology—as if asking a man questions about a murder really were insufficient grounds for disturbing the smoking of a fine cigar—and Frank smiled to himself as he wondered whether Don would dare to get out his own, infinitely humbler, small cigars. For the moment, though, the D.I. seemed content merely to inhale the room's atmosphere. For his part, Frank reckoned they could have done with a window open. It was a lovely smell right enough, no disputing that; but it would have been nice to have been able to see each other across the room. There again, perhaps Mr. O'Brien had his flat hermetically sealed, so the priceless smoke would last from one Christmas to another.

"Don't worry," O'Brien assured Don. "Actual physical torture might ruin this cigar, but not much else will." His weather-beaten face, seemingly permanent smile, and jaunty Liverpool accent combined to project good humor. "Would you like some coffee?"

"We'd really love a—" Don began.

"Only I got a new coffeemaker for Christmas, and I'm enjoying playing with it."

"Lovely," said Don. "Thanks."

"Come through to the kitchen, then, gents. We can talk while it's making."

"What do you do for a living?" Don asked, though Frank had told him not ten minutes earlier.

"I'm a milkman."

"Good heavens. I didn't know there were any left."

"We are a dying breed, it's true. But there's still a few people prefer getting their milk on their doorstep instead of at the supermarket. Older people, mostly, it has to be said."

"Top of the milk," said Don, with feeling, and for a moment Frank thought it was some sort of cod-Irish greeting. "That's why milk's better out of a bottle. You don't get top of the milk in a carton. Remember fighting over that, as a kid?"

"It was the only thing worth having on a bowl of cereal, wasn't it?" O'Brien agreed.

Frank thought it was about time they moved on. "I understand you were playing hide-and-seek this afternoon?"

"That's right," said O'Brien. "We're the Great Britain Olympic hide-and-seek squad, you know."

"You're—are you?" Could nothing bring this conversation to its senses, Frank wondered.

O'Brien held up his hands. "Well, we reckon we are—no one else is, after all. Let's say, we await the call."

"Champions in waiting," Don suggested.

"Quite so. And we hold our Olympic trials every year, on December 25."

"I see. Sounds great fun," said Frank, hoping his tone matched his words. "And who was hiding, do you remember?"

"It was Greg's turn."

"And did anybody find him?"

"Oh, yeah. We found *him*. Then we sent out the call. I don't know if you remember the rules of hide-and-seek?"

"Just about," Frank assured him.

"Right, well, once the hider has been found, he and the finder go round calling in the other seekers. You with me?"

"And everyone came back, except one?"

"That's it." O'Brien nodded, and at last, Frank saw, the smile had gone. "At first we thought maybe he was having a slash behind a tree, or…I don't know, something. Then after a while, he still hadn't come back, we set out looking for him."

"Were you worried yet?" Don asked.

O'Brien frowned. "I don't know, to be honest. I don't think I was, I can't speak for the others. I suppose I thought, like, maybe he was hiding. Having a laugh, you know. But really, I don't think I thought about it all."

"So who finally found Paul?"

"Greg did. He was—oh, well, you know where he was, in that hollow amongst the hollies."

"Why do you suppose Greg found the body, rather than anybody else?" said Frank.

"No reason." O'Brien shook his head. "I mean, just chance, you know. He found Paul, because he went where Paul was. That's all."

"He went into the bushes ahead of everyone else?"

"Yeah…" O'Brien drew the word out, giving it a skeptical tail. "He was a second or two ahead of us. *Not* long enough to have killed anybody, in my opinion."

"Fair enough," said Don. "Have you been a member of the Movement for long?"

The smile was back, as O'Brien replied, "Since the beginning. Me and Greg are the only two who've attended every meeting."

"You've never married then, or lived with anyone?" Don laughed. "At least, that's what I'm guessing."

"You guess right, Inspector! No, never been blessed in that way. My working hours aren't conducive to romance, that's the trouble. I'm usually in bed by eight of an evening."

"You must be a very keen 25th December Resister, Neil, to have attended every meeting."

"Well," he waggled his hands. "At the start, maybe. To tell you the truth, I'm rather hoping this sad business will be an end to it. Fact is, it's become a chore—just like any other

Christmas arrangement you can't get out of!" O'Brien clapped a hand over his mouth, miming guilt with his eyes. "Oh shit, don't tell Greg I said *Christmas* instead of December 25th!"

"We won't shop you," Don reassured him.

"How it all started—don't know if you know the history— we all drank at the same pub. For me, for a lot of us, most of us, it was just a laugh, a way of passing Christmastime. I'm not from London originally."

"We guessed," said Frank, knowing from his several years' experience as an adopted Londoner that this response was obligatory.

"Right, and the inspector here perhaps remembers what it was like twenty-odd years ago. Things really did shut down for a few days, from late Christmas Eve. Not like now, there's even shops open on Christmas Day, now."

Don shuddered. "I remember."

"Like, almost all the pubs were closed Christmas night," O'Brien continued, warming to his hideous theme. "If you weren't going home for Christmas for some reason, it could be bloody lonely. Say you're a young lad, on your own, living in some dismal bedsit, don't happen to have a girl on the go that year." He paused to take a good toke on his cigar. "And, to be fair, there *is* something bloody irritating about Christmas. It's all about couples, isn't it? And children. It's all so smug. All that bogus religious nonsense, and all the commercial crap."

"Know what you mean," Don said, his nostrils dilated and his head tilted as he attempted to passively smoke the milkman's Christmas treat.

"So, we all got talking about it, those of us in the same boat down at the pub, and jokingly we talked about setting up a resistance movement, and then the idea came up of getting together on the dreaded day itself and…well, basically doing what we usually did at the weekend. Few beers, a curry, play some records, talk rubbish, possibly certain other activities not to be discussed in front of officers of the law." He grinned at both of them, one after the other. "Long time ago!"

"Of course," said Don. "Before you discovered Havanas. So, if the original pleasures of the Movement have worn off, why do you keep going?"

He shrugged. "I don't know. Partly laziness. Habit. And partly, so many people have dropped out—I don't want to let Greg down. He's a good friend, been a good friend over the years, and the Movement is important to him." He took a final deep draught of luxury smoke, and placed the last inch or so of his cigar in an ashtray. No vulgar stubbing out, Frank noticed. "But if all this puts an end to the Movement naturally, so to speak…well, that wouldn't break my heart." His face suddenly fell, as he heard his own words. "Sad about this poor kid, of course—more than sad, horrible, terrible—but I didn't really know him that well."

"Did he seem like a nice bloke to you?" Frank asked, knowing that Don would want to watch, rather than hear, the witness's response to that question.

"Yeah, he seemed sound, sure. Didn't say a lot, really, come to think of it, but then that's no bad thing, right? A good listener. Well, that's what you look for in youngsters when you get to middle age, isn't it?"

Too bloody right, Frank thought, writing industriously in his notebook, and being careful not to catch Don's eye.

FIVE

"THEY'LL CALL US from the incident room if there's anything new," Don said, looking not at his watch but at the night sky. "Meanwhile, you should get back to whatever's left of Christmas with your family."

"Right, Don, I will. Thanks." As he drove Don back to his car, Frank wondered whether he ought to invite the D.I. back with him for a festive drink. Or some supper. Debbie wouldn't mind. She'd be a bit surprised, but she wouldn't mind, as such. On the other hand, if he did invite him and he had other plans, would he feel obliged to accept?

The journey back to Jubilee Park passed mostly in silence.

As soon as he got out of Frank's car, Don went straight to his own. Frank waited, to make sure his boss's car started, and was a bit puzzled when Don's first priority wasn't putting the heating on but checking the contents of the boot. Whatever it was he was checking on was still there, judging by his relieved smile. For a moment, Frank thought he was going to find out the identity of the mystery object. Don leaned in as if to take the thing out—only to change his mind after another scrutiny of the sky, and a sad shake of his head.

Frank lowered his window. "Everything all right?"

Don waved him on, but Frank decided this was daft, he was going to get this done, so he pulled up alongside the D.I. "Listen, Don, you're very welcome to, you know, if you fancy a…like, or if you. You know, you'd be more than welcome."

"No, you're all right, Frank, you get on. Early start tomorrow, you get what time you can with your family. That boy needs his dad at Christmas."

And so, relieved but frustrated, Frank drove home, still wondering what, if anything, Detective Inspector Packham did for Christmas.

Just after midnight, Frank and Debbie were about to turn in. Joseph had finally tired to the point where he had fallen asleep standing up, holding on to the furniture and humming in an attempt to fool onlookers. He had been caught by his father when he eventually succumbed to the merciless effects of gravity. Then Frank's mobile rang.

"Bet I know who that is," Debbie said, but she was wrong. It wasn't Don, it was the D.S. in charge of the incident room.

"Frank, have you got your jimjams on?"

"Not quite yet, Sarge. Will I need my coat?"

"I fear you might. I've just processed reports from the officers tasked with informing the deceased's mother—there's no father—and we've got a bit of a puzzle here."

"Oh, aye?"

"Mum has a different address for the deceased than the one you and the D.I. visited earlier. Different story altogether in fact."

"That is a puzzle," Frank agreed.

"It is," said the D.S., "and one which I will leave you to tell Mr. Packham about, if you don't mind."

Frank wondered whether he should phone Don with this odd bit of news, but Debbie talked him out of it. "You'll be seeing him in a few hours, won't you? And whatever he's doing for Christmas, it's unlikely to be improved by a midnight phone call from a colleague."

"Let's hope you're right," Frank said.

MUCH OF THE COUNTRY was still asleep at eight o'clock on Boxing Day morning, but it takes a lot to interfere with trade at a motorway services. Don and Frank sat over cups of strong but flavorless coffee, helped down, in the D.I.'s case, by a Danish pastry that had a particularly prefestive bite to it.

"Bloody places," said Don. "Background music composed by Herr Tinnitus."

Frank couldn't disagree about the strange aural conditions that always seemed to prevail in such locations—a kind of echoing silence, full of underwater pops, cracks and burbles—but he also couldn't resist the unspoken retort: You chose the bloody meet, not me; I'm not the one with a violent aversion to police stations.

"He was neither unemployed nor a casual worker, according to his mother," said Frank, précising the report in front of him. "He worked for Customs and Excise. And secondly, he didn't live alone in a crummy bedsit, but with his girlfriend in a nice, two bedroom flat in Uxbridge. So what was he up to?"

"Well, that's the point, isn't it," said Don. "We know now that he *was* up to something. And whatever it was, it's quite possibly something to give one of his four supposed mates a motive for murder."

"Where to first, then? Straight to the new flat?"

"No," said Don. "Tell you what, let's have a proper chat with Greg Mulford first. He's the centre of this group, its ideological chief. If there's anything we need to know about the Resistance Movement, we'll most likely get it from him."

Frank took out his phone. "Better give him a ring first, seeing how early it is—this is Boxing Day, after all."

"Balls," said Don. "He doesn't recognize the existence of Boxing Day, does he? It's just another Friday to him. He should have been up ages ago."

GREG MULFORD WAS, indeed, treating Boxing Day like a normal weekday. They discovered this by phoning his home, and speaking to his wife. He'd already gone into work, she told them.

"He has a wife?" Don said. "And he spends every Christmas Day with the lads?"

"So it seems," said Frank.

"That's unbelievable. I'm looking forward to having another talk with this man."

Mulford's workplace was a warehouse on a trading estate a couple of miles from his home.

"Garden bird-watching," he explained, in answer to Don's initial question. "It's all in kit form, that's why you don't recognize it. But if you take one of these, for instance, and attach it to that...see?"

"A bird-table," said Frank. "Got something similar in my own garden."

"Well, all these are for export. I send them all over the world. It's a rapidly growing hobby."

"Ornithology?"

"No, see, specifically *garden* bird-watching. People haven't got the time these days to spend a week at a nature reserve in the Hebrides or whatever. But virtually any garden, no matter how tiny, can be packed with birds all year, if you use the right gear to attract them. I do tables, feeders, nestboxes, the whole caboodle."

"It's your own business?" Don asked.

"It is indeed. Started from scratch, built it up slowly, and now it's not doing at all badly, if you'll forgive my lack of modesty."

"Well done. Always good to hear a success story." As Mulford turned away to replace his bird-table bits, Don raised his eyebrows at Frank, trusting that the D.C. would receive his message: Could be money here.

"Thanks. Look, come on through to the back, I'll stick the kettle on."

Amid the ordered clutter of his office, Mulford answered

questions about the 25th December Resistance Movement with an enthusiasm bordering, Don felt, on the fanatical.

"Anti-Christmas isn't quite it," he insisted. "We've got nothing against Christians celebrating their own festivals—or Hindus, or Shiites, or anyone else. All we're saying is they shouldn't force it down the throats of the rest of us. *And* they shouldn't get away with pretending that it *is* a Christian festival in the first place."

"But it is, isn't it?" Frank asked. "I mean, it's got the word Christ in it."

A smile spread across Mulford's big face. "That, Constable, is where people make their mistake. Fact is, if history had gone a little differently a couple of millennia ago, you wouldn't be sending Christmas cards—you'd be sending Mithras cards. Have you heard of Mithras, a god worshiped by many Romans before Christ?"

"Just about," Frank said, remembering the answer to a quiz question on TV a few weeks back.

"Well, let's see…" Mulford rocked his swivel chair from side to side, and made a great show of scratching his chin. "Mithras was born in a cave on December 25, of a virgin, attended by shepherds. He died and was resurrected to redeem sinful mankind. He had twelve disciples, who ate the blood and flesh of God at mass, and he treated them to a last supper of bread and wine."

"You're straying from your brief a little, aren't you?" said Don, unable to resist. Not actually trying to resist, if the truth be told.

"How do you mean?"

"Still," said Don, mimicking Mulford's display of hard thinking, "I suppose you couldn't have set up an anti-Easter group. Easter's a movable feast, so you wouldn't have known what to call it. The Sometime In Late Spring Resistance Movement—nope, it ain't got that swing."

Mulford gave him an uncertain smile, then turned his attention back to Frank. "Point being, Sol and Apollo were also born on December 25. That date was only chosen for Jesus's birth about three hundred years after the supposed event. It's a midwinter festival, that's all, a way for rural people to mark an astronomical event, and it's been kidnapped by every bloody religion going since forever."

"You must be pretty happy with the way things are heading then," said Frank.

"Happy?"

"There was a couple of bishops on the radio just the other day, complaining that it's a consumerist celebration these days, not a religious one."

"No, no, no." Mulford shook his head, causing a slight whiplash effect around his jowls. "No, that's just as bad. Worse, even. If you refuse to take part in a religious Christmas, the worst anyone can call you is an atheist. If you don't want anything to do with the modern Christmas, they'll call you a tight bastard. Besides, it's only another religion, isn't it? Worshiping the almighty pound."

That was probably enough theology for one morning, Don decided.

"So you never miss the 25th December meeting of the Movement, I take it?"

With his hand on his heart—was that bit a joke? Don wondered—Mulford said, "Never have missed, never will. My life has had its ups and downs, I've no shame in saying so, but my role in the Movement has, throughout it all, been something concrete and worthwhile. Something to be proud of, something—"

"What does your wife think about the Movement?" Don said.

"Fact is, she knew about the Movement long before we ever got serious, so she can't really complain."

Which doesn't mean she doesn't, Don thought. "Is she a member?"

"She did come along one year, as it happens. But it wasn't really for her." He played with his tea mug for a moment, then added, "To be honest with you, there's no actual ban on bringing partners, but it's not what you'd call encouraged."

"Because…?"

"Because, it makes it too much like—well, you know, like a family Christmas!"

"You've no children yourself?"

"No. We married only a few years back."

"The death of Paul Alsop," said Don, "must be a terrible blow to you. A personal loss, I mean, and a loss to the Movement."

There was no hint of a joke about Mulford now. This bloke wasn't just putting on a mourning face, Don was sure. He was clenching his jaws against tears.

"It's awful. I mean it's just…it's awful. Like you say, Inspector, a young man dead, that's bad enough. That's terrible. But then, you have the loss of young blood from the—sorry, 'young blood,' clumsy expression, you know what I'm trying to say."

"How did Paul come to join the Movement, being so much younger than the rest of you?"

"He originally came along with someone else, someone who was a member for a while, but who's since dropped out. Moved in with his girlfriend, if I recall."

"Does that often happen?" Frank asked. "People bringing along new members?"

"Now and then. Anyway, we were all glad to see Paul. He was a breath of fresh air."

"It didn't matter that he was a different generation?" Don asked. "That he didn't share your history?"

Mulford shook his head. "In fact it was a good thing, it

meant that we didn't just stagnate into a nostalgic bunch of old pals. See what I mean? Having someone new, it meant that the Movement really was a movement: a living, dynamic, growing movement."

"That's important to you, Greg?"

"Of course! It'd be nice to think you might pass something like this on to a new generation. And having Paul there meant we had to observe the rituals and that, do the thing properly. I mean, amongst ourselves we could just say, like, 'Old Harry, eh? And the egg timer?' and everyone falls about laughing. You can't do that with a newcomer at the table. You have to make an effort."

"He was an enthusiastic convert, was he?"

Mulford nodded. "Very much so."

"Nice bloke?"

"He seemed so, yeah." He sighed. "Fact is, very sadly, we didn't really get to know him much. Only saw him the twice, this year and last."

"You never met him other than on those two Christmas Days?"

"December 25ths, you mean," said Mulford, smiling again. "No, I didn't. I see a bit of Neil during the year, and Simon very occasionally, but that's about it."

"Tell us about the others," said Don, "those few Decembrists who are still left. Diehards, are they?"

"I've known Simon and Neil for a long time. Neil the longest—he's a founder member like me."

"And are they both as enthusiastic as you?"

Mulford met Don's expression of innocent enquiry with one of injured disappointment. "I'm not daft, Inspector. I know the boys aren't as committed as I am to every dot and comma of the Movement. That doesn't bother me."

"Why do they keep coming, then?"

Mulford laughed. "Well, I don't know where else Neil

would go on the twenty-fifth! And what could be better, anyway, than spending the day with your old friends?"

Fair point, thought Don. "And Simon? Does the same apply to him?"

"Well, now, Simon does believe in the cause. They both do, I should say, but Simon has, if you like, a closer understanding of it all."

"Even so," said Don, "he stopped attending for a few years, didn't he?"

"Only because he got married. That didn't work out." Don couldn't quite tell whether Mulford was trying not to be glad about Simon Young's failed marriage, or just trying not to *sound* glad.

"And what about Derek?"

Mulford fished around in his breast pocket for some chewing gum. "Well…everyone's welcome, you know."

"But…?"

"Yeah, but. Look, being honest, Derek's a bit of a hanger-on. I suspect, to be brutally frank, that he is one big reason why attendance has dropped in recent years."

"He's not one of the original lads from the pub, I take it?"

A look of bemusement came over Greg Mulford's face. "Well, this is it! He wasn't someone from the pub, he wasn't a friend of a friend or anything like that. He just…what can I say? *Attached* himself to us one year when we were having our annual lunch in an Indian restaurant. In Hampstead it was, that year."

"And you haven't been able to shake him off since?"

"More a case of haven't had the heart to shake him off. I mean, how do you tell someone something like that? He's not the sort to respond to gentle hints, believe me."

"What sort is he?" Frank asked.

"He's not a monster or anything, don't get me wrong. He's rather loud, foulmouthed—I mean, okay, I'm not claiming

I'm the Archbishop of fucking Canterbury, but I do know when to moderate my language. For instance, not effing and blinding at three million decibels in the middle of a crowded restaurant, yeah? He's sarcastic, can't hold his drink—just generally not good company." Mulford seemed to run out of breath, and devoted himself to scratching the side of his nose for a little while, before adding: "Still, I will say this for Derek—he sticks with it, which is more than some others I could mention. Anyway, maybe it's just me. Paul didn't seem to mind him, and I've never heard Simon badmouth him, especially."

Back in the car, Don and Frank were of one mind.

"Takes it pretty seriously, doesn't he?" said Frank.

"He certainly does, Frank, he certainly does. And if he had found out that Paul Alsop's reasons for joining his Movement weren't genuine…"

"Yeah," said Frank. "He could be very angry indeed, couldn't he?"

SIX

THERE WOULD BE MORE TEARS to come. Frank knew that sudden death wasn't something which had finite consequences. Its effects lasted forever—but for now, Bet Thomas seemed calm enough, sitting on a brand-new sofa in the living room of the flat she had shared with Paul Alsop. She wore no makeup on her chalk-white face, her eyes looked as if they'd been inexpertly transplanted from a marsupial, and she was shredding tissues like someone with a grudge against origami, but at least she was speaking in full sentences.

Don and Frank had agreed not to mention her boyfriend's other address to her at the moment—for investigative rather than humanitarian reasons—and so they started by asking the twenty-seven-year-old florist why she and Paul hadn't spent Christmas Day together.

"He had to work."

"I see," said Frank, writing that down as if it were new information. "And where did he work?"

"He's a civil servant. Customs and Excise."

"Okay," said Frank, busy with his pen.

"He got a phone call on Christmas Eve. Said he had to go in."

"What time was the phone call?"

She seemed to be experiencing some constriction of the talking muscles. While swallowing with evident effort, she flapped her hands spasmodically at ear level. *I don't know, I don't remember, who cares?* was the general message.

"We could get that from your phone company, no doubt,"

said Don, a remark that was rewarded only with further flapping and hard swallowing. "Was it usual for him to have to work over Christmas?"

She looked over at an unoccupied armchair the other side of the smart, flame-effect gas fire, and it seemed to Frank as if she was seeking advice on how to answer the question. But, of course, her adviser wasn't there. "Not—well, no, not really."

"Were you upset?" said Don. "That Paul was called in?"

She shrugged, with just one shoulder. "Well, we're saving up for a bigger place. So, you know, the overtime was handy. Anyway, he said we'd go round to my parents today, Boxing Day. Have a proper Christmas then."

"But," Don said, "you've been told by other police officers that in fact Paul died yesterday in a public park in Cowden?"

"Yes," she replied, speaking quickly and swallowing almost simultaneously, so that she choked slightly on the combination of words and saliva. "But I don't understand it. I don't know why he was there."

"Have you ever heard of the 25th December Resistance Movement?" Frank asked.

She shrugged again. "Is it a band?"

"No, it's a sort of club. Paul was a member."

"No." Her voice was firm. "No, I don't know about it."

"All right, Bet," said Don. "That's fine for now. You've done very well. I think the other officers you spoke to told you that they will want to conduct a proper search of your home a bit later on? Right, but in the meantime, would you mind if Frank and I had a quick look round? We'll be very careful with everything, and we'll be as quick as we can."

"Okay." Her voice was very small, and her hands were very active, tearing at the tissues in her lap.

In the short hallway, with the living-room door closed behind him, Don whispered, "We'll send the search team in once we know what we're looking for, if anything. But there's no harm in conducting a bit of a preliminary."

The couple's bedroom yielded nothing that struck either officer as a member of the clue family, but the spare bedroom was a little more intriguing. It seemed to be in use as a combination of home office and storeroom, much like every other spare room in the country, since the invention of the personal computer—except that in this case, there was no computer.

"Look at that desk," Don said. "There's a perfect space for a computer, judging by the dust pattern, but I don't see the machine itself."

"Maybe they were buying themselves a new one for Christmas," Frank suggested. "Already got rid of the old one."

"Could be." Don dropped to his knees, somewhat disconcerting Frank, who wasn't used to seeing the D.I. take such an interest in physical evidence—evidence which couldn't be argued with, charmed, harangued or joshed into indiscretion.

Funny time of year, this, Frank thought. "Spotted something down there, Don?"

"Indentations," Don said. "In the carpet, see? There's been something standing here for a while."

Frank joined him on the floor. "Chest of drawers?"

"Smaller than that." Don stood up, looking around the small room with growing animation. "Whatever it was, it's not in here anymore. You staying down there, Frank? Thinking of making her an offer for the carpet?"

"They've got a splitter, look."

"They've got a what? And I'm not looking, you'll have to tell me. One full-body squat per day's my limit."

Frank stood, and pointed to the skirting board behind the desk. "In the telephone socket. It's a fitting that allows you to run a phone and a modem from the same socket, without having to unplug one to put in the other. It's not new, either; it's quite grubby. It's been there a while."

Don smiled, and sniffed the air. "Money troubles," he said. "They've been flogging stuff off."

"Do you want to put it to her?" Frank asked, pretty sure he knew the answer.

"No, not yet."

There was something else Don wanted to ask Bet Thomas, however. As she was showing them out, he said, "By the way, you say it's not usual for Paul to be called into work at Christmas?"

"That's—yes. That's right," she said.

"In which case, can you tell me, where did he spend *last* Christmas Day?"

"He…" She looked away to one side, again, as if seeking guidance. Clearly she didn't find any. For a full thirty seconds, she blinked and swallowed, before replying, "Actually, now you come to mention it, yeah, he was working then, too. I forgot."

THE FIRST ALL-DAY PUB they came to would "do fine," Don insisted, and in fact wasn't that bad. The music was quiet and the beer was drinkable. Don took a savoring, head-tilted-back throatful of his drink and sighed happily.

"Used to be the best pint of the year, Boxing Day lunchtime."

Frank smiled. "You mean because they're closed the night before?" Despite the smile, he couldn't help wondering why "used to be"—why not still? Does he mean because he's in his forties, or because he's a copper, or because the times they are a-changing? Frank himself had married quite young, joined the police service quite young, and so he'd joined the adult world early. He hadn't really known those few years between mother and wife, which all men were supposed to look back on forever after as their best. Therefore, he didn't quite feel, firsthand, what Don was talking about. But he'd grown up with enough lads who would have. It wasn't that they were particularly big drinkers, most of them. It wasn't the drink that mattered. It was just that they were mostly single blokes and their social life centered on the pub, radiated from the pub, and there was just one night a year when the pub was closed—they got withdrawal symptoms, a bit of a panic attack. They felt the dawning of the 26th December as a day of liberation. No wonder Boxing Day was a national holiday, because it was the day that everything, for pub-goers, returned wonderfully, miraculously to normal, after the midwinter madness of the twenty-fifth.

"This 25th December Resistance thing," said Don. "I can understand it as an excuse for a get-together, but all that anti-Christmas stuff Greg Mulford comes out with—it's crap."

"Really?" Frank was a bit surprised. If he'd been asked to bet, he'd have guessed Don would have some sympathy with the Decembrists. Mind, he'd learned that there was little point in being surprised by anything D.I. Packham did or said.

"I'm not saying he's wrong—I'm saying who cares? So his precious December 25th has been hijacked by religion and consumerism. Big deal! Christmas existed long before the Christians, long before capitalism, and it'll outlive both. You've got to have a midwinter festival if you live in the northern hemisphere, otherwise you'd go bonkers. Just enjoy it!" Don said.

"Aye, I suppose so."

"We're lucky in this country—you can celebrate it any way you want. Greg Mulford is kicking against an open door."

"How do you mean?" Frank asked, his voice a little quieter than Don's, in the hope that his boss might subconsciously imitate him.

"Think about it, Frank. How many British people do you know for whom Christmas is a religious festival? And as for commercialization ruining it—tough luck. It's essential to the economy, it's essential to the mental health of the nation, and above all, it's voluntary. Millions of people just get in a few bottles, a box of chocolate mints and a couple of videos, and take the rare chance to put their feet on the sofa for a few days in a row."

Emboldened by the setting, Don's mood, and perhaps the date, Frank was about to ask just what it was that the D.I. himself did for Christmas; but the D.I. had only paused to wet his throat and refill his lungs.

"And you know who the fiercest anti-Christmas people are?" Don continued.

"Ah—"

"Hard-line Christian fundamentalists—that's who! They reckon it's all pagan nonsense, a complete disgrace, and good Christians should have nothing to do with it. Christian fundamentalists ban Christmas whenever they get into power. They have done for centuries."

"Well, that's very—"

"And straight after them, the next most extreme Christmas-haters? The free market fundamentalists." Don sat back with his arms crossed and a pleased smile on his face.

"No," Frank said. "No, you've lost me. Why are the free market fanatics anti-Christmas? I thought you said the whole economy depended on Christmas spending?"

Don employed his cigar to wave away any trifling dialectical discrepancies. "They reckon it's uncompetitive, Frank, that's the point. For the whole country to shut down for a fortnight once a year. Instead of having a communal Christmas, they reckon we should all have a day off in lieu during the year, individually."

"Do they really?" Frank had, right enough, noted some pretty daft ideas from the free market think tanks over the last couple of years, but he seemed to have missed that one somehow.

"If they don't, they soon will," Don assured him. "Uncompetitive! Well they're right, it *is* uncompetitive and here's to it!"

And so, in a quiet pub on Boxing Day, the two colleagues raised one pint of bitter and one glass of tonic water, and the toast was "Christmas."

"Two main questions," said Don, when the sandwich plates had been cleared away, and the detectives' minds returned to the matter at hand. "What was Paul Alsop doing in the Movement, and who killed him?"

"And are we assuming that the first question will answer the second?"

"Not *assuming*," Don said, "but it does seem likely. We're agreed that there's something odd about Paul being in the Movement, yes? He isn't single, for a start."

"Neither is Greg."

"Okay, but Greg's a zealot. That's different. For the other members, it seems to me, the whole purpose of the Movement is to have an annual ritual of your own, something you look forward to or which, at least, occupies you during the one day of the year when it is socially unacceptable not to have anything planned. And the only reason you need that ritual is because you're single."

"Paul lied to his girlfriend about where he was—assuming she's telling the truth, which I'm not convinced about."

Don nodded, and his small cigar nodded with him. "I'm with you there, Frank. She's giving us a version, no doubt about it. Not sure why, but she is."

"Then, if we're right that there are only two legitimate reasons for joining the Movement," Frank said, hoping his slight stutter had gone unnoticed; he'd almost said *if you're right,* which he thought Don might have misinterpreted. "That they're either fanatics or bachelors, and Paul fits neither category, then I can only think that he joined in order to get close to someone."

Don beamed. "Spot on, Frank. By which I mean, obviously, that your view accords with mine. It has to be that, doesn't it? But for what reason?"

"Revenge?" Frank offered.

"Blackmail?" countered Don.

"Information?"

"Lust? Never mind, Frank, we could go on all day with that. Was the murder premeditated or not?"

"Surely not. If it was, he'd have brought a knife, or something."

"Not necessarily. A tree branch is easer to dump, can't be raced back to you by an entry on your credit card bill. You don't have to carry it around with you all day, risking someone seeing it."

"But you are relying on finding it conveniently lying there, where and when you need it."

"True," Don admitted. "The killing could still be premeditated but opportunistic—I'm going to kill that bastard next chance I get, and I'll use whatever comes to hand."

"All right," said Frank. "Now, they all say they didn't see anyone else around in the park. Theoretically they could be wrong. The killer could be someone from outside the group. But there's no evidence of robbery, or attempted robbery, or sexual assault or anything that could supply a reasonable motive for an outsider."

"Plus, no struggle. And nothing from the scenes examination to suggest a sixth person at the locus. No, I'd be very surprised if this was done by a stranger. Wouldn't you?"

"It seems unlikely," Frank agreed. "In which case, we're saying that Paul joined the Movement to target an unknown other for an unknown purpose, and that this other then killed him—with premeditation or otherwise—as a result."

"Sounds about right," Don said. "Could do with a few more details, perhaps, but basically sound."

SEVEN

THEY BROKE FOR ANOTHER PINT for Don, and a coffee for Frank, and a bit of chat about Joseph's Christmas. The D.I insisted on a comprehensive list of the little lad's presents Then they resumed their hunt for the unknown other.

"Was Paul after someone who'd done him wrong at some time?" Don asked. "Robbed him, abused him, stolen his woman stolen his dog? If so, how come they didn't recognize him?"

"On the other hand, the killer might well have recognized Paul, and strung him along until he could kill him."

Don grimaced, and ground out his cigar. "No, I don't like the revenge theory; it's too complicated. If Paul knows the bloke, why not just do him?"

"Well, maybe he doesn't know for sure if it's the righ man—the offence happened when he was very little. O maybe the offence was against his family, or a friend, no against him. Or his girlfriend, maybe?"

"Even so, this is his second Christmas with the Move ment—surely he knows by now, if he's ever going to?"

"Yeah, I suppose so."

"Back to blackmail, then. Something he's discovered through his work as a Customs man? Are we having the sus pects' bank accounts checked?"

"It's in hand," Frank said, making a note to chase that up "Though even if they don't show anything, that could merely mean that the killer had killed *instead* of paying."

"If it is something he discovered at Customs—unless on

of them's a master smuggler or something—that surely points at Greg Mulford? His export business."

They drank in silent contemplation for a while, until Frank said, "Sticking with blackmail, what would you kill to cover up?"

Don suggested embarrassment—which won Frank a small bet with himself—and Frank offered shame. Or anything carrying a significant custodial sentence.

"Anything which," Don said, "if it was revealed, you'd have to top yourself."

"Can't see anything like that in the investigation so far. None of them are known to police."

"What, nothing at all?"

"Well," said Frank, flipping through his notes, "strictly speaking, *all* of them are known."

"Which isn't quite the same thing, Frank!"

"Yeah, but Derek Fleet was done for brawling when he was seventeen, Neil O'Brien for failing to report a motor accident, very minor. Greg for possession—only a couple of joints, and again, he was a teenager—and Simon Young was cautioned after making a row outside his mother-in-law's house when his marriage broke up."

"See what you mean, nothing very significant."

"None of them's got a real criminal record, no interesting known associates, none of their names have ever come up in another investigation, none of them are flagged by Customs or drug squad or anyone."

"All that means is they got away with it," Don said. "All the more reason for Paul to seek his own justice."

"I suppose," Frank said, "that Paul might have found out something about Simon which might interfere with his access to his kids."

"That's more like it." Don rubbed his hands. "What about Neil?"

"The only thing I can think of there, and it sounds daft…"

"Go on," Don encouraged him. Frank knew that, whatever D.I. Packham's other faults, he did genuinely welcome ideas from colleagues.

"Well, suppose in an unguarded moment, Neil told Paul that he was fed up with the Resistance Movement—which is pretty much what he told us—and Paul threatened to tell Greg." Frank hid his blush behind his cold coffee cup. "No, forget it, that's a pathetic motive for murder."

"On the contrary, Frank. That's excellent thinking. That bloke in the papers last month, stabbed his wife, his next-door neighbor and a passing postman, and then tried to kill himself, all because his mother-in-law said his new beard made him look like a weather forecaster. Now, *that's* a pathetic motive, but it almost bankrupted the National Blood Service. Happens all the time."

"I suppose so."

"I've told you before, Frank, never overlook or underestimate the possibility of a motive based on the emotional dynamics of the group. And certainly, Neil's friendship with Greg is important to him."

"Only one thing…" Frank began.

"You're determined to talk yourself out of this, aren't you?"

"Well, no, it's just how would that fit with Paul joining the group with blackmail in his mind?"

"True. All right, who's left? Derek. Well, I'd put him in the same basket as Greg. A businessman of some sort. We don't know what shady dealings he might have been involved in during his career. But, my God, if we're going to have to explore the past misdemeanors of every one of them for the last twenty-five years, we're going to be here until next Christmas. And that's assuming we are ruling out revenge. I mean, if this guy was seriously unstable, he could have been stalking someone who queue-barged him in a pizza takeaway in 1993."

THEY APPROACHED Simon Young first—on the grounds that his custody troubles at least gave them some sort of starting point. But he begged them to give him a couple of hours. He had his children with him for their official Christmas visit, and they'd be back at their mum's by teatime.

Don agreed. You should never come between a man and his kids. That was an important principle, and another equally important one was that if Simon felt indebted to them he was more likely to be loose-lipped. Of course, they might just be giving him more time to compose his lies, but that was a risk worth taking.

"Meanwhile," he told Frank, "we'll see the milkman again. Maybe he'll let me take the contents of his ashtray home with me."

"What's the approach? I mean, how much do we tell him, about what we now know about Paul?"

Don pondered, and just before they reached Barnet, he said, "All of it. Or most of it. See how much it rattles him."

O'Brien seemed shocked by their revelations, but you never could tell—not really. Don knew a lot of cops thought they could, but they were fooling themselves. He'd been sent on a body language course once and been amused to realize that, according to the signs the instructor taught them to look out for, she was lying every time she lectured them.

"Man, that is amazing! I mean, what was he doing in the Movement, in that case?" O'Brien asked.

"We were wondering the same thing," said Don.

"I just don't get it. Greg's going to be gutted. The thing is, Paul reminded us of how we were when we were younger. He gave the whole thing new energy." O'Brien ran his hands through his hair. "This is going to devastate Greg. You haven't told him yet?"

"Not yet."

"I thought not—he'd have been straight on the phone if you had. Poor sod."

"And," Don added, "we'd prefer it if you didn't mention it to him, until we've had a chance to discuss it with him ourselves."

"Right." O'Brien nodded that he understood. "Yeah, I'm with you."

"You can't imagine what Paul's motives might have been," Frank asked, "for joining the Movement?"

"I really can't, mate, I really cannot think—unless, you know, it was just a joke to him. A piss-take. Spending the day with a bunch of pathetic, middle-aged has-beens, and then going home to his girlfriend for a good laugh."

"Seems some length to go to just for a piss-take."

"Well, yeah," said O'Brien, "to you and me, normal people, but some people are like that, though, aren't they?"

"Was Paul like that?"

"I couldn't say. I'm sorry, I just didn't know him well enough to have an opinion."

FORTY MINUTES LATER, they found Simon Young tidying up after his kids. Though it seemed to Don, as he watched the actor flitting around his living room, that he wasn't actually clearing anything away, just moving bits of wrapping paper, fizzy drinks cans and eviscerated Christmas crackers from one surface to another.

"I'm only allowed them for three hours," said Young, as he finally abandoned his domestic efforts and sat down, "but they manage to make the place a tip even so."

"Which is good, isn't it?" Don said. "Means they feel at home here."

"Yeah!" said Young, the enthusiasm of his response putting Don in mind of an amphetamine fan deciding to paint his spare bedroom at midnight. "Yeah, *exactly,* that's exactly what I think. If they thought of themselves as visitors, they'd be all neat and tidy, wouldn't they?"

"Of course they would," Don said, "being well-brought up youngsters."

They told Young exactly what they'd told O'Brien. He, too, seemed initially astonished by the news, but then a sad smile crept over his face, and he began nodding his head, rhythmically. "Funny thing, power of hindsight I suppose, but I always did get the impression he wasn't really with us. Too keen to join in with everything, if that makes any sense."

"Paul never talked about having a girlfriend?"

"As far as I can remember, he talked about girlfriends—plural, you know. That's partly why we were so keen to have him, truth be told. He seemed almost like a replica of our younger selves, unattached and fancy-free, sort of thing." He rubbed his nose. "Or perhaps I should say, like a replica of how we imagine ourselves to have been, when we were his age."

Don opened his mouth to ask the next routine question, when it suddenly struck him. *My God.*

"Okay, Simon, that's all for now. Thanks very much. Come on, Frank."

"Ah—right, sir. Thank you, Mr. Young, we'll see ourselves out."

They were hardly beyond earshot, on the other side of Young's front door, when Don grabbed Frank by the arm. "Paul Alsop's got a mother, right? But no father."

"Right."

"Right. Never *had* a father, in fact."

"Yes…"

"Frank, don't you see? There's another possibility. Not blackmail, not revenge, but *paternity.* Paul was looking for his father!"

IT WASN'T A BAD FIT, Frank had to admit. Somehow or other— by chance, or by deliberate effort—Paul Alsop had got a lead on the 25th December group, or on one of them specifically, and the best way of pursuing his search for his father was to get to know them socially, chat them up about their past. Everything that worked for a blackmail theory worked for this, but better.

Even so, he hoped the D.I. wasn't going to go off bonkers on this, as he had sometimes been known to. Unless Frank could rein him in, they were going to end up arresting anyone with a decent sperm count.

"So who's the daddy?" Don asked, as they drove aimlessly.

"Or *assumed* daddy," Frank cautioned. "DNA would tell us, presumably."

"Yeah, I know, Frank, the wonders of science. But we'd have to have a bloody good reason to get five DNA tests done—not least to get the request past the Guardians of the Sacred Budget."

"More than we've got now, you mean," Frank said, with as much emphasis as he deemed diplomatic on the word "now."

"Hell of a lot more. The Super would just give us his usual tedious lecture about evidence."

"That old thing."

"Besides, it'd take too long. No, as I said yesterday, this one's going to be solved the old-fashioned way. We'll have to talk to them all again, with this new trick in our magic bag."

"A touch of the old dialectics," Frank said, scarcely the first policeman to take comfort in a catchphrase. "Simon Young's not on the paternity list, I suppose—too young."

"Culturally," Don said. "Not biologically."

But within an hour, Don's paternity theory was dead in the water.

Frank's mobile phone tracked Alsop's mother down to the flat Paul had shared with his girlfriend. Mrs. Alsop herself opened the door to them, explaining that Bet was lying down.

"Of course," said Don. "In fact, it was you we wanted a quick word with."

"Certainly. Come in and sit down. What is it you want to know?"

Don managed to get halfway through his opening sentence before Jessica Alsop leaped from her seat with such velocity that Frank feared she was headed straight down the D.I.'s throat.

"I just cannot believe this! What are you like? You're supposed to be catching Paul's murderer, and instead you're coming round here trying to smear his family!"

"Mrs. Alsop, if I could just—"

"Of course my son knew who his father was."

"He did?" Don said. "Oh…"

"I should think he did. The useless, cheating bastard only lives two streets away!"

"Ah," said Don, and then went very quiet. He looked up at the ceiling, and chewed his lip. After a while, Mrs. Alsop seemed to become bored with staring at him and getting no response, and returned to her seat. The sound of her slight panting, and the faint humming of the central heating, was the room's only noise.

Fearing that Don was sinking along with his brilliant theory, Frank decided he had to get the D.I. away from human company. But how? Doing a complete runner was out of the question. It would involve too many explanations and apologies, so instead Frank asked if he and the inspector might have another quick look around the flat.

"Oh right, you're expecting to find the killer under the fridge, are you?" She dismissed his attempted explanation with a wave of her hand. "Keep out of the bedroom, you hear? I don't want Bet disturbed."

That didn't leave much flat to search. Frank managed to persuade a docile Don to regain his feet, and to steer him into the kitchen. The kitchen and bathroom were as clue-free as ever—at least, as far as Frank could tell from a cursory inspection. And so it took them only a few minutes to end up in the spare-room-cum-office. Don leaned against the wall, staring at his shoes—made a change from the ceiling, Frank supposed—saying nothing. Frank assumed his boss was breathing, but couldn't have given a sworn statement to that effect.

What to do? Leave him here, make peace with Jessica Alsop, then come back and collect him? No, that was too close to acting out an urban legend; not the granny on the roof rack, but the inspector in the spare room.

He'd have to try to get Don talking.

"Oh well, looks like back to blackmail, then." He remembered that in his detective training he'd been told, when attempting to establish a dialogue with a recalcitrant witness, always to use sentences that invited a response. "Don't you reckon, like?" he added.

To Frank's astonishment Don said, "There's definitely something missing."

Oh God, he thought. Was that a philosophical remark? Does he mean "missing" in his life, "missing" in a cosmic sense? "Something missing, you say?"

Don clicked his tongue and made an impatient gesture with his foot. "That indentation on the carpet has faded, which means that when we saw it yesterday, it must have been fresh. So whatever's been moved from there, it was moved very recently."

He pushed himself away from the wall, and hurried from the room. Frank hurried behind him, rushing to catch up with Don's thought processes, too. If the piece of furniture, whatever it was, had been moved *since* Paul's death…

They found Paul Alsop's mother and girlfriend in the living room, clutching each other and both shredding tissues. "Mind if I look in your loft, Bet?" Don said, smiling widely. Or was it wildly?

"We haven't got a loft," she replied.

"Must be in the garage, then. You have got a garage, yes?"

"We've—" Frank could see, in Bet's darting eyes, her attempts to come up with a lie which couldn't be instantly disproved. She failed. "Yeah, there's a garage."

"May I have the keys then, please? You don't mind us having a look?"

She fetched him the garage key from a hook on the back of the kitchen door, all the time avoiding eye contact with Jessica Alsop, who said nothing, but looked plenty.

The garage yielded its prizes quickly and without drama. "There they are," said Don, squeezing between the car and the wall, and pointing at a bulky, rug-covered shape in a far corner. He removed the rug to reveal a computer and an old-fashioned, four-drawer filing cabinet.

"Frank, get on the radio—tell them we need a full search doing straightaway. And make sure they know there's an IT aspect."

"Sir."

"Now then, Bet." Don emerged from the garage to bestow upon the mourning girl what he presumably thought was a comforting smile. "What are we going to find, when we take your files apart?"

She shredded air between her twisting fingers, having left her tissues indoors. "I don't know, I really don't know—that's all Paul's stuff, I never touched it."

"You never touched it?"

She shook her head.

"You do know, love, that it'll take them about thirty seconds flat to establish whether or not you have touched it?"

Bet Thomas began crying, quietly, and turned to her boyfriend's mother for comfort. Mrs. Alsop's arms did eventually find their way around Bet's shoulders, but Frank noticed that they did so only hesitantly, and that there was little warmth in the embrace.

"And having done that," Don continued, "it won't take them much longer, I daresay, to prove that *you* moved those items from your spare bedroom to your garage. It could even be—I'm not going to lie to you, Bet, I'm not a forensics expert, and I'm only guessing here—but it could be that they can tell *when* you moved them. Which, I'm guessing again, was after you heard of Paul's death. Wasn't it?"

She concentrated on crying into Jessica Alsop's shoulders, until Mrs. Alsop gently—well, fairly gently, Frank thought—turned her around to face the inspector.

"Come on," said Don, "what was the scam?"

Scam? thought Frank.

"It wasn't anything as melodramatic or dangerous as blackmail, was it?" said Don.

"Blackmail?" said Mrs. Alsop, taking a step toward Don herself.

Don held up his hands, palms out. "Don't worry, a theory from earlier in the investigation, which has now been abandoned."

Has it? thought Frank. Thanks for telling me.

"You're calling my dead son a blackmailer?" Mrs. Alsop had her hands on her hips, and—Frank reckoned—at least seven pints of blood in her face.

"Certainly not, madam," said Don, with—did Frank imagine this?—a short bow toward the angry woman. "I wouldn't want you to get that impression at all."

"Well, all right…"

"We're calling him a *con man*. Aren't we, Bet?"

EIGHT

THERE WAS A SCAM; Bet Thomas was willing, in the end, to admit that. Though she was keen to make sure the policemen understood that she had known very little about it, and definitely wasn't in on it in any active sense. It was obvious to Frank that she had panicked when her boyfriend had been killed. She told them the lie about him having lied to her about where he was, hid his files, both paper and digital, in the garage and distanced herself, however inexpertly, from any potential consequences.

"Just so we're clear on this," Frank said, "Paul didn't actually believe that one of these men was his father?"

"No. He knew who his father was. Never spoken to him in his life, but he knew who he was."

"But he intended to convince one of the 25th December men that he, Paul, was his son?"

"Yes." She nodded. "That's right. Or at least," she added, "I mean, that's the impression I got from what little Paul told me about it." And then she started crying again, and Don and Frank waited for her to finish because they knew what crying for effect looked like, and they knew what crying because the boy you loved had been murdered looked like, and they knew that it wasn't at all surprising or unusual to see one person do both things in the course of a single interview.

"And he needed to get to know the men in order to make his story convincing in its detail? Okay," Frank said. "Now how did he come to target this particular group?"

"Just their lifestyle, I suppose. You know, guys who've been single a lot, so they might have kids they don't know about."

"You remember what I said to you, back at your garage, about the computer being moved?" Don said. "Well, this is the same story. If there is a connection between either of you and any of the 25th December lot, then sooner or later our investigation will uncover it. You understand?"

She thought about it for a moment, but it was obvious that she did understand. "We met this guy—well, Paul met him. I think I might have said hello to him once or twice, but that's—"

"Tell us about the guy, Bet," Don said.

"He was one of these December Resistance saddoes—but not like a hardcore member, you know? Just on the fringes, he'd been along once or twice. And Paul met him through work or something like that, I don't know the details. I suppose they got nattering about Christmas, or whatever, and this guy must have said, 'Oh, before I got married I used to belong to this club, it was a real laugh,' or something." She took a sip of water and swallowed noisily. "Something like that, anyway, I don't know."

"This was a couple of years ago?"

"Yeah, but early autumn. I think."

"And this gave Paul an idea for a scam?"

"I suppose so, yeah."

"Or was it something he was already planning, and talking to this chap helped him select a target?"

"I don't know. I think the idea just sort of came up in conversation."

"Conversation between—?"

She looked away. "Well, between Paul and me."

It was her idea, Frank was certain then; the whole thing had been her idea, and that's why she was in such a state about

it. Not only had she initiated a conspiracy to defraud an innocent man—she'd managed to get her boyfriend killed in the
process.

"You understand why we're so interested in all this?" said
Don. "There's a very good chance that the man Paul was
planning to rip off is the man that killed him. So, we need to
know—who was the target?"

"I honestly don't know." She pressed her palms against her
cheeks. "I don't know. I think what it was, I think Paul
couldn't decide who he should go for."

"So what you're saying is, he hadn't made his move yet?"

"I just don't know. Maybe. He never told me much about
it, but I don't think he'd done anything yet."

Except get killed, thought Frank.

I DON'T KNOW," Don said. "She could be lying, or she could
be wrong. I think we've still got to assume that the target of
the paternity scam is our chief suspect."

"Or to put it another way," Frank said, "our only lead."

"That, too, yeah. You have to admit, Frank, it's the most
promising hypothesis so far."

Whatever happened to blackmail? Frank wondered.
"We're saying he—whoever he is—killed the man he believed to be his own son?"

"Possibly." Don lit a cigar. "Or perhaps—and more likely,
I suspect, given the amateurish nature of Paul's scam—the
killer killed the man he knew or guessed to be *pretending* to
be his son."

"Why? Why not just tell him to sod off?"

"That's a good question, Frank. We'll have to ask him
when we get him. Anger, probably. Maybe he can't have kids,
or he has a son he's estranged from, or whatever."

Frank wasn't convinced, but then he hadn't been convinced about the blackmail, either, and the fact was they had

to follow up something. "Either way," he said, "if money is the ultimate motive here, we're agreed that Greg's the only obvious target?"

"Looks like it, so far. What's happened to the checks on bank accounts?" Don asked.

"Be a couple of days yet, apparently."

"Bloody Christmas. But in any case, I think we can assume for the moment that the milkman isn't sitting on a secret fortune, while still getting up at two in the morning every day just for the fun of it."

"Probably. But what about the retired management trainer and the voiceover actor? They'd earn a bit more than a milkman, you'd think."

"They'd have decent, middle-class incomes while they were working, sure. But retired is retired, even on a good pension. And aren't actors on the dole most of the time?"

"On the other hand, it depends what Paul Alsop was after—a one-off sting, or a source of long-term handouts?"

"That's true, Frank. And how high he—or he and his lovely girlfriend, to be accurate—set their sights. A retired management trainer could presumably raise a decent sum by liquidating a few assets. Not a fortune, maybe, but enough to impress Paul and Bet."

"Come to think of it," Frank said, "these days, most people could, if they really had to. If it was worth that much to them. Most people have got a mortgage, a car, maybe a private pension fund. Even the milkman, he's probably got savings."

"And if he hasn't," Don said, "I daresay his parents own their own place, which he'll inherit, or partly inherit, when they die, assuming he hasn't already copped for it."

"So we're back where we started? Any one of them could be the target."

"It's got to be a short, sharp sting, though," Don argued,

"because it'll fall apart if anyone breathes on it. DNA testing would destroy it, but only if it survived long enough to get to that stage."

"Agreed."

"So, the target should be someone who has immediate access to a lump sum. Someone with cash flow. Which still sounds more like Greg Mulford, and his birdie export business, than anyone else."

Frank felt they were getting ahead of themselves—a familiar feeling, when you were working with D.I. Packham. "Are we absolutely clear yet on the details of Paul's con?"

Bet Thomas had insisted that she didn't know any more than she'd already told them, and it was pretty obvious she wasn't going to be easily budged from that position. They hadn't arrested her. As Don had said when they discussed it, "She *has* just been widowed, whatever else she's been up to. And with what we've got on her, we'd never get her to court."

Now, Don said, "We're guessing, to some extent, but I feel on pretty firm ground. Paul would get to know the group, and select his target from among the Decembrists, simply through hanging around with them. Talking to them about themselves, about each other, about their pasts. Flattering them, making them feel young, tempting them to boast to him a bit, to prove that they weren't just poor old middle-aged has-beens."

"From all of which he is able to piece together a reasonable story of who his mother might have been."

"Exactly, 'You remember that girl you spent three nights with in a tent at Glastonbury Festival in 1977? Well, she's my Mum, and I'm twenty-five years old, and I think I've got your nose.'"

"'Oh and by the way,'" Frank filled in, "'I need ten thousand quid to get out of debt, or set myself up in business, or go back to college.'"

"'Or fly your grandson—who've you've never met but

you're really going to love him—to Switzerland for a pioneer-ing operation.' It's something like that, Frank, I'm sure of it. Paul and Bet bank the cheque, then they vanish."

"Doesn't seem the most brilliantly worked-out scheme in criminal history."

"I won't deny that. Thing is, Frank, I've met a lot of scam-mers in my time, some of them quite successful, but I've never yet met a criminal mastermind. It works on the force of the scammer's personality, and the strength of his luck, or it doesn't work at all. The details, in the end, really don't mat-ter that much. It's psychology, not brain surgery."

"Right enough," said Frank.

"There's something else that makes me fancy Greg for this. If he found out anyone was misusing his precious Resistance Movement for monetary gain, he probably would kill them."

"Whether or not he was the target of the con," Frank agreed.

"Like I said, Frank, never underestimate the emotional motive in murder cases."

"As if I would," Frank said. "As if I would."

"ALPHABETICAL LAST TIME, wasn't it?" Don asked, as they walked to the car. "Wasn't that how you chose the order in which we interviewed the suspects?"

"Oh aye," said Frank, pleased to see the D.I. in a mischie-vous mood. "Something like that."

"Well this time, how about assigning numerological val-ues to the letters of their names and then reversing them?"

"Too easy," Frank said, sneering. "Too obvious."

"I suppose you're right. You have to make allowances, I am getting on a bit."

"Besides which, I assumed we were going straight to Greg Mulford, as he's the one you like the look of?"

"No," Don said, sliding into the passenger seat of Frank's

car, and peering up at the sky. "Frank, do you reckon that sky is turning from dull gray to bright gray?"

Frank checked the sky on his side of the car. "Bright gray? Is that an actual, recognized color?"

"I mean, it doesn't look quite as damp as it did an hour ago. Don't you reckon?"

Frank started the car. "Could be, I suppose." He was beginning to pride himself on his ability to produce ambiguous, yet perfectly legitimate answers to mysterious questions. Whether or not this was a skill which he was right to be proud of was another matter, and a matter for another day. "So you don't want to do Greg next?"

"No, not yet. What's the point? We've really not got much now that we didn't have last time we spoke to him. No, tell you what. I wouldn't mind another crack at the old fella— Mr. Management."

"Derek Fleet. Right you are."

"Derek Fleet, that's him. See if he's had time to complete that correspondence course yet."

"Correspondence course?"

"Yeah, the one from the charm school."

"Ugggggghh." Don shuddered and pulled his jacket tighter around him. "These places give me the willies."

"You don't ever use the gym at Division, then? Tone up your triceps a touch, on your day off?"

Don caught the Christmas twinkle in Frank's eye. "Don't be cheeky, Constable." It wasn't only the smell—various sweats masked by various perfumes—of gymnasia that upset him. It wasn't only the vile unnaturalness of the whole idea: people who didn't sweat enough in their real lives—whose ancestors, indeed, had fought for generations for the right *not* to sweat excessively in their real lives—who now worked ever-longer hours at their nonsweating jobs so that they could afford to pay to be sweated in their dwindling leisure time. And what were they training *for?* To go back to their desk jobs! And it wasn't only the repugnant, unrepentant narcissism of the whole idea, a vice which people hid from themselves by renaming it "health." It was all of that, of course, but more than anything it was the simple, undeniable, scientifically verifiable fact that everyone other than professional boxers who had ever belonged to a gym was a lard-headed, pebble-brained, fully-fledged tosspot of a pillocky twat.

Derek Fleet a member of a gym? Gosh, thought Don; there's my nomination for Big Fat Surprise of the Year.

"Have him hoiked out of whichever Dantean circle he's hiding in, will you, Frank?"

Fleet had, apparently, been on an exercise bicycle when he'd answered his mobile—ecstatic, no doubt, at the opportunity the ring tone gave him to demonstrate his indispensability. Don would be buggered if he'd interview him on a stage of his own choosing. At home was one thing; there, the suspect's territorial advantage was offset by the detective's opportunities for espionage. But trying to grill a man about murder while he runs seven miles on a conveyor belt? No, thanks; why, Don would almost rather take him to the cop shop than put up with that.

The interview eventually took place in an abomination called a "juice bar," where Don declined to join Frank and their guest in a glass of grapefruit, priced to rival a champagne cocktail in a West End hotel. Instead he demanded a glass of tap water and was significantly put out when he was served with just that, nice and cold, in a sparklingly clean glass, and accompanied by a graceful smile from the girl behind the counter.

"Now then, Derek. We're more or less at the end of this investigation, just tying up some loose ends before we make an arrest, you understand. So, I'd be glad if you could tell me when Paul Alsop first told you about his family history?"

Fleet sipped his fruit juice. "Don't know what you're talking about, pal. Sorry."

"Don't know what we're talking about? Don't know anything about Paul learning everything he could about you and your fellow Decembrists, with the intention of falsely claiming paternity from one of you, and hitting you for a sum of money?"

"No." Fleet raised his glass to his lips, looked at it and put it down again. "Not a clue, I'm afraid."

"Well, that's fine," Don said, half rising from his seat. "If that's the truth, then that's fine. I ought to mention, I suppose, just to be fair, that Paul's computer and paper files are being examined by police experts as we speak." On Boxing Day? he thought; fat bloody chance!

Fleet's bluff was not called quite so easily. No doubt he'd taught classes on the subject during his management training days. His expression was more calculating than panicky. Even so, there was enough there, Don reckoned, to be worth persisting with.

"Could you pass me the ashtray, Derek?"

Fleet was sufficiently distracted from his surroundings to almost fall for that. He looked around for a second, perhaps two, before shaking his head at Don. "Very funny, Inspector. If you want to smoke, I suggest you go and stand out by the dustbins along with all the other losers."

"You seem distracted, Derek. Anything you want to tell us, before we find it out ourselves?"

"Only this," Fleet said, spinning his empty glass slowly around on its coaster. "That if that boy was running a scam on us, trying to find out details of our past lives like you say, then he wouldn't have found it at all difficult, I'm afraid. We're all a bunch of blabbermouths."

"Even you?"

"All of us. None more so than any other. It's only natural, under the circumstances."

"But you weren't his target?" Frank asked.

"No, not me." Fleet shook his head, firmly. "I've always practiced safe sex."

"Really," Don said, standing for real now, and signaling Frank to do likewise. "Both times?"

NINE

"GOT HIM WORRIED, anyway," Frank said, in the fitness center car park.

Don was glad to hear that; he'd thought the same, but you never knew how it looked to someone else and it was good to have his own feeling confirmed. "What's he worried about, though? That's the question. I hate to say it, but I don't get the sense that he was the victim of the plot. Do you?"

"No, it was something else, wasn't it? That bit about being a bunch of blabbermouths sounded from the heart."

"Yes, I noticed that. Could be that's what he's feeling guilty about—that he's the blabbermouth who led Paul to Greg."

"That something he said allowed Paul to target Greg for his paternity scam?"

Something in Frank's tone made Don look up. "Yeah. You don't like that?"

"I'm not sure. The thing is, Derek's not one of the originals. And he's not exactly Greg's favorite person, whatever he might think to the contrary. So would he actually know that much about Greg's past?"

"How long does it take to get to know someone? Paul didn't necessarily need to discover deeply buried secrets about his victim—just some little, casual hint that could set him on the right road."

Greg Mulford was neither at home nor at work, but they got him eventually on his cell phone. He told them he was in a business meeting—in a pub or restaurant, judging by the background sounds—and suggested that, if the detectives really needed to see him urgently, they join him for a car conference.

"For a what?" Don asked, when this proposal had been conveyed to him.

"A car conference," Frank repeated. "I imagine it's import-export speak for talking to someone whilst sitting in a car."

"How big's his car?" Don demanded. "Has his car got a kettle in it?"

"I'll tell him yes, shall I?"

"When he holds one of these car conferences, are there full creche facilities for those delegates with ongoing child care responsibilities?"

"Thank you, Mr. Mulford, that'll be fine," Frank said, as he wrote down Mulford's directions. "Next to the tenpin bowling, okay; I've got you. We'll be about fifteen minutes."

"Tell him we'll meet him at reception, and if we miss him there we're sure to run into each other during the induction session in the Rear Bumper Ballroom."

It took them ten minutes—Frank never underestimated in such cases—and they decided to hold the conference in Frank's car, rather than Greg Mulford's. "No offence, Greg," Don told him, "but you just don't offer the amenities which the modern conference-goer takes for granted. At least Frank's got a CD player, even if he did forget the bowl of fruit and the scented handwipes."

Greg sat in the back, with Frank; Don took the jam sandwich seat. "We've made a fair bit of progress since we last saw you, Greg."

"That's good news." His accent made it sound like a question; Don decided to treat it as one.

"Well, we think that is good news, yes. Whether you'll think so, I'm not so sure."

"Anything that gets you nearer to catching the murderer, of course it's good."

"All right then, Greg. Something that might get us a lot closer to catching the murderer is for you to tell us about Paul trying to con you."

Mulford looked from one cop to the other. His face said, *You're playing a game, but I don't know what it's about.* His voice said: "What are you on about? What con?"

"We have reason to believe," Frank said, acting on a nod received from the D.I., "that Paul Alsop joined the 25th December Resistance Movement with the sole intention of running a scam."

"Shit," Mulford said. His mouth stayed open, but he didn't seem able to say anything else.

"His files are being examined at the moment, and we expect to learn more details from them, but we understand that the nature of the con was that Paul approached one of the members of your group with the fraudulent intention of claiming to be that man's illegitimate son."

"Bloody hell."

Again, Mulford seemed unlikely to expand on these few syllables, so Don decided it was time to loosen his chords a bit. "A paternity scam, Greg, you see? And we think that's probably why he was killed. And one other thing—we think perhaps it was you that Paul was trying to con."

"Me?" Now his mouth closed—snapped shut, in fact, before flying open again. "No, you've got it wrong, mate. He never mentioned anything like that to me. Christ, if he had, I'd have— I mean, he never so much as hinted at anything like that at all."

"All right, Greg, let's say it wasn't you that he was—"

"It wasn't!"

"But can you remember any conversation you ever had with Paul which now, in the light of this information, strikes you as odd? Did he seem to take an unusual interest, for instance, in any—"

"Oh, my God," Mulford said. "So that's what all that was about."

Don waited, patiently, for about two and a half seconds. "What *what* was about, Greg?"

"On Christmas Eve," Mulford began, and then fell quiet again, his brow wrinkled and his fingers tapping against the car door.

"On Christmas Eve?" Don prompted, excited by Mulford's liturgical slip. That the Resistance Movement's leader had called December 24th 'Christmas Eve,' must surely mean that whatever it was he was about to tell them was something pretty earth-shattering.

"Neil O'Brien phoned me. About ten, eleven at night."

"What did he want?"

"He was asking about a girl called Trudy … "

"Yes," Don said. "Who is Trudy?"

"She used to drink in the pub, where we all met. Years ago."

"How many years ago?" Frank asked.

"Well, that was it—we were trying to remember. Neil was on about that. He was, like, really insistent about it. How many years ago was it when we'd all known her."

"And did you come to any conclusion?"

Mulford shrugged. "Best we could work it out, it was about twenty-five years ago. Give or take." He clicked his tongue. "Which, given what you've just told me, is possibly…significant, shall we say?"

"How well did Neil know this Trudy?"

"Yeah, well—I'm afraid you're going to like that bit, too."

"There was a sexual relationship between them?"

Mulford made no verbal reply. He merely moved his eyes and mouth in a way which made it clear that, much as he would like to, he couldn't actually deny the nature of Neil and Trudy's friendship.

"Did this relationship last long?"

"I don't know. I don't think so. It wasn't anything very serious, I don't think—just a casual thing, as far as I remember. We were all a lot younger, you know, and a pretty sociable bunch. Lots of parties, and all that. Lot of pairing off."

"What else did Neil ask about her—apart from how long ago he'd known her?"

"Just, what had become of her."

"What did you tell him?"

"Couldn't tell him much. Said I thought she'd got married, moved up to Scotland, that was the last I'd heard of her. And that was years ago."

"How did he react to that?" Frank asked.

"He wanted to know if anyone we knew was still in touch with her, so I gave him a couple of phone numbers, e-mail addresses, of people I'm in touch with who might possibly be in touch with people who might—"

"And was that the end of the conversation?"

"Pretty much. He thanked me. I said 'See you tomorrow?' He said, 'Yeah, don't worry,' and that was it."

"It didn't seem odd, all this?" Don asked. "That he should suddenly ring you out of the blue, when he was going to be seeing you the next day, and start interrogating you about a woman he hadn't seen in decades?"

Mulford looked irritated by the question. "You're asking that with hindsight. At the time, no. We've been friends a long time, we often talk crap late at night. I assumed he was just having an attack of nostalgia, to be honest—possibly alcohol-related."

"Yeah," Don allowed, "well, it was Christmas, after all."

"RIGHT," DON SAID, as Frank drove. "Let's try and get a chronology of this worked out. Paul gets in touch with Neil some time in the last few days, probably Christmas Eve itself—"

"Hence the urgency of Neil's call to Greg."

"Exactly. So presumably Paul has found out about this old girlfriend only recently."

"Must've. I can't imagine Paul, from what we know of his limited con man skills, sitting on his information for long."

"Neil O'Brien checks out Paul's story, as far as he can, and with results we can't know at the moment. But either way—whether he believes that Paul's his unknown son or not—he has a confrontation with him at the December 25th meeting, and caves his head in."

"Has a confrontation?" Frank asked. "Or engineers one?"

Don nodded enthusiastically. "That's the question, isn't it! The only remaining question—was this killing done in a rage, or was it planned?"

The milkman was in bed when they arrived at his flat. Don had rather hoped he would be, and for that reason hadn't rung him to say they were on their way.

"I didn't ring you to say we were on our way, Neil," Don told him, "because I wanted to let you sleep as long as possible."

"I wasn't asleep," O'Brien said, blinking and pale in his tartan dressing gown. "Just having a read."

"Anything good?"

"P. G. Wodehouse. I felt the need of an uplift, as you can understand."

Don understood well. "Jeeves, was it?"

"Blandings," said O'Brien.

"Ah, that'd do it. You can always rely on the Empress to lift the fallen wotsits."

"It is what she does best," O'Brien agreed. "And what can I do for you, tonight?"

Still smiling, Don replied, "Stop fucking lying, for starters."

"Okay." O'Brien sat down. Then he stood up to put the fire on. "All right, Inspector. Fair enough. I'm sorry."

Don twitched in Frank's direction, and was gratified to see

that the lad already had his notebook in his hand. If there was a pre-caution confession coming, they'd at least have it down verbatim and contemporary. "You knew about Paul Alsop's nasty scheme before we did, Neil. And we ask ourselves—why didn't he tell us about this? I can think of one obvious reason."

"There *is* an obvious reason," O'Brien said, "but it's not the one you mean. I didn't kill the little shit, and I don't know who did."

"But he did attempt to con you? And you chose to conceal this fact from police officers investigating his death."

Huddled over the fire—although, as far as Don could tell, the central heating was already doing a perfectly good job of maintaining a comfortable temperature—O'Brien spoke with his back to the policemen. "I knew how it looked, Inspector. And, no offence intended, but once the police have a hot suspect, they're not exactly famous for being unable to find evidence to match. I just hoped you'd get a confession, or at least a lead or something, before I *needed* to say anything." He turned his head to look the D.I. in the face. "I would have said something eventually, of course. I'm not completely irresponsible. But the fact is, it wasn't relevant, and you'd have thought it was, so all you'd have been doing by following it is wasting time."

There were certain people, Don reflected, who could chop your head off and then explain why they'd done you a favor, probably with reference to toothache and catarrh. He knew, because he'd spent much of his adult life being paid to listen to them. "I'll be straight with you, Neil—if you want to convince us not to nick you on suspicion of murder, you're going to have to do better than you're doing at the moment. You admit you had a motive."

"Not for murder, I didn't! For giving him a good slap, perhaps, to teach him not to be such a little turd—except that he wasn't all that little, not compared to me. And he's a lot younger than me."

Don wasn't having that, and he made sure his face showed it. "This wasn't a wrestling match, Neil. He was killed by being whacked on the bonce with a lump of arboreous matter."

"Yeah, well. Not by me, he wasn't."

No confession, then. Just as well, Don thought; save that for the formal interview, with the tape running and the solicitor sitting in. "Paul told you he was your son, by a girl you knew years ago?"

"Trudy, right."

"And when did you realize he was lying to you?"

O'Brien laughed. "Half a second after he said it! He was a useless con man. Pathetic. Anyway, just for peace of mind, I checked it out. I spoke to Greg. He gave me some names. I followed it up and it very quickly became obvious that his story was one hundred percent bollocks."

"And this angered you so much that you killed him the next day."

"No way. I was going to have a word with him, that's all."

"And did you?"

"Didn't get a chance to, he got himself killed."

"But not," Frank said, "by the one person who had a motive to do so?"

"Tell you what, Neil, that's a good point," Don added. "If you didn't kill him, who did?"

"I've been asking myself that, nonstop, ever since it happened." He turned the fire down to minimum; didn't seem able to make up his mind whether he was hot or cold, Don thought. "The only thing I can think of is, perhaps he tried his con job on someone else, too."

"Any idea who?"

"No, no. I don't even know *if*. I'm only guessing."

"Nobody else has mentioned anything to you?"

"No, nobody's said anything."

"And you haven't spoken about any of this to anyone else?" Frank asked. "So, who do you think Paul got Trudy's name from?"

O'Brien's face showed disgust. "Could be any one of us, to be honest. We like to talk, he liked to listen. He wasn't much of a con man, but he got that bit right."

"He did indeed," said Don. "And I think I know who he got the name from."

TEN

DURING THE DRIVE to Watford, Don kept half an eye on the sky, but he didn't think he could see much change. Not many stars out; another cloudy night, another gray day to follow. So much for Christmas.

He just about allowed Derek Fleet to get his front door open before putting to him the one question they'd driven all this way to ask.

"It was you that told Paul Alsop about Neil's old girl-friend, wasn't it?"

Fleet tried to look unconcerned, attempted a bit of bluster, but the results were pretty feeble by his standards. "Might have been, for all I know. So what?"

"So I'm arresting you on suspicion of murder," Don said. "You do not have to say anything, but it may harm your defense…"

NO DENOUEMENT SUIT, Frank noted; perhaps because of the practicalities of the season. In major cases like this he was used to seeing the D.I., in preparation for a formal interview with a suspect under caution, change into his suit, have his hair trimmed, do his breathing exercises. None of that, this time. Indeed, Don seemed edgy, and that made Frank feel a little uneasy, too. Barring a confession, they'd got basically nothing on this bloke. And looking at the confident, sneering face of their adversary as he sat opposite them in the inter-

view room, it was hard to imagine what might shake a confession loose from his tight lips.

"This is the theory we're working on, Derek," Don said.
"Let's see how it accords with your version of reality, shall we?"

"Should be interesting, Inspector. Carry on."

At least his lawyer hasn't insisted on the no-comment
route, Frank thought. But probably only because he doesn't
reckon his client's in any danger.

"We believe," Don continued, "that you killed Paul Alsop
in anger, having discovered that he was attempting to blackmail one of your fellow members with a paternity con. And
worse, that it was you yourself who had inadvertently provided him with his ammunition. Whether this was premedi-
ated or a spur-of-the-moment act, we don't yet know, but we
do know how important to you that group—"

"Sorry to interrupt, Inspector." Fleet treated his solicitor
to a relaxed grin. "Bad manners, I know, but I think I can probably put an end to this nonsense right here."

"Oh, yes?"

"Oh, yes." Fleet rubbed his hands together. "How exactly
did I find out that my friend Neil was being blackmailed by
the deceased?"

Bloody good question, Frank thought, while concentrating
on keeping his face as blank as possible.

"Did Neil tell me? I don't think he did, and I don't think
he's told you he did. In fact, if you ask him, I think he'll specifically tell you that he didn't." Another happy grin.

"Well, that's all very—"

"Or did Alsop himself tell me? That seems exceptionally
unlikely, doesn't it? Be an odd way for a con man to proceed,
I'd have thought."

"Naturally there are details which we don't yet—"

"And the thing is," Fleet said, this time with a smile each
for the solicitor, for Frank, and even for Don, "if I didn't know

about this scam you're going on about, then what, exactly, was my motive for killing the little creep?"

The solicitor coughed. "Derek."

"Sorry. Apologies. I should have said 'the late lamented deceased.' I don't mean to be disrespectful." Fleet took a drink of water. "To the verminous little crook."

Frank glanced at his boss. He couldn't help it, and he was disconcerted to catch Don glancing back at him. The look that passed momentarily between them said it all: *It was definitely him. He's as good as boasting about it. But we can't prove it, and he won't admit it.*

Evidently the despairing glance did not escape the lawyer's eye. "You must admit, D.I. Packham, that my client makes a fair point. With no prior knowledge of the victim's 'scam,' as you describe it, you are going to have a hard job establishing motive. And since you seem to have very little else…" He sighed, and looked at his watch. "Well, I really think we might all be getting home to our beds, don't you?"

"Sad thing is," Don said, clearly driven beyond the point of discretion by Fleet's sarcastic smile, "there was no point you killing Paul. The other three couldn't have a lower opinion of you than they do now, even if you were arrested for badger baiting, child molesting and unsolicited telesales all on the same day."

Fleet erupted from his seat. "That's lies!" he screamed. "You don't know what the hell you're talking about!" His solicitor pressed on his shoulders, trying to force him back down into his chair, at the same time whispering urgently in his ear. Frank moved his right hand toward the panic button, just in case. "I have had it up to here with bastard liars," Fleet said quietly, his eyes boring into Don's face.

"Is that right?" Don began, but Frank was too fast for him.

"Time for a tea break," he said, thinking that he and the solicitor were like seconds at a duel, trying to keep their men

to the gentlemen's code while the men themselves would
rather tear each other's throats out and be done with it. "Interview suspended at ten-thirty…"

DON WASN'T SMOKING. Frank was sipping coffee from the
machine, but Don was just pacing the corridor in small circles, muttering. He didn't seem depressed, exactly, Frank
thought; more anxious than anything. As well he might be,
of course. If it turned out he'd mistimed the arrest… Still, it
couldn't be a good sign that, despite all the No Smoking
signs, Don wasn't smoking.

"We're going to have to prove that he knew about Paul's
scam," Don said, after a few minutes of circling.

"The thing is," Frank said, trying not to sound too tentative, because this had to be said, "what if he didn't?"

"What?" Don asked. "You think he's innocent?"

Frank held up a peacemaking hand. "No, of course not. He
did it. But I can't answer his question to my own satisfaction.
How did he know about the scam? Neil says he told no one,
and Paul certainly wouldn't have told anyone."

"Look," Don explained, the patience in his voice sounding forced, "if he didn't know, he wouldn't have killed Paul.
We're sure he *did* kill Paul, ergo he *did* know, ergo we have
to prove it. All right?"

The logic sounded a little circular to Frank, but he knew
when he was beaten. "Fair enough, Don, aye. Where are we
going to get the evidence from?"

"Nothing new from forensics, or the computer files?"

"Nothing expected from the former. The men all spent the
day together, so they all carried traces of each other. And nothing imminent from the latter."

"Because they're on a seasonal go-slow," Don guessed.
"Lazy sods. Okay, I think what we'll do now is bail him,
make sure his so-called mates in the Resistance Movement

know what's happening, and hope one of them might have seen something—maybe without realizing it—and that Derek's arrest will jerk their memories. Or consciences, whichever."

Frank opened the door to the interview room, and immediately his field of vision seemed filled by Derek Fleet's hate-filled face. Fleet was looking at the D.I., not at Frank, but even so the obvious strength of his antipathy was almost a physical force. Frank was about to enter the room, when Don clutched at his arm and hauled him back out.

"You're right, Frank—you're bloody right!" Don stared at the ground, his lips working silently and his fingers still spasmodically gripping at his colleague's arm. "Yeah…I'd put money on it. You're right."

"Oh, good," Frank said, slightly distracted by the pain of the first wrist-burn he'd received since primary school.

"Are you wearing a protective helmet, D.C. Mitchell?" Don's tone was so intense that Frank actually raised his free hand halfway to his head, before realizing that the question had to be rhetorical. "Just follow my lead in there, all right?"

"As always."

"And don't be in too much of a hurry to punch the panic button. Okay?"

Panic button…? Oh great, Frank thought, it's going to be one of *those* sessions.

Don didn't hang about. As soon as the tapes were running and the caution had been restated for the record, he carried on where he'd left off.

"They can't stand you, Derek. They think you're an out-and-out tosser."

Fleet growled. "You know nothing about it. You've got no friends, what do you know?"

"They're not your friends, Derek. They're desperate for an excuse to dump you. They reckon you're a drunk, a loudmouth, a parasite. You ask the constable, here—he's got it all written down in his official notebook."

Frank tapped his breast pocket, nodded, and smiled while raising his eyebrows. He stopped when he had a sudden mental image of himself as Stan Laurel.

"To be fair, mind," Don continued, "they'll probably be glad you killed Paul. Because it means they'll never have to see your sarky face again."

That seemed to do the trick. Fleet's lava flow of abuse continued uninterrupted for one and a half minutes, by Frank's watch. The solicitor did his best, but his best was, to be blunt, useless. He looked to Frank for help, but this time Frank kept his face frozen and his arms folded.

The crucial words occurred about halfway through the ninety-second tirade. "It was lies when that bastard said it, it's lies when you say it! They'd do *anything* for me, that lot."

Right man, wrong motive, Frank thought, now seeing what Don had seen. Enlightenment clearly fell on Fleet's solicitor at the same moment, and he redoubled his efforts to silence his client.

"Shut up nagging, baldy, or I'll sack you," Fleet told him. But he did at least sit down.

"Excellent motivational technique, Derek," Don said. "I can see why you did so well in the competitive world of management training."

Frank shot Don a warning look and, thank the small god of coppers' Christmases, the D.I. wasn't too far gone in his triumph to heed it. In fact, he did better even than Frank had hoped, and asked Fleet if he would like time to consult with his lawyer.

"Do I, bollocks!"

"You're quite sure? Well, Derek, any time you wish to break off from giving us your statement in order to talk privately with your brief, you only have to say. That is your right at any time, you understand?"

Derek assured all present—and posterity's representative, the tape machine—that he understood. His fury seemed spent now. Frank had witnessed this moment in the process so often in so many interview rooms. It was time for the story.

Derek Fleet and Paul Alsop had met up from time to time during the past year, for a pint, a curry, a chat. It wasn't necessary for Fleet to state the obvious, even if he'd allowed himself to acknowledge it: that Paul had been the only other member of the Movement who had been willing to spend time in his company between the December 25th get-togethers. To the two detectives, at least, the reason for Paul's sociability was equally obvious: he was pumping Fleet for information useful to his plan.

That plan nearly complete, Alsop knew his time with the Movement was almost over. He never expected to see any of them again once he'd collected his pay-off from Neil O'Brien. He had nothing to lose—and pleasure to gain—by telling Fleet the truth.

During the hide-and-seek in Jubilee Park, the two men had happened to find themselves sharing the same hiding place. Fleet asked Alsop if he fancied getting together for New Year's Eve.

"What did he say?" Don asked, his voice sympathetic, his eyes sparkling with tension.

"He laughed. 'No way!' he said. I just shrugged, you know. No big deal, I said, if he didn't fancy it. I'd probably be seeing some of the other lads anyway."

"And he laughed again?"

Fleet swallowed, and took a deep breath. "Little bastard. He came out with all these lies—same as you, Packham. He couldn't stand to see how close I was to those boys. He started going on about how they all hated me and they wouldn't spend New Year's Eve with me if I paid them a million quid each. All sorts of lying crap."

"And so you killed him?"

"Didn't mean to kill him. I just pushed him."

"Thumped him?"

"Pushed him! That's all. Then he came back at me, swinging at me. I tripped, I went down. I grabbed a stick or something, stood up, whacked him with it." He looked at his solicitor, and then at Frank. He wouldn't look at Don. "Must've hit him harder than I thought. Anyway—that shut him up, him and his lies."

Again, the dutiful solicitor suggested a break for consultation; again, Don asked Derek if that was what he wanted; again, Derek declined.

"Do you think they'll kick me out of the Movement?" he asked Don, and then he started crying. "Next Christmas is going to be crap, away from my friends."

"You never know," Don said. "Look on the bright side—maybe you can set up a branch of the 25th December Resistance Movement in prison."

"SAD BUSINESS," DON SAID, hours later, the formalities all complete for the night.

"Murder usually is," Frank said.

"No, I meant the Movement. Bunch of friends, been through it all over the years—there's just no saying whether they'll get over this. No saying what they'll all be doing next Christmas."

"I suppose not. Bound to be fallout."

"I hope they're still together." Don sighed. "Still—at least it got us out of Christmas, so it can't be all bad."

"Will it stick, do you suppose?" Frank asked. "An unsupported confession."

"Touch and go. We'll have to hope Paul Alsop was a good note-taker, and that something corroborative comes up in his files."

But that would corroborate the wrong motive, Frank thought. And then he thought about getting home, and reminded himself that he should let the lawyers worry about the rest of it. *Our job was to identify the killer, and we've done that.* "I suppose it is a pretty full confession—not much wriggle room."

"And made in front of an impotently protesting lawyer," Don added, with a smile. "How many times did I ask Derek if he wanted to consult his brief in private—seven, eight? Besides, his account contradicts the physical evidence that there was no struggle; he's still lying, and that'll count against him."

Frank started to say good-night, but Don interrupted, said there was something he wanted to show him. "Come over to my car for a moment, would you? Bring your torches."

"Sure," Frank said, stifling a yawn.

"I'd have given it to you last week," Don said, opening the boot of his car, "but I kept hoping it would snow."

"It's…Don, I don't know what to say, it's a beauty." It was, in truth, the flashiest, best-made, most expensive-looking sled Frank had ever seen in his life. It was as far removed from the tea tray of his own childhood as a space rocket is from a paper airplane.

"It's for young Joe."

"Aye, I guessed. Thanks, it's fantastic. He'll be thrilled."

Don sighed again, and looked up at the dull sky. "No sign of snow. I'm sorry, Frank, there's nothing I can do about that."

Frank started to make a joke about detective inspectors and gods, but just in time he realized that Don really meant what he said; he was actually apologizing for the lack of snow. He thanked his boss again, promised him that a thank-you letter from Joseph would be on his desk by 0800 hours Monday next, and finally got away before Don could apologize again about the weather. He wasn't sure why, but he really didn't want to hear that twice in one evening.

He was just turning into his drive when his mobile rang.

"Yes, Don?"

"Frank, have you got any relatives in Scotland?"

"Have I what?"

"I just checked the weather map…they're expecting snow up there. If you want a few days off, take Joe up north, I can swing that for you no problem."

Frank switched off the engine, took a deep breath, saw the hall light come on in his house, and said: "Don't worry about it, Don. It's got to snow sooner or later. It always does."

THE THREE
WISE WOMEN

by Linda Berry

ONE

As I studied my partially trimmed Christmas tree, I was definitely letting myself get into the mood. Some part of every Christmas season of my life has been spent in the old house that now belongs to me. No wonder, then, that when Christmas decorations start popping up in malls and stores I fall into an orgy of seasonal nostalgia. That's good and bad. I'm beginning to think nostalgia is just a rose-colored word for loss.

A good part is thinking of the warmth and love that seemed to emanate from the tall tree that always stood in the bowed front window. The couch would be moved farther into the room to make space for it so that the tree and its nook seemed like a special magical room. That warm magic sustained me through the loss of my parents in a car accident, the loss of my husband in a hunting accident, which made me a widow before I reached thirty, and the loss of my grandmother, who left the family home to me.

Good, too, is choosing my own tree from all the possibilities in the woods behind the house to fit its special spot, and going through the ornaments and decorations, deciding, just as though it's never been decided before, exactly where to put each one.

Less good is having to puzzle, maybe even fret, over what gifts to get for my near and dear, which includes Phil Pittman—growing nearer and dearer all the time—and the family of Henry Huckabee, my cousin and my boss. Hen's the chief of police here in Ogeechee, and I'm the first and so far only female officer on the force, hired by Hen under duress since he's not convinced he ought to be putting women, especially women in his own family, at risk. We have an ongoing tug-of-war between what I see as his protective, paternalistic, chauvinistic instincts and what he apparently sees as my willful, petulant boredom with any jobs fit for womenfolk. Hen's family, which is, after all, my family, includes his wife, Teri; his daughter, Delcie; and his mother, my aunt Lulu. It was Aunt Lulu who tipped the scales in favor of my becoming a police officer by threatening to quit making banana pudding for Hen if he didn't hire me.

Also on the not-so-good side of the ledger is disappointment. How can Christmas possibly be all we want it to be? I never did get a sled, for instance, in spite of asking for one year after year, and it was a long time before I understood that even if I had a sled it wouldn't bring the necessary snow to south Georgia with it.

Really not good is facing the fact, unavoidable for a police officer, that the Christmas season always brings an increase in burglary, robbery, domestic violence, suicide, and driving under the influence of a wide range of Christmas spirits. Just the week before, Christmas gifts that had been collected by area churches for distribution to families served by the Department of Family and Children's Services had been stolen from a van in a parking lot over in Vidalia. Who could have needed those toys and warm clothes more than the people they were intended for? I was holding a broken ornament—How in the name of creation, as my grandmother would have said, can something that was packed away in one piece come out broken?—and trying to resist the sinking of my Christmas spirit when I realized it was time to get downtown for the Christmas parade. Interesting as it is to see what the businesses, schools, churches and civic organizations will come up with from year to year, that wasn't the reason I needed to watch the parade. I'd promised Hen's daughter, the delightful, darling Delcie, that I'd be there to wave at her when she rode past on the fire truck with Santa Claus.

The parade would wind its way up Main Street from the staging area south of town to the courthouse, where it would take a left on Court Street just past the judging stand and wander west for a while before petering out. I live a couple of blocks north of the intersection of Main and Court, so a brisk walk would bring me to a spot near the end of the route in good time, and, if I was lucky, improve my mood. I slung on a jacket against the late-afternoon damp chill and started walking, aiming to catch the parade from the upper gallery of the old hotel that houses the historical society and visitor information center. When I got there, the narrow gallery was occupied by a trio of senior citizens who'd settled into the cane-bottomed rockers on the gallery. I recognized Ellis and Bernice Hodges and Stella Strickland, all of whom had at least eighty years behind them.

"Room for one more?" I asked.

"Sure, if you'll pardon me if I don't get up," Ellis said. He was wearing a neon-orange knit hunting cap and had a woolly blanket around his shoulders. Practically nothing of him was exposed except his face, a wizened little object that brings to mind a walnut, until you notice the mischievous eyes. Then, monkey is a better comparison.

"A gentleman would offer her his chair," Stella said. She's small and wiry and wears a short spiky haircut that sets off what even at her age are sultry good looks.

"Thanks, anyway," I said. "I'll give you full points for manners, but I'd just as soon stand."

"Thought I never would get these women up those stairs," Ellis said.

"You didn't know better, you'd think he had to walk behind us to catch us if we fell, not the other way around." This came from Bernice, Ellis's wife. Her round face and white curls made me think of Mrs. Santa Claus, especially since she was wearing a bright red jacket. "Truth is," Bernice went on, "Stella and I had to take turns goosing him to get him up here."

"And I've got the bruises to prove it," Ellis said. "You want to see?"

"No, thank you."

"Here it comes." Ellis leaned forward.

A sleek red convertible bearing a sign advertising Dawson Motors turned the corner and headed our way. It carried the mayor, this year's parade marshall, since Miss Georgia Sweet Onion had a prior commitment.

Little Miss and Mr. Ogeechee Christmas came next, then cheerleaders from the county high school, performing elaborate choreography, then a clown in a rainbow wig, tossing candies to bystanders.

"You bein' the po-lice, you probably know all about the murder they had here," Ellis said, darting a quick glance in my direction before he turned back toward the clown.

A murder they had here? Like it was a party, or something? Here? "Where?" I asked.

"Right here in this hotel," he answered.

"I don't remember a murder here," I said.

"No way you could remember it, hon," Stella said. "It was back in the thirties, way before you saw the light of day."

"Poor man had his head bashed in. Was it a hammer, Bernice?" Ellis asked.

"Why're you asking me?"

Her husband might not have heard her question. He clearly didn't need her answer to his question. "His own hammer, they said. He was a carpenter, one of them helpin' build the prison. Never solved it, either. Policin' bein' what it is these days, you'da probably solved it right off the bat, with DNA or somethin'."

"Modern technology makes a big difference," I admitted.

We watched a flatbed truck with Mary, Joseph and three wise men all waving and smiling, while the pig and goat filling in for the more usual camels, oxen, and sheep, squalled and burrowed in the pine straw that surely wasn't what they had in the manger in Bethlehem. The baby in Mary's arms began bawling along with the animals, and a golden star bounced from the end of a fishing pole suspended from the cab. Outstanding!

"Man got killed," Ellis said, "and it took 'em a while to find him. Startin' to smell."

"Was not. Don't make it sound worse than it was," Bernice said. "They found him the next day, the next afternoon. He'd just been dead overnight, as far as anybody could tell."

"Y'all sure do seem to know a lot about it," I said.

"Ought to. We worked here back then, me and Stella." Bernice said. "And old numbnuts here was always hanging around." Her husband's eyes glittered.

Bernice continued. "Back in the thirties, when they were

building the prison, that was the heyday of the hotel business in Ogeechee. They needed all kinds of workers, builders, you know. Carpenters, plumbers, electricians, everything, and most of the ones who didn't live right around here would take a room by the week. That's who got killed, one of them."

"Josh Tippins." This came from Stella.

"Josh Tippins. That's right." Ellis nodded agreement. "Got his head bashed in right there in his room one night."

Conversation stalled, drowned out by the marching band from the high school. When they were out of earshot, Ellis darted a sly glance at Stella. "They'da found him sooner, and maybe done a better job of findin' out who killed him if they'd had a better idea when it happened, 'cept the maid who shoulda cleaned his room, and woulda found him, called in sick that day."

"I *was* sick," Stella said.

"Cost you, too," Ellis said, apparently pleased to have gotten a rise out of her. "If you'd showed up, you coulda beat the police to the box of chocolate-covered cherries they found on the dresser. That's always been your favorite candy, hasn't it?"

"Always has," Stella said, with a meditative look. "I don't remember any talk about chocolate-covered cherries, but if you know so much about it, Ellis, you being on the inside track and all, you should have snagged it for me. I'd've been ever so grateful!" She added this last with a mischievous glance at Bernice.

"Nuh-uh. Nuh-uh! I was goin' with Bernice at the time and if she'd caught me givin' candy to another woman I never would have been able to get her to marry me. There might even have been another murder. She's jealous as all get-out."

"Better step back, y'all, in case a lightning bolt hits him,"

Bernice said. Then, to Ellis, "What you think I got to be jealous about? Anybody'd take you off my hands'd be doing me a favor."

A float featuring strings of twinkling colored lights that wound up around supports and roof-poles came our way. Girls in festive dresses danced while a musical ensemble—guitar, accordion, trumpet—played "Feliz Navidad."

"Nice," Stella said.

"About the murder," I asked. "You say the police never did solve it. Did they have any suspects?"

"Not that they were willin' to admit," Ellis said.

"There was always so much coming and going at the hotel, you know," Stella added, "it was hard to keep track of people."

"That was a long time ago," Bernice said. "I remember telling the police back then I didn't know anything about it. If I didn't know then, I sure don't know now. This isn't anything to be talking about at the Christmas parade. Why don't y'all just watch the parade? I don't know why you're bringing it up in the first place."

"Well, I don't know, either," Ellis said. "Sittin' here right outside the room where it happened made me think of it, that's all."

"It was a shame," Stella said. "He was a nice, quiet boy. Seems like I remember he'd been planning to go off for the weekend, since it was so close to Christmas, and then came back for some reason. Is that what you remember, Bernice?"

"I told you I don't remember."

"I'm surprised y'all remember as much as you do, since it was so long ago," I said.

"Well, he was somebody we all knew," Stella said.

"And it was the biggest excitement we'd ever had around

here," Ellis added. "Not to mention that the police talked to everybody, which sort of fixed it all in our minds."

We turned our attention to the entry from one of the onion farms. They'd tried to construct a snowman out of cold-storage onions, and I didn't think it was much of a success.

"Some people had the opinion the police didn't try too hard," Ellis said. "They said since he wasn't from here, nobody cared much, so nobody stayed after 'em."

Was he harping on the subject simply to get a rise out of me? I was trying to decide whether it was worth my trouble to come to the defense of that long-gone police force when the fire truck turned the corner. "There's my niece," I said, waving at Delcie. She'd managed to get right up next to Santa Claus.

The Santa Claus-fire truck-Delcie entry was the end of the parade, so I bid farewell to my fellow spectators and ambled over to the food booths on the courthouse grounds. By the time I'd worked my way through a bowl of chili and most of a funnel cake, the judges had worked their way through the dozen or so categories that would receive trophies. My choice for best overall would have been the one from the library—children prancing around encased in what looked like oversize Christmas storybooks—but the judges went with the one from a church, featuring carolers dressed as if they expected snow.

I swallowed the last of my funnel cake and went to watch Phil Pittman photograph representatives from the winning entries with their trophies. Best Church, Best Non-Motorized, and Best School were milling around, waiting when I got there. As publisher, editor, writer, and photographer of the *Ogeechee Beacon*, Phil makes his bread and butter letting the community know what's going on, or, according to some people, merely confirming what everybody already knows, but with pictures. He's serious about every aspect of his work, but it's the photography he loves. He took his time arranging the groups, taking several shots of each, fiddling with his glasses and his camera between shots in a mannerism I used to think was irritating but am getting more and more attracted to.

When Phil was finished with the trophy winners and had dropped off his camera at the nearby *Beacon* office, we walked back to my unfinished decorations, part of my mind still occupied with the old murder and Ellis Hodges's insinuations about the police not trying to solve the murder of an "outsider."

Phil and I had popcorn and hot apple cider and finished decorating my tree. By the time the day was over I wasn't thinking of the old Christmas murder or my old disappointment at not getting a sled. Good old Phil.

TWO

EVEN ON A SUNDAY MORNING after an evening with her near and dear improved her morale, a police officer must be on the job, to serve and protect. So I was driving around, putting the required number of miles on the cruiser to convince Hen I'd actually been patrolling instead of spending my entire shift eating donuts somewhere, when I came upon a girl who seemed to be in need of some kind of help. Detective that I am, I reached that conclusion from her dejected posture and the fact that she was crying.

She was sitting on a bicycle, bracing herself against a lightpost in front of the Ogeechee Mall, under one of the electrified candles the town hangs from every lightpost during the Christmas season. If she was waiting for the stores to open, she still had quite a wait, since practically everything is closed till noon on Sundays in Ogeechee, where the righteous are presumed to be spending the morning in church and roisterers are presumed to be getting over their roistering. Either way, it doesn't pay to open for business very early, and all six stores at the mall were still closed.

The girl looked up at the sound of my car, and I saw a round, tear-stained face that looked to be nine or ten years old, a couple of years older than Delcie. Alarm chased sorrow and worry away when she saw me, and she pushed away from the lightpost so forcefully that she fell off the bike. Her frantic agitation as she struggled to her feet reminded me of the half-wild kittens that live under my house.

She looked around, dark eyes wide. The spiky ponytail and shaggy bangs, which I recognized as fashion, not neglect, flopped this way and that. Seeing no one to save her from me, she crouched over the bike and began to weep again.

"Hey, honey, you look like you've got a problem."

No response.

"Part of my job, besides chasing bad guys, is helping good girls."

No response.

"*¿Habla inglés?*" We have a much larger Spanish-speaking population than most people realize. The living isn't necessarily easy for them here, but it must be somewhat easier than in other parts of the United States, and staggeringly easier than in Mexico or Guatemala, which accounts for Georgia's Hispanic population having nearly quadrupled in the last decade. Most are field laborers who come and go with the seasons, working in onion fields and peach orchards. Some stay year-round, working at the poultry processing plants, gathering and baling pine straw for landscapers, or doing domestic work. Some of them have the proper papers, arranged by the employers. Some of them don't, which makes for tricky interpersonal relations, especially if you're wearing a uniform. As Hen likes to put it, the racial situation in our little corner of Georgia isn't as black and white as a lot of people think.

¿Habla ingles? is just about the extent of my Spanish, and I was relieved when the girl sniffed a tear away, smiled crookedly, presumably at my accent, and said, *"Sí."*

"Can you tell me what you're crying about?"

"My brother."

"What about your brother?"

"I can't find him."

"Are you supposed to be taking care of him?"

Apparently, my question was even funnier than my accent. She smiled. "My big brother."

"How big?"

She smiled again. "Really big. Bigger than you." Really big, then. At least five-seven.

I changed my question. "How old is he?"

"Nineteen."

"So why are you worried about this b-i-g nineteen-year-old man, your brother?"

Her sunny smiled clouded over again. "He wasn't home this morning to take Mama to Mass."

"Maybe he's with friends and forgot."

"No." The ponytail and bangs flopped emphatically. "No. He doesn't forget. He didn't come home at all last night."

"And you thought he'd be here waiting for the stores to open?"

"No." She didn't actually tell me not to be ridiculous, but I read in her eyes that she didn't think my sense of humor fit her situation. "I was afraid maybe he got in a fight and got hurt and can't come home, so I was looking."

"Does he get in fights a lot?"

"No. Not a lot. Sometimes."

If she knew of any at all, there were probably more. "I haven't heard about any fights where somebody got hurt so bad they couldn't go home," I told her. "But part of my job is looking for people who are lost. Tell me about your brother and I'll help you look for him."

She thought it over and apparently decided to let me help

Her name was Connie Reyes. She spelled it for me and I got another smile from her as I perfected the pronunciation, RAY-ess, not rays or reez. Her brother, Carlos, had brown skin, brown hair, brown eyes, no moustache or beard, no tattoos or piercings, no wooden leg—which got me another smile, when I asked.

"How about I give you a ride home? Maybe your brother has come home by now. It would be a shame for you to be out here worrying about him if he's already home." A strict interpretation of the department's regulations would not permit me to give the child a ride, but my sense of the situation overrode that prohibition. Sure, I could be ambushed by a little girl, but I wasn't worried about it.

Connie had to act on faith, too, weighing the dangers of fraternizing with the police—being seen to be fraternizing with the police—against the novelty of the experience. Novelty and my engaging sense of humor apparently won the battle, or maybe she just figured nobody she knew would be out and about on a Sunday morning to see her in my company. She let me put her bicycle in the back and she climbed in front with me. Still, she didn't give me an address, claiming she didn't know it, but would just tell me where to turn.

I was obediently following the winding path she pre-scribed—patrolling is patrolling, after all—and wondering if she really thought she was trying to get me lost in my own hometown, when my radio crackled.

It took me a moment to translate the seldom-heard code 1044—into a meaningful message.

"Okay, hon, I've got to quit fooling around and take you home. Where do I turn?" I didn't feel the need to explain that my presence was required at a scene where somebody had discovered a body, but she must have sensed some urgency when I picked up my pace from leisurely to impatient.

She looked up, big brown eyes wide, and pointed in the direction I needed to be going.

The crime scene was at the parade-staging area south of downtown, an empty field roughly bounded by Main Street to the west, sparse housing tucked among pines to the north, thicker pine woods to the east, and a group of ramshackle trailers to the south. Near Main, on the side of the field nearest the trailers, was a restaurant-bar called El Milagro, the miracle, which occupied a run-down building that had been a succession of dim, and ultimately unsuccessful, restaurants. The miracle might be that the building still stood, the wonder of owning a business, the benefits of alcohol, the fact that there wasn't actual bloodshed every Saturday night or the gathering of a community of compadres in our little town. Belatedly it occurred to me that it might have been the miracle of the promise of a new life Ogeechee offered. My low Christmas spirits reasserting themselves.

"Let me out here," Connie said when I slowed to turn off Main onto the dirt road north of the field.

Her needs had sunk to the bottom of my priority list. I removed her bicycle from the back of the car and she wobbled off as I hurried to join the small knot of people gathered near a shed and flatbed truck. I was pleased to see that I was the first officer on the scene. Hen, thinking he had the morning off, probably got paged while he was at church, while I was already on the job and moving. Still, it was a good feeling to be there first.

A man detached himself from the others and met me at my car.

"Roscoe Little," he said. "I came to clean up my truck from the parade mess, and that's when I found him."

"You're the one who called?"

"That's me."

"Where's the body?"

"On the truck."

"You sure he's dead?"

"I'm sure."

I took a look for myself. The flies gathered around the body confirmed Mr. Little's opinion.

Having verified that we had a body, and not somebody in need of medical attention, I sent Mr. Little back to the others while I made generous use of yellow tape to mark off the scene to try to prevent any further contamination.

I was just finishing that task when Hen arrived, so we got most of the story from Mr. Little at the same time.

He'd let the Maranatha Baptist Church use his truck for their float in the parade. After the parade, they left it under the open-sided shed where we now stood. When he came to clean off the truck he discovered more than pig and goat droppings among the piles of pine straw. One of the wise men had a knife wound that was no longer bleeding. Mr. Little called the police.

Anybody watching might have been surprised by the lack of bustle in the scene. Bustle would come later, with the crime scene techs from Statesboro, nearly forty miles away, and it would take them a while to arrive. Meanwhile, my job was to keep everybody away from the truck and to begin a log of what was going on. The first order of business at a crime scene: seal, secure and evaluate. In a police investigation, there's no instant replay, no overs, no retake. Any evidence lost now is lost to the investigation forever. I needed to be thorough and meticulous.

Engaged in this, I looked up to see that Connie Reyes, on foot, had joined the onlookers. She sidled behind a large man when she saw me looking at her.

Hen talked with Roscoe Little and the slowly gathering group of onlookers. Most of them would be neighbors. It was possible one of them had heard or seen something that would be helpful.

"On Saturday nights there's always noise from that joint over there," a robust black woman, Vonetta Andrews, offered, "but I didn't hear anything extra." The joint she indicated was, of course, El Milagro.

"I saw somebody hanging around after the parade was over, after the rest of 'em left," said a boy. "I wanted to come play in the pine straw but she—" he indicated Vonetta Andrews "—wouldn't let me."

"See there? I was right, too. Mighta been you up there dead instead of that poor man."

"Did you see one somebody or several somebodies?" Hen asked the boy.

The boy wasn't sure.

"We haven't established a time of death yet," Hen reminded everybody. "It could have happened early this morning. Did anybody—"

At that moment, Connie Reyes, who'd slipped past the police tape and climbed up on a tire to get a better look, let out a wail.

"It's Carlos! Carlos!"

I grabbed her. "Connie! Hold on, honey." She struggled frantically.

"Ain't no Carlos, neither." Roscoe's drawl rose above Connie's wails. "Don't know what she's talking about. I told you, his name's LeRoy Hopkins. Been LeRoy Hopkins as long as I've known him."

Connie looked from Roscoe Little back to the dead man, and stopped squirming.

"Well?" I asked.

"No. It's not." She was squirming again, so I took her away and set her down outside the tape.

"You ought to go on home now," I said. "This is no place for you."

She nodded, but when I turned back toward the truck, she still had made no move.

"I called the church right after I called the po-lice," Roscoe was saying.

"What church would that be?" Hen asked.

"Maranatha, the one that used my truck in the parade. They need to know about LeRoy."

It would have been hard to deny that, although when a car bumped across the field and rocked to a halt near the truck, and half a dozen people—obviously dressed for church—got out, I wished he hadn't been quite so quick to call.

"LeRoy?" The screaming woman was the one I had last seen wearing a blue choir robe and trying to calm a bawling baby when the float passed the hotel. I didn't have to restrain her as I had Connie Reyes, though. An imposing man in a black suit did that, putting an arm around her without a word, as Roscoe Little nodded, confirming her fears.

"Who's this?" Hen asked.

The big man answered. "This is Starr Taylor, she's LeRoy Hopkins's sister. If it's true that the Lord has taken LeRoy from us…"

"And you are?"

"The Reverend Oliver Palmer."

"Well, Reverend Palmer," Hen said, "it's good you're here. Not that I doubt Mr. Little's identification, but maybe Miz Taylor better have a look."

Hen lifted the police tape so the two could approach the truck, holding up a hand to restrain the others who'd come in the car with them. Starr Taylor looked at the dead man for such a long time I began to wonder if she was seeing anything at all, then her face crumpled and she sagged back into the ready arm of her pastor. Identity confirmed. Out of the corner of my eye, I saw Connie Reyes dodge back inside the tape. When I turned to shoo her off she dipped to the ground, picked up something, then turned and ran, ponytail flying. Finally going home? I took off after her, catching up only because she stopped for her bicycle.

"What you got there?" I asked breathlessly, when I'd jerked her to a stop by grabbing the back of the bicycle seat.

"*Nada*. Nothing." She was more concerned with trying to stuff the nothing into her jacket pocket than with her perilous position on the bike.

I helped her get her feet on solid ground. "Better show me. You could be in a lot of trouble for tampering with a crime scene."

Reluctantly she pulled her hand out of the pocket and opened it, revealing a silver cross about two inches long, which appeared to be made of several hammered silver beads. A loop at the top suggested it had hung from a chain. .

"You're going to give me that cross, and we're going back over there so you can explain to the chief of police what you're up to." Connie obviously wasn't impressed with me, but experience has shown me that Hen impresses people. Not only is he male, he's bigger than most people, and he is the chief of police. He could try his luck. I hauled Connie back toward the shed.

Hen broke off his conversation with Starr Taylor, the Reverend Oliver Palmer, and Roscoe Little, and met Connie and me at the tape.

"Got your fugitive, I see," he said.

"Meet Connie Reyes," I said. "Connie and I met earlier. She says her brother, Carlos, is missing."

"Uh-huh," Hen said. "Carlos." He nodded, with a glance back at the body on the truck. "And what's this ruckus about?"

I showed him the cross. "She was trying to take this from the scene."

"Reckon there's a connection?" he asked.

I shrugged.

Hen glowered.

Connie cowered.

"Want to tell us about it?" Hen asked.

Connie looked at her shoes.

"All right," Hen said, still glowering. "You think about it. I want you to stay right there—right there—till I'm ready to talk to you. You understand me?"

"*Sí.*" But Connie's eyes drifted to the bicycle.

"If Officer Roundtree has to run you down again you're gonna have some explaining to do. You understand me?"

"*Sí.*"

Hen went back to talking with the other possible witnesses. I went back to making notes, listening to the witnesses, and keeping an eye on Connie, just in case.

"He was so proud that he got to be one of the three kings,"

Starr Taylor said. "Brother Oliver told him that his name, LeRoy, meant king, in French, and he just wouldn't let us alone till we agreed."

"LeRoy was a little slow, you understand," Reverend Palmer said. "But he got along just fine, with help from Starr and his brethren and sistren at the church. Even had him a little job, thanks to Brother Leggett. We were all proud of him."

"And he did just like we told him in the parade, too," Starr said. "Who did this to him?"

"We don't know yet, Miz Taylor, but we plan on finding out," Hen said. "Maybe you can help us. Your brother on bad terms with anybody?"

"No. Not a soul." She wiped at her tears with the back of her hand. Reverend Palmer handed her a neatly folded tissue and she flashed him a watery smile before continuing. "He was as gentle and sweet a man as you'll ever run across. Nobody could have had anything against him."

We've heard that before, and Hen didn't take it at face value. "What if somebody teased him about being a king, if he was so proud of that. Would he have fought with 'em?"

"No, Chief Huckabee," Reverend Palmer said. "That wasn't LeRoy's way. He'd have had his feelings hurt, but he'd have come to me, or to Starr, and asked us to pray for his enemies. He just did not understand meanness."

"Robbery?" Hen suggested.

"They didn't get much if that was it." LeRoy's sister was letting her pastor do the talking. "LeRoy wasn't good with money, so we...so he never carried but a dollar or two."

"Married?" Hen asked.

Sister and pastor shook their heads.

"Girlfriend?"

No. Hen turned to the woman. "When did you last see your brother alive?"

Starr Taylor wailed again, and Hen waited till she composed herself. "After the parade. I went right on home. My baby was our baby Jesus, and it was past time for him to be fed, so as soon as we got back here, I left."

"Was there anybody here with your brother when you left?" Hen asked.

She frowned in thought. "No. When the parade was over, it was starting to get dark, and most everybody was ready to get on to whatever else they had to do, like I was. Freddie and Adele took the animals with them, and Roscoe had told us not to worry about the truck, he'd take care of that, so we left."

"Just how slow was your brother?" Hen asked.

"He was slow to think bad of anybody," Palmer answered. "Slow to anger, slow..."

Hen nodded understanding, but interrupted, speaking to LeRoy's sister, "Did you usually leave him to himself?"

"Oh, yes. He needed help to get along, but it wasn't like he had to be watched all the time. And he'd enjoyed being a real king, dressing up and all, so I thought it would be mean to make him hurry to be through with it. Look." She teared up as she pointed to a pile of folded cloth with a tinfoil crown sitting on top. "He folded up his costume, so he wouldn't be a bother to anybody else."

"That's the kind of man he was," said Reverend Palmer.

"He have any special friends?" Hen asked.

Starr looked to her pastor. They both shook their heads and she answered, "No, not any special friends that I can think of. Most people liked him well enough, but there wasn't anybody he spent a lot of time with."

"The work of the devil," said the Rev. Palmer.

"Whoever killed him couldn't have been anybody that knew him," Roscoe said.

"He was so sweet," his sister said.

"Pure-D hatefulness," the pastor said. "Random evil."

Hen was nodding agreement, in general, with that opinion, when the pastor added, "Random, unless it was because of his color."

Hen took a deep breath and I imagined him counting to ten before he said mildly, "We have no reason to think it was that, Reverend Palmer, but we will certainly take the possibility into account as we investigate, along with robbery, and revenge, and a whole roster of other possibilities."

Reverend Palmer nodded.

Starr was crying into her tissue again and shaking her head.

"We'll be talking to you again," Hen said, his glance including Roscoe Little. "Before you go, though, I want you to take a look at this."

He held out the silver cross. "Any of you know who it belongs to?"

No.

"Any of you ever see it before?"

No. Not even a pause to think it over.

"Okay, then." He dropped the cross into his breast pocket and buttoned the flap securely over it. The textured surface of the small silver cross wouldn't have taken any fingerprints, and any other evidence it might have held had already been contaminated. The cross would be safe in Hen's pocket for the time being.

The arrival of the van full of crime scene techs from States-boro changed the rhythm of the investigation from chatty to intense. Chatty is where Hen shines. Intense technical analysis is where they shine. As they began examining, measuring, weighing and photographing, Hen edged Starr Taylor and the Reverend Palmer away from the body, interposing his bulk between them and the activity behind him.

"Let's leave these expert technicians to their work of finding whatever they can find to help us figure out what happened here. We'll be in touch. And you let us know if you think of anything that could help us."

"What about LeRoy?" his sister asked.

"We'll let you know when we can release the body," Hen said. "As soon as we can."

He nodded, man to man, at Reverend Palmer, who rose to the occasion, taking Ms. Taylor's arm, and leading her away.

"And you and me, now," he said, turning to me, "we'll have to talk to the rest of the neighbors."

"Goody," I said.

"This cross is unusual enough somebody might recognize it, and I think we might as well start with your little girl."

She wasn't my little girl, but I had to admit that if I had a little girl, I wouldn't mind her being as energetic and persistent as Connie Reyes. Although Hen doesn't always agree with me, I happen to think energy and persistence are two of my better qualities.

THREE

CONNIE DIDN'T SEEM HAPPY to see us turn our attention back to her, but she was still standing more or less where Hen had told her to.

"You live over there?" Hen asked, indicating the group of trailers.

Connie, eyes on the ground, nodded.

Hen spoke to one of the techs. "Looks like you'll be here for a while, son. We don't want to get in your way, so we'll be over there at those trailers if you need us." A loose translation of that, I knew, was that the tedious, meticulous crime-scene work was not nearly as interesting to Hen as talking to people.

"Sure, Chief."

Hen turned back to Connie. "Show us."

Except for the people who'd come to gawk at the goings-on at the shed, nobody was in sight as we followed Connie toward the trailers. That suited me, since I know we made an odd procession, Connie leading out, forlorn; Hen impressive, as always; me, stoically wheeling the bicycle along behind.

The half-dozen trailers sat on weed-fringed cinderblocks, and were distinguished from each other mainly by the color of the rusty paint. We made for a mostly blue unit with a well-worn conventional plastic Mary, Joseph and babe in front. As

we approached, the door opened and a woman hurtled down
the uneven steps. She looked to be in her mid- to late-forties,
but my impression might have been skewed toward age by the
shapeless slacks and shirt she wore and the harried, worried
expression on her face.

She aimed a torrent of Spanish in Connie's direction, glancing at me and Hen and back to the girl. Connie returned fire.

"No," Connie responded, shaking her head. Besides "Carlos," that was the only word I understood. Connie took her bicycle from me and leaned it against the trailer, behind the
kneeling Joseph.

"Has your brother come home?" Hen asked.

"No," Connie said again, turning to face him.

"What was all that about?" Hen's waving hand indicated
swirls of Spanish words. Connie seemed to understand.

"I told her about the man on the truck."

"Uh huh. This your mother?"

"*Sí.*"

"What's your name, ma'am?" Hen asked the woman. He
was raised well.

"Esperanza Reyes," Connie answered.

The woman's face hadn't lost the worried expression she'd
worn when we first saw her.

"Espe…" Hen began.

The girl repeated, "*Es-puh-rahn-zah.* In English it's Hope,
if that's too hard for you."

"Esperanza," Hen said. "Señora Reyes."

Good for him, not taking the easy way out. Even if the meaning is hope, in English, it wouldn't sound the same in her ears.

Hen went on with his question to the woman. "Did you see
or hear anything unusual after the parade yesterday?"

"There's always noise over there." Connie answered for her mother, jerking her head in the direction of El Milagro and giving a shrug. "We don't pay attention."

"Nothing else?" Hen asked.

Señora Reyes shivered.

"Would you like to go inside to talk?" I suggested.

"No. Too messy. Too crowded." Connie hadn't needed to consult with her mother about it.

"Ask her if she saw or heard anything," Hen said.

The girl spoke in Spanish and listened to her mother's response before she answered Hen. "We didn't hear anything, or see anything, and Carlos didn't do it."

Why did they assume we thought he had? Maybe there was a connection, after all, something we hadn't noticed. "How do you know that?" I asked. "You don't even know where Carlos is. Maybe he killed him and ran away."

A change of expression on the woman's face suggested that she was understanding at least a part of what was being said.

"No," Connie said again. "He didn't. He wouldn't."

"You said he fights. Maybe they had a fight." I couldn't have said why I kept at it, except for wanting to hear what Connie would say and see if her mother's expression would change again. They both disappointed me, so Hen and I exchanged glances and he took up the slack. With full, slow dramatic emphasis, he unbuttoned his shirt pocket and pulled the silver cross from his pocket.

"Does this belong to you?" he asked Esperanza Reyes.

Connie and her mother exchanged a quick glance, then Connie said something in Spanish, maybe translating the question, and her mother shook her head, and looked nervously back at Hen. Connie shook her head, too.

"Do you know who it does belong to?" Hen asked.

They didn't confer again. No.

Hen and I conferred with our own glance. *"Hasta la vista,"* I said. I know enough Spanish to know that means we'll be back. This time when I tried my Spanish, Connie didn't appear to be laughing at my accent. As her mother turned to go inside the trailer, she clasped the cross hanging from her own necklace, as if for comfort.

Outside and at a little distance from the trailer, Hen said, "I'd bet you a bowl full of Mama's banana pudding that Señora Esperanza Reyes understands more English than she lets on."

"That's fair," I said. "Since you understand more Spanish than you let on." In fact, I think one of the reasons Hen's such a good policeman is that he generally knows a lot more than he lets on. He likes to give people a chance to underestimate him.

"What do you think?" I asked.

"I think Connie tried to take that cross because she recognized it and knows who it belongs to," Hen said. "They're a religious family and it's a religious symbol. It might have caught her eye because it's pretty, but I don't think she was trying to steal it."

"Do you think Carlos Reyes and that cross and the killing of LeRoy Hopkins are connected?"

"It's way too early for me to think much of anything, but it sure looks like his mama and his sister are afraid of just that, doesn't it?"

I had to agree.

Hen and I canvassed the other trailers and the houses on the fringes of the field, talking to everybody we could find, posing the same questions we'd posed to Esperanza and Connie Reyes. Had they heard or seen anything out of the ordinary going since the parade yesterday? Did they recognize the necklace? *Nada*. That left El Milagro, but Sunday morning is not the time you'd expect to find anybody at a Saturday night hot spot, so we agreed we'd done all we could for the time being. We'd have to wait for a report from the crime lab. Maybe they'd be able to tell us something useful about the time of death or the murder weapon.

FOUR

A CALL TO A FRIEND WHO WORKS at the Department of Family and Children's Services led me to Father Miguel Lucero. Recent growth in Spanish-speaking Catholics in our area has been a mixed blessing for the churches, I'm sure. Most churches believe growth is good, but the many needy newcomers have stretched the facilities and resources of older churches. The white-painted cinderblock extension attached to the original red brick building was evidence of growth at St. Elizabeth's, Father Lucero's church.

The priest, a wiry man with silvery highlights in his dark hair, was still at the church when I got there that afternoon, picking up litter from the churchyard. Protected by his faith, his collar, and his secure citizenship status, he was less affected by my uniform than Connie and Esperanza Reyes had been.

"Trudy Roundtree," I identified myself.

"Father Miguel Lucero. Father Lucero, if you want to be formal; Father Miguel would be friendlier. Sometimes Father Mike."

"I'll try Father Miguel," I said, wondering if this was a test. "Would that be friendly but respectful?"

"*Sí,*" he said. "How can I help you?"

"I'm not sure how, or if, you can help me. A couple of things, maybe. Do you know Carlos Reyes?"

A sigh escaped the priest. "Ah, Carlos. He's not in trouble, is he?"

"Would you expect him to be in trouble?"

He shook his head and gave me a rueful smile. "Carlos is a good boy, a good son, a good worker."

"But you asked if he's in trouble."

He gave me a charming rueful smile. "But he is young and hotheaded. The Latin temperament, you understand."

That time, I was sure he was testing me. Remembering Hen's mild, neutral response to Reverend Oliver Palmer's provocation, I smiled. "I'll try to avoid stereotyping if you will, Father. Actually, Carlos's sister, Connie, tells me he's missing and she's worried about him."

His face clouded. "Oh. I noticed they weren't at Mass this morning. That would explain it. I'll go and see them. If Carlos is missing, they must be worried. His mother depends on him for so much. Do you have any idea—maybe he was in an accident?

"We've had no reports of accidents. You asked if he was in trouble. Did you have any particular kind of trouble in mind?"

He bent to pick up a scrap of paper. "No. Nothing in particular."

"In general then?"

"He's the kind of boy who sees things in black and white, good and bad, right and wrong, and he doesn't have much patience with people who don't see things the same way." He folded and refolded the scrap of paper as he spoke.

"If you don't mind my saying so, that seems like an odd comment from a priest. Isn't it your business to see things in terms of right and wrong, good and bad?"

He stalled by bending to pick up another piece of litter, but he was smiling when he straightened up. "Carlos is even worse than a priest in some ways, meddling in people's lives, telling them what they ought to do."

"It sounds like you do have something particular in mind."

"It's possible. Yes. I hear Carlos has been causing trouble with some of the farmers that use the seasonal labor, trying to stage a protest to get better housing and some changes in how they work, to make it safer."

"Did all that meddling get him into trouble with anybody special that you know of?"

"I hear he made people on both sides mad at him. The farmers didn't want to change things, and some of the workers, too, didn't like him stirring things up. They have little, and work hard for that little. They're afraid they'll lose what they have, that the farmers will find other workers."

Fat chance of that.

"So all I have to do is interview all the employers and all the laborers and ask if they've done something to stop his troublemaking?" I stooped to pull a plastic grocery bag from under a bush.

"That would be a start." He wasn't smiling now. "But that's not all. Carlos got it in his head that the man who'd arranged to bring some of the workers here was cheating them."

"Cheating them how?"

"Maybe charging them, and then blackmailing them, to bring them here. Or maybe taking a big bite out of what they are trying to send back to their families. I don't know. For the most part, the coyotes, the people who prey on their own people, aren't the people I know. The ones I know, the ones who come to church, trust me for their souls, and for my help, but they don't always trust me with their immigration status. I hear things, but not always directly."

I nodded. "I understand. And you might not want to tell me everything you do know."

"I might not."

I held out my plastic bag and he put his scraps of paper in it.

"But you can tell me this, I think, Father. You paint a picture of a young man who has many causes, and possibly many enemies. Does Carlos Reyes have friends?"

"Oh, yes," he said. "Carlos is a handsome, charming boy, with many friends. Now, you tell me something, Officer Roundtree."

"If I can, Father Miguel."

"From what I understand, it's unusual for the police to be looking for an adult person who has been missing such a short time. This is why I asked about trouble. I think there must be more than you've told me. Do you think Carlos has done something wrong? Is that why you're so interested?"

"It's possible he's committed a crime, but, as I said, it was Connie who called him to my attention."

"A handful, that girl," he said, smiling again. "But?"

"Yes, Connie's a handful." I smiled back. "But, besides Connie's concern for her missing brother, somebody discovered a body this morning near where the Reyes family lives."

"Oh. The body isn't Carlos, surely."

"No."

"Then, some trouble at El Milagro?"

"We don't know of any trouble there, but we'll check it out," I admitted. "People do keep mentioning El Milagro."

"Do you have some reason to think the body has anything to do with Carlos?"

"We don't know that yet, either. All I can say for sure is that the dead man is not Carlos, and not your coyote. The victim was a black man."

"I see, at last. You think Carlos may have killed him."

"I need to find that out."

His eyes met mine. "My mission, my job, is to help people, these people who are working hard to provide a good life for their families."

"Yes, I understand that," I said, when he stopped.

"They come to me because they trust me not cause trouble for them."

"Of course." He seemed to be talking himself through some moral dilemma and I couldn't help him.

"But I'm no good to them if they can't trust me, and I'm no good to anybody if I can't trust myself."

I thought about that. "My job is to help people, too, Father, and I can't do that without putting the bad guys out of business."

"Carlos isn't a bad guy."

"If that's true, it wouldn't hurt for you to help me find him, would it?"

"Probably not." He smiled at me then. "Maybe not."

"Especially if he had nothing to do with our murder," I suggested.

"Especially then."

"From what you've told me, he might be in trouble from some of those bad guys, needing us to look for him."

"Yes." He still looked troubled, but thoughtful.

I risked this fragile thread of rapport by adding, "His mother wasn't very helpful, but I got the feeling she understood more of our conversation than she let on. Maybe she knows what kind of trouble he's in, if he's in trouble, or maybe she suspects."

"She would be very worried," he said.

"Maybe she didn't tell me everything she knows."

"It's possible." He smiled briefly.

"What if you talked to her?" I asked. "She'd tell you if she knows where he is, wouldn't she?"

"She trusts me, if that's what you mean," he said, then, "I've heard that the police say Hispanics are like pool balls."

I knew what was coming. I'd heard it, too.

He looked me in the eye. "The harder you hit them, the more English you get out of them."

I drew a deep breath, but kept my gaze steady.

"I've heard some people say that. Not me. Not Chief Huckabee. Our job is to keep the peace, not create trouble. Do I look like the kind of person who'd slap a woman around?"

He shrugged. "There are other policemen."

I shrugged and brought out the silver cross. "Do you recognize this?"

His frown might have indicated concentration. Or sorrow. Or deceit. "Maybe."

I waited.

"I'm no expert on jewelry, you understand, but that is a beautiful, unusual piece of art, the kind of thing you notice. Yes, I think I may have seen it before."

"Around the neck of one of your people?" I'm a Methodist, and don't speak Catholic, so I fumbled for the right word. Unfortunately the word I came up with made me sound racist. "Your church people," I said. That might have made it worse, but he seemed to understand my problem.

"Parishioners," he said. "They belong to my parish. Does this cross have something to do with the dead man?" he asked.

"That's another thing I don't know. It might. It was found

near the scene. It doesn't look like something a hotheaded young man would wear." Humor had helped with Connie. I'd find out if it would work with Father Miguel Lucero.

He didn't look happy, but he said, "It looks like one that belongs to a girl named Rosa Cruz. She's another reason Carlos might be in trouble."

"What do you mean?"

"Rosa and Carlos are friends, but Rosa has a boyfriend, and from what I've heard, he's not the kind of man who would be tolerant of that friendship."

Could LeRoy and Carlos have gotten into a fight over Rosa Cruz? Going by what LeRoy Hopkins's sister had told us about him, it was unlikely he'd been Rosa Cruz's boyfriend, but you never know.

"What's the boyfriend's name?"

"Hector Torres."

I wrote it down. "Is he one of your parishioners?"

"No."

Father Miguel didn't seem inclined to amplify, which I took to mean that Hector Torres never darkened the doors of the church.

"Can you tell me how to find Rosa Cruz?"

"I could be wrong about the cross."

"She'll be able to tell me if you are."

"Yes. I hope I am wrong, and this murder has nothing to do with Rosa or Carlos, but if Carlos is in trouble, if he's had to hide somewhere and his family doesn't know where, Rosa's the only other person I can think of who might know."

"If he's committed murder, you don't want to shield him," I said, "and if he hasn't, if he's not in trouble, we don't need to waste our time looking for him instead of looking for the killer. If Rosa Cruz can help us clear this up, you need to tell me how to find her."

He bent to pick up a flattened beer can. "She does house-keeping at one of the motels. She would probably be home now. This might be a good time to talk to her, too, without the men around."

I knew what he meant. The field workers are on the job, as Hen puts it, "from can to can't"—from when there's enough daylight that they can work until it's so dark they can't—every day, including days the more privileged of us don't have to work, days like Sunday, Thanksgiving and Christmas. Talking to Rosa Cruz about Carlos Reyes would surely be more productive without Hector Torres around.

"Where does she live?" I asked. "And how good is her English?"

"I'll show you."

We'd been getting along pretty well so far, but I didn't think we were good enough friends for me to ask if he wanted to go along to protect her from me, from pool ball syndrome.

FIVE

"OH, YEAH. The old Rogers place," Hen said when I told him Father Miguel Lucero's idea of who might own the silver cross, and gave him the directions the priest had given me. "I heard there was a bunch of people living out there. I'll meet y'all there."

A wobbly wire fence ran alongside the road near the property, stopping where the gravel driveway crossed a cattle guard. Red plastic bows that had seen many Christmases were tied to the gateposts and stirred in the disturbed air when we drove past. A big old farmhouse and several outbuildings were scattered in a loose circle, like beads strung on…a rosary, since I was thinking along Catholic lines. Hen had parked his cruiser at the base of the circle, the noose, if your mind runs to comparisons like that instead of religious ones, creating an obstacle to incoming or outgoing traffic. I pulled to a stop at another awkward angle. Anybody coming or going would have to be very determined.

"I can see why El Milagro is so popular," Hen said as the three of us walked toward the house. "Gotta be more cheerful than where most of these workers are living. I wonder if this old place even has running water."

It was a good question. Various Rogerses had moved away from the homestead for, no doubt, various reasons. Modern conveniences might have been one reason—and the lack of modern conveniences might have made it affordable for workers who didn't make much money to begin with, and who wanted to send as much money as possible to family they'd left behind.

"She may be frightened of the police," Father Miguel said when we reached the porch. "Let me call to her."

Hen and I stepped back.

"Rosa?" Father Miguel called. His knock at the door went unanswered for so long that if we hadn't heard creaks and rustles and seen a slight shadow moving through the window we might have thought nobody was there.

"Too bad," Hen said theatrically, voice pitched louder than necessary to reach the ears of anybody on the porch with him. "Here we got this nice piece of jewelry to return. Be a shame if we can't find anybody to give it to."

Father Miguel looked from one to the other of us in confusion. "Rosa?" he called again.

"Do you want to wait for her?" I asked, loudly.

"Well, dinner's not for a while, so I'm not in any big hurry. Why don't we just wait here till somebody turns up?" Hen leaned against one of the pillars supporting the roof of the porch, batting a trailing red ribbon away from his face. He hastily stood erect again when the pillar shifted under his weight.

"Or maybe I'll stretch my legs and take a look around. You want to come, Father?"

They weren't ten yards away when the door cracked open.

"Father?" The voice was low and musical.

With a sly smile in my direction, Father Miguel answered my question about Rosa's command of English. "Rosa, are you all right?"

A nervous glance at Hen and me was her only answer.

"These officers have some questions for you," the priest said. "I thought I might be able to help."

"You're Rosa Cruz?" Hen asked.

A glance at Father Miguel. "Yes."

"We'd like to talk to you. Can we come in?"

More thought. Then, like Esperanza Reyes, she chose to come outside with us.

In the light of day, we saw that the low, musical voice belonged to a young woman. Esperanza Reyes had seemed older because she was careworn. This woman's youth and beauty were distorted by a swollen, discolored lip and a bruise high on one cheekbone. A red welt along the right side of her neck looked like a section of a thin red necklace. If she'd walked into a door, she must have been such a slow learner she did it two or three more times.

Hen didn't mention the bruises, but led with the silver cross. "Is this yours?" She began to reach for it, but he held it away. "We can't let you have it just yet, but you can identify it?"

She drew her hand back. "I have one that looks like that."

"You have it?" Hen asked.

"Yes."

"So this couldn't be yours?"

"No." She said it quickly.

"We'd like to see yours," Hen said.

She didn't bat an eye, or make a move to go get it to show to us. "Maybe this could be mine. I lost it."

"Can you tell us how you lost it?"

She shook her head emphatically.

"Do you know a man named Carlos Reyes?"

She darted a glance around, behind, up, down, as though looking for escape, but she didn't deny it. "I know Carlos."

"Do you know where he is?"

Like the other questions, that one should have been easy. I sensed rising panic. "Why do you want Carlos? He…" But she didn't finish her non-answer.

"Esperanza and Connie are worried about him," Father Miguel supplied.

"We need to talk to him," Hen said. "He may be able to help us with an investigation. Is he here?"

Her voice said no, but a stiffening in her posture said otherwise, and I noticed that she didn't look at her priest when she spoke. Call me a cynic, but I wondered if she could manage to lie to the police but not directly to her priest.

"Will you let us know if you hear from him?"

She didn't say she would, but I gave her a card, which she put in a pocket.

"Thanks for your time," Hen said.

As Hen and I turned away, Father Miguel lingered, speaking quietly to the woman. Suddenly I saw movement near the shed.

"What?" Hen asked, when I stopped in my tracks.

"I must be hallucinating. I swear I saw Connie Reyes."

"Where?"

"Over there."

When we turned back, I caught an expression on Rosa's face that looked like fear.

"I thought I saw Connie Reyes," I said. "Was she here?"

To my surprise, the answer came quickly. "Yes. She was looking for Carlos. I told her he isn't here."

"Maybe he's hiding in one of those other buildings," Hen said. "Mind if we look around?"

"He isn't there."

"We'll look, anyway," Hen said. "Father, you stay here with her. We wouldn't want civilians getting caught in the middle, in case we find somebody who shouldn't be hanging around out there."

Hen and I started for the shed, leaving Rosa Cruz and Father Miguel. I noticed she didn't invite him inside, either.

I hadn't seen any more movement. Either I really had hallucinated or Connie was smart enough to stay out of sight as she melted into the fields and wood. We conducted a careful, thorough search of the barn, garage, an open shed with a closed end that was probably a workshop, and a smaller building that looked like what was left of a tobacco barn. Piles of blankets and remnants of food—empty cans and grocery bags—were evidence that several people were calling the old Rogers place home, regardless of deficiencies in amenities, but we saw no further sign of Connie, unless you count the track of a bicycle wheel, and no sign at all of Carlos.

"You ever think of learning Spanish?" I asked Hen.

"*Sí,*" he said. "Something tells me if we're gonna keep on top of our jobs, we're gonna need to do better than be able to do more in Spanish than ask for a driver's license."

Father Miguel met us in the driveway.

"Do you think Carlos Reyes is here?" Hen asked.

The priest looked startled. "I didn't see him."

"Okay," Hen said. "You know that boyfriend of hers? What's his name?"

"Hector. Hector Torres."

"Hector Torres. You know him?"

"Not well. I know who he is."

"You know him well enough to know if he's the kind that would beat up a woman?"

"No. I don't know."

"What about Carlos Reyes? He that kind of man?"

"Not Carlos. No."

SIX

I WAS UNPREPARED for what met me when I showed up at the stationhouse the next morning.

Starr Taylor and the Reverend Oliver Palmer had obviously been there a while. Starr Taylor was in a new role, neither Mary the Mother of Jesus nor the bereaved sister of LeRoy Hopkins, but, maybe, Joan of Arc, challenging authority for the sake of her convictions. Or somebody's convictions. Had she been cast in the role, which, as far as I could tell, was more stage dressing than speaking, by the Reverend Oliver Palmer? She was dressed all in black and carried a delicate white handkerchief, and he was doing the talking.

"Some of my people asked me to speak for them, Chief Huckabee," Reverend Palmer was saying, leaving ambiguous who "his people" might be, and making me think of my tongue-tied stammering in the presence of Father Miguel Lucero. Maybe it isn't simply Methodists speaking to Catholics who have trouble finding the right word.

"Speak, Reverend," Hen said majestically.

"My people, they're concerned that LeRoy Hopkins, poor soul that he was, might not have been important enough to command the respect necessary to cause you to…"

"Let me stop you right there, Reverend," Hen said, "before you accidentally say something both of us will have trouble swallowing later on. If things are going too slow to suit you, all I can say is you probably watch too many police shows on television, where they get everything done in an hour, minus whatever time the commercials take."

"Are you going after those hoodlums that hang out at that so-called restaurant over there? If it's some kind of gang headquarters, they might have killed LeRoy for nothing more than being black and on their turf." I had to give the man points for tenacity, if not for good sense. I gathered Hen wasn't giving him points at all.

"With all due respect, Reverend," Hen said—and with no respect that is not due, I thought— "You think about it, you'll realize I don't go over to your place of business and try to tell you how to do your job." He whined into, " 'I'd like a little more fire and brimstone, Pastor, and could you please come down a mite heavier against drunkenness and adultery, to get my husband's attention?' See how ridiculous that would be?" he asked in his normal tone. "Although I want to give you credit for meaning well, I don't think you're qualified to come over here and tell me how to do my business. We are interviewing people of all colors, shapes, sizes, sexual orientation, religious persuasion and—lessee, did I leave anything out? Oh, yeah, ages, people of all ages, too—if we think they can tell us anything about the way Mr. Hopkins died. That's what we do in a murder case, it's what we always do, and it's what we would do whether the victim's name happened to be Pancho Gonzales, Mohammed Abdullah Sahib, or Martin Luther King." He paused for breath. Even Hen has to do that.

"We want to bury him," the bereaved sister said.

"Yes, ma'am," Hen said. "Of course you do. I know this is hard on you, and we'll let you get on with saying goodbye to your brother just as soon as we can, just as soon as he's told our crime scene techs everything he can about what was used to kill him and when he died. You don't want us to rush that, because that's what'll help us catch whoever killed him and bring a solid case against the killer."

Hen's own comment seemed to remind him of Reverend Palmer again, and he turned back to the minister.

"Somebody always knows something about a crime like this, and we'll find whoever that is. If you know something, or if you know somebody who knows something we ought to know, send 'em over and we'll listen to what they have to say. But what we need is evidence, not preconceived ideas about what happened and who made it happen. We don't aim to go off half-cocked. When we do go off, we want to be firmly cocked, fully loaded, and carefully aimed. Am I making myself clear?"

"I believe so," Reverend Palmer said, looking somewhat dazed.

"We don't have much to work on so far, but we are working with what we have. We will be keeping you and your people—" I'm sure he winked at me when he said that "—and the rest of the public informed about developments that will not compromise our case. It will not help us any for you to go around muddying up the waters of the investigation by stirring up the muck so we can't see what's going on.

"I would like to point out that as a group, the people you are trying to put at the wrong end of the pointing finger at the end of the long arm of the law, are hardworking people who do not do anything to get the attention of law enforcement of any ilk. Don't you start sputtering, now, till I've said my say. In general, I'm saying our Spanish-speaking population is made up of that kind of person. In particular, now, there's likely to be a rotten apple or two in just about any barrel, and if there's a Spanish-speaking rotten apple, we'll do our best to find him. Or her," he added with a glance at me.

I love it when he says something that shows he sometimes listens to what I say, and I'm always having something to say to remind him that women deserve equal status with men. He wasn't through with Reverend Palmer, though.

"Just like there might be a black sheep among your flock," he said, which struck me as a reckless turn of phrase in this particular company. Maybe he did it on purpose.

Starr Taylor and I, audience, held back our applause for his performance. Hen did not take a bow, but somehow Reverend Palmer knew the show was over and it was time to leave.

"Wow!" I said as the door closed behind the reverend and the sister. "And I'd been thinking I should model my behavior on your manly restraint in the face of provocation."

"Uh-huh." He wasn't interested in my provocation. "You got anything useful to say or you just want to hear yourself talk?"

"Don't snap at me. I'm on your side. You don't watch out, Santa's gonna bring you a lump of coal," I said.

Well, I considered that useful.

SEVEN

WHEN WE CAN, Phil and I meet for a quick lunch at Kathi's, a small restaurant near the center of town with a loyal clientele that appreciates home-style cooking and reasonable prices. It's convenient for both of us, just a few blocks from the *Beacon* offices and from the station house.

I got there first and chose a table away from the front windows with the festive row of tiny pines decorated with gold-sprayed pecans and pictures cut from old Christmas cards. Our habit is for the first one there to order for both, since neither of us has much time to spare for lunch. This arrangement is not at all risky since you can't go wrong with Kathi's cooking. It's been a growth experience, too, besides the fun of wondering what I'll have for lunch. Once Phil ordered liver and onions for me, definitely not my fave, but I ate it and found it wasn't as bad as I'd always thought,

Today, Phil would be having meat loaf, green beans and canned pear salad, followed by mincemeat pie. He used to feel about mincemeat the way I used to feel about liver and onions, which I ordered for myself today just to confuse him. Live, learn and grow. No pie for me, unless I got a bite of his, which I might do, since stolen calories don't count.

While I was waiting for Phil and our lunches to appear, Ellis Hodges hitched his way into the restaurant.

"Well, hello there, Officer Roundtree," he said.

"Season's greetings, Mr. Hodges," I replied equally formally.

"I'm glad I ran into you," he said. "Bernice has been on me for stirrin' up that old business about the murder the other day and I'm feelin' bad about it."

"Oh?" I didn't believe it. If he had felt bad, he wouldn't be bringing it up again.

Uninvited, he sat across from me. He propped his walking stick against the chair beside him, leaned forward and immediately confirmed my skepticism by launching into the subject. "I always felt the police coulda solved that one if they'da tried."

"I gathered that. Do you have a specific idea about where they went wrong, or do you just have a quarrel with the police in general?"

"They didn't catch the killer, did they?"

"I haven't researched it, but I'm willing to take your word on that."

He nodded triumphantly. "So they didn't catch 'im, they didn't do their job. Can't argue with that, can you?"

"Do you know something the police didn't know?"

"Me? If I did, it wouldn't be my business to tell, now, would it?"

"It certainly would!" I paused and then added, "But maybe I misunderstood your concern. Maybe you're more interested in criticizing and stirring things up than in being helpful."

He adopted a crafty look. "Sometimes bein' helpful can get you in trouble. Anyway, it's not my job. I've got my civil rights to think about."

"You do not have a right not to testify if you have knowledge of something that would assist in a murder investigation.

Maybe you need to worry less about your civil rights and more about being prosecuted for obstruction of justice or being an accessory to murder."

My threat didn't faze him.

"I'm sittin' here tryin' to be helpful, wouldn't you say?"

"Is that what you call it?" A narrowing of his eyes suggested he'd noticed my sarcasm. I continued. "You do understand that the police don't ever take a murder off the books if it's unsolved. For your information, murder is right up there with treason as something the law doesn't ever get over."

"That's what I been sayin'. You ought to be interested, even if it did happen before you were born," he persisted.

"Of course I'm interested, Mr. Hodges. Yes, indeed, I am interested not only because I'm a good citizen, but also because it is my job. Tell me, though, do you think the killer is still around waiting to be brought to justice?"

"Ha!" He laughed so explosively he knocked his walking stick to the floor. When he'd recovered himself and the stick he said, "That's the question, isn't it? Could be. If he was, he'd be as old as I am, one foot in the grave, whether you put 'im in jail, or not."

"Are you telling me you have your own statute of limitations on murder?"

"What? I didn't say that."

"You said there'd be no reason to put him in jail. Him. Does that mean you think you know who the killer was?"

"Huh? Oh. Well, no, I wouldn't want to go that far. Mighta been a woman, if that's what you mean. When I was in school, saying 'he' was good enough, but that's not good enough any more. Okay, then, 'he' or 'she,' 'him' or 'her.' Whoever. Tell you what, though, if you're interested.

Maybe, just maybe, Stella Strickland could help you solve this one."

"Why do you say that?"

"Stella was always what the young'uns today call a 'hottie.' I won't deny there was a time I coulda gone for Stella, myself, before I met Bernice, naturally, and she convinced me to quit sowin' wild oats or she'd take a rollin' pin to the situation and make oatmeal."

"I'm sure you and Stella would have made a lovely couple," I said, not even trying to hide a teasing grin.

"Don't let Bernice hear you say that." His eyes flashed. "She's always been the jealous type. Anyway," he added, "I'm just tryin' to be helpful."

"Helpfully pointing the finger at Miz Strickland?" I looked around hopefully, but neither Kathi nor Phil was coming to my rescue.

"I didn't say that. You must not be all that good a policeman if you go puttin' words in people's mouth."

"If you'd stop hinting around and come out with whatever it is you want to say, I wouldn't have to guess."

"All I'm sayin' is that maybe Stella knew Josh Tippins better than she let on."

"Well enough that she killed him?"

"There you go again! I didn't say that! Stella's looks didn't do her any good, anyway. Harold didn't treat her right, and neither did her second husband. Rumor had it that she was already carryin' on with him while she was married to Harold."

"Harold would be her first husband?"

"That's right. Harold Cowart. The next one musta been somebody Strickland, but I don't remember much about him. He didn't last very long."

"And the 'him' she might have been carrying on while she was married to Harold was?"

"Huh? Oh, Whatshisname Strickland. Did you think I meant Josh?"

"Just trying to understand things as we go. Honestly, Mr. Hodges, it sounds like you're telling me Miz Strickland had such bad taste in men it wouldn't have been much of a compliment if she had been interested in you."

A grin crossed his monkey face. "I never thought of it like that. Uh-huh, that's probably why we never hit it off. That and the fact that I'da had to stand in line waitin' for a vacancy. She was always carryin' on with somebody else." A bogus expression of sincerity chased the grin away. "But Bernice is the only one for me."

I nodded and tried to stifle a sigh. "Is there anything in particular that makes you think the police didn't do everything they could to solve the murder?"

He looked uncomfortable, like so many opinionated people do when they're asked to back up their pronouncements, so I decided to amuse myself by probing even more. With a little luck, I could intimidate him with my superior knowledge of police procedure, and he'd give the subject a rest.

"Did they secure the crime scene?"

"Secure? You bet your booties. Old Jimbo Todd found the body and set up such a holler nobody coulda got in there to have a look even if they'da wanted to. Jimbo was about the size of two horses, so if he wanted to keep the door closed till the police got there, it stayed closed. Anyway, Cooter Nail was the boss dawg at the time, the Chief of Police," he clarified for me, "and he was downstairs waitin' for the poker game to start, so there wasn't much of a wait."

"What did the boss dawg do then?"

"He identified the body and got the doc in to look at him. Not as scientific as y'all can do it these days, but that's what they had. The doc did his mumbo-jumbo and said he figured Josh had been dead since sometime the night before."

"So far, it sounds like a good way to start the investigation," I said. "What next?"

"Well, Cooter started askin' everybody to account for their movements the night before. Waste of time, if you ask me, since the doc couldn't say exactly when it happened."

"Did he try to pin down when Josh Tippins was last seen alive?"

"Matter of fact, he did. Josh came back to the hotel kind of late that night, and everybody noticed when he turned up because we hadn't been expectin' to see him. He'd told everybody he was goin' home for the weekend, but he said his folks were all down with the flu or somethin' so he figured he'd be better off back at the hotel, lettin' Stella and Bernice cook for him. Ha. Better off. Shows what he knew."

"He came back to the hotel and went to his room, and that's the last time anybody saw him alive?"

"That's right. Unless you count when Harold went up to see if he wanted to play cards."

"You'd have to count that. Did he come down and play cards?"

"No. Harold came back and said Josh was worn-out from goin' all the way to Pembroke and back and thought he might be comin' down with somethin', himself, so he didn't want to play."

"Were you staying at the hotel, too?"

"Me? No. I lived here in town. Why'd you ask that?"

"You seem to have spent a lot of time there."

"Well, between Bernice and Stella, and their cookin' and
ll the people who were stayin' there, it was probably the live-
est place in town. One way or another, those women at-
racted just about everybody. Except the other women,
aturally."

"Naturally."

"Did your friend Cooter Nail come up with any kind of move for the killing?"

"Not that I ever knew, and that's another thing that made
ie think there was a cover-up. There had to be a motive, and
at would have led them to the murderer, even if they didn't
ave all this DNA stuff like they do now."

"Did you have an idea about a motive?"

"Can't say I did."

"So, then, there we are. You still haven't told me what you
iink the police didn't do what they should have done."

"That's not my job."

Mercifully, just about then, Phil came through the front
oor and Kathi, who keeps a close eye on things, came out
rom the kitchen carrying our lunches.

"Mr. Hodges," Phil said, "you trying to beat my time with
rudy?"

Ellis Hodges grinned at the implied compliment to his
ex appeal. "Wouldn't think of it," he said. "Just passin' the
me till Bernice comes back for me. She props me up in
ere so I don't slow her down when she's doin' her grocery
hoppin'."

"That hip still bothering you?" Phil asked.

Ellis Hodges cackled. "I'll never play quarterback again,
ut that's not the problem. Bernice don't like it when I add

things to her shoppin' cart when her back's turned. She don
appreciate my help the way a good wife ought to."

"Not properly submissive?" I asked, knowing that was
hot issue among Southern Baptists, and Ellis Hodges was
loyal Baptist.

"Not even halfway," he said. "Well, don't let your foo
get cold."

He struggled to his feet and made his way to the counte
where he asked for coffee and pecan pie.

Phil slid into the chair Mr. Hodges had vacated.

"Ah, meat loaf! Or did Kathi get our lunches switched?'

I just smiled and hoisted a forkful of liver, with sautéed on
ions dripping seductively from it.

"What was that all about?" Phil asked, forking a bite o
meat loaf.

"I'm not sure, but I can understand why his wife doesn
want him in the grocery store with her. I think he's trying t
irritate me by maligning the police, based on a murder cas
they didn't solve seventy years ago."

"What murder?"

"It happened at the Anderson Hotel, back in the thirtie
Ellis Hodges keeps hinting that Stella Strickland did it. Or a
least knows who did. Or maybe he just wants me to think sh
did it or knows who did. It sounds like he had a crush on he
back then, so maybe all it is is sour grapes, spurned love
something like that."

"Why's he bringing it up now?"

"I don't know. He acts like he thinks I ought to investigate.

"Well, that's your job, isn't it, fighting crime?" he aske
sounding like Ellis Hodges. "I'll admit, the trail is pretty col
but you are so good at what you do!"

"I've already bought your Christmas present, Phil. You can let up on the heavy-handed flattery."

"I meant every word," he protested. "How would you go about investigating a case that old, assuming you were interested and had the time and weren't snowed under with more pressing crimes?"

"I don't know, beyond talking to people like Ellis Hodges and Stella Strickland. Too late to talk to Cooter Nail."

"Hmph?"

"Don't talk with your mouth full. Cooter Nail was the chief of police back then. Rings a lot better than Henry Huckabee, doesn't it?"

"Um-hmm." He swallowed. "Cooter Nail. I'll look back and see what the *Beacon* had to say about the murder at the time. In the thirties, you said?"

"Right. Late thirties. That's a great idea. And it would be interesting to see what kind of files Cooter Nail left behind, too, wouldn't it?"

"It would." He put his fork down and looked soulfully into my eyes. "Since my stock with you is high right now, this might be a good time to tell you…."

"You have my attention."

"The *Beacon* has received a rabble-rousing Letter to the Editor, along the lines of how the police aren't working very hard on the LeRoy Hopkins murder because of the color of the victim. It's full of unpleasant innuendo and outright attacks on our local law enforcement, and it calls for our citizens to stand up for their civil rights."

"Oh, heck. Did it come from Ellis Hodges?"

Phil laughed. "Not unless he signed somebody else's name."

"Sounds just like what he's been saying about Cooter Nail."

"Maligning an historic police officer is one thing, Trudy. This is something else. I felt like I needed to let you—and Hen—know that I'm going to run it next week."

"Oh, Phil!"

"Yeah, I know. I'm not crazy about it, knowing it could cause trouble, but if the *Beacon* is supposed to serve the entire community, it has to reflect the opinions and interests of the entire community."

"I know that, but…"

He tried a smile, and I could tell he wasn't particularly happy about this commitment to his own code. "Think of it as a ticking bomb, Trudy. If y'all get this wrapped up before we go to press, I'll fill in the space with Christmas clip art."

"Okay, Phil. I understand. I'll warn Hen. He won't like it any better than I do, than you do, but he'll understand. I think."

"I hope. I've got to run it, whether he does, or not."

I sighed. "Okay. A ticking bomb. In the meantime, can I have a bite of your pie? Maybe just the point?"

EIGHT

"LET'S SEE WHAT WE'VE GOT," Hen said, waving the sheaf of papers that was the report from the crime scene techs. "Hmm. Hmm. Hmm."

"Hmm?" I inquired.

"Oh. Nothing here that comes as a surprise. Our Mr. Hopkins died of stab wounds inflicted by…here it is…a one-edged blade about three-quarters of an inch wide. He was stabbed in the back and the wound reached the heart, after which he was stabbed in the chest."

"Poor guy." I tried to picture the knife. "Does the report mention any other injuries?"

Hen didn't even have to refer to the report. He smiled at me. "Very good, Officer Roundtree. Very good. There were defensive wounds, cuts on the palms and fingers, no doubt received as he twisted around to try to see what was happening to him. Tissue and blood under his fingernails."

"Presumably tissue and blood from his killer. Sure would be nice if we had somebody to look at for signs of that fight."

"Sure would."

I continued to quiz him. "And the time of death?"

"About ten o'clock on Saturday night, give or take an hour."

"I suppose that's not too early for it to be the result of somebody getting juiced on too much *cerveza* at El Milagro."

"How come a good Methodist girl like you knows a word like that?"

"I read a lot, and it shows up on menus. Give me a little credit."

"Okay, Miz Officer Roundtree. Earn a little credit. Let me hear your theory of the crime."

"Yessir, Your Excellency." But I didn't have one.

"Yes, ma'am?"

When in doubt, start talking, start anywhere. I said the first name that came into my head. "Maybe it was Rosa Cruz."

He didn't laugh in my face, which tells you that he really is a good police officer, not willing to discount even me and my off-the-top-of-my-head ideas without giving them a hearing. "Okay, let's start with her. Why'd she do it?"

"Maybe, in spite of what his sister and his pastor say, LeRoy Hopkins was a sexual predator. Maybe he attacked Rosa and she had to defend herself. That would account for her bruises. Maybe there were scratches we didn't see."

"Good," Hen said, but he said it meditatively, as if weighing arguments in a debate, not as if he believed me, which, at this stage of our investigation, was exactly what he should have been doing. "If she's the killer, it would also account for that dingle-dangle, the cross that looks like it might have come from a broken necklace, at the scene. And why she wasn't willing or able to tell us where she lost it." He looked up. "Okay, then, maybe we could place her at the scene, and we have a motive. Maybe. You want to go bring her in?"

"You're trying to call my bluff, Hen. You win. LeRoy Hopkins was stabbed in the back. I can't see Rosa Cruz as a knife-wielding killer who'd sneak up on somebody from behind, and that scenario shoots down the defending-herself theory, anyway. No. Rosa strikes me as more of a victim than a killer."

"People can surprise you, Trudy."

"Sure they can, but there's no way LeRoy Hopkins was killed by Rosa Cruz defending herself against him. She got her bruises from walking into a door, or that boyfriend we've heard about."

"Likely, you're right. So we cross her off. You got another theory?"

"Well, there's Carlos. He's a big question mark. I should have mentioned him first. Father Miguel told me Carlos and Rosa are friends. If LeRoy attacked Rosa, and Carlos came to her defense, that explains Rosa's bruises and the cross."

"Right. From what you said, Father Miguel made Carlos sound heroic, all right. Maybe so. You go find him and we'll check him over for scratches. Put that on your to-do list."

"Yessir." I pulled out a notepad and wrote that down, pretending to think he really was delegating that task to me. "Neither one of these theories fits with what we know about LeRoy Hopkins, though."

"People can…"

"I know, I know. People can surprise you."

"We need to have a talk with some people besides LeRoy's sister and his pastor about LeRoy Hopkins. See if we get a different picture of him. He mighta been up to a thing or two his sister and his pastor wouldn't know about. Add that to your list."

I scribbled again.

"Anything else you can think of?" Hen asked.

"If we're trying to cover all possibilities, we don't want to forget the popular theory that some of them furriners, them illegal aliens, killed him because he was the wrong color and too near their turf."

Hen opened his mouth, but I hurried on to stave off an unnecessary lecture. "But if that's what happened, some sort of gang attack, there'd have been more of a mess at the scene, wouldn't there? And the victim would probably have been more battered."

"Possibly." He rattled the papers again. "Everything here is consistent with its being one assailant, not a mob. I dropped by El Milagro when they opened up and had a chat with the manager. It will probably not surprise you to learn he was extremely eager to be helpful and tell me anything I wanted to hear so I'd go away."

"And?"

"Freely paraphrasing, El Milagro's manager, Robert Lopez, Berto to his friends, tells me he's never seen anybody at El Milagro drinking too much or exhibiting any antisocial behavior whatsoever. All his employees are trained to stop serving people who seem to be drunk, aggressive or in any other way the worse for drink, but that seldom comes up because all his patrons are models of sobriety and self-control. Many of the Spanish-speaking element patronize his place because they like hearing their native language and being able to relax among others like themselves, but he's never, no never, well, hardly ever, well, you know."

"I think I know," I agreed.

"Berto tells me he was aware of the parade, but didn't go watch it, since he had work to do getting ready for the night's business. He noticed when the truck with the parade entry on it was brought back, but it's a good distance across the field and he didn't pay much attention. Saw some people leaving. That's all."

"We need a break," I said.

"Go find us one, then. That's what I hired you for, ain't it?"

"Yessir, Your Honor. I'll put it on my to-do list."

So I went, completely forgetting to ask Hen for his theories of the case. Probably I'd covered them all.

NINE

THERE OUGHT TO BE A SPECIAL LAW, or special penalties, against committing crimes during December, when police officers, like most everybody else, are trying against all odds to be people of good will. Thanks to Phil, I did have my Christmas decorating done to suit me. I had also managed to find gifts for the people on my list, all books. I gave careful thought to the subject matter of interest to the recipient: photography for Phil, camellias for Aunt Lulu, cooking for Teri, classic children's fiction in the form of the Little House on the Prairie books for Delcie (who, I'm pleased to see, is turning into an avid reader), and, for Hen, a couple of self-described police procedural crime novels that I knew would set his teeth on edge and maybe even give him indigestion. Ah, yes, the holiday spirit was alive and well, except for the nasty business of a murder.

Make that two murders. There was the death of LeRoy Hopkins, which threatened to make racial tensions break through the superficial seasonal good cheer of the community. Even though only a few days had passed, the pressure on the *Beacon* to print an attack on the police for not trying hard enough to bring LeRoy Hopkins's killer to justice was weighing on me. I knew Phil would bend over backward not to let his relationship with me and Hen affect his responsibility to the community. He couldn't, in good conscience, ignore the issue. You've got to admire a man like that.

Since we seemed to be stymied on the LeRoy Hopkins case, I let my thoughts range over the possibilities in the Josh Tippins case, which, thanks—or no thanks—to Ellis Hodges, I couldn't get out of my mind. I let my thoughts range over the possibilities in that old case. Maybe backing off from the immediate problem and thinking about something else would clear my head and give me a fresh perspective on the newer case.

A man had been found with his head bashed in, if my senior citizens were to be believed, and the body wasn't discovered immediately, which meant alibis had been difficult or impossible to verify. The murdered man was a friend of a woman who had a reputation for being…friendly. Thinking of Ellis Hodges's hints and Stella Strickland's quick recollection of the victim's name in the old case, I did wonder if there was a connection between her and the murder. After all, she had called in sick that day. Was that because she knew the body was there and didn't want to be around when it was discovered?

As Hen says, there's always somebody who knows something that would help in an investigation. I wondered if Stella was that somebody in this case. And, if she was, I wondered how I could get her to tell me.

The journey of a thousand miles begins with a single step. My first step was to call Stella and ask if I could drop by her house and talk to her. I told her I'd bring fruitcake. How could she refuse?

"THAT ELLIS HODGES never has had enough sense to put his brain in gear before he starts running his mouth," she said, when we were seated at her kitchen table with coffee and fruitcake in front of us. "Bernice calls him numbnuts, which I'm here to tell you I'm not able to verify, but he's always been a numbskull, too, if you ask me."

"I *am* asking you. Why do you think he brought up that old business now?" I picked a cherry out of the fruitcake so I could enjoy it all by itself.

"Who knows how the old goat thinks? Maybe being laid up with that hip has given him time to get all nostalgic about when he was young and frisky." She shrugged and picked a cherry out of her own piece of cake, smiling. "Maybe he really thinks I killed poor Josh Tippins and he was being clever pointing me out to you."

"Did you do it?" I meant for the question to sound friendly and casual, but even so, I instinctively watched for her reaction, which was a grin, an easy, innocent grin as far as I could tell.

"You think I'd just say 'yes' after keeping quiet about it all this time?"

"Maybe a guilty conscience has been eating at you and you want to get it off your chest," I suggested.

"More likely, a guilty conscience is what won't let Ellis leave it alone. For all I know, he did it. With all the hullaba-loo that was always going on down there, it might have been a team of trained elephants and nobody would have heard 'em. Ellis, now, he's been born again and supposed to be such a good Baptist, he might be feeling guilty about all the time he spent lusting after women, like Jimmy Carter, now he's getting closer to his own personal judgment day. He was always hanging around the hotel, around me and Bernice."

"You don't seem to think much of him."

She shrugged.

"What do you think Bernice saw in him?" I asked.

"Mainly somebody she could push around, if you ask me. She had a lot of boyfriends, even went with the chief of police for a while, but she couldn't push the others around like she does Ellis. Serves her right, if that's what she had in mind, that he got so religious. Took what fun he ever had right out of him. But it isn't like there were a lot of great choices. Look at what I wound up with before I got smart."

"What about Mr. Hodges's suggestion that you were having an affair with the victim, Josh Tippins, and his murder was a crime of passion, the result of a lover's quarrel?"

That earned me a hearty laugh. "I wasn't interested in Josh, but I think Bernice was. Maybe Ellis killed him out of jealousy. That could be your crime of passion. No. I'm just kidding. Not Ellis. He's always been way too wishy-washy for anything that would take that much gumption. More likely, he's just got bored with his life, and he's trying to stir up trouble."

"Why does he keep bringing you into it? Do you think he really believes you were mixed up in it?"

"Beats me all hollow. Maybe he's getting even because I never gave him the time of day, and if he can believe I'm a murderer he won't have to feel so bad. But making trouble's always been his way. Stirring up mischief may be all the fun he gets. Men like him never get over an insult to their idea of themselves."

Who does?

"That Josh was a sweet boy, but not nearly up to my speed. No, I wasn't having an affair with him, any more than I was with Ellis. To tell you the truth, though—don't be shocked, now—I did have a romance going." A wry smile twisted her lips.

"Being a police officer has had just the affect on me that

Hen was afraid it would, Miz Strickland. I've become jaded, cynical, coarse and hard to shock."

We toasted each other with another pair of cherries, and then I said, "Mr. Hodges suggested your husband wasn't good to you."

"Old Ellis is chock full of suggestions, isn't he? Well, he hit that nail on the head, all right. It wasn't much of a secret that Harold—Harold Cowart was my first husband—roughed me up once in awhile, but people didn't talk about it out in the open back then like they do these days. I guess they thought a man owned his wife and had the right to do whatever he wanted with her. To her."

"He beat you?"

"Yes, ma'am, he did. Shocked?"

I sighed.

"I don't know why I feel embarrassed to admit it," she continued. "But that's why when somebody came along that knew how to sweet talk, it turned my head, even if I did know I was asking for trouble." She plunked her coffee mug down decisively. "What I forgot was that old Harold knew how to sweet talk, too, before we got married, and then he forgot it real quick, before the honeymoon was over. It wasn't much of a honeymoon, either, just a trip to Tybee so he could do some fishing and we could walk around on the beach. Maybe I was supposed to be glad he was the jealous type, take it for a compliment or something, that I was important enough for him to be jealous about, and be grateful he never hit me with anything except his fists."

"Did he hit you a lot?"

"Not often enough to make me leave him, but often enough. I had trouble acting brokenhearted when he got mangled in an accident out at the sawmill and died. I'll shock you again, but I couldn't help thinking it was kind of appropriate. That was just a couple of years after the murder, come to think of it. Lucky for Harold he didn't have some lingering disease and expect me to nurse him. I might have committed murder then, or suicide. Since we're on the subject, though, I will make a confession."

"Oh? Somehow I don't think you're about to clear up an old murder for me."

"No, not that, but the truth is I wasn't exactly sick the day they found poor old Josh, like Ellis said. Not with the flu or a cold or the kind of thing you might think. I couldn't go to work because I was too sore to move. When Harold got home that night he was madder'n a hornet about something and he beat me up one side and down the other."

All I could do was shake my head in sympathy. It struck me then that whatever her lurid history with men, Stella's house was aggressively feminine. Spindly tables and chairs, dainty china cups and saucers, floral motifs on upholstery, curtains, and wallpaper—it had the look of a woman who didn't give a thought to what it would take to make a man comfortable.

After a moment, I asked, "Did you know what set him off?"

"No. Mighta been he had a bad night at cards. You'd better believe I had enough sense not to ask. I think, in general, he operated on the principle that if he tried to tell me where I'd come up short he might leave something out, and this way I'd feel guilty for whatever it was I'd done. If that makes sense."

"I'm afraid I do see why that might make sense to somebody like that."

"May he rot," she said pleasantly.

"How did you learn about the murder?"

"Good old Harold brought the news home with him, seemed to enjoy talking about it. That's the kind of man he was. He had gone by the hotel to tell them I wouldn't be in to work, and he hung around, jawing with the other men. If I remember right, he was there when somebody went up to see Josh about something. He's the one that found him dead."

"Had you been at the hotel the night before?"

"Sure had."

"Did you see Josh?"

She laughed. "Sure did, and it was an unpleasant shock, I don't mind telling you."

"Are you going to try to shock me again?"

She grinned, again showing the personality that would have made her a hottie, even if she hadn't had the looks, which I was willing to believe she did. I was sorry I had missed knowing her when she was younger.

"I doubt that this will shock you," she said. "I was using his room. Oh, no, you don't have to be that shocked. I wasn't what they call a working girl, not that kind, but with me work-ing at the hotel like I was, I could usually find a room to meet my boyfriend in, and then clean it afterward, which was my job, anyway. Added spice to the whole business."

"What do you mean?"

"I knew Harold was a mean, jealous son of a biscuit, so it was fun to fool him. Oh, he suspected I was running around on him, and at the time I thought Ellis was spying on me for him. That would be Ellis's style, sneaking around, getting his kicks from somebody else's fireworks."

"Were there fireworks that night?"

"At the hotel? Almost, but not quite. My personal fire-works exploded after I thought I was safe at home, and Har-ld came busting in. See, Josh was supposed to go off that weekend, but he came back. I was up in his room with—oh, I might as well tell you, since he's dead, too—with Johnson Strickland, who was my second husband and pretty near as worthless as Harold—when Josh turned up back at the hotel. Johnson and I got out of there and down the back stairs in jig time, I'll tell you. Pretty funny, looking back on it, I guess. I hadn't thought about all that in years till Ellis brought it up the other day. Another thing I hadn't thought about in years, Johnson had brought me a box of candy, those chocolate-cov-red cherries Ellis was going on about. We left in such a hurry, we left the candy. I guess it's a good thing I didn't take it with me."

"Why's that?"

"The mood Harold was in when he got home that night, he might have killed me if he'd found me with a box of candy he hadn't bought himself."

"Did you ever have an idea who might have killed Josh?"

For the first time in our conversation filled with shocking revelations about her sexual exploits, her abuse, and her plea-ure over her husband's grisly death, Stella Strickland seemed to hesitate.

"You did, didn't you?" I pressed.

"Well…"

I waited, sipping cool coffee while she decided how to fin-ish the thought. It took a while, but just as I was about to speak, she looked up, smiling. "Old Harold was capable of just about anything."

I wasn't at all sure that's what she'd started out to say. If she'd wanted to accuse him, a man whose death had set her free from abuse, a man she'd already verbally trashed in our conversation, why hesitate? My vague idea that Stella Strickland might know something she hadn't told about that old case had proved valid, but talking with her hadn't done anything more than feed my interest. It certainly hadn't shone a bright light into the dim corners of the past.

"What about Cooter Nail? Mr. Hodges keeps saying he didn't try to solve the case. Was he lazy? Dishonest? Stupid? How well did you know him?"

"Not as well as he wanted me to, I'll tell you that. About all I know for sure is he was as randy as any of the rest of 'em."

I left the rest of the fruitcake with her and went on my way, musing on the fascinating glimpse I was getting into lives of people I'd almost discounted.

And then I asked myself, "How do you suppose Ellie Hodges knew about the chocolate-covered cherries?"

TEN

ON MY WAY BACK to the station house, I passed First Baptist Church, and saw Ellis Hodges getting out of his car, no doubt headed for the weekly senior citizens' lunch and social. I pulled the car alongside.

"Could I have just a minute?" I asked.

"Certainly, Officer," he said.

I parked and walked along with him toward the building. "Where's your wife?"

"She don't like these lunches. Says it makes her feel old to come down here with all the geezers and gum the casseroles. So she stays home and watches the soaps and I come over here and give us both a break from each other. Tell you the truth, I get on her nerves." He had never looked more monkeylike, but behind the shrewd humor I sensed something else. Sadness? Satisfaction? Resignation? Spite?

"What you want me for?"

"A couple of things," I said, thinking of the assignment Hen had given me. "Did you know LeRoy Hopkins?"

"Black guy they found dead the other day?"

"That's right. Did you know him?"

"Saw him around. Kind of slow, wasn't he?"

"That's him. Where'd you see him around?"

"Oh, just around. Post office. Video store. Grocery store. Around. Walkin', even in the heat."

"Ever talk to him?"

"What about?"

"Anything at all? Oh, never mind." On to the real reason I wanted to talk to Ellis Hodges. "Since you've been so interested in that old murder, I'm giving you the opportunity to assist the police."

"That don't mean you're arrestin' me, does it, like it does in those British cop shows on television?"

"It means I'm grieved that you think the police didn't do their job in that old investigation and I want to restore your confidence in law enforcement by taking another look at the case."

"Uh-huh. And how you gonna do that?"

"Reconsider the evidence."

"After all this time? What evidence?"

"Just your testimony, Mr. Hodges, so it's important that you be as impartial and as exact as you can."

"Sure. Impartial, exact, that's me."

I shared a smile with him. "Do you know if the police ever learned anything about that box of chocolate-covered cherries in Josh Tippins's room?"

"What they gone learn about a box of candy? I don't remember the brand, if that's what you're after."

"No, not that. Did they seem to think it was important? Ask where it came from?"

"I never heard them mention it at all. Probably figured Josh brought it back with him."

"But you knew it was Stella's favorite candy. A lot of people must have known. Didn't you mention it to them?"

"Don't remember that I did, but see here! There it was, a clue, and they didn't follow up on it. That's just what I've been sayin'!"

I let that sit there long enough to make a point. "If the police didn't question you, how did you know about it?"

He leaned on his walking stick and gave me a calculating look while he thought it over. "Oh. Well, somebody musta told me."

"Didn't you say your big friend Jimbo kept everybody out of the room?"

"Yes, I did say that. Yes, he did. I see where you're goin' with this. You think I was in the room, killin' Josh, and that's how I know about the candy."

"You do have to admit that would explain everything about the case except why you've been bringing it up lately."

"Maybe I saw the candy in his room before."

"Before what? And what would you have been doing in his room? My grandmother used to tell me when you start slinging mud some of it's bound to stick to you. All this might have started out with you trying to tease Miz Strickland, but you've made me wonder about your interest in the case."

"I'm a concerned citizen, that's all."

"Of course you are."

"I told you I had a sort of a thing for Stella back then. Whoa! I remember now how I knew about the candy."

"Really?" I infused as much skepticism as possible into the word. "You wouldn't lie to me on your way in to the church, would you?"

"No, not then or any other time. Here's the truth. It was Harold Cowart mentioned it, and said somethin' or other about how much Stella liked chocolate-covered cherries. That's it. That's how I knew."

"And how did he know about it? Was he with the police?"

"No, he wasn't with the police, unless you count sittin' around a card table playin' poker with the chief."

Now there was a thought. What if the chief, the marvelously named Cooter Nail, had eased up on the investigation because he suspected one of his good buddies of killing somebody who was, after all, an outsider?

"Thank you very much," I said.

"You're welcome very much," he said.

"Enjoy your lunch."

"That's askin' a lot, but at least it's a change from what I get at home."

We went our separate ways.

"GOT A MINUTE, YOUR REVERENCE?" I asked, seeing that Hen was doing paperwork at his desk when I got to the station house. He hardly ever minds being interrupted from paperwork, and this was no exception. Even in the face of a murder investigation, time has to be made for paperwork. But a diversion is always welcome.

"About the murder," I said.

"What you got?" He pushed the papers aside and leaned back, clasping his hands together over his head and stretching. Hen doesn't ever act like he thinks I'm good at my job, so I generally have to be satisfied with involuntary revelations, like this one, that he thinks I might know something. I almost, almost, hated to ruin the moment by telling him I was thinking of the old murder.

"You back on that? We got more current cases, Trudy, in case you hadn't noticed."

"Just give me a minute." Hen is a celebrated storyteller, so I considered it a tribute to my own abilities in that line that after a few more sputtered questions as to why I was wasting my time and his on such a very cold case, he began paying attention to my telling of that old story.

"What do you think?" I asked, when I'd finished.

"No way to know for sure," he hedged.

"No," I agreed.

"I don't see Ellis Hodges as the perpetrator of a crime of passion, even when he was young and juicy and had two good hips."

"I don't, either," I said. "And nothing I've learned hints at any reason for Stella to do it, either."

"Maybe that police chief."

"Why?" I asked.

"Who knows? But it would explain why he didn't do much investigating. If he didn't."

"I'm appalled at your low opinion of law officers," I said piously.

"I know you are," Hen said. "Naive and simple as you are. Glad to know doing police work hasn't coarsened you. I'd never forgive Mama for making me hire you."

"What do you think, seriously?"

"Seriously? I'd have to bet on that husband of Stella's. What was his name?"

"Harold Cowart," I supplied.

"Harold Cowart. He went up there to invite the victim to play cards, saw the box of candy, assumed the innocent young man was his wife's elusive lover, lost his feeble grip on his mean temper and bashed the poor feller's brains in with his own hammer. All he had to do was report that Josh didn't want to play cards and let the passage of time confuse things enough for him to get away with it."

"I couldn't have put it more clearly, myself," I said. "It all fits, complete with means, motive, and opportunity. A brutal jealous husband kills the wrong man. He was still in a fury when he went home, and took it out on Stella. Even if his friend Cooter Nail suspected, he might have turned a blind eye to it. There's no way for anybody to prove it after all this time but it sounds right. And if he did it, he got his punishment." I told him what Stella had told me about the way Harold Cowart died. "Hen, as I was listening to you, something else occurred to me."

"Got an old dognapping you want me to put my little gray cells to work on?" He reached for the papers.

"No. Listen. I think one reason I haven't been able to get that old case out of my mind is that there are a lot of similarities with LeRoy Hopkins's murder. When I think of one, the thoughts sort of slip over to the other."

"Okay, this time I'll be the straight man. You explain what you mean, and I'll play like I knew it all the time and am agreeing with you," Hen said.

"Okay. Stella Strickland and Rosa Cruz were both the victims of abuse at the hand of their men."

Hen nodded. "We're just guessing about Rosa Cruz, but I think it's a good enough guess for now. Go on."

"Okay. Both cases involved a delay in finding the body leading to confusion over the time of death, which gave the killer time to get away and made it hard to pin down an alibi."

"Uh-huh." He started picking at a fingernail.

"I'm almost through. So what if both cases involved mistaken identity? Well, not exactly mistaken identity. If Harold Cowart killed him, he knew it was Josh, but mistook Josh for Stella's lover. What if whoever killed poor LeRoy Hopkins got the wrong man, too? It was dark when and where he was killed. And remember, at first Connie thought the body was her brother's."

Hen abandoned his fingernail. "That's a good angle, Trudy.

We haven't been able to find any reason for anybody to want to kill LeRoy Hopkins. Have we?"

"No. I've talked to several people who knew him, including the Brother Leggett that Reverend Palmer mentioned, who gave LeRoy a job, helping customers out with their groceries. I haven't found anybody who ever saw a show of temper or a mean streak in him, no reason for a sane person to want to hurt him, much less kill him. The worst thing I heard against him came from Elmo Leggett, who said LeRoy would get to talking to the customers instead of letting them go after he put their groceries in their cars, but since Mr. Leggett wasn't paying LeRoy much of anything he was willing to put up with it, as long as LeRoy wasn't actually running customers off."

"That's about what we expected," Hen said. "Now, following your line of thought about the confusion of victims, we've heard of a lot of people who might have been after Carlos Reyes for one reason or another. If he'd been the victim, we'd have a lot more leads to follow."

"That's what I think, too," I said, grinning. Hen knew perfectly well, and knew that I knew, that I'd listened to him feel his way to the conclusion I'd reached earlier.

"If Carlos Reyes is not our killer, maybe he's ahead of us in making this connection," Hen said. "Maybe that's why we can't find him."

"And maybe if we start looking for somebody who'd want to kill him, we'll get that break you sent me looking for," I said.

"Those possible enemies your priest brought up. What were they, some of the other workers? The employers? A go-between, coyote, smuggler? It opens the investigation up a whole lot more than if we're looking for somebody who didn't like LeRoy Hopkins."

"Yessir," I said. "I'm glad you thought of that."

"Let's get hoppin', then. We've got that ticking bomb to worry about."

"Yessir."

"And as a Christmas present for you, I'll send Sutton Tatum over to root around and see if he can find the old files on the Tippins case for us to take a look at. Sutton's not good for much else and he's been getting on my nerves lately, so spending some time up in that storeroom at the courthouse may be just what he needs."

"A Christmas present for both of us, then," I said. "Discipline for Sutton and the chance to satisfy my—our—curiosity about the old case."

"You couldn't just say thank you, could you?"

"I'm sorry. It just isn't in me."

"Maybe you'll thank me for this, then. While you were out doing whatever you do while you're out, our friend Esperanza Reyes called to say that Carlos is still missing and now Rosa Cruz is missing, too."

"Reckon our visit scared her off?"

"Could be. Miz Reyes says she wasn't especially worried at first, because she knew Carlos was with Rosa, but now…"

"Her English must have improved," I said.

"Uh-huh. A dose of worry and a vote of confidence from Father Lucero did more good than an ESL class. What it comes down to is she's worried."

"You want me to go back out to the Rogers place and see if I can find anything?"

"Already looked there. Nobody there at all, which isn't surprising. Checked the motel where Rosa works, too, and she didn't turn up for work."

"You think they've run away, Carlos and Rosa?"

"No. I don't think so. I don't think he'd worry his mother like that. But it does look more and more like there's a connection between Carlos Reyes and LeRoy Hopkins. I went over and had me another chat with Berto Lopez at El Milagro. He stands by his statement that he didn't notice anything in particular going on that night, but he thought maybe somebody else would be more help, maybe Johnny or Jimmy Chavez, who work on the same crew as Carlos out at Carter Farms."

"Johnny and Jimmy?" I asked.

"I'm pretty sure that's Juan and Jaime, *en español*," Hen said, looking smug.

"So you're learning Spanish?"

"Well, if our buddy old Berto feels like he has to go to the trouble to translate those names for me, I think I can put myself out a little."

"Did you already talk to J and J?" I asked, steering clear of taking sides linguistically.

"Not yet. You want to go with me?"

Like he had to ask.

ELEVEN

J AND J CHAVEZ, according to Berto Lopez, worked in pine straw out at the Carter place a few miles north of town. We found the crew chief, Tomas (Tommy, maybe) Trujillo near a semitrailer which was being loaded with pine straw.

Trujillo confirmed that Carlos Reyes worked on his crew—was supposed to work on his crew—but wasn't there and hadn't been seen since Saturday. There was a certain nervousness in his manner. He relaxed noticeably when Hen said we wanted to talk to Juan and Jaime Chavez and it had nothing to do with work permits, green cards or immigration status. Actually, it was a relief to us to be able to skirt those issues, too. Once, several years back, under intense prodding from Immigration and Naturalization Services, we made a sweep and came up with about 80 undocumented workers, far more as it turned out than INS could deal with. This caused Hen no end of amusement. If you'll pardon the comparison, we felt something like a cat who's brought in a mouse and expected praise from its human companion and got a big "Ick!" instead. The effect on Hen seems to have been to make him even more tolerant of whatever problems the workers create and less tolerant of the INS.

The way he summarizes the tale, the INS took about half of the people and put them on a bus headed south, and an agent told the rest, "We'll be back later." The agent did not say, but might as well have said, "You'd better run and hide." There are few enough entertaining aspects of the problem of undocumented (or illegal) (workers) (or immigrants) foreign aliens, or guest workers—take your pick—so we pretty much laugh at whatever we can find that is laughable.

Trujillo introduced us to the Chavez brothers, lanky, muscular men wearing faded jeans and plaid flannel shirts. Hanging from each belt was a sheath that held a knife, a basic tool for cutting the twine used to bind the pine straw.

"Were you fellas at El Milagro Saturday night, after the parade?" Hen asked, including Tomas Trujillo in the question.

Juan and Jaime glanced at each other and Juan, slightly taller and skinnier than his brother, the one wearing the red plaid shirt, confirmed. "El Milagro. Saturday. Yes."

Trujillo nodded.

"Carlos Reyes with you?"

The brothers again consulted with a glance, and again Juan spoke. "Carlos? No."

"You friends of Carlos?"

Two shrugs and one abstention. Maybe.

Hen's glance took in all three men. "Carlos Reyes has disappeared. Any of y'all got an idea where he might be?"

No need to consult with a glance. Decisive negative head shakes from J and J. "No," from Tomas.

"We heard Carlos had been stirring up trouble," Hen said. "You know anything about that?"

Blank looks.

"Any of you know anybody who'd want to hurt Carlos?" Hen persisted.

The three men seemed to be competing to see which of

them could look most like a man who didn't know anything about anything. I had the idea that if it hadn't been too late, all three of them would have denied knowing a word of English. I thought of Father Lucero's pool ball story and turned away in annoyance—with myself and with the men—in time to see a man dodge behind the trailer. If his sudden, furtive, movement hadn't caught my attention, I'd never have noticed him. The guilty flee when nobody is pursuing.

"Who was that?" I asked, foolishly, because the man had disappeared. Not surprisingly, all four men looked at me with puzzlement.

"Big guy," I said, "gray shirt. He ducked behind the trailer."

"Not Carlos," Tomas Trujillo said. "Carlos isn't here."

"Hector," said Jaime, under his breath, without moving his lips.

"Hector Torres?" I asked.

"You know Hector?" Tomas asked.

"Not yet, but I think we ought to meet him," Hen said.

"They can go back to work?" Tomas asked.

"I don't see why not," Hen said. "Come on, Trudy. Let's go introduce ourselves to Hector Torres."

But instead of waiting patiently behind the trailer, eager to make our acquaintance, the man I had seen was now loping off in the opposite direction.

"Stop! Police! We want to talk to you!" Hen yelled as we started after him.

Somewhat to my surprise, he did stop. The decision was surely prompted less by an impulse to assist the police than by the fact that it was fifty yards to the nearest cover and any hope of escape. He turned, hands held high, revealing a certain acquaintance with the ways of the police.

"Hector Torres?" Hen asked, when we were close enough that he didn't have to yell.

"What you want with me?" He seemed to be measuring both Hen and me, measuring our strength against his own.

"We've been looking for Carlos Reyes," Hen said. "Heard he's a friend of yours."

The slightest of gestures indicated that maybe he and Carlos weren't friends. Hen tried again. "Maybe what I heard was he's a friend of your girlfriend."

Hector turned his head and spat. No manners at all. Worse than that for Hector, with his neck stretched out like that I could see scabby scratches that had been concealed by his shirt collar.

"Rosa give you those scratches?" Hen asked. He doesn't miss much, either.

A snort indicated that Hector thought that suggestion was beneath his contempt.

"Maybe when you gave her a few bruises?"

"She tell you that?"

"Just a guess," Hen said. He took a long look at the sheath and knife at Hector's belt. "Or maybe you got those scratches somewhere else."

Our previous theories of the murder of LeRoy Hopkins shifted dizzyingly in my mind in another of those convergences with the old case. Of course. LeRoy Hopkins hadn't been killed by somebody protecting Rosa but by somebody jealous of Rosa, who'd mistaken him for Carlos.

"Were you at El Milagro Saturday night?" Hen asked.

Hector's glance back toward J and J, who were having a hard time getting their work done since they were looking in our direction, must have convinced him that they'd have already told us that. I'm sure they would have if we'd thought to ask.

"Drink with my friends. Anything wrong with that?"

"No," Hen said. "Nothin' wrong with that. What we're interested in is a murder that took place near there. We're looking for anybody who might know something about that."

"I don't know nothing about that."

"Mind if we look at your knife?" I asked.

Oh, yes, he minded. The knife positively leapt to his hand, and he fell into a defensive crouch.

"Hold on there, son. Just drop it on the ground and step back," Hen said. He'd been only a fraction of a second behind Hector in unholstering his own weapon.

Hector spat again and dropped the knife.

"Back away. That's right. Over there."

When Hector had backed away enough so I could retrieve the knife without getting between him and Hen, I picked it up. Then, since we were getting along so well, on new footing, he couldn't refuse our invitation to come to the station house, where we could talk more comfortably.

As we stowed Hector safely in the back of Hen's cruiser, I became aware of Tomas Trujillo, making crablike gestures that I finally interpreted to mean he wanted me to come to him, away from where Hector could see.

"Hector's a troublemaker," he confided in a whisper. "He's a good worker, but a troublemaker. Nobody goes against him. If something happened to Carlos, ask Hector about it."

When we got back to the station house with him, we did ask Hector about it, whether he'd done anything to Carlos Reyes, along with the other questions we had for him. The scratches, he said, he got on the job, not from Rosa Cruz or

LeRoy Hopkins. Pine straw is scratchy. The knife is something he needs in his work. Pulling the knife was a natural reaction to a threat from the police, not the instinctive move of a brutish killer.

J and J Chavez and Tomas Trujillo must have been connected to an invisible communication network that would rival the internet. We had scarcely delivered Hector Torres to the lockup when Carlos Reyes and Rosa Cruz turned up at the station house, together, in the custody of Esperanza and Connie Reyes.

Like Trujillo earlier, once they were assured that Hector was in no position to harm them, they wanted to talk, to explain, to set the record straight.

Although it was probably too late to do much good, we split them up just in case details of the stories didn't mesh. Just in case they were more perfidious than they seemed and had hatched a plot to get rid of Hector. Leaving Esperanza and Connie to their own devices, Hen took Carlos to his office and I took Rosa to the conference room to talk.

When we shuffled their stories back together, we found no discrepancies. Both said that the night before the murder, Friday night, Carlos and Hector had gotten into a fight, Carlos attacking Hector when he got rough with Rosa. Naturally this made Carlos a hero in Rosa's eyes and in mine, since it was obvious now that we'd seen him that Carlos, although well built, was no physical match for Hector. At a guess, Hector had four inches and fifty pounds on Carlos, and they looked like meaner inches and pounds.

During the fight, Hector had torn Rosa's necklace from her neck. He threatened both Carlos and Rosa if they didn't do what he said. Carlos was to stay away from Rosa and Rosa was to behave like a woman is supposed to behave. Never-theless, Carlos and Rosa, knowing Hector and his buddies would be at El Milagro on Saturday night, and thinking they were safe, were together when LeRoy Hopkins was mur-dered. They alibied each other. Thinking of young, battered Stella sneaking around on her abusive husband, somehow I believed them, in spite of the recklessness of their behavior.

Hector wasn't the type to confess, and his command of En-glish deserted him, but that was a minor matter since we had good enough reason—probable cause—from the story Rosa and Carlos told, plus the cross that was found at the scene, to hold him until the lab had a crack at giving us some hard ev-idence.

"I told you there's always somebody who knows some-thing, Trudy," Hen said. "The secret is getting them to tell you what they know."

"I knew that," I told him.

TWELVE

SUTTON TATUM MUST HAVE BEEN more motivated—or more afraid of Hen—than I would have expected. He showed uncharacteristic enthusiasm for the grubby task Hen had set him and, miraculously, found files going back to Cooter Nail's day.

In the relative lull that came after we locked up Hector Torres for pulling a knife on us and while we were waiting for the results of tests on Hector's knife and scratches, I had time to look over the files on the Josh Tippins murder that Sutton unearthed.

At first glance, the files didn't seem to be any more helpful than the skimpy newspaper stories Phil had found in the *Beacon's* archives. According to the paper, Chief Sidney Herman Nail was pursuing several leads in the mysterious death at the popular Anderson Hotel of Mr. Joshua Tippins, formerly of Pembroke. I assumed that language came from the reporter, not Chief Nail, because the only part of the story in quotation marks had an entirely different style. "Right now, we're stumped. We're looking into his business in Pembroke, to see if that sheds any light."

Nail's police files had a similar laconic quality. They contained the barest of facts in the case: time and place, identity of the victim and a report from the medical examiner saying he'd been done in by a couple of sharp blows from a hammer. These were all in line with what my informants had told me. The most interesting thing to me, because by its very nature it broke out of the confining report form, was a sketch of the hotel, showing the two sets of stairs: a wide, open staircase at the front of the lobby and gathering room, where I imagined the poker games and socializing had taken place, and another one, closed from view by a wall, accessible at the end of a hall near the kitchen. The hotel sketches were grimy, as though Cooter Nail had pored over them looking for answers. Maybe he really had tried to solve the case but couldn't find any evidence. Of course, any physical evidence, such as Josh Tippins's hammer, was nowhere to be found.

"Looks like the po-lice can solve a murder case when they put their minds to it." Ellis Hodges waylaid me at the post office.

I was getting tired of him. "With the Hopkins case solved, Mr. Hodges, we're reopening the Josh Tippins case. New evidence has come to light and…"

"What? New evidence? What…"

"You bring your wife and Miz Strickland to the station this afternoon about one o'clock and I'll tell you."

I left him there with his mouth agape, and I thought that was the end of it. And then one o'clock rolled around and there were the three of them, Ellis Hodges looking triumphant, his wife looking annoyed, and Stella Strickland looking a little worried. Ellis had called my bluff and I had no choice but to usher them into the conference room we share with the city council.

"Am I invited?" Hen asked.

"You bet." Even if he was doing nothing more than avoiding paperwork, I'd be glad for the backup.

"Y'all wait here while I get the files," I said. I grabbed the old police file, the copies of the newspaper story Phil had given me, and another handful of papers, to give visual weight to the actual facts.

I began by outlining the theory of the crime that Hen and I had hatched earlier, the theory that had Stella's first husband, Harold Cowart, killing Josh Tippins in a jealous rage.

"That could be," Ellis Hodges said. "I wouldn'ta put it past old Harold."

Stella looked sad. Bernice looked pleased.

Since the hotel sketch was all I had, I pulled it out. "I never realized there was a set of stairs back here," I said, pointing to the hidden staircase near the kitchen.

"Mostly for the maids," Stella Strickland said. "Easier to get around with the kitchen and housekeeping stuff."

"You could get to all the rooms from there?" Hen asked.

"Sure. That was the whole point," Stella said.

"Wouldn't do to haul the dirty linen up and down the fancy front stairs," Bernice added. "They were for show. These were for work."

"If I'm reading this sketch right, a person could go up and down these stairs without anybody seeing them," I said. "Isn't this a wall?"

"That's right," Stella said. "See here?" She pointed. "You could get to the stairs from the lobby, but you could get to them by going through the pantry, if you were in the kitchen."

"And you were the cook?" I addressed this question to Bernice mostly to include her in the conversation. I wasn't prepared for the look of surprise in her eyes. Another dizzy-ing shift, like the one in the Hopkins case when we saw Hector Torres's scratches, occurred in this case. Once again, I realized I had had everything backward. Thinking the old case paralleled the new one had opened up some lines of thought that proved productive, but it looked like I had put everything together wrong.

"You'd been seeing Josh Tippins, hadn't you?" I asked Bernice Hodges.

Slowly, she nodded. She was looking less pleased at this turn in the conversation.

Ellis Hodges and Stella Strickland leaned back in their chairs. I thought I heard a sigh from both of them.

"Ellis always knew I had other boyfriends," Bernice said. "No news there."

"Lots of 'em," he confirmed. "Those back stairs were real convenient, weren't they, Bernice?"

Before Bernice Hodges could answer, Stella Strickland spoke, looking surprised. "That's right. And that night, when I was scooting out of Josh's room so Harold wouldn't catch me, I remember passing you on the stairs. I remember wondering what business you had upstairs when you were supposed to be in the kitchen. Maybe you were going up to see Josh. Remember, Bernice?"

"No, and you don't, either. You're making things up."

"No, I'm not," Stella said.

After a pause, I recklessly continued with the fairy tale, taken with the way it was all fitting together. "And when you got to Josh's room, your lover's room, you saw that box of chocolate-covered cherries and thought he'd brought them to your rival, Stella."

"Whoo-ee!" said Bernice's husband. "She wouldn'ta liked that much!"

"I saw her throw a skillet at a man once for saying something she didn't like," Stella said. These two would never be friends again.

"Really?" Ellis asked. "Wish I'd known that before I married her. Maybe I wouldn't be breakin' in a new hip."

"Slow down, now," Hen said. "Sounds like a lynching party here."

But he was too late. He couldn't stop the momentum. Nobody actually said Bernice picked up the hammer and killed Josh Tippins, but nobody had to.

"You got a good imagination, I'll give you that, all of you," Bernice Hodges said, looking from one to another of us. Her scornful glance settled on me. "I thought you'd decided to blame it on Harold."

"That was just a theory," I said. "It had holes in it. Stella told me he never hit her with anything but his fists. Hitting with a weapon wouldn't have been his style."

"Harold liked the feel of it, I think," Stella said.

"And it explains why old Cooter didn't ever catch 'er, too," Ellis said. "Started goin' out with him right after that, didn't you, Bernice?"

"You are trying to lynch me, you old…" Bernice started, but Stella cut in.

"Or maybe you took up with him to keep him from arresting you," Stella suggested.

"Same difference," Ellis said.

"I've never heard anything so spiteful in all my life," Bernice said. "Are you two trying to get rid of me so you can get together again?"

"We never were together, Bernice," Stella said.

"Well, I'm not admitting anything. Not confessing, if

that's what you think," Bernice Hodges said. "And I'm not forgetting how you're treating me, either. Nobody knows, nobody will never know what happened back then, and whatever did happen, it's like it happened to different people, anyway."

Ellis Hodges's monkey-face crumpled, and he said to nobody in particular, "I knew I was her sixth or eighth choice, but I still thought I'd got myself a prize."

Stella Strickland had begun to cry. "I always thought Harold had killed him and it was my fault. This is like a weight off me after all these years. Yeah, Bernice, we were all different then, but I've been suffering all this time. Have you?"

"THE MORAL OF THAT STORY, Trudy," Hen said later, in his most irritatingly, patiently, instructive tone, "is that whether she did it or not, and I'm inclined to think she did, we can't go to court based on sixty-year-old recollections from eighty-year-old witnesses. Cooter Nail may have been a disgrace to law enforcement, but he was smart enough to get rid of the hammer, and circumstantial evidence isn't good enough."

"Not in this case," I said.

With the pressure off, Hen was feeling philosophical. "People like to compare a murder case to a jigsaw puzzle, like the pieces are all cut out from a solid picture, and all you have to do is assemble all the pieces and put them together."

"And what's wrong with that, oh, learned one?" I asked. "Please enlighten me."

He was impervious to my sarcasm, choosing to treat it as a humorous but sincere request for information.

"What's wrong with that is that there is no one picture. You don't start out knowing that this particular puzzle has five hundred or a thousand pieces and all you have to do is fit 'em together, so you never know if you've found all the pieces. Physical evidence. You gotta have that."

"I'll try to remember," I said, hoping he'd quit lecturing, but he wasn't quite through.

"Both these cases, now, we worked up a good story, using our little gray cells, but that wasn't enough."

"That's the truth," I said.

"Don't feel bad about following the wrong rabbit trail for a while," Hen said. "Both of these cases were a lot more like a kaleidoscope than a jigsaw puzzle. Every time you looked at it, the pieces shifted a little bit. Still made a pretty picture. Not our fault if it was a different picture every time. That's where the physical evidence comes in."

Right. Some details of the Hopkins case were still debatable, but the physical evidence had given us the true picture. The technical guys had matched Hector's knife to the wounds in LeRoy Hopkins, matched residual blood near the knife's handle to LeRoy's blood, and matched the human tissue under LeRoy's fingernails to Hector Torres.

Hector Torres never did get chatty, but from what the others told us, we pieced the story together this way. When Hector, filled with *cerveza* all the way up to his beetling eyebrows, was told by the chatty Tomas Trujillo that Rosa was with Carlos, he went looking for them. In the dark, his fuddled state led him to mistake LeRoy Hopkins for Carlos. By the time LeRoy turned around to defend himself and Hector realized his mistake, Hector had already dropped the cross. He didn't tell us whether he dropped it by accident or in a drink-inspired, clumsy attempt to implicate Rosa, or warn her about what would happen if she didn't stay in line. Maybe he didn't know.

By the time he realized he'd killed the wrong man, he couldn't find the cross in the dark.

Even before they learned of the murder, Carlos and Rosa had been afraid Hector would do something bad to Carlos, and she had talked Carlos into hiding out till Hector cooled off. Then, when they heard about the murder and the cross that had turned up at the scene, Rosa understood that even she wasn't safe. Then they both disappeared, moving from the Rogers place to the Reyes trailer, where Connie and Esperanza could be trusted to keep the door locked until they could figure out what to do next.

"Hard, physical evidence," I said. "Got it. You know, Hen, in spite of everything, I feel bad for Bernice," I said. "Just look how quick her husband and her lifelong friend turned on her."

"Let it be a lesson to you," Hen said. He always has to get the last word. I was left to puzzle over what lesson he had in mind.

THIRTEEN

THE REMAINING DAYS before Christmas still held surprises.

First, Starr Taylor and the Reverend Oliver Palmer turned up at the station house again, but this time their roles were reversed. Starr was doing most of the talking, and I had the feeling she'd done a whole lot of talking before they got there.

"Oliver, Reverend Palmer, sometimes tries too hard to do what he thinks everybody expects him to be doing," she said. Reverend Palmer looked out the window.

"Yes?" Hen encouraged.

"And that means he comes across a little strong to people who don't know and understand him."

"You could be right," Hen said.

"What I'm trying to say is, he doesn't really, necessarily speak for everybody when he...well, he feels bad that he took off on y'all like he did about not trying to find who killed LeRoy."

Reverend Palmer nodded agreement.

Starr continued, "So, besides coming to apologize to y'all to try to make things right, I thought I might go talk to Miz, Señora Reyes, and apologize for thinking her son killed my brother when I didn't have any real reason to think so. See if there's anything I can do to make it up. I'm a little nervous about it, but I think it's the right thing to do."

"What about Miz Reyes?" the reverend asked. "Will she need an interpreter?"

"I doubt it," Hen said. "Señora Reyes does better in English than I do in Spanish."

When they left, Hen and I both shook hands with both of them, making peace.

The next development was when Starr Taylor called to say she and Esperanza Reyes had really hit it off, cried together some over the loss of LeRoy and the plight of so many of Esperanza's friends and family, commiserated over how hard it was to find a place to live, or money to put food on the table, or clothes for the young'uns. "That doesn't have anything to do with how dark or how light your skin is, or what language you speak."

"No, it doesn't," I said.

Starr said she and Esperanza wanted to see if they could do something to bring their communities together. "What do you think about that?" she asked.

"I think it's a great idea," I replied, my own Christmas spirits rebounding. "But why limit it to you and Miz Reyes, the blacks and the Hispanics? What about bringing in some anglos? We could use some coming-together, too."

"Keep talking," she said.

My automatic impulse was to put her in touch with Aunt Lulu, who has fingers in just about every community pie, but then I thought of Stella Strickland. That turned out to be a stroke of genius, if I do say so myself.

"This project is just what I needed, Trudy," she told me later. "Without any family, Christmas is usually a bad time for me, but this year will be different. I feel like I've just come out from under a cloud, and I'm ready to celebrate."

The project the women came up with was a Christmas party at the hall at St. Elizabeth's. Esperanza Reyes and Father Miguel Lucero had mobilized the Catholic and Spanish-speaking people; Starr Taylor and Reverend Oliver Palmer got after the black and Baptist population; Stella Strickland celebrated by turning her considerable energy into twisting the arms of local merchants for donations of food, clothes and household goods. And Phil Pittman used the space opened up by not having to run an attack on the police to print a handsome open invitation to the community at large.

The result of all these efforts was a mixed throng of people at St. Elizabeth's and a truckload of largesse for distribution to the neediest of the community, as well as a bag of candy and a toy for every child.

"We want to thank you all for coming," Father Lucero said to the crowd. "Welcome. We're hoping this small step toward peace on earth will become a tradition."

He stepped aside and Reverend Oliver Palmer stepped up, beaming just like the whole thing had been his idea. "I won't take but a minute of your time," he said, "but I want to add my thanks and appreciation to the three women whose idea it was to bring us together today—three wise women, heh, heh, heh."

That line did earn him a smattering of applause and a few chuckles. "Before y'all make a mess out of that refreshment table the ladies have worked so hard on, let's have a round of applause for Starr Taylor, Esperanza Reyes and Stella Strickland."

Those three wise women, and they surely were that, made a striking picture that Phil captured and presented to the world at large in full color in the next issue of the *Beacon*. Starr Taylor, in the center, taller than the other two, wearing a white suit, with a large star-shaped gold pin and matching earrings, hair in corn-rows like a halo, was the perfect centerpiece. To her left, Stella Strickland was in green, a dress of a shiny knit fabric that showed she still had a nice figure. Her pin and earrings were crocheted poinsettias that didn't photograph well, but with her spiky dark hair, she looked a little like an elf. Esperanza Reyes wore red, a shade that brought out a glow in her complexion. She looked ten years younger than she had the first time I saw her, confident and happy. It's wonderful what a little makeup and the release from worry over Carlos did for her. Her one piece of jewelry was Rosa Cruz's silver cross, on a new silver chain.

"Looks like y'all were wise enough to plan ahead for this photo-op," I said when I congratulated the three on the success of the party.

"Gracias," said Esperanza Reyes.

"Knew that boyfriend of yours would show up with his camera," Stella Strickland said.

"Speaking of boyfriends, are you taking up with Ellis Hodges? I hear he needs a good woman," I retaliated.

The gleam in her eye was distinctly mischievous. "Uh-huh. I hear Bernice got her feelings hurt, I can't imagine why, and moved out on him. Went to stay with their daughter for a while. Their children are scandalized, but Ellis looks better than he has in years. All the other old ladies are doing a good job of taking care of him. More women than men at our age. He's finally getting the kind of female attention he's always thought he deserved." Her grin made her look even more like an elf. "But not from me."

Carlos Reyes and Rosa Cruz were there, too, of course. Like

Esperanza, Rosa had been transformed. Without bruises and with an attentive man in tow, she was beautiful and vivacious.

The other women who had provided the food found that to talk about while the men, not excluding Reverend Palmer, Father Lucero, and Henry Huckabee, mostly stood on the sidelines and watched. On the whole, the children mixed better than the adults did, partly because there was no language barrier with them, the children having learned in school.

"Trudy, listen!" This was Delcie, Hen's daughter, with Connie Reyes beside her. "Connie just told me *reyes* is Spanish for king, sort of like Le Roy is in French. Did you know that?"

"I never thought about it," I hedged. It served to remind me that we all have connections with each other, even if some of them are hidden.

I won't say the Baptists as a whole enjoyed the tamales as much as some of the others, or that the Spanish-speaking contingent as a whole went for the local fruitcake with the same enthusiasm as the natives, but on the whole, I felt the party was a success. Like Rosa, maybe we were all looking better than usual now that our bruises had healed. I'm too modest to claim to be the fourth wise woman, but I think I deserve some credit.

FOURTEEN

IN THE AFTERNOON OF Christmas Day, Hen, Teri, Delcie, Aunt Lulu, Phil and I were gathered around my Christmas tree. Having wrecked all the pretty gift wrapping paper, the adults were drinking coffee and eating Aunt Lulu's pecan pie while we fatuously watched Delcie reveling in her take. I was especially gratified to see that she was curled up on the floor behind the couch, in that magical Christmas tree room, with a blanket and pillow and the first of the Little House books.

Not to brag about my own take, but Phil gave me a sled. We put it on my front porch right next to the steps, not because I really thought it would bring snow, but as a vote of confidence for *esperanza* in general. It does snow here sometimes.

When Phil and I got back inside, Teri and Aunt Lulu were headed back to the kitchen with empty plates. After we were all settled again, lazily watching the lights on the tree, Hen said, "Oh, yeah, something I've been meaning to tell you," as if he'd forgotten till now, when we all know him well enough to know that whatever was coming he'd been waiting for exactly the right moment with his audience in exactly the right mood.

"What, Hen?" Teri said. Sometimes I pretend to think he's wonderful. She really does think so as far as I can tell, and she's his reliable prompter at moments like this—even if he hadn't softened her up with the Christmas gift of a beautiful

apphire ring, her birthstone, which she was studying as she
ncouraged him.

He beamed, very pleased with himself. "I got a call last
ight from one of our good Christian ladies, who shall remain
ameless. She never has been happy that the house next door
o her has been rented out to what she calls 'a buncha those
vetbacks,' and she got a little perturbed when they started as-
embling last evening. I tried to tell her that we're a long way
rom the Rio Grande and they probably didn't swim."

I nudged Phil gently with my elbow, and we smiled at
ach other, happily imagining Hen telling the woman—who
vas not nameless in my mind, no matter what he thought—
vhere the Rio Grande was located.

He continued. "But she told me I knew very well who she
vas talking about, which I did, and she said they were mak-
ng a lot of noise and there was a bunch of 'em in their old
unker cars and some of them parked up on the grass, some
of them coming real close to her yard and she didn't know
vhat they were up to, but she thought I ought to look into it."

"Did you look into it?" Phil asked.

"Yes, indeedy, I did. I eased around over there to take stock
of the situation."

"And what was the situation?" Aunt Lulu's even more in-
atuated with Hen than Teri is. He's a lucky man.

"She was right. Had told me God's honest literal truth.
There was an assembly. People had driven up in whatever cars
hey had, none of 'em what you'd call fresh off the assembly
ine, and they had parked them up on the grass, like people
lo, and one or two of them were kind of close to Miz…to my
nformant's…driveway. Not on it, you understand."

"We understand," I assured him.

"And she was right about the noise, too. Lotsa noise, people, lights. A real party."

"Maybe Miz…your informant…had her feelings hurt that she wasn't invited."

"You know, Trudy, that hadn't occurred to me."

"So what did you do?"

"I stayed and listened for a little while and then I left."

"You didn't call for backup."

"Nah, and I'm sorry about that, but I figured they'd be through singing before anybody else could get there, which woulda been too bad. 'Silent Night' is a grabber in any language."

"Noche de paz, noche de amor." Delcie's voice floated up from behind the couch.

It sounded even better in Spanish. Peace. Love.

And *esperanza,* no matter how much patience it took.

Witness
in Bishop Hill

Sara Hoskinson Frommer
A JOAN SPENCER MYSTERY

A Christmas sojourn to the scenic hamlet of Bishop Hill turns out to be murder for Joan Spencer and her new husband, Lieutenant Fred Lundquist, when Fred's mother witnesses the vicious murder of a local.

Disoriented by Alzheimer's, Mrs. Lundquist cannot clearly identify the killer, but she's still a threat. With her mother-in-law's life depending on it, Joan must sort out which secrets are worth killing for in peaceful Bishop Hill.

"Frommer is a brisk and clean writer, she handles the rueful ambivalence of middle age very well indeed."
—*Booklist*

*Available November 2004
at your favorite retail outlet.*

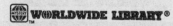
WORLDWIDE LIBRARY®

WSHF510

ARE YOUR MYSTERIES DISAPPEARING?

As of January 2005, your Mystery Library™ books will no longer be available at retail locations. The good news is, you can still get them delivered right to your door! Fill out the form below to guarantee you'll keep getting these great books each month.

SECOND ADVENT

T O N Y   P E R O N A

A NICK BERTETTO MYSTERY

When the beloved patriarch of his hometown dies of a shocking suicide, investigative reporter Nick Bertetto is called in to investigate what Martha, the victim's granddaughter, insists is not suicide, but murder.

It's clear that Martha has the most to gain from a murder investigation—suicide would void her grandfather's bequest of his fortune to her religious organization—Children of the Second Advent. And as Nick digs deeper, a dark picture emerges of fanaticism, con artists, "miracles," and a killer dead set on making sure there will be no second coming…or second chances.

"My kind of writing, my kind of characters."
—Ed Gorman, author of the Sam McCain mysteries

"A winning first novel."
—*Mystery Scene*

Available December 2004 at your favorite retail outlet.

MURDER IN THE BLOOD

A FRANK DECKER MYSTERY

When local history teacher Lou Cameron disappears, Farrell County sheriff Frank Decker is puzzled by accusations of embezzlement from wealthy Nathaniel Wetherston. Was the history teacher really stealing money from Wetherston's company?

Unconvinced, Decker sets out on a bizarre case where the only answers lead to a twisted trail ending in a face-off with a killer....

GENE DEWEESE

"A highly professional dip into moldering Americana."
—Kirkus Reviews

"...fabulous police procedural."
—Harriet Klausner

Available December 2004 at your favorite retail outlet.

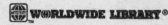

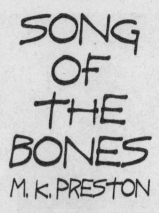